THE CRYSTAL STAR

Books by Ellen Argo

JEWEL OF THE SEAS
THE CRYSTAL STAR

THE
CRYSTAL STAR

Ellen Argo

G.P. Putnam's Sons
New York, N.Y.

Copyright © 1979 Ellen Argo

Published simultaneously in Canada by Longman Canada Limited, Toronto.

SBN 399-12297-4

Library of Congress Cataloging in Publication Data

Argo, Ellen.
  The Crystal Star.
  Sequel to Jewel of the seas.
  I. Title.
PZ4.A69Cr   (PS3551.R417)   813'.5'4   78-13325

PRINTED IN THE UNITED STATES OF AMERICA

FOR
MILDRED AND FRAN WRIGHT
Friends Beyond the Realm of Friendship

THE CRYSTAL STAR

Chapter One

1842

White crests had been topping the waves of Massachusetts Bay, but once the *Crystal Star* passed between Deer Island and Long Island, the wind dropped off. Only a creamy lace foam was left sliding from the smaller peaks down the side of the waves. Heavy laden vessels waiting in the Roads for a change of wind, which would set them free to fly across the oceans of the world, strained at their anchor chains and pointed directly into the course of their desire.

As Julia watched them from her place near the weather rail of the quarterdeck, she saw the glint of telescopes that were trained on the *Crystal Star*. A surge of pride in the ship she had helped design and build added to the exhilaration she already felt. Despite the jury rig and the fact that they were towed by a pair of schooners, she knew that none of the seasoned observers would fail to see the beauty and sweet lines of this latest addition to the East India merchant fleet.

What she was not aware of was how many of those telescopes were trained upon her as she stood braving the cold wind of late March. Perhaps at such long range, they wouldn't see the sparkle of her sapphire eyes beneath their finely arched brows nor the

9

flush that stained her winter white skin. Yet none could miss the cloud of black hair, teased loose by the sea breeze from the pins and combs that had held it earlier in the day. Neither would they miss her proud bearing nor the loveliness of the face that was raised to inspect their rigs.

For Julia, this was the day, the moment, when the door that had been closed to her for so long was finally opening. Instead of dreams, this was reality, and it was far more glorious than even she had ever imagined.

There had been the years of childhood, when she had played on the pebbled beaches of the Cape and had yearned to play instead upon bleached decks beneath those towering canvas sails she saw out on the blue-green waters. As a young girl, she had stood upon the tall dunes and watched the gulls and clouds fly out across the Bay to join the freedom of the sea. Until his sudden death, she had followed her first husband, Jason Thacher, in her imagination as he traveled the ocean highways and she had looked forward to the time when she would sail beside him.

Throughout her life, the rhythm of the sea had beat with every stroke of her heart. The waves, whether they flung themselves in crashing violence upon the land or whispered softly on a summer's day, had called her to come, to come. And now, at last, she was able to answer that call.

As she turned to watch the passage between Castle Island and Governors Island grow wider before them, she shivered inside her long, rough, grey cloak, and Stephen Logan, who had been standing beside the mate and the helmsman, noticed it as he noticed everything about her, even when his mind was on other matters.

He nodded at the mate and said, "Carry on." Then he moved to the rail and put his arm lightly around her waist. His cap was pulled low over his light brown, sun-bleached hair, and his grey eyes were shaded by the visor, but she could see the amused twinkle in them.

"Cold or excited?" he asked in a low voice that wouldn't be overheard by the helmsman or the mate.

"I don't know." She pressed against the sheltering warmth of his body. "A little of both, I expect."

"Well, there lies our first port, my lady," he said with a grin.

She looked at him and her face was suffused with the radiance of her smile. Her husband. Her captain. In the two weeks they'd been married, she had found what an ever-growing thing their love could be, and now all the world, with its seas and oceans and far-flung harbors, lay before them to explore.

"The first, but think of all the ports to come. Oh, Stephen, I wish we were outward bound with the cargo stowed safe below, the hatches battened, our sails set and flying, and the crew in the rigging."

"Aye." And he could no longer hide his own excitement beneath a master's professional veneer of indifference. He was entering Boston Harbor for the first time in command of his own ship! He'd fought so hard for so many long years for this moment, and now that it was here, it was difficult not to savor it to the utmost. Yet there was a need for calm, and so when he spoke, it was as much to sober himself as to remind her. "There's still a lot of work to be done before we'll be able to sail. Masts to be stepped, sails to be cut, and miles of rigging to be roven."

"I wish Papa was with us." As Julia sighed, a slight frown creased between her eyebrows. "I've been with him when he's come down to Boston to oversee the fitting out of our vessels, but I've never handled it alone before."

"You're not alone, Julie. Not so long as I'm with you, and I do know a fair bit about rigging a ship myself, you know."

"I know, but you didn't build her. Till she's fully rigged, she's still Papa's responsibility . . . and mine. Captain Asa won't blame you if anything goes wrong with his ship before she sails. He'll blame the Howard Shipyard."

"That old codger will blame everyone in sight, but nothing's going to go wrong. Not with the ship I command."

Julia looked thoughtfully at her husband, and through the joy he couldn't entirely conceal, there was a hint of steel in his grey eyes. "You're very sure of yourself, aren't you, Stephen?"

"Very," he said and he pushed his cap back on his tawny hair with a grin. "At least when it comes to ships, I am."

"And just about everything else," she laughed and thought of how he had set out to win her not long after they'd met. It had been a day in late June just nine months ago when he had suddenly appeared at the Howard Shipyard in search of a vessel and an owner who would have sufficient faith in him to give him his first command. At first, his light charm and gaiety had amused

11

her. Later, as his pursuit of her became more intense, they had irritated her. Finally, when she had understood the more serious depths they overlay, she had no longer been able to resist him, and she had been swept into a love that she had believed she would never find again after she had lost Jason.

"I've yet to see you act uncertain about anything," she said.

"That's one thing no shipmaster can afford. The sea's too unforgiving." He was suddenly more sober as he scanned the water ahead of them. Then he gave her a quick squeeze and moved away from her.

Julia smiled as he left her. She knew he was barely aware of her existence as they approached the passage between the islands that led to Boston Harbor. His attention was completely focused upon his ship. As she leaned on the weather rail and watched him resume his place beside the helmsman, she thought that her husband was lithe as only a man who'd spent years at sea could be. But he was also charged with an electrical vitality she'd never encountered in anyone before.

Despite his blithe approach when they had first met, she had sensed that he would make a fine deep sea captain. Until this short trip, she hadn't been able to observe him in action, but now she knew. He was perfect.

Stephen narrowed his eyes as he silently watched the wind on the water, noted the speed of the current, and observed the men working the ship. It was a makeshift crew, composed of men from the shipyard and a few from the village who'd come along for a ride on the new ship. Nevertheless, it was a good, experienced crew. He had already decided which village lads he would sign on for the voyage.

One by one, the three hills of Boston appeared, and Julia could see how the city had grown since she'd last been there. Construction on the new Customs House between Long Wharf and Central Wharf was well under way. New houses, shops, and buildings were going up everywhere. Even when seen from the water, the prosperity of Boston of 1842 was obvious.

Of more interest to her than the city, though, were the vessels lying along the wharves and at anchor in the harbor. There were hundreds of them of every conceivable design and age. There were coasting schooners, their decks loaded with lumber, barrels, and livestock; small packet sloops with a mixture of cargo and passengers; fishermen and whalers, which were followed by screaming flocks of gulls on the lookout for scraps that might be tossed overboard; but best of all were the deep sea merchantmen loaded with the treasures of the earth. As they skirted by the anchorage, Julia recognized the ensigns of almost every nation in Europe, but most of them were American.

Not all the craft were tied up or at anchor, however. There was constant activity as sloops, skiffs, dinghies, and longboats joined the traffic that flowed in and out of the harbor. Many of them, upon sighting the *Crystal Star*, changed their course in order to see the new ship up close, and although most stood well clear of their path, it took all the skill of the skippers of the schooners and the men on the ship to avoid an occasional collision.

It was with a feeling of relief, therefore, that Stephen saw that their approach to the long granite wharf was clear. He nodded to Kenneth Wilson, who was acting first mate. "Cast off the schooners."

"Cast off the schooners," Wilson echoed, repeating his captain's command. It was a necessary habit of the sea, where words misunderstood could lead to disaster. Under his direction, the crew cast some of the lines to the schooners that had towed them from Cape Cod. Other lines they took aboard and quickly stowed.

"Man the jib downhaul," Stephen said, and under the mate's shouted orders, three men ran to the lines, ready to lower the jib.

"Let go the halyard when you're ready." The rough cut cotton sail came flapping down to the deck and was rapidly made fast by those who stood waiting for it.

"Luff her up." And the spokes of the wheel moved rapidly under the helmsman's expert touch.

The ship was steadily slowing, but she still had headway on.

"Put the helm down."

"Putting the helm down, sir."

"More!"

"Aye-aye, sir."

The *Crystal Star* began to swing up into the wind as she neared the seaward end of the wharf.

"Take in the mainsail. Make her fast."

A few men, who had been waiting for the order, rapidly clewed up the remaining sail while others, springing to the wharf with the shore lines in their hands, were able to tether the ship to giant bollards despite the press of a crowd that was rapidly gathering. Boys, with a dream glittering in their eyes, pushed their way through the porters and hawkers. Merchants stepped out of their counting houses and warehouses to inspect what could mean either new competition or new business or both. But it was the idlers who haunted every seaport of the world and the newsmen that considered themselves the real experts.

With a hundred eyes staring at her, Julia felt as though the quarterdeck of the *Crystal Star* had become a stage, and she moved away from the rail to stand near Stephen with her back to the crowd. Throughout the operation, she had remained silent and tried to stay out of the way of the men working the ship, but now she wanted to be the first to congratulate her husband.

"Really beautiful, Stephen," she said.

"Not bad for a jury-rigged ship and a pickup crew," he said with a modesty that lay more in the words than in his voice. His features relaxed into the slow, lazy grin that always made him seem younger than he was, but Julia could see the pride in his eyes. "We'll still have to warp her up the dock when we find out what berth we've been assigned, but for all intents and purposes, we've made port."

"Aren't we going ashore for dinner tonight?" She swept her tumbled black hair behind her shoulders and tied a blue ribbon around it to hold it in place.

"Tired of ship's fare already?" he teased her. "After only three days? What are you going to do after three months?"

"Once we're at sea, I doubt I'll care what I eat. Just being there will make up for almost anything. But as long as we're in Boston, there's no reason not to eat well. Especially tonight."

"Why especially tonight?"

"To celebrate, of course. Do you realize this will be the first time we've had a chance to be alone together?" she asked as she thought of the days since their wedding when they'd stayed with her family. There'd been no time for a wedding trip between their marriage and the launching of the *Crystal Star*. Neither had bringing the ship down to Boston been a pleasure cruise. There had been little privacy and even less time to share it.

"Now I'll feel as though we're really married," she added.

One tawny eyebrow shot up and Stephen grinned at her wickedly. "You mean to tell me you don't feel married? After all the effort I've been putting into it?"

14

Julia could feel the color rising in her face and she looked around quickly to see who might have heard him, but none of the crew was nearby, and the crowd remained on the wharf.

Stephen, watching her, laughed.

"Come along, my lady," he said. Despite the number of eyes that were on them, he put an arm lightly around her slender waist and led her to the companionway that ran below to the officers' quarters. "We'll dine ashore this evening, and tonight we'll enjoy a soft feather bed at the Tremont House with no family on the other side of the wall."

Julia was dazzled by the chandeliers, the candlelit tables, and the reflected glow of silver as she and Stephen entered the new French restaurant. When she had come to Boston with her father in the past, she had eaten in public dining places, but never one like this. She couldn't believe the luxury that lay before her eyes.

Draperies of rich gold cloth were drawn at the windows, and an enormous fireplace blazed at each end of the long room. In a corner alcove, a string quartet competed softly with the laughter and lilting voices of the diners. Fine linen covered the tables that were scattered throughout the room, and the men and women seated at them outshone the silver and sparkling crystal. Julia felt a little unsure of herself in the bright blue satin dress that had been made for her wedding. She had thought it so beautiful and stylish, but now she wondered.

To reassure herself, she touched the long strand of pearls at her neck, the pearls that Jason Thacher, her first husband, had given her as a present one long ago Christmas. Stephen had no idea whose gift they were, and she had resolved never to tell him. The mention of Jason's name was enough to bring a brooding look to Stephen's handsome face.

She glanced at him and smiled. In his well-cut frock coat and blue trousers, he certainly seemed to fit into this room. The fawn of his coat set off the fresh sea-color of his tan face, and even the willful lock that so often fell across his forehead seemed to have been subdued tonight.

"Ready, Julie?" he asked as he smiled back at her.

She glanced once again at the room and was aware that quite a

15

few of the diners were looking in their direction. Then she nodded, and as they began to follow the headwaiter, she straightened her shoulders and lifted her chin. Staring directly at the headwaiter's back so that she wouldn't have to meet anyone's eyes, she was nevertheless aware that Stephen was nodding and smiling at people as they progressed through the room.

After the headwaiter had seated them, Stephen grinned at her. "Did you see them, Julie?" He seemed to be elated.

"See what?"

"The way everyone was looking at you. Now they're all trying to decide who you are."

"Why on earth should they bother to do that?" she asked, her delicately arched eyebrows shooting up in surprise. After all, it wasn't likely they yet knew about the *Crystal Star* or, even if they did, that they would connect her with it.

"Because it's not every night they see a woman as beautiful as you." He had the same glow of proud ownership that he'd shown earlier in the day when he'd given a few merchants and newsmen a tour of the *Crystal Star*.

"Stephen, how can you say that? I'm all wrong. You should have warned me. Look at those gowns and those hairdos." She touched one of the long curls she had arranged as a simple frame to her face and glanced at the elegant coiffure of the woman at the next table.

"You really don't know how lovely you are, do you, my Julie?" He reached across the table to touch her hand. His smile had turned to one of warm affection that was touched only slightly by amusement. "You walk through the room like a queen and then don't understand why everyone stares at you."

"To tell the truth, I was scared to death."

He laughed then. "That's the first time I've ever heard you admit to being scared. I thought you were never afraid of anything."

"Well, I'm not usually."

"And a few unimportant people like these are enough to do it?"

"They don't look all that unimportant to me," she said.

"Well, not all of them are. There's a handful of people here worth knowing." He let his eyes roam casually around the room. Occasionally they paused at one table or another, as though he were speculating about the people who sat there. Then he nodded. "Some of them could be useful contacts. I'm glad we came."

When the waiter approached with the elaborately penned menus, Stephen released her hand. After giving the menu a long and careful scrutiny, he beckoned to the waiter. Julia listened in surprise as her husband spoke with the man in a French so fluent and rapid, she understood very little of it.

"You really do amaze me," she said after the waiter had gone. "Just when I think I know everything there is to know about you, you go and surprise me. What else can you do?"

"Why don't I let you discover that for yourself? It might make life a bit more interesting," he said, but there was a touch of pride in his voice that showed how pleased he was that he had managed to impress her. As he smiled, his face was filled with that special radiance that was for her alone. It was so intense, she glanced away for a moment. It wasn't a look meant for public places, and she hoped no one would notice.

Over Stephen's shoulder, she noticed a tall, dark-haired young man with very pale skin. He seemed to be approaching their table.

"There's someone coming over," she warned him. "Maybe one of your important contacts."

Stephen turned and looked back over his shoulder, then swung quickly around again. He frowned with impatience.

"Not a contact. An acquaintance. One I'd rather be without. I knew him at Harvard, and he's a bloody nuisance."

Julia smiled at the young man, who was wearing the most flamboyantly embroidered waistcoat and the most elaborate cravat she'd ever seen, when he came up behind her husband, but Stephen kept his back firmly turned and took a sip of wine. However, this didn't discourage the man.

"Steve Logan! Didn't know you were home. How's the bounding main?" His voice was surprisingly deep for so slender a man.

Stephen's impatience turned to pure irritation, but by the time he'd put down his glass, swung his chair around and stood up, he managed to look pleasantly surprised.

"Herbert! Good to see you." He held out his hand.

Julia noticed that Herbert winced when Stephen shook his hand, but he managed to retain his poise and his smile.

"You're looking well, Steve," he said.

"All a matter of clean living. You should come to sea with me. It'd put a little color in your cheeks."

"Thank you, no. I get seasick." The young man looked pointedly at Julia. "Aren't you going to introduce me, Steve?"

"With pleasure. Julia, this is Mr. Taylor. He writes poetry and gets seasick. Herbert, my wife, Mrs. Logan."

"I'm delighted, Mrs. Logan." His dark brown eyes were warm with admiration. "I didn't realize Steve had such good taste. You're not from Boston, are you?"

"No." Julia, enjoying the unspoken compliment in his attentive smile, smiled back at him. "I'm from East Dennis on the Cape."

"Really? How interesting. I'd like to hear all about it. May I join you?"

"No, you may not." Stephen was still standing impatiently with his napkin in his hand. "My wife and I are discussing the fitting out of my new ship."

"*Your* ship?" Herbert Taylor raised both eyebrows. "You've risen in the world, Steve. But that must be a terribly tedious conversation for such a beautiful young lady."

"Not for my wife," Stephen said firmly. "She helped her father design and build the *Crystal Star*. Mrs. Logan doesn't get seasick, Herbert, and she doesn't write bad poetry. I think you'd find you have very little in common."

"Well, if you're really talking business, I won't intrude." He looked at Julia again. "Some other time, perhaps? Dinner at my house?"

Julia recognized the flint that had come into Stephen's eyes and the tightening of his jaw muscles. She thought she'd better put an end to the conversation before he said something really outrageous.

"That's kind of you, Mr. Taylor, but until the ship is fitted out, I'm afraid our plans are uncertain."

"Then perhaps I could show you around Boston while Steve's hard at work. The Athenaeum has two interesting new paintings I'm sure you would enjoy."

"Does it have to be spelled out for you, Herbert? My wife will be working with me."

Herbert Taylor looked incredulous. "You don't mean it!"

"I do. Now, if you'll excuse us . . ." Stephen sat down, effectively putting an end to the conversation.

"Of course. Some other time, then." The young man bowed and left them.

"Stephen, that was rude," Julia said as soon as Herbert Taylor was well out of earshot.

"Not as rude as I wanted to be. What you just saw was a dazzling display of good manners and restraint on my part. He couldn't keep his eyes off of you. For a moment there, I thought he was going to order you served up on toast points with hollandaise sauce."

Julia laughed. "Do you know, Stephen, I think you're jealous!"

"Not really." As he reached across the table and touched her hand, his eyes smoked with tenderness. "It's just that I want so to be alone with you. We never really have been for long. There have always been intrusions and I resent them."

"Even from friends you haven't seen for a long time?" Julia asked, but she was glad that he wanted to be with her above all others. "After growing up in Boston, there must be a lot of people you'll want to see before we sail."

"No. No one but you, my lady. As a child, I never really did have many friends, and those I had, I've grown away from. The sea has separated us for too many years."

"But you had friends at Harvard. There was Aaron Martin," she said as she thought of her sister Sarah's husband. If it hadn't been for Aaron, Stephen might never have come to the Cape in search of a ship. Then she would never have known him.

"Aaron." Stephen's lips twisted with distaste as he said the name. "I would hardly call him a friend any longer. Not after he insinuated to your father that the reason why I wanted to marry you was for your money. No. He's gone the way of almost everyone I ever considered a friend."

A sadness flickered over his face, and Julia felt the loneliness in him that she had sensed a few times before. He refused to speak of his childhood except in the most general terms, and even then, a certain yearning that was almost desolation crept into his voice and across his face.

She squeezed his hand to comfort him. "There'll be other friends. A lot of them."

"I don't need friends," he said, and as he gazed into her deep blue eyes, his face softened into happiness. "As long as I have you, my lady, I'll be quite content with acquaintances, and as you can see, I have more than enough of those."

While they dined, the room that had seemed so filled with people grew dim, for the area that surrounded their table became a very private and magic place, where they were alone. Other

19

diners watched them and smiled, but no one else intruded. It was obvious that these two had a bright and shining newfound love. For a few, the sight of Julia and Stephen brought back the memories of their own youth and the bittersweet sadness of times that would never return.

It was late when they returned to their two-room suite at the Tremont House. In their enjoyment in dining alone, they had eaten slowly, more interested in each other than they were in the food, and had dawdled over their coffee.

Yet even after they had entered the small parlor and the boy who had lit the lamps and built up the fire had departed, they made no move towards the bedroom. Knowing that it was there and that most of the long night lay ahead of them, they enjoyed prolonging their anticipated joy. The certainty that no family member might wander in, that no member of the crew would interrupt their solitude, was a luxury they had never before experienced.

Stephen extinguished all the lamps but one, and then he came to sit beside Julia on the small velvet-covered love seat.

"Are you tired?" he asked and lazily stretched one arm out behind her.

"A little sleepy, perhaps, but not tired. It must have been the wine."

She leaned her head back against his arm and he dropped his hand onto her bare shoulder. As he pulled her towards him, he brushed her forehead with his lips.

"Then shall I tell you a bedtime story?" he asked.

"Yes," she said drowsily. "Tell me about Ombedia. You haven't mentioned it since our wedding night. Tell me about that imaginary land where you are king and I am queen."

"It's not imaginary, my lady, my queen. It's real. All we can do is pity the rest of the world because they are blind to it."

"Truly real?"

She curled up against him, and Stephen slipped his hand under her legs to pull her knees up onto his lap.

"Truly real," he assured her.

"Then tell me about it. Do we have a castle?"

"Of course. The most beautiful castle ever built. It's stoutly made of the finest oak, hackmatack, cedar, and pine. No one will ever be able to breach its walls. Its turrets soar up into the clouds, and from the topmost walls, you can look into heaven."

"And can you watch the sea from them?" She tilted her head back against his shoulder so that she could gaze up into his face.

"Ombedia must be surrounded by the sea, mustn't it?" He smiled lovingly down at her, and with the tip of one finger, he drew a line down the center of her nose. "Otherwise, the queen would be miserable, and the king would never permit that to happen. But you can't watch the sea from the highest towers. From them, the view is of angels and cherubim playing their ethereal music."

"And at night when we sleep, the sound of the sea will fill our dreams?"

"Always."

"But will we have to stay in Ombedia? The king and queen can travel, can't they?"

"Anywhere they wish. But of course, the realms they visit will fall to their invading footsteps as soon as they enter the country. Cheering crowds will line the streets as they pass because their subjects know that their rulers bring only lightness and joy and laughter."

"And no one is ever unhappy in Ombedia?"

"No one. It's against the law." He pulled her even closer so that he could reach behind her back to unfasten the buttons of her blue satin dress.

"Are there any children there?"

"Yes. Many children. The courtyards and halls ring with the laughter of princes and princesses, who play together with golden balls and silver hoops, emerald tops and crystal marbles."

"They're beautiful children, aren't they?" she murmured.

"The most beautiful children ever born . . . and the happiest."

He pulled her dress down and she slithered out of it so that it landed in a heap on the floor, but they were so entranced with one another, neither noticed the pool of blue satin on the carpet or thought of the possibility that it might be ruined. When Julia shivered, Stephen picked up his coat from the arm of the love seat and draped it around her shoulders and then pulled her close so that the heat of his body would warm her.

For a few moments, they were silent as they held tightly to each other. They heard no other sound than the two hearts that beat in closely timed rhythm. They saw no other sight than the face each loved better than any other. There was no need for speech, for the essence of their beings mingled as though the two had always been one.

Finally it was Julia who spoke. "When will we go to Ombedia?"

"We're already there. I'll show you." And as his lips touched hers, she became part of him in the reality of Ombedia.

A few days later, the morning was clear and the sun warm, but a cold wind blowing over the water piled waves up against the ebbing tide and capped them with back-blown white. The scent of salt, borne by the onshore breeze, mingled with but could not overpower the rich odor of spices that emanated from the warehouses that lined Central Wharf. Inland there would be hints of spring, but here on the waterfront, there were none.

Julia stood in the lee of a tall brick building and watched the men who were attaching lines from a crane to the huge timber that lay in a wagon on the wharf. The foremast for the *Crystal Star*.

As they hoisted it up from the wagon and down to the deck of the ship, she felt uneasy. Something was wrong, but she couldn't decide where the trouble lay. Whatever it was, she felt responsible.

She wondered if her uneasiness sprang from the fact that this was the first time she had been given such full and ultimate accountability. The Howard Shipyard had a reputation for building fine vessels with skillful care and out of the best materials. It was up to her to maintain that standard. Had her father been wrong when he had trusted her with the task?

But she had watched them step the mainmast, and she'd had no doubts then.

She left the shelter of the building and walked across the wharf to the side of the *Crystal Star*. The riggers were resting for a moment before they moved the crane into position to step the mast.

She made up her mind. No matter what Stephen said about staying off the ship while heavy work was in progress, she was going on board to have a look at it. After all, she'd been climbing around on vessels for years, and she'd never been injured. Since their marriage, Stephen had become overprotective, constantly afraid that she was going to be hurt in some way. She found it annoying even while she recognized that it was his love for her that caused it. Lifting her skirts, she walked down the gangway.

Without a glance at Stephen, who stood on the quarterdeck, she went directly to the mast. Strolling the length of the timber, she checked it, not only with her eyes, but with her fingers, feeling the finish and texture of the wood. Occasionally she thumped it with her knuckles. When she reached the end, she turned to walk down the other side of it. Her concentration was so deep, she didn't notice Stephen's approach across the white-bleached deck.

"What is it, Julie?"

"I don't know," she said, her arched eyebrows drawn together in a frown. "There's something wrong."

He looked at her quizzically, then rubbed his clean-shaven chin. "But you saw it over at the spar yard. You thought it was all right then."

"I know." She lowered her voice so the nearby men couldn't hear her. "Do you think it's the same one?"

"Certainly. John Newman's an honest man. Your father's done business with him before, hasn't he?"

"Yes." She turned her attention once again to the mast and glared at it as though daring it to show her its weakness. "We've dealt with him for years."

"Well?" He pushed his cap back and a wayward lock fell across his forehead.

"I've got to find out what's wrong," she said and pressed her lips together.

Slowly she walked the length of the mast once more, and Stephen, following behind her, also gave it a careful inspection. When they had reached the other end, Julia looked at her husband.

"Tell them to take it back and bring us another one."

"Julia, we've already approved it," he said impatiently. "It's cut to your specifications."

"I don't care," she said, lifting her chin and looking at him stubbornly. "I don't think it's the same one. Tell them to take it back. There's something wrong with it."

"For God's sake, what is it?"

"I don't know, but I don't like it."

"Well, without good reason, I can hardly tell them to take it back. You're the one who'll have to tell them." He looked at her intently, his eyes a smoky grey. "And you do realize, don't you, that if they take it back, it'll take time to make up another? It's not only going to cost more, but it'll hold us in port much longer than we'd anticipated."

"Damn!" Julia said and impatiently pushed back tendrils of hair that had escaped from her bonnet. "They won't listen to me. They think I'm just some meddling woman. I wish Papa was here. He'd know what's wrong."

She stooped down so that she could sight along the top of the mast. It ran straight and true. Damn, she said again to herself. Then she stood up and looked at her husband with a defiant challenge in her indigo eyes.

"If Papa was here, *he'd* make them take it back."

"Be reasonable, Julia. I've seen hundreds of masts, and there's nothing wrong with this one." His rising annoyance showed in the tightening of his square chin. "Absolutely nothing."

The boss rigger came up to them as they stood rigidly staring at each other. "We're ready to step the mast now, Captain Logan."

Stephen glanced for a moment at Julia. Then he shrugged. "Go ahead," he said to the rigger. "Julia, you'd better go ashore. If you stay here, you're likely to get hurt."

She stood her ground for a moment and glared at him.

"Well, don't say I didn't warn you!"

Her skirts swirled as she turned and strode across the deck to the gangway. Without looking back, she went ashore.

Keeping an eye on the men stepping the mast, she began to pace the granite wharf as she tried to work off her feelings of frustration. At home in the shipyard, men listened when she spoke and they carried out her orders. They didn't ask why.

Even Daniel Sears, who was second only to her father, listened to her and respected her judgment. But here in Boston, they wouldn't listen. Just because she was a woman, they wouldn't believe her knowledge and abilities could be as keen as a man's. She'd found out soon after they had arrived that she had to give every order through Stephen.

At least they followed his orders, and as far as shipbuilding and fitting out went, he believed in her. Usually. 'Twas lucky he'd spent so much time with her while she worked in the shipyard at home. He knew she was able. Maybe Papa'd counted on that when

24

he'd told her to handle the fitting out of the *Crystal Star* without his own help.

But why wouldn't Stephen listen to her this time? It was so important. Was he so eager to get to sea, he'd sacrifice almost anything for it?

As soon as the mast was in place, Julia returned aboard. Ignoring the men who were running temporary lines to hold it in position, she walked slowly around it. Now that it was upright, maybe a flaw would show up.

She couldn't find one.

Frustrated, she walked aft to where Stephen stood watching her from the quarterdeck.

"Satisfied now?" he asked when she reached the top step.

"No. But I can't find what's wrong."

"There's nothing wrong."

"There is!" She put her hands on her hips and glared at him.

His face hardened and the white lines at the corners of his eyes showed more clearly in his tanned face.

"Then, for God's sake, tell me what it is."

"I don't *know* what it is, but you'd better listen to me, Stephen Logan. That foremast is important. If you want to bring the *Crystal Star* home safe again, you'd better listen to me."

"Don't tell me what's important on a ship, my lady. I was at sea when you were still in apron strings."

"Oh, no you weren't. I was helping my father in the yard before I was twelve. Furthermore, I was *born* at sea, and you never set foot on a deck till nine years ago when you were twenty."

"Didn't I?" He raised one eyebrow and looked at her tauntingly. "I never told you about the summers I put in on the coastal trade while I was in school."

"I don't believe you. You're just making it up, trying to impress me. If you had, you'd have told me about it a long time ago. That's certain."

"I don't tell you everything, my lady." His eyes were cool. They might have been enemies rather than lovers. "And you may have been born at sea, but you haven't been back since you were five years old. That's sixteen years ago, almost seventeen. You can't remember much about those early years."

She straightened her shoulders and flung back her head. "I most certainly do!"

"I doubt it. You may know how to build a ship, but you don't know how she works at sea. You don't know what it's like in a gale or a hurricane in the North Atlantic. You don't know what it's like to fight your way around Cape Horn."

"I've got a pretty good idea."

"No, you don't. No one can have a 'pretty good idea' until they've done it. You're so anxious to go to sea. Well, you're going, but I'm not sure you'll thank me for taking you."

"I can put up with anything you can!"

Stephen shook his head and, taking a step closer, tried to tower over her, which wasn't easy. She was just a few inches shorter than he was.

"You're as bad as the farmboys who run away from home to go to sea, thinking it's a romantic thing to do," he said. "They soon find out what the sea's like. It doesn't take long to discover there's nothing romantic about it. They grow up fast and so will you."

"I've already grown up, and I know that mast is wrong."

"Prove it!"

They glared at each other, blue fire meeting grey flint.

So intense was their silent battle, they failed to notice the heavy-set man in the well-cut grey suit, who had been walking along the wharf beside the *Crystal Star* while he subjected her to the closest scrutiny.

Chapter Two

1842

Seeking no one's permission to board, the man strolled down the gangway. With the arrogant air of an owner, he inspected fittings and joinery work through the gold spectacles that were perched on his nose. Slowly he made his way aft until he reached a spot just below the quarterdeck. Neither Julia nor Stephen was aware of his presence until they heard his voice.

"Well, Stephen," he called up to them. "I see the rumors are true."

The sight of the newcomer did nothing to lessen Stephen's anger. In fact, his face hardened when he glanced down at the portly middle-aged man.

"Hello, Uncle Brenard," he said. There was no welcome in his voice.

The older man came lumbering up the steps of the starboard ladder, which was crafted like an elegant staircase, to the quarterdeck. It seemed an effort for him and he leaned heavily on a gold-headed ebony cane.

"So you've been in Boston a week and haven't even stopped by the counting house to see me," he said.

"After our last meeting, there didn't seem to be much point in it," Stephen said abruptly.

"Now, now. We've had harsh words in the past. Never stopped you from coming back before."

"As I said when I left, there seemed to be no reason for me to come again." Stephen's anger had turned from fire to ice.

"Meaning you think you don't need me anymore now that you've gone and gotten command of a ship on your own." Brenard Logan's eyes swept over the length of the ship.

About one hundred forty-four feet long with a thirty-one-foot beam, he shrewdly estimated. A little long amidships and too fine in the bow for his taste. Still and all, that seemed to be the modern trend. Probably run about six hundred and fifty tons.

Stephen watched his uncle as he surveyed the *Crystal Star*. The older man might purse his lips and shake his head as though he disapproved of the radical design of the ship, but Stephen knew that he was impressed. The pleasure this gave Stephen only heightened the animosity he felt for his relative.

"It's more than you would give me, Uncle," he said. "You own a dozen ships, but never had one for me."

"I would have sooner or later. You still had a few things to learn as supercargo, and you were more valuable to me and the firm that way. But if I'd known you *really* wanted a ship, I'd have found one for you."

"When hell froze over."

"Now, now, Stephen. Is that any way to talk to me?" The older man's dark eyes were innocently injured behind his spectacles. "You know I've always tried to do what was best for you. Gave you a good home when your parents died. Nothing but the finest schools. Sent you to Harvard. Gave you a good job in my business. Brought you up like my own son."

"Yes, you did. But somewhere, a few years back, you stopped."

"I never stopped trying to do what was right for you."

Stephen pushed his cap farther back on his head and grinned. Julia had never seen so much malice in a smile before.

"Want to know what I think, Uncle? I think you raised me the way you might raise a prize pig. For your own profit. I'm twenty-nine years old, and I'm finally going to sea as master of a ship. You could have given me a command when I was twenty-four or twenty-five, and you know it. But you didn't."

Uncle Brenard pulled out a large white handkerchief and,

taking off his spectacles, began to polish them. Uncovered, his eyes were smaller and harder than when seen through the magnification of his spectacles. They were absolutely chilling, Julia thought.

"I'll give you a ship right now if you'll resign command of this one," he said, still concentrating on his spectacles.

"I hope you're joking."

"No, no. I'm not." Satisfied that they were clean, he settled the spectacles back on his nose. "I mean it. I give you my word. The *White Cloud* needs a master. You can have her."

"You really are incredible, Uncle." Stephen stuck his hands into his pockets and leaned back against the wheel. Though his body was more relaxed, the contempt in his grey eyes intensified. "You really expect me to give up this ship and break my contract with her owner just to take that old hulk of yours to sea?"

"It's a family vessel, Stephen," Uncle Brenard said placatingly. "I'll give you better terms than a stranger would. Family should come first."

"I never noticed you putting *me* first before. Besides I own some shares in the *Crystal Star*."

The older man was immediately suspicious. "Where'd you get the money?"

"I saved it. Believe it or not, out of that miserable salary you paid me, I saved it."

"Now, I was never that miserly. Not with my own brother's boy."

"It wasn't a captain's salary. Wasn't even a proper salary for a supercargo."

"No. Thought if I paid you too much, you might do something foolish. Like getting married."

"I see you've heard all the rumors, Uncle."

"Oh, yes. I don't miss much. I presume this young lady is your wife."

"Yes."

For a moment, Julia thought Stephen wasn't going to introduce her, but then he straightened up from the wheel and turned towards her. When he looked at her, their quarrel seemed to have been forgotten. Love as well as pride softened his eyes and a slight smile appeared at the corners of his mouth.

"Julia, as you've probably already gathered, this is my Uncle Brenard."

29

His voice hardened when he looked at his uncle. "Uncle, this is Julia."

The older man took a step towards her and, sweeping off his tall grey hat, revealed a balding head with a few strands of dark hair plastered across the top. When Julia extended her hand, he bowed almost imperceptibly over it.

"Pleased to meet you, my dear. The gossips haven't exaggerated a jot when they said how lovely you are."

Julia sensed that he was very much aware of the rough and faded grey cloak she was wearing. She didn't care. It was warm and it was ideal for climbing around on a ship. She straightened her shoulders and lifted her chin.

"Thank you, Mr. Logan," she said sweetly. "It's a pleasure to finally meet you. Stephen's told me *so* much about you."

"Has he?" Uncle Brenard glanced suspiciously at Stephen. "Yes, I imagine he has. I hear you come from the Cape."

"Yes, I do."

"Ben Howard's daughter, I hear. A good man. Now that we're related, I'll have to see if I can't find my way clear to having him build a vessel or two for me. I understand he can use the business."

Julia drew herself up very straight and looked directly into Brenard Logan's eyes.

"Then you've been misinformed, Mr. Logan. My father has more orders than he can handle."

"Good, good. Glad to hear it. Always pleasant to hear a man's doing well." He looked at Stephen. "So you've married wisely after all, Stephen. Got some money into the bargain. I was always afraid you'd marry some little slut out of the gutter. They seemed to be more your type." He glanced at Julia, and from the look he gave her, she wasn't so sure he didn't consider her a slut. "You turned your nose up at enough lovely girls of good family, money too, right here in Boston."

"I think you'd better leave, Uncle."

Julia could see that Stephen's hand, though hanging at his side, was clenched into a fist.

"No offence meant, Stephen. I'm just complimenting you on your good sense. If you'd displayed it earlier, I might have given you a command then."

"Well, perhaps, Uncle, things have worked out for the best,"

Stephen said acidly. "I'm master of a fine, fast, new ship. She's not one of your old barges. Captain Crofton has complete confidence in me. He doesn't keep me on a leash the way you do some of your masters. And if I hadn't had to go up to the Cape to find my own ship, I might never have met my wife. I might have had to settle for one of your empty-headed 'lovely girls of good family.' I think I'm the winner, Uncle."

"Well, we'll see about that." Brenard Logan put his hat back on his balding head. "The wheel goes around and around. Sometimes you're at the top, but then you sometimes find yourself suddenly at the bottom again, Stephen. Very suddenly. You might be glad to have me for a friend someday."

"Is that a threat, Uncle?"

"No. Just some good, sound advice from someone who's lived a lot longer than you have. Well, I'll be off. Look me up the next time you're in Boston." He raised his hat slightly to Julia. "It was a pleasure meeting you, my dear. I hope you won't find living with this young rascal too difficult. It's hard to keep him in line."

"Good-bye, Mr. Logan," Julia said simply.

"Good-bye, Uncle," Stephen said coolly. "Give my regards to the family."

"I will. They'll be glad to know you're still alive."

Julia and Stephen stood in silence as they watched the portly man make his way down from the quarterdeck and over the gangway. He didn't look up at them, even when he walked along the wharf beside the ship.

When he was out of earshot, Julia turned to her husband.

"He's unbelievable, Stephen! Asking you to break your word to Captain Asa just like that!"

"Asa Crofton may be crotchety, but he's more of a father to me than that man ever was," Stephen said. His eyes were narrowed as he looked up the wharf at his uncle's receding back. "Uncle Brenard gave me the best, but only on the surface. Just enough so everyone would say how good he was and praise him for how well he treated me. But affection? Any show of really caring what I thought about or felt? Never."

"What an awful childhood you must have had," Julia said, and she could not help comparing it with the warmth and love she had received from her own family."

"No. Not awful. Uncle Brenard never resorted to violence or

anything of that sort, and Aunt Wilma was all right. A little humorless, but she meant well. But they had their own children, and I was always the stranger in the house." He smiled at her then, and there was no more than a touch of melancholy in it. "The best thing to be said about it is that it's over now, and I'm finally free of them all."

"It just seems sad."

Ignoring the riggers who were leaving the ship, he put an arm around her waist and drew her with him to the starboard rail.

"Nothing to be sad about. You and Captain Asa are my family now."

"But that doesn't make up for your childhood."

"I think it does." He gazed at her face and brushed a few stray tendrils of black hair away from it with gentle fingers. "At any rate, I probably learned a lot more about life than if my parents had lived and brought me up with all the love in the world. And as Uncle Brenard said, he gave me a good education. The best. I don't know whether my father could have afforded it or not."

"What did your father do, Stephen? You've never told me."

"He was Uncle Brenard's partner."

"Really?" Julia's sapphire eyes widened in amazement. "And yet your uncle's rich and you inherited nothing?"

Stephen looked away from her and at the two newly-stepped masts. He seemed to have forgotten her in his concentration upon them.

"Stephen?"

"I don't know, Julie." He took a deep breath and leaned back against the rail. "I've had more than a few suspicions about that, myself."

"Shouldn't you do something about it? Can't you find out?"

"I tried once. Even hired a lawyer to look into it for me."

"What happened?"

"Nothing, except that I wasted a lot of my money on lawyers' fees. There's no proof. My father was ill for a couple of years before he died. During that time, he signed everything over to Uncle Brenard. The papers are legal. My father's signature appears to be genuine."

"Well, I don't trust that uncle of yours. I don't even like him. All that talk about Boston girls and giving my father a couple of orders. As though Papa needed charity!" Julia lifted her chin and her eyes sparkled with blue fire as she remembered the anger she hadn't allowed to show in front of Brenard Logan.

Stephen laughed at her.

"Don't take that seriously, Julie. It's just his way of getting information. If he riles people enough, they might tell him something."

"Well, he riled me."

"And you told him something."

"I guess I did," she said ruefully.

"That's all right." He grinned at her, the slow, lazy grin that so contrasted with his usual vitality. "It didn't hurt. He doesn't respect anyone if he can run over them . . . or buy them. I think I went up a few notches in his opinion today."

"Well, I don't want to see him again."

"I doubt you'll have to. You'll notice he didn't ask us to call at the house."

"Probably because he thinks you consider it your home."

"No." Stephen looked away from her and watched a barkentine that was sailing into the harbor, trim and loaded with a heavy cargo from halfway across the world. "He doesn't think that at all."

Julia looked at his profile. She was puzzled. He was trying to tell her something, and yet at the same time, he was trying to avoid telling her. She studied his clear forehead, his straight nose and strong chin, searching for a clue in his tense face. Then she had a suspicion.

"But he would have invited us if I'd been a 'lovely Boston girl'?"

"Most likely." He still wouldn't look at her.

"In other words, he thinks you married beneath yourself?"

Stephen was silent, but she could see the flicker of a muscle in his jaw.

"Well, I'll have you know, Stephen Logan, that at home, everyone thought I was marrying beneath *myself*. What's so grand about Boston, anyway? The people at home are just as rich, they're better sailors, and they're a lot nicer than anyone I've met here."

She whirled away from him and swept across the quarterdeck to the opposite rail. She leaned on it and stared angrily into the water that was swirling out of the harbor with the ebbing tide. Even the water in Boston was dirty!

Stephen came up behind her and put a hand on the rail on

either side of her. His body was pressed closed against her back, trapping her at the rail.

"*I* didn't say I'd married beneath myself, Julie," he said softly, his lips almost touching her ear. "I doubt even Uncle Brenard thinks so."

"Then what *does* he think?" She continued to stare stubbornly into the water, refusing to acknowledge the warmth of his body, which was like a caress.

"He's very proud of his social position. I don't think I enter into it at all. He has a strange set of values."

"Well, I don't care what he thinks! I'm Julia Howard and I'm proud of it."

"You're Julia *Logan*, and you still don't have to care what anyone thinks." He moved one hand from the rail and, putting an arm around her, pulled her back against him. "Except me," he whispered huskily.

Julia gave up and leaned against the strength of his hard body.

"Except you," she agreed. "But *you* care about what people think."

"Only people a lot more important than Uncle Brenard. If I'm to make that fortune I promised you, I need contacts with the people who really hold the power."

"Oh, Stephen, I don't care about a fortune." She watched the gulls swooping down over the harbor, picking bits of garbage out of the water. "But I know you want it. How are those people, those important people, going to look at me?"

"The same way they looked at you at dinner the other night. With appreciation and respect. Anyone who doesn't will end up being very sorry for it."

Three weeks later, the *Crystal Star* was fully rigged, her lofty spars and crosstrees held in place by an intricately woven network of lines. Now the decks belonged to the sailmakers, who went to and fro with their measurements, while in the sail lofts, yards of cotton duck were being sewn into two suits of sails. There was no longer any need for Julia or Stephen to be constantly present aboard the ship.

Julia shopped for the personal things they would need during the long months at sea and Stephen searched for a profitable cargo. He spent hours tramping through the streets of Boston, sitting in coffee houses and Topliff's News Room in the Old State House. Wandering through insurance offices and into merchants' counting houses, he picked up a promise of Lowell cotton and lead in one place, heard of an auction of English wares he could buy for China in another.

Captain Asa Crofton had arranged for a shipment of valuable sea otter, much prized by the Chinese, to be picked up by the *Crystal Star* in Oahu, but he'd left the rest of the arrangements in Stephen's hands.

On a sunny April afternoon, Julia was dressing in the bedroom of their suite at the Tremont House. She listened absentmindedly to the street vendors who called their wares in the street beneath her window as she admired her new rose silk dress in the long pier glass, but her thoughts were of Stephen.

The dress had been his choice, and as in all the clothes he had delighted in helping her select, she'd been amazed by his knowledge of fabric and workmanship as well as by his unerring sense of good taste. Stephen enjoyed shopping and bargaining as much as he'd enjoyed the building and fitting out of the ship. She understood now what people meant when they spoke of her husband as a shrewd trader, and she knew why his uncle, reluctant to let him go, had wanted to keep him on forever as his supercargo.

To Stephen, business seemed to be a game, which he entered with zest. He often came back from his quest for cargo glowing with the excitement of having made a good purchase. He would spend hours telling her in great detail just how he had managed to find the goods, how he'd beaten down the price, and how much he thought he could sell them for in the islands or in China.

When she heard the door from the hall to their parlor open, she hurried with her buttons. Stephen had promised to take her to the Athenaeum this afternoon, and she'd meant to be ready when he returned.

She heard the door close, but then there was only silence. Strange. He usually called out and came to give her a kiss the minute he arrived. Could someone else have gotten the key to their rooms?

"Stephen?" She quickly fastened the last button.

"Yes." He sounded subdued.

She went to the bedroom door, her many petticoats rustling against the silk of her dress. Stephen was standing with his back to her, pouring a glass of rum from the crystal decanter that usually stood on the small mahogany corner table.

"You sound low, Stephen. What is it? Weren't you able to get the lumber for the Sandwich Islands?"

He turned and she could see that his usually impeccable cravat was twisted and rumpled. The willful lock of hair had tumbled over his forehead, and he had that withdrawn air that she hated. From the way he was looking at her, she might have been a stranger.

"I signed the papers for it this afternoon," he said listlessly.

She wanted to go to him, to hold him against whatever it was that troubled him, but the grey bleakness of his eyes held her back.

"Well, what is it, then?" she asked as she unconsciously pressed a pleat of rose silk between her fingers. "I thought you'd be happy about the lumber. You've already got the needles and thread and rum, and you've been promised a load of codfish for the islands, haven't you?"

"Yes, but it's that damned opium." He strode to the window and stared out from between the red velvet curtains that smelled of dust and smoke after the long winter. Then he impatiently pushed the curtains away from him and slumped down on the nearby settee. "I still haven't been able to get in touch with Hiram Richardson. I suspect he's avoiding me."

Julia looked at him uncertainly for a moment. The late afternoon sun coming through the window haloed his hair and touched his face with warmth.

"Why should he avoid you?" she asked and went to sit beside him.

"I don't know." He held his glass up to catch the sunlight and watched the dark amber turn golden.

"Could it be your uncle's doing?" she asked slowly.

"I wonder?" He looked at her thoughtfully, then took another sip from his glass. Stretching his legs out in front of him, he laid his arm across the settee behind her. "No, probably not. I don't think Uncle Brenard has any influence over him."

"What else could it be?"

"That's what I'd like to know. I hear Richardson's having an enormous summer house built at Nahant. Seems to be spending most of his time out there."

"But he has a large firm to run," she said and frowned slightly with the intensity of her thoughts. "One of the largest in Boston. He must be here part of the time."

"He should be, with his vessels constantly coming and going, but whenever I go to his counting house, his chief clerk tells me he's not in."

He let his arm drop around her shoulders, then pulled her closer to him. Julia looked at him tenderly and pushed his sun-bleached hair back from his forehead.

"Do you know him well enough to go to his house?" she asked.

"Not really, but I *have* tried it. His butler came up with the same story. He wasn't in."

"Then maybe you'd better hire a buggy and go out to Nahant and see if you can't find him there," she said firmly. She couldn't stand this strange listlessness in Stephen. It was so unlike him, he who would never admit to defeat.

He lifted an eyebrow and looked at her for a moment. Then he grinned. "Always direct, aren't you, my lady?"

"If you want something, that's the only way to get it."

"Not always. It might be the way to build a ship, but it's not the way to deal with a merchant, especially not one like Hiram Richardson."

"You won't know whether it is or not till you've tried it."

"And if you're wrong, he might very well refuse to sell me any opium at all."

"Stephen," she said as she lightly brushed some dust from his light blue frock coat. "Is the opium all that important? You've got cotton goods and English wares for China. Can't you find something else besides the opium to round out the cargo?"

"It's important," he said and his arm tightened around her. "I want it and I'm going to get it. Captain Asa says that ship must be paid for on her first voyage, and I intend to see that he's satisfied."

"There *are* other goods."

"None like opium. There's a big profit to be made if I can lay my hands on it. In China, it will sell for five times the price I'll pay for it here, and it won't take up much cargo space."

37

"That *is* a nice profit," she said thoughtfully.

"Damned right it is. *If* I can get the opium." He drained his glass, then stared at it as though it would show him the future. "The problem is that, at the moment, Richardson seems to have the only supply of it in Boston, outside of Perkins and Company. They import most of it from Smyrna, but they ship it all out in their own vessels. They won't deal with me."

He got up abruptly and walked over to the table that held the crystal decanter. After pouring more rum into his glass, he turned and looked at her.

"Damn it, Julie! Aside from buying it on Captain Asa's account, that's what I wanted to put our money in. That five hundred dollars Captain Asa gave us for a wedding gift can turn into twenty-five hundred in China. The profit's equal to twenty months pay."

Julia watched him prowl restlessly around the room. He had obviously completely forgotten that he'd promised to take her to the Aethenaeum. Seeing the paintings there might distract him from the opium problem. On the other hand, she hesitated to suggest it. She'd already learned that, when Stephen was in this kind of mood, he was quick to anger. A neutral subject seemed the safest course.

"I ran into your friend, Herbert Taylor, on Broad Street today," she said casually as she watched to see what effect her words would have on him.

"Oh?" He looked at her intently. She had obviously gotten his attention. "I hope you're not making a habit of seeing him."

"Of course not, Stephen. 'Twas the first time I'd seen him since the night you introduced us."

"What did he have to say?" Stephen leaned against the window frame and looked down at the street below. After seeing the truth in her face, he had lost all interest in Herbert Taylor, whom he considered a dandified fop.

"Just that his mother's having a musicale on Thursday evening. He invited us to come."

"I hope you said no."

"Yes. I knew you didn't like him."

Stephen was silent for a moment, his mind still on the opium. Then he quickly straightened up and turned away from the window. "Well, I've changed my mind," he said. "We're going." He was suddenly charged with energy and purpose.

"We are?" Julia was bewildered.

"Yes, we are." He put the glass down on the table decisively. "The Taylors and the Richardsons have always been good friends. We might just be lucky enough to meet Hiram Richardson there."

"But I've already told Herbert Taylor we couldn't come, Stephen."

"Well, now we'll tell him we're coming. I'd be willing to wager he's hanging around the Athenaeum right now." He looked in the mirror while he straightened his cravat and brushed back his hair. Then he picked his hat and gloves up from the table where he had laid them. "Are you ready to go?"

As they approached the front steps of the gracious three-story Beacon Hill house, which Stephen told her had been designed by Bullfinch, Julia was a little apprehensive. She wondered just how Stephen's friends would welcome her. Her meeting with Brenard Logan hadn't been exactly reassuring. Once inside, however, she found that she needn't have worried.

After leaving their cloaks with the butler, they entered the drawing room, and just beside its entrance, Mrs. Taylor, with her fair-skinned, dark-haired, poetic son beside her, greeted Julia as though she'd known her all of her life. Her confidence continued to rise as she glanced at the guests and saw a few familiar faces. Some she'd met only recently, when they'd come to see the *Crystal Star*, but others were friends of her father's whom she'd known for many years.

The drawing room itself was warm and inviting with its rose brocade curtains and luxurious, deep-piled Turkish carpets. The light of many candles was refracted from the prisms of the crystal chandelier and reflected in mirrors strategically placed near the sconces on the wall. It gleamed on the bared shoulders of women in lustrous silk dresses and mellowed the glowing colors of the men's formal coats and gaiter-strapped trousers. Most of the richly upholstered furniture had been drawn into small groupings along the walls, and there the elderly ladies and gentlemen held court.

Almost immediately, people drifted up to meet them, and their names came at her so fast, Julia felt she'd never sort them out. Stephen seemed to know everyone and many seemed anxious to meet his new wife. When she saw the jealousy that tinged the curiosity in the eyes of several young matrons and their even younger sisters, Julia was amused. She hadn't realized until now that her husband was considered quite a catch. Yet glancing at Stephen in his light blue frock coat and his tight white trousers, she understood why. He was certainly one of the best looking men in the room. However, the older women were kind and a few asked her to call on them.

More often, though, as they progressed through the room, Julia found that she and Stephen were drawn into conversation with small groups of men who wanted to talk about the *Crystal Star*. As shipowners, merchants, and captains, some retired and some still active, they were interested in the controversial design of the ship. Some considered her radical, oversparred, and unseaworthy. Others were excited by the prospect of more speed that her lines seemed to promise.

Stephen was enjoying the interest that both his ship and his young wife excited, but as soon as they had entered the room, he'd seen that Hiram Richardson was not amongst the guests. Each time the door opened, he glanced at it expectantly.

Then, while they were talking to two older captains in a corner of the room, Julia saw Stephen stiffen ever so slightly. She followed the direction of his eyes.

The man who had just entered the room was an imposing figure. Even his chestnut hair, sprinkled with grey, had a vibrant quality. His head was held high and his bulky shoulders, in an emerald green coat, were square with the knowledge of his own importance. While speaking to his hostess, he glanced casually around the room.

"Who is it, Stephen?" Julia asked.

"Hiram Richardson," he said while pretending to look at Julia, but in reality watching the merchant prince out of the corner of his eye. He noted that, when the man's casual search of the room came to Julia, his face lit up with interest.

"Aren't you going over to talk to him?" Julia whispered. "Now's your chance."

"Let him come to me." There was an amused secret in Stephen's smile.

"But how can you be sure he'll come?"

He looked at Julia. Her cheeks were flushed deeper than the

rose of her low-cut gown, her eyes were wide with dark blue puzzlement, and lustrous blue-black curls framed the delicately molded features of her face. My wife, he thought. His pride in her was not due to her beauty alone. She was unique, different from any of the hundreds of women he had met either in Boston or during his travels. She was a prize that any man would like to have won, and she was his. Life might have shortchanged him until recently, but now he was coming into his own. His smile deepened.

"I'm sure, my lady. Very sure." He drew her arm through his and turned to the grey haired, portly man on his right. "And you say, sir, there are no real difficulties to be encountered entering the harbor at Riga?"

"Not if you remember just a few things," the older man said, happy to impart some of his hard-won knowledge.

Julia was astonished by Stephen's assumed nonchalance. She watched Hiram Richardson, who was slowly making his way from group to group, always pausing to have a few words with each. Finally, he did seem to be coming in their direction. From the increased pressure of Stephen's arm on her hand, she knew that he was aware of it, too, even if he was pretending great interest in the latest news from the Baltic.

"Captain Logan?" Hiram Richardson's voice was rich and deep.

Stephen turned slowly and nodded formally to the merchant prince. "Good evening, Captain Richardson."

"I hear you've found a ship." Hiram Richardson warmly shook hands with Stephen. "Congratulations."

"Yes, sir, I have." Stephen seemed to be utterly relaxed, but Julia could sense his tension. "I was fortunate in being given command of the *Crystal Star.*"

"Sorry I didn't have a vessel for you when you came to see me last spring, but perhaps from your point of view, it's just as well." There was nothing but candor and goodwill in Richardson's light blue eyes. "I've seen the *Crystal Star* over at Central Wharf. She's a fine looking vessel."

"I think she is," Stephen said.

"Built by Benjamin Howard, wasn't she?"

"Yes, sir. Julia," Stephen said as he turned to her. "May I present Captain Richardson? Sir, my wife is the former Miss Howard."

"I'm enchanted, Mrs. Logan." The older man, bowing slowly

over to kiss the hand she held out to him, observed her low-cut bodice closely as he did so.

"And so am I, Captain Richardson." Julia smiled an innocently charming smile. "My husband has often told me how much he admires you."

"Really? I'd like to hear more about that," he said as he straightened up. He glanced at Stephen. "Would you permit Mrs. Logan to be my partner at supper, Captain Logan?"

"Of course." Stephen found he was beginning to dislike the gleam in the other man's blue eyes when he looked at Julia, but he couldn't afford to let his antagonism show. Damn it! This was his chance, maybe his only chance, to get the opium. "I've been trying to contact you for several days, sir."

"So I've heard." Richardson was absorbed in looking at Julia when he spoke and didn't bother to glance in Stephen's direction.

"I wonder if I might set up an appointment to see you within the week." A muscle twitched in Stephen's jaw.

"No business tonight," the merchant said. His teeth flashed unbelievably white when he smiled. "Tonight is for pleasure."

The sound of instruments tuning up in the other room caught their attention. People began drifting in that direction.

"Shall we take our seats?" Hiram Richardson said and offered his arm to Julia.

Trapped, Stephen followed closely behind them. He wasn't going to let Richardson have any more time alone with Julia than was absolutely necessary. In the richly paneled library, the merchant led the way to a pair of delicate crewel-covered chairs in the back of the room. The light was dimmer here.

"Is this all right with you, Mrs. Logan?" he asked.

Julia was disappointed. She had wanted to be near the front where she could watch the musicians, but she smiled at him. "Yes, it's fine," she said.

After she was seated, Hiram Richardson, quickly appropriating the chair beside her, left Stephen standing alone. In order to sit beside his wife, he had to draw up a chair from another grouping. He was beginning to dislike Hiram Richardson. Very much.

Julia was aware of Stephen's irritation, but there was nothing she could do about it, and once she heard the first notes of the Beethoven violin concerto, she forgot both men who sat beside her. The beautiful precision of the rising cadence, the clean force

42

of the composer's strength, reminded her of the sweep and the power of the sea. The music completely claimed her.

However, it did not claim the two men beside her. Stephen's exasperation mounted when he saw Hiram Richardson watching his wife. The man seemed far more entranced with her than with the music, and Julia was doing nothing to discourage it. On the contrary, he thought. Leaning back in his chair, he watched her. Her blue eyes were sparkling between her thick black lashes and her lips were slightly parted as she listened to the music. She was too damned beautiful.

His instinct was to take her away from here, out of this house, as soon as the music ended. Yet he needed the other man, and if it hadn't been for Julia, this opportunity might never have arisen.

Supper was served in the elliptical dining room almost immediately after the music had reached its conclusion, and although the oysters and partridges that were served were amongst his favorite delicacies and the ices were a culinary triumph, it was an endless and excruciating affair for Stephen. The prismed candles and hothouse flowers that decorated the long center of the table failed to impress him, for he was separated by half its length from Julia. He tried to make polite conversation with the girl who sat beside him. She was quite pretty with long blonde curls that swayed forward as she talked with him and she was well versed in all the proper phrases and responses. Once he would have enjoyed flirting with her, but now Stephen was far more aware of Julia's dark head bent toward Hiram Richardson. He saw her eyes flash and her mouth curve with laughter as she talked. Damn it! Why couldn't she be more sedate?

When the supper finally ended, Stephen went directly to Julia. He'd had enough.

Perhaps Hiram Richardson read the intent in Stephen's tense face. If he did, he received it with amused gallantry and a warm handshake.

"Thank you, Captain Logan, for sharing your lovely lady with me. This has been the most pleasant evening I've spent in many a day. You're a fortunate man."

He bent, quite correctly this time, over Julia's extended hand.

"The pleasure was mine, Captain Richardson," she said gravely, aware that Stephen was intently watching her with suspicion.

"I must be off," Richardson said. "I have a busy day ahead of me." He looked at Stephen with quiet calculation. "Be at my counting house at ten tomorrow morning. And bring Mrs. Logan with you. I'm sure she'd be interested in some of the models and paintings I have in my office."

"We'll be there," Stephen promised.

He stood silently beside Julia while they watched the man leave. Then he asked the butler for their cloaks. After thanking their host and hostess, he wrapped Julia's cloak around her shoulders and quickly led her from the house.

Once outside, Julia took a deep breath of the crisp night air that was underlaid with the balminess of coming spring. "Well, now you've got your opium," she said gaily. "Isn't that grand?"

"I'm not so sure." He helped her into the hansom cab that waited for them in the street.

"What do you mean? He all but promised it."

"I'll tell you when we get home," he said brusquely and got into the cab beside her.

Driving back to the hotel and on the way up to their rooms, Stephen remained rigidly silent, and Julia became tense as she sensed the mounting darkness of his mood.

When they entered their parlor, he stiffly helped her off with her cloak and threw it, together with his own, over a chair.

"Well?" She turned to face him, determined to meet whatever was coming head on.

"I will not have you flirting with other men." His jaw was tight and his eyes cold as grey iron.

She stared at him in complete surprise. What on earth had come over Stephen?

"I was just trying to get you an appointment with Captain Richardson," she said quietly. "That *was* the purpose of our going to the Taylors', wasn't it?"

"You don't have to sell yourself on the open market. I pay for my cargoes with money, not with my wife's favors."

"Stephen! That's terrible. How can you even suggest such a thing? There weren't any favors involved, and you know it. You're the one who said he could be my partner at supper. I didn't."

He moved a step closer to her.

"I saw you. Laughing and talking, flirting with him like a coquette, making promises you can't fulfill."

She opened her mouth to reply, but the words wouldn't come.

Her mind wouldn't work. She was absolutely stunned. She shook her head.

"I didn't make any promises."

"Promises aren't made by words alone, my lady. Beautiful women make promises with their eyes. Don't think I didn't see you. I never took my eyes off you all evening."

She turned away from him and sank down on the nearest chair. As she passed her hand across her forehead and closed her eyes, she tried to think, but images only slid over her mind without lingering long enough to acquire any coherence. She couldn't believe that this was Stephen. The man she loved. The man she'd married. She had known that he tended to be jealous, but she'd never dreamed that his jealousy was so intense it could lead him to interpret her actions so wildly.

Even with her eyes closed, she was aware that he had followed her and was standing over her. She opened her eyes and looked up to see that his fists were clenched by his sides, his face was taut, and a glimmer of violence lit his eyes. Never before had she seen him this way, never had she believed him capable of such fury. More frightened than she had ever been, she tried to placate him.

"Maybe it would be best if I didn't go with you tomorrow."

"Oh, you'll go with me. That was part of the bargain. Without you, there'll be no opium." He grabbed her by the arms and hauled her up out of the chair. His fingers were pressing tight into her flesh.

"We don't need the opium that badly." If only he would stop it. If only this terrifying stranger would leave and the Stephen she loved would return.

"Oh, yes, we do. You'll go tomorrow, but from now on, you'll let me pursue my trade without any of your damn meddling."

She nodded dumbly as tears swam into her eyes. She would agree to anything if only he would let her go.

"And tomorrow, you'll act with more discretion . . . and modesty."

"Yes, Stephen."

He shook her so hard, she could feel the pins and combs, which held her heavy hair in place, falling out.

"Go take off your dress," he said roughly, and with one final shake, he pushed her at the love seat. "I don't want to tear it."

She staggered, then caught her balance on the arm of the love seat. Without looking at him, she fled into the bedroom and closed the door behind her. She looked for a key, but there was none in the lock. There was nowhere to hide, no place where he wouldn't find her. She would have to live through this nightmare as best she could.

The ivory buttonhook shook in her fingers while she tried to free the tiny pearl buttons, which ran down her back, from their satin loops. Glimpsing herself in the long pier glass, she was startled to see another stranger with disheveled hair, scarlet stained cheeks, and blue eyes wide with agonized fright. Then the door burst open and Stephen was reflected in the glass behind her. He had shed his coat and his cravat, his brocaded vest was open, and the power of his arms and shoulders was clearly visible under his fine lawn shirt. He stood in the doorway without moving, but angry vitality radiated from him.

"You're a wife now, Julia. My wife. And if you don't know what that means, it's time you found out."

There was no reply possible. Julia looked away and continued to struggle with the buttons. She heard him cross the carpet and froze. There was no telling what he would do next.

He wrenched the buttonhook from her hand, and working down her back with smooth efficiency, he soon had her dress unbuttoned. He pulled the sleeves down from where they barely touched her shoulders until her dress dropped to the floor. She stood immobile as he loosened petticoat after petticoat, and they piled up in a froth of white upon the rose colored dress.

When only one petticoat remained below her lace ruffled chemise, he carried her to the bed, which had been turned down earlier in the evening by the chambermaid. After he had her settled upon it, he proceeded to remove the rest of her clothes very slowly, all the while telling her how a married woman should conduct herself, how *his* wife was going to behave. She listened without really hearing his words. He had done nothing to hurt her so far, but all of her body, her mind, were tensely waiting.

When his kiss came, it was hard with the determination of mastery, but even to this, she found herself beginning to respond. Then her body, which had known so many nights of glory with him, betrayed her, and she was caught up in the web of his lovemaking.

But much later, when he finally slept, she was left alone with a body that ached and a mind that was filled with angry disillusionment. Jason had never treated her this way. His love had always been free and joyous. He had delighted in calling her his wife, but never in the tone of voice Stephen had used.

She felt the weight of her wide wedding ring and thought of the light and slender band that Jason had given her. She could remember so well that day when Jason had put it on her finger. It had been over five years ago in the autumn of '36, and yet she could see so clearly the pride in those emerald green eyes set above high cheekbones and could hear his voice ringing out strong and clear in the small oak-lined Boston chapel.

He had been much on her mind lately. Feeling a traitor to Stephen, she had tried to push him from her thoughts. But now she felt free to think about him, to remember the sensation of her fingers buried in thick hair almost as black as her own, to linger over the pleasures he had given her with his tall, lean body.

Perhaps it was because she was in Boston again with a man she loved that she saw Jason on every street. The memory of herself as a young bride, who had watched her bridegroom sail away from her, appeared every time she and Stephen went down to those same granite wharves.

She could hear Jason's words of concern when he had met her on that chilly dawn of their elopement. "I was worried about you. Alone and the night so dark."

And I'm so alone now, Jason, and the night is so dark.

The fabric of the curtain that separated life from death seemed very thin then, as it had many times before, and she felt that Jason was with her, comforting her. And strangely enough, the love she felt from Jason made her realize that she still loved the man who lay sleeping beside her. Despite this evening, Stephen had usually shown himself to be a tender and loving man. She would have to try to understand him, to protect him from jealousy. Although others had courted her after Jason's death, she had wanted none of them until Stephen had come along. And she understood truly for the first time what women meant when they spoke of the work of a marriage.

Chapter Three

1842

The next morning, Stephen was up early. Before Julia had even opened her eyes, she could hear him rummaging through the wardrobe. It must be early, she thought, for the streets were relatively quiet. Only the calls of market vendors and the clatter of delivery wagons broke the morning peace. The sounds of large crowds and carriages rumbling over cobblestones, which never seemed to cease by day, were missing.

"Here. Put this on."

She opened her eyes to see Stephen, still in his long white nightshirt, standing by the bed. He was holding one of her new dresses in his hand.

She sat up sleepily and pushed the loose hair away from her eyes with one hand while she took the dress from him with the other. With a high collar and long, buttoned sleeves, the dress was one of the most modest they had made.

Julia fingered the blue and white cotton that was still so crisp, then she looked up at Stephen. Last night, she'd thought he had worked off his anger. She could still feel its imprint on her sore body, but from the look on his face, apparently he hadn't.

"Are you going to argue with me?"

"No, of course not," she said tiredly. All she wanted to do was to curl up and go back to sleep. She wished that the morning and the meeting with Hiram Richardson were over. Afterwards, she was sure, Stephen would calm down.

"Then hurry up and dress. Our appointment's for ten, and it's almost seven now."

That seemed more than enough time to Julia, but she wasn't about to argue with him over it. It was easier to get up and dress and try to ignore his wretched mood.

All through breakfast, Stephen kept glancing at her plate and then at the gold watch he had laid on the table beside his place. Julia ate as fast as she could, but she was still hungry when he pushed back his chair.

"Whether you've finished or not, it's time to go," he said.

They walked in silence through the early morning over brick sidewalks that were beginning to come to life. Shopkeepers were opening their stores, and women with baskets over their arms appeared. The waterfront, when they reached it, was already busy. Julia wondered if it ever slept.

When Stephen turned down Central Wharf, Julia was surprised enough to speak.

"Stephen, Captain Richardson's warehouse is on India Wharf."

"I'm well aware of where it is. I *have* been there a few times, you know."

Damn! she thought. I'm not even going to *try* talking to him until that blasted meeting is over.

Once they were on the granite-paved wharf, Stephen slowed his pace, and as they strolled along it, they inspected the tall-masted vessels that lay on either side until they could see the *Crystal Star*. With only light ballast in her holds, she rode high on the flood tide.

Her black paint glistened in the clear spring air and her white waist shone as though it had been scrubbed overnight. Beneath her soaring bowsprit, the blonde-haired figurehead, the embodiment of the ship's spirit, smiled serenely at the sky. Her white gown and her halo of stars glowed faint pink as reflections cast by the early morning sun on red brick buildings caught and held her.

Here Stephen paused, as he always did on catching sight of his ship, to admire her. He never tired of it. Julia was content to stand quietly beside him. Just as her husband had pride in his first command, so Julia had pride in her creation, for it was, she reminded herself, partly *her* mind and *her* hands that had built this ship.

Once the rigging of the ship had been completed, Julia had sometimes felt rather useless. All important decisions were now Stephen's, and she seemed to have become less real to herself, as though she were his shadow or a mirrored reflection. As much as she had wanted to go to sea, to escape from her land-bound home, there were times now when she thought with longing of the bustle of the shipyard and the peace of the large white house that faced across the marsh.

The ship gave her strength. It was her link with home. It was also a part of her, a part she could look at and touch. It was tangible proof that she was who she was, and as long as the *Crystal Star* and other vessels she had helped build remained afloat, no one could take that away from her.

"Come on," Stephen said, breaking into her thoughts. "I want to check on that lower fore topsail."

They went up the gangway, and after inspecting the sails, Julia went to the quarterdeck, where she could lean on the rail and watch the traffic in the harbor. When she saw the Cunard's Royal Mail steampacket leaving East Boston, belching smoke while its side wheels churned the water, she shuddered and was thankful that they would never be able to replace the graceful sailing vessels. It was all very well for them to track back and forth across the Atlantic, but steamships still were dangerous. She had heard too many tales of boilers exploding and of fire consuming vessels and passengers alike ever to want to set foot on one herself. And they were incapable of long voyages since they consumed at a great rate the power that drove them. The wind was free and would carry ships around the world and back at no expense to their owners. She looked fondly up at the three tall masts of the *Crystal Star.*

Stephen watched the steamship, too, but soon he was back to a restless prowling of his own ship. Going from sailmaker to sailmaker, he watched each man work. He tested the many halyards of each mast and yardarm as he had already done dozens of times before. He went below into the holds to check on the twelve eighteen-pounders that had been delivered yesterday. Even in the dim light, he could see the brass cannon gleaming. With the

Opium War still crackling between the British and the Chinese, this armament and the long pivot guns gave him a feeling of security. He wondered briefly how wise it was to take Julia on this voyage, but then he dismissed it from his mind. She was determined to go and be damned if he'd leave her ashore for vultures like Richardson to prey on.

As the sun rose higher and the hour for their meeting approached, Julia wondered if Stephen had decided not to go after all. It would be a relief if he had changed his mind, even if it meant making an enemy of Hiram Richardson. At exactly ten minutes before the hour, however, he appeared out of the midship's hold and dusted off his hands.

"Are you ready?" he asked her curtly.

"Yes. Here's your hat." She handed him the tall top hat he had left beside her. "Thought maybe you'd decided not to go."

"It doesn't pay to be early for an appointment." He smoothed his light brown hair back with his hand and put his hat carefully on his head. Then he tilted it slightly to one side. The angle of the brim made his lean face look arrogant. "If you're early, you appear too eager, and I intend to have all the advantage on my side."

His timing was perfect. As a clerk led them through rooms where other clerks perched on high stools, their quill pens moving constantly as though ruffled by a breeze, they could hear a ship's clock somewhere striking four bells.

Hiram Richardson was waiting at the door of his office to greet them. This morning, he was dressed in severe black and white, which contrasted with his fresh coloring and chestnut hair. He seemed wide awake and even more freshly alert than he had been the evening before. Julia wondered if Stephen really would have all the advantage on his side.

"Come in, come in," Hiram Richardson said, smiling warmly and holding the door open wide.

"Good morning," Julia said with an answering smile. No matter what Stephen said, she liked the man. His open heartiness and candor made her feel at ease.

While he was greeting Stephen, Julia looked around the sunlit office curiously. She had been in other counting houses before, but the luxury of this one surpassed them all.

Unlike the outer rooms, the office was paneled in warm walnut, and on the floor lay a deep, richly patterned Oriental carpet of red, black, and gold. On the walls hung half-models of ships and the portraits of many vessels, pictured both at sea and in foreign harbors. Although the day was growing warm, the small-paned windows were shut and a fire burned in the fireplace near a large and handsomely carved desk.

"I've ordered coffee to be served," Hiram Richardson said. "Or would you prefer tea, Mrs. Logan?"

"No. I'd enjoy coffee," Julia said, trying to remember to be sedate.

"No trouble having tea sent in as well." Hiram Richardson was puzzled by the change in her manner since the previous evening.

"Oh, no." She smiled at him appreciatively despite Stephen's warning presence. She just couldn't be rude. "I'd rather have coffee. We always had it at home in the shipyard about this time every morning."

"It won't be long. Would you care to look around while we're waiting?" He gestured at his walls with obvious pride. "I'm sure you'll recognize some of my ships, Captain Logan."

"Yes," Stephen said rather impatiently. He hadn't come on a social call, to look at pictures and drink coffee. He wanted to contract for the opium and get out. However, there was nothing to be done but to follow the other man's pace. He nodded at the nearest painting. "The last time I saw her was in Trieste."

"She sailed from there not long ago." Richardson's chestnut eyebrows met in a frown. "Unfortunately, she's a month overdue. She was seen passing through the Strait of Gibraltar, but no one's reported sighting her since. I'm afraid she may be lost."

"Captain Parker still her master?" Stephen asked.

"Yes. An able man. He's been with me for fifteen years."

"Yes," Stephen said gravely. He stared at the painting and thought of the many ships and men he had once known that were now buried forever beneath the sea.

"Still, I've had ships turn up after a longer absence," Hiram Richardson said cheerfully. "It's bad luck to count your losses before they're confirmed. All the rest are still afloat." His wide gesture included the four walls of the room.

"You own all those vessels, Captain Richardson?" Julia asked, amazed. She had assumed that many were ships from his past.

"Every last one of them. When I sell one, I take down her

picture and replace it with that of a new vessel. I don't believe in dwelling on the past. The future is the thing. Don't you agree, Captain Logan?"

"Yes, I do," Stephen said with a new intensity that brought a spark of blue to his grey eyes and sharpened the contours of his face. As he thought of the future, he momentarily forgot about Julia and his jealousy of the man before him. "After centuries of bluff-bowed barges, we're finally beginning to learn how to build ships, fast ships. Look at the *Crystal Star*. She's going to set new records and after her, there'll be another and another, each one going faster than the one before."

"Yes, yes," Captain Richardson agreed with him, pleased to find another who shared his beliefs. "Takes a few Americans to show the rest of the world what can be done. Not that we don't have our skeptics. I've heard plenty who've said your ship's too fine in the bow and, with that long midship section, she'll break up in a rough sea, but I think they're wrong."

"They're wrong," Stephen said, "and I'm going to prove it."

"I'm sure you will." The merchant didn't allow the amusement he felt to show in his smile. He remembered what it was like to be a young man with his first command. "This country's proving a lot of things to the world, thanks to men of imagination and daring. Men like your father, Mrs. Logan. He has a fine eye for design."

"Thank you." Julia, in turn was amused by the older man. She wondered what he'd say if he knew how much she'd had to do with the design. She was sure he couldn't believe a woman capable of anything but running a house, caring for children, and looking pretty. "I'll pass your compliment along when I see him next week."

"You're not going to desert us so soon, are you?" Richardson's light blue eyes widened in mock alarm.

"No. He and my mother are coming down to Boston before we sail."

"Good. Boston would be a duller place without you." He smiled when he noted the tightening of Stephen's lips. Do the young man good to worry a while. He always had been too cocksure. "While they're here, you'll have to have dinner with me. I'd like to see if your father would consider building a ship for me. One like the *Crystal Star*."

"I'm sure he'd be glad to talk about it," Julia said. Though

Stephen had relaxed for a moment, she could feel the tensions rising again. She was wondering if *she* should bring up the matter of the opium when the door opened and three clerks entered the office. They carried trays loaded with a silver coffee service and Rose Medallion china as well as plates of small cakes.

"Will you pour, Mrs. Logan?" When the merchant smiled, his teeth seemed incredibly white. "I'm sure the coffee will taste much sweeter if it comes from your pretty hands."

"Yes, of course." Julia was glad to have something to do. She was uncomfortably aware of the two pairs of eyes fixed on her while she poured the coffee. Even while concentrating on the cups, she sensed the frank admiration in Hiram Richardson's gaze. She knew it wasn't lost on Stephen. She could feel his disapproval without glancing at him.

She was relieved when, as soon as she had handed the men their cups, the merchant launched into a brisk discussion of the opium. Once on the subject of business, his entire attention was concentrated on Stephen. Julia was content to sit quietly, to listen and to learn.

As soon as the two men had reached a bargain agreeable to both, Stephen stood up and held out his hand. He seemed pleased. "Thank you, Captain Richardson. We'll have to be going. I've promised the sailmakers I'd be on hand for a final inspection of a few sails."

The merchant smiled. "Always the man of business, aren't you, Logan? I'm sorry now that I didn't have a ship to give you last spring."

"As you said, sir, perhaps it's all for the best."

"Please send me a note when your father arrives," he said as he bowed over the hand Julia held out to him.

"I will." She wished he would let go of her hand.

"We'll see each other before that, of course." He escorted them through the rooms of his counting house, past the wooden chests that held his vessels' records, past the clerks who never looked up from their leather-bound books and fluttering pens, to the top of the stairs.

Once they were out of the building into the bright sunlight of noon, Stephen took her arm and hurried her up India Wharf.

"Not if I have anything to do with it," he said in a tight, angry voice.

54

"What?" Julia, who had been admiring the lines of a newly arrived topsail schooner, didn't know what he was talking about. "I said he won't be seeing you often if I have anything to do with it."

"Oh, he was just being polite."

"I doubt it," Stephen said curtly and quickened his stride.

"Well, it doesn't matter," Julia said as she hurried to keep up with him. "There's no reason for us to see him again, is there?"

"None that I can think of and I'd advise you to think of all the reasons why you can't."

"Stephen! For heaven's sake." She looked at him in amazement, but he never even glanced in her direction. Really! He could be infuriating. "The man's old enough to be my father."

"But he's not your father, and I wouldn't call his interest in you exactly paternal."

"Stephen, do you really think I'd be interested in a man who has false teeth?"

"False teeth?" He stopped abruptly and stared at her.

"Yes." She laughed when she saw the startled look on his face. "Didn't you notice how white and perfect they were? Looked more like porcelain than enamel to me."

"False teeth!" he grinned. Suddenly, he whipped off his hat, threw back his head, and laughed up at the gulls who swooped down over the garbage in the harbor. Then as he clapped it back on his head, he whirled Julia around, and, despite the curious stares of the passersby on the stone wharf, he kissed her with an enthusiasm that left her breathless.

Two days later, the sails were completed and stowed below. One set was folded, ready for bending on. The second was stored in sealed barrels to preserve it against mildew and rot. Captain Asa Crofton and Julia's parents were due to arrive in Boston on the packet from East Dennis the next day, but when the winds died in the morning and a flat haze hung over the harbor, Stephen hired a carriage to get away from the city and the sight of his ship lying ready but idle at the wharf.

Julia enjoyed the drive through the open countryside filled with fruit trees blossoming in the sun. Like girls in pastel dresses, dancing in the meadows, she thought. Soon there would be no trees for her. No flowers, no lambs and colts gamboling in the lush, new grass. Her trees would be masts, her flowers the ocean foam and seaweed, her animals the porpoise and flying fish. She smiled. It was a fair trade.

However, after one taste of fresh country air, Stephen turned the horse and headed back for the noise and dirt of Boston. Until they sailed, there would be no staying the demons that drove him restlessly from place to place.

As it turned out, it was fortunate that he had decided to return when he did. They had been in their suite at the Tremont House only a few minutes when they heard a loud banging on the door. Julia was splashing fresh water on her face to rinse away the dust from the road. She looked at Stephen in surprise.

"You expecting someone?"

"No." He picked up the coat he had just taken off and put it on as he went to the door.

Before he was able to open it, though, there was more banging and a voice shouted through the panels.

"Ahoy there! Anyone on board?"

Julia laughed and wiped her face quickly with a towel. It was Captain Asa at his foghorn best.

"Come on in, you old sea dog," Stephen said as he opened the door. Then he saw Julia's parents standing beside the short, white-haired captain in the hall.

"Come in, come in," he said, shaking hands with Benjamin and giving Lydia a light kiss on the forehad. "Julia, your parents are here."

Julia flung the towel on the washstand and ran into the parlor.

"Oh, Mama! Papa! I'm so glad to see you!" She threw her arms first around her mother, then with greater warmth, around her father.

"Well, it hasn't been that long, child. Are you all right?" Lydia started to remove her bonnet from her thick, silvered-gold hair. There was worry in her light green eyes. She hadn't expected such an exuberant welcome, but then she never did know what to expect from Julia.

"I'm fine. I'm wonderful!" Julia's sapphire eyes sparkled as she looked up at her father, still hugging him tightly. She'd forgotten how tall he was and how distinguished he looked with his vigorous black hair only lightly touched with grey. Already she was becoming accustomed to Stephen's shorter stature. "You look grand, Papa."

"Probably because I haven't had you around to fret me." Benjamin gave her an extra squeeze and smiled at her, his deep blue eyes a reflection of her own, but he was worried, too. "I've missed you, my jewel," he said in a lower voice.

"Oh, Papa, I've missed *you*. Nobody would listen to me when they rigged the ship. Stephen had to tell them everything."

So that was it, he thought with relief. For a moment, he'd been afraid that something had gone wrong with the marriage.

"Did Stephen listen to you?" he asked.

"Yes. Usually."

"Usually?" Benjamin released her and took her hands between his. He looked down at her, suddenly serious.

"He did, Papa." She decided not to mention the foremast. Though she had looked at it a hundred times, she still couldn't figure out why it made her uneasy. "He ordered them to do what I wanted. It's just been so frustrating."

"I'll have a word with John Newman. He should know that you speak for me. I don't want this happening again."

"Don't bother, Papa. Now that I'm going to sea, I probably won't be involved in rigging any more ships."

"You'll come back to the shipyard someday, Julia," he said gravely. "When that happens, I don't want anyone questioning your authority."

"What do you mean going gallivantin' off," Captain Asa was saying, "leavin' the *Crystal Star* with no one on board but an addle-pated shipkeeper?"

"She's in good hands, Captain Asa." Stephen's lazy smile was filled with affection for the wiry, white-haired owner of the *Crystal Star*. "We didn't expect you'd make it today."

"That's obvious!" The old captain was trying to keep a straight face, but his watery blue eyes gleamed with amusement. "Well, where are your cargo listings? Where's your mate? Why aren't you loading? I can't afford to pay wharf fees forever."

The corners of Stephen's grey eyes crinkled as he laughed at the crotchety old man. "Just waiting for you to approve the cargo, Captain Asa. Thought you'd want to be present when the officers were hired."

"Nonsense! Told you the ship was yours. Get on about your business and stop dawdling afore I change my mind and find another master. I'm beginning to wonder about you, young

Stephen. Not even the courtesy to offer us a drop to drink. I'm parched."

"I'll have some tea sent up," Julia said, turning away from her father.

"Tea is it? Don't tell me you don't have a bottle of rum handy."

"A bottle with your name on it, sir." Stephen lifted the crystal decanter from the table. "Would you care for a glass, Captain Howard?"

"No. Later, maybe." Benjamin was still watching his daughter intently.

"I was hoping Amelia would be with you," Julia said to her mother. She *had* wanted to see her youngest sister again before she sailed.

"She was hoping, too," Lydia said, "but Michael's mother is finally dying. Doubt she'll be there when we get home, poor soul."

"She's been in pain a long time," Julia said. "It's Amelia I'm sorry for. She was so looking forward to coming down to Boston. And now Michael will go to sea and leave her. He always said he would when his mother died."

"Well, Amelia knew that when she married him," Benjamin said gruffly. He was thinking of the days when Jason had been a first mate like Michael and had gone off to sea and left Julia. Gone off to sea and never come home again. He knew Julia was thinking about it, too.

"Don't worry about Amelia," he said. "She'll be all right."

"Yes, I guess she will."

"Let's go out and have our tea . . . and rum," Benjamin said, turning to Captain Asa and Stephen. "Then we can get on down to the wharf and see the *Crystal Star*."

"I think I'd rather stay here with Julie, Benjy," Lydia said, sinking down onto the red velvet settee. "Why don't you men go on and we'll have a nice little chat."

Benjamin looked at his daughter and then at his wife. "Be best if Julie comes with us, Lyd," he said quietly. "She's the one who'll be to blame if anything's amiss."

"I'll take the responsibility, sir," Stephen said, squaring his shoulders, "but I think Julia should be with us when you go over the ship."

"Still won't let her out of your sight, eh?" Captain Asa cackled and slapped the young man on the back. "Can't say as I blame you.

Boston's a wicked place. Come along, Lydia. You might as well take a look."

"Yes. Come on, Mama." Julia held out her hand to her mother. "You can advise me on the saloon and our cabin. I'm sure I've forgotten dozens of things. After all, you've been to sea with Papa. You know what's needed."

"No." Lydia pushed the heavy hair away from her forehead with the back of her wrist. "I've had enough of sea-going craft to last me a week. I can still feel the motion of that packet. I'd rather lie down here and rest."

"I hate to leave you alone, Mama. I'd better stay," she said, looking up at the men apologetically.

"No, no. Go along. I might be able to get some sleep once you've gone."

"I'll have some tea sent up for you, then," Julia said dubiously. She felt she should stay with her mother, but she could see Stephen's impatience, and she did want to spend as much as possible of the short time they had left with her father. She went into the bedroom to get her bonnet.

It was the busiest part of the day at the waterfront. Central Wharf was crowded with wagons, carts, and carriages clattering over the granite stones with their loads of goods and passengers. Julia and her father, who walked beside her as they followed Stephen and Captain Asa, had to stay close to the buildings to avoid the traffic.

They were so absorbed in conversation that, at first, they didn't notice the well-dressed man, swinging a gold-headed ebony cane, who came out of the doorway of a building just down the wharf from the *Crystal Star*.

Stephen was the first to spot Hiram Richardson, and then it was too late to avoid the man. It was almost as though he'd been lying in wait for them; Stephen thought. However, instead of showing his irritation, he smiled at the merchant. The opium wasn't in his hands yet, and until it was, he would have to be polite. After that, though, be damned to the man!

"Mrs. Logan, Captain." Hiram Richardson tipped his tall hat, revealing the crisp chestnut hair touched with grey.

"Good afternoon, Captain Richardson," Julia said demurely, aware that Stephen had dropped back to stand close beside her.

"Benjamin!" the merchant said and extended his hand. "It's been many a year since we've met. I've been looking forward to seeing you. Mrs. Logan promised to let me know as soon as you arrived, and here you are without a word from her." He glanced at Julia with mock reproach in his light blue eyes.

"It *has* been a long time, Hiram," Benjamin said, "but don't blame my daughter. She didn't know when we'd be coming till about an hour ago. Asa, may I introduce Captain Hiram Richardson? Captain Crofton."

The merchant shook hands with the old man. "It's a pleasure to meet the owner of such a beautiful ship."

"That she is! You been aboard?"

"No. Regretfully not. I've been waiting for Captain Logan to invite me."

"Stephen! Such manners, lad! You come along now, sir, and see what you think." Captain Asa took the merchant by the elbow and steered him over to the gangway.

Benjamin and Stephen exchanged glances. Neither of them liked the intrusion, but there was nothing to be done about it. Stephen took Julia's arm and kept her near him as they followed Captain Asa and Hiram Richardson to the ship.

"I'm delighted to have the opportunity of looking her over," the merchant was saying, "but the real reason I wanted to see you was to invite you to be my guests at dinner tomorrow night."

"Fine, fine," Captain Asa said, answering for them all. "I've heard about that house of yours. Wouldn't mind taking a look for myself to see the truth of it."

"I'm afraid the truth will seem paltry compared to the gossip."

"That's what I figured. Now you just come on board. See if this isn't the finest vessel you ever sighted." Captain Asa waved him up the gangway.

After inspecting the rigging and spars, the old man insisted that they go over the ship inch by inch. When they climbed down into the holds and fo'c'sle, Benjamin went with them, but Stephen, keeping Julia with him, stayed on deck.

"That bastard knows how to play every advantage," he muttered once the others were safe below.

"We couldn't avoid him forever. The waterfront isn't that large."

"I'll sign Kenneth Wilson on as mate tomorrow, and we begin to load immediately. We sail within the week."

"Is that enough time?"

"Yes. There's no more reason to delay and plenty of reason not to."

He was grimly silent as he watched the three men ascend from the fo'c'sle.

Captain Asa, out of breath from his exertions, propped himself against the pinrail that ran around the foremast for a moment. He looked up the mast with loving eyes. Then he frowned. He leaned over and ran a hand over the wood.

"Ben," he said quietly. "Come here."

"What is it, Asa?"

"Take a look at this mast."

Benjamin glanced at it, then walked slowly in a circle around it, his eyes traveling up and down the tall timber.

"Looks straight and true to me. No flaws I can see."

"Feel it."

Benjamin raised his bushy black eyebrows and shot a quizzical look at the old man. Then he stroked the wood and rapped on it.

"Don't see a thing wrong, Asa."

The old captain scowled at the mast. Then he circled it slowly as though stalking a flaw. He ended up standing in front of Stephen.

"You see it before they stepped it?"

"Yes, sir. It seemed to be all right."

"What about you, Julie?"

"Yes. I saw it." She glanced at Stephen, wondering what she should say. The old man thought the world of Stephen. Treated him like the son he'd never had. But when it came to putting his ship into a master's hands, it would be another thing. Captain Asa wouldn't settle for second best. She couldn't raise any doubts about her husband's judgment in the old man's mind. It might cost Stephen the command of the *Crystal Star*.

"Well?" Captain Asa was still staring intently at her.

"I couldn't find anything wrong with it."

"Hmpf! I don't like it."

Hiram Richardson, who had been watching them idly, now stepped up to the mast and ran his hand over it. "It looks sound to me," he said.

"I paid for the best and the best is what I want."

"I don't think you have any cause for complaint." The merchant suddenly smiled. "If it worries you, why not sell the ship to me? I'll

61

pay you all costs, including what you've invested in cargo and master's salary, plus twenty percent."

Stephen's arm tightened, clamping Julia's hand to his side. She glanced at him and saw that, although his features remained expressionless, he was staring at Captain Asa, as though trying to will the old man to refuse. It was, they both knew, a tempting offer.

Captain Asa hesitated for a moment and pulled on his white beard as though seriously considering the offer.

"No, no," he said finally. "I plan to make a lot more out of her than that. This young man's goin' to make her pay for herself before he comes home again." The old man's pale blue eyes glimmered. "Least that's what he promised. That right, Stephen?"

"Yes, sir. That's my promise." Stephen grinned his relief at the old captain and relaxed his hold on Julia's hand. He couldn't possibly consider sailing under Richardson's ownership. Not after the way he'd acted with Julia. There would be constant petty humiliations. Yet to lose the *Crystal Star* would be more than he could bear.

"You're gambling on that," Hiram Richardson persisted, "whereas my offer is a sure thing. A tidy profit in your pocket and no worries."

"Maybe I like to worry." Captain Asa shot a stream of tobacco juice over the rail. "Don't expect to do much of it, though. I know the ship and I know the man."

"Think it over."

"No thinkin' to be done. Come along aft now. I'll show you something none of your ships've got."

"Oh? What's that?"

"The fanciest captain's quarters afloat, that's what. Nothing but the best for my master and his wife."

"I certainly hope so." The admiration in the merchant's eyes was directed at Julia. "She deserves nothing but the best."

For once, Benjamin approved of the way Stephen kept Julia close to his side. He and his son-in-law might not always see eye to eye, but as far as Hiram Richardson was concerned, evidently they did.

Benjamin had known the merchant in his youth, when both had come up before the mast, and he'd never trusted the man. They'd never sailed on the same vessels, but he'd run into Hiram in ports around the world and had heard enough gossip about him back in the days when they were both captains of their own ships.

He had a suspicion that not all the merchant's fortune was honestly come by. There had been talk, too, about his connection with slave ships. Nor did he like the way the man's eyes returned again and again to his daughter. Hiram might be a widower and free, but Julia certainly was not. He had to admit he'd rather have her in Stephen's hands than in Richardson's.

When they arrived at the five-story brick house on Louisburg Square the next evening, they were met at the door by a giant black butler, whose muscles threatened to split the seams of his well-tailored uniform. He ushered them into a long, high-ceilinged room, where Hiram Richardson stood before the fire ready to receive them. The opulent taste, which the merchant permitted to glimpse through in his office, was here allowed full rein.

The treasures of the earth that streamed through the port of Boston on his ships seemed to have been funneled into this house. Crystal chandeliers sparkled in every room. Huge Chinese urns, filled with branches from flowering trees, stood against the walls. In cabinets that lined the walls were ivory figurines, mellowed cream with age, cloisonné bowls, ebony statues, and elaborately patterned silver goblets.

The richly dyed, multicolored rugs were thick and deep. Julia wondered what it would feel like to walk barefoot on them.

It was hard not to be impressed by the luxury with which Hiram Richardson surrounded himself. Captain Asa didn't even try.

"Looks like there's more truth to the tales than I figured," he admitted as he turned slowly around and eyed the room. "Must have cost you a pretty penny."

"Glad you like it." From his satisfied smile, it was obvious that the merchant was proud of his possessions.

"Seems a bit much for a man living alone. Now if you had a wife, might make more sense."

"I don't intend to live alone all my life. Someday I'll remarry."

"Don't think you'd have any trouble finding a wife. Not with the bait you've got." The old captain's pale blue eyes sparkled with amusement in his puckered face.

"I've found her. Unfortunately she's not available." He glanced at Julia, and she was angry to find herself blushing. Stephen was looking at the merchant with expressionless slate grey eyes.

"Then find yourself another. Plenty of women in this world." Captain Asa picked up a small landscape carved in ivory and peered at it nearsightedly. "You goin' to show us the rest of this palace? Or don't the rest measure up?"

"I'll leave that answer up to you." Hiram Richardson turned to the others. "Would you be interested in a tour of the house?"

"That would be right nice," Lydia said as she fingered her jade necklace. She hadn't wanted to come this evening, but with the merchant's easy hospitality and the warmth of the sherry, she was beginning to enjoy herself.

Upstairs the rooms were quieter in tone and, Julia thought, in better taste, though the sight of so many empty, well-furnished rooms depressed her. They seemed to be tenanted by unborn ghosts.

The master bedroom and adjoining study, however, were obviously used. Here, amongst the massive, carved Spanish furniture, there were even a few objects that were slightly shabby. An old chronometer and a sextant, a few books with well-worn leather covers, a ragged American ensign in a glass frame. Above the mantel in the bedroom there was the portrait of a woman. She was wearing a low-cut green dress that had long been out of style.

Julia studied the narrow, delicately boned, pale face, which was framed by long brown curls. There was a forgiving sweetness to her expression. Her lips were slightly parted as though she were about to smile.

"My wife," Hiram Richardson said, coming up behind her.

"She was lovely."

"Yes, she was. I wish I'd known her better." He sighed as he looked up at the portrait. "I was at sea when she died. We'd only been married a couple of years. Then she died in childbirth. It happened just a few days before I reached home."

"I'm sorry."

"It was a long time ago."

"And the child?"

"He died with her."

"I *am* sorry."

"Well, it's better not to dwell on the past," he said briskly. "Let me show you the next room. I think you'll be interested in it." He took her elbow and guided her to a door opposite the one that led to his study, and the others followed them.

The adjoining room had obviously been planned with a woman in mind. The bed was canopied in pink silk to match the quilted coverlet, and the curtains echoed the color. On the highly polished floor were several pale green Oriental rugs, which had pink and white flowers running around their borders. The Chinese wall-paper mingled all three colors in its portrayal of flowers and exotic birds perched on delicate branches.

"Must have been your wife's room," Lydia said, her green eyes wide at the frivolous luxury. She wasn't sure she approved of it.

"No, I'm afraid not. She died before the house was completed. The room's never been occupied. It's waiting."

"More bait," Captain Asa muttered.

"It's very pretty," Julia said tartly, "but how do you know the woman you marry will like it? Maybe she'd rather decorate her own room."

"I can only hope she will." There was an uncomfortable compelling intensity in his clear blue eyes as he looked at Julia. "If she doesn't, she'll be free to make changes. Can you think of anything I've forgotten?"

"That's not for me to say. It's up to the woman you marry." She turned from him abruptly and started for the door.

"Yes. I suppose so. Shall we go down?" he said to Lydia, who had been following the conversation with tight-lipped disapproval.

As they returned down the swirling staircase, the butler announced that dinner was served. Throwing open the double doors to the dining room, he revealed a long table covered with heavy damask linen and lighted by four massive silver candelabra.

Hiram Richardson offered his arm to Lydia and escorted her to the head of the table, where he seated her to his right.

"My dear," he said to Julia, who had followed them on her father's arm, "would you be kind enough to act as hostess this evening?" He indicated the end of the table opposite his own.

Why does he insist on embarrassing me? Julia thought irritably.

Her father pressed her hand, reassuring her with his presence. She smiled at him gratefully when, after seating her, he sat down in the chair to her left. With an empty ache, she suddenly realized how much she would miss him in the months ahead.

"To the Howard Shipyard," Hiram Richardson said as he raised a glass of wine after dinner had been served. "May it fill the seas with vessels as fine as the *Crystal Star*."

"Thank you," Benjamin said. "We intend to do just that."

"And the next keel you lay, I want to belong to me." The merchant set his glass carefully down on the white linen and looked seriously at Benjamin.

"I'm afraid that's impossible." Benjamin was intent upon the piece of meat he was cutting.

"Why not?" Hiram Richardson's chestnut eyebrows shot up. He was not used to receiving no for an answer.

"I've made promises to a lot of men before you." Benjamin was also determined never to do business with the man.

"For ten percent on top of your normal profit, I think you might find a way to fit me in ahead of them."

"Nope. Can't do it. My word is my word. Never gone back on it yet. Don't intend to start now." Punctuating his statement, Benjamin stabbed a piece of meat.

"How long would it be then?"

"There's plenty of good yards around. Samuel Hall's right over in East Boston. Got a good reputation, too. Why not go to him?"

"He already has an order from me."

"Then leave it with him."

"I intend to, but I want a Howard ship, too."

"Why?" Benjamin shot him a deep blue look from under black eyebrows that seemed to bristle.

"Because the Howard family produces the best," he said, smiling at Julia through the glass he raised. "Nothing but the best."

"Then you'll have a few years to wait," Benjamin said bluntly.

"I'll wait. Put my name on your list for the largest ways. I'm a patient man. The best things are always worth waiting for. Don't you agree, Captain Logan?" His eyes were innocent in their question.

Stephen had kept a careful check on his emotions all evening. He had seen from the first that the man was deliberately goading him over Julia, and he was determined not to let the merchant guess that some of his barbs had met their mark. Each time he had felt his anger rising, he had looked at the merchant's mouth and had smiled to himself. He was sure Julia was right. The teeth were false.

"It depends," Stephen said quietly, "upon whether you're sure of getting what you want in the end. Some things a man will never have, no matter how patiently he waits."

"If he has the money to go with the patience," the merchant said, rolling a piece of bread between his fingers, "he'll get it . . . eventually."

"Time and money won't buy everything." After looking with calm measurement at his opponent, Stephen took a sip of wine.

"Perhaps not, but I've yet to see the combination fail."

"I'll heed your advice, Captain Richardson, since the years must have taught you a little wisdom. Perhaps I'll be able to use it to advantage."

"But first you have to have the money," the merchant taunted him.

"I'll have the money." Stephen's smile was lazy, but his eyes were grey steel. "And *I* have a great deal of time."

Chapter Four

1842

Julia stood on the quarterdeck of the *Crystal Star* as the ship lay in Boston Harbor. The moment of anticipation had stretched into hours that covered the long day. The sun, which had been rising when they'd arrived on board, now lit the hills of Boston from the southwest, and still no wind. It had come only briefly once when the tide had turned and begun to flood.

Belonging now neither to the land which they had left nor to the sea which had yet to claim them, they rode the long, slow swells at anchor. The water was a lightly rolling mirror that reflected the hulls and spars of vessels that surrounded them. Some of them, too, were waiting for the wind.

Julia wondered if any on board those other vessels felt the same restless, hushed excitement that filled her. It reminded her of being in the eye of a hurricane when the wind is stilled. When it returns, it always blows from a new direction, she thought, and she felt her skin prickle as she wondered in which directions the winds of life would blow her.

To distract herself, Julia looked back at the land. Red brick buildings and stone towers were clearly visible amongst trees that were freshly green. Seen from this distance, the wharves where she had walked and the vessels lying alongside them looked like toys. No sounds of the city carried across the water. For once, Boston seemed quiet.

The *Crystal Star*, however, with her full complement of crew aboard, had sprung to life. The men, in their black varnished hats, checked shirts, and flowing, full bottomed trousers, filled the decks and rigging as they put up chafing gear, crossed royal yards and rove studding sail gear. There were several familiar faces amongst them, faces from home.

It seemed strange not to be able to speak to them, but as the wife of the captain, her place was on the quarterdeck or below in the master's quarters. Theirs was forward and there was no mingling.

Despite their activity, the sailors worked in a silence that was broken only by the cries of the swooping gulls, the gentle lapping of the waves on the wooden hull, and the shouted commands of the mates.

Stephen stood beside her, alert and watchful but silent, issuing no orders, making no comments on the performance of his men. He seemed far less interested than she was in the preparation of his ship for the sea. Instead his eyes shifted constantly from the ship to scan the water, then aloft, where an occasional breath of air stirred the lift lines and fluttered the house flag with its white star emblazoned upon a royal blue background. He watched the small, scattered clouds that moved slowly overhead and searched the horizon for a sign of wind.

The ship swung as the tide began to ebb, and the long black shadows of her masts crossed their length across her bleached decks. The hens in their small houses in one of the long boats began to cackle uneasily, and the sheep moved restlessly in their pens, but the piglets continued to suckle at their mother, as content as though they were still on the farm.

Stephen shook his head as he watched the bow point towards Boston. "I thought we'd get a breeze at the turn of the tide, but I don't see any sign of one."

"Maybe it'll come at sunset," Julia suggested.

"Maybe, but that'll be a while yet. We may as well go below and have supper. When the breeze comes, I want to be ready for it."

In the small saloon, water-reflected sunbeams streamed in through the stern windows, and dancing across the ivory painted walls and curly walnut paneling, they warmed and brightened them. They touched bookshelves laden with leather-bound books and gleamed on brass lamps that hung from gimbals. Light from the overhead skylight brought out the rich colors of the Brussels carpet that covered the deck, and the red velvet that covered the settee looked new and fresh. The wooden armchairs, as well as Julia's special upholstered one, were already bolted down in preparation for the sea, and the gimbaled table, covered with damask, was laid with silver for two. In the center was a bowl of golden daffodils.

"Stephen!" Julia was untying her bonnet when she saw the flowers. "Where on earth did they come from?"

"You like them?" He was still standing near the door while he waited for her reaction.

"I love them, but with everything else you had on your mind when we boarded, that you should think of flowers!"

"You should have them. They won't keep long, but they're the last you'll see for many a day."

"Oh, Stephen!" She threw her arms around him and hugged him. "Sometimes you can be so wonderful."

"Like this?" he asked and his lips met hers, soft with a taste of salt. Under the sweetness of them, she felt herself melting, and as his hand traveled up a secret path to her neck, she thought of their soft bed in the next cabin.

"I've been wanting to do that all afternoon," he said huskily.

"You didn't even know I was there."

"I did." He smiled. "It's going to be very distracting having you on board, my sweet lady. Just now, I should be hurrying through supper so that I can get back on deck. Instead, I find I'm not hungry, not for food." He took her arms from around his neck and held her a little away from him. "But food's what we need. Don't tempt me anymore, my sweet, or this ship will never sail."

"But after we set sail . . ." Julia smiled at him temptingly.

He shook his head. "Not until we've cleared Race Point."

Julia pretended to pout. "Guess I might as well tidy up then."

"Might as well," he agreed, his attempt at solemnity betrayed by the laughter in his eyes.

In the captain's cabin, which adjoined the saloon on the starboard side, Julia poured a very small amount of water into the bowl that fitted snugly into the walnut washstand, and as she rinsed her face and hands, she smiled. The seagoing habit of her childhood had instinctively returned. Water was a precious commodity aboard ship, never to be wasted.

Smoothing her hair with her ivory-backed brush, she studied her reflection in the small mirror that reflected the cabin background. There was the wide feather bed covered with her wedding quilts, and it faced out to the sea through the stern window. There was also the brass porthole, open now for ventilation, which would be closed as soon as they sailed. Already their clothing hung from pegs on the wall and filled the built-in drawers that lined the inboard wall. Aside from the bed, the only other piece of furniture that was not built in was one straight chair.

This is me! she thought. I'm really here. After all these years. Papa promised me I'd go to sea again, but I've had to fight for it. I swore I'd never marry a man who couldn't take me voyaging. It was worth waiting for Stephen to come along, no matter how many others were pushed at me after Jason's death.

"Julia, what in God's name are you doing in there?"

She put the brush quickly back in the drawer. This was no time to be daydreaming, she thought guiltily. Opening the door, she latched it back.

"Just making myself presentable for you, sir," she said in her best Boston accent, and curtsied to him. "Do I pass inspection?"

"Yes. Come and eat now." He gestured toward the table where Tomaii, their Polynesian steward, stood ready to serve them. "Once we weigh anchor, there'll be no time."

"You think it will be soon, then?" she asked as she slipped into her chair.

"Only God knows, and he hasn't seen fit to inform me. The sooner, the better. As long as we lie here at anchor, we're feeding the men with no return on the money."

"And besides, you're itching to get back to sea," Julia said, teasing him as she picked up her fork.

"Yes. We've a schedule to keep. Furthermore, I want to see how this ship of yours performs."

"She'll be a lucky ship," Julia promised him.

"That remains to be seen, my lady," Stephen said between mouthfuls, eating hastily now that he had begun.

71

"Oh, no. She's already been lucky. Brought us together, didn't she? If it hadn't been for the *Crystal Star*, you most likely wouldn't have looked at me twice."

"I . . ." Stephen began and suddenly stopped. The cadence of the water swirling around the hull had changed. He threw his napkin on the table, rose and went to the aft window.

"We're swinging," he said just as a knock came on the saloon door. Stephen nodded at Tomaii, who opened the door to reveal the short, brawny figure of the first mate.

Kenneth Wilson carried his hat in his hand, and for the first time, Julia noticed how his straight black hair was thinning on top. It surprised her because she knew, from their childhood days, that he was only two or three years older than she. Maybe that was why he had recently grown the small, neat moustache. To make up for what he was losing on top. When at home, she knew he considered himself quite a ladies' man, but now he did not glance at her, but looked directly at Stephen.

"Wind from the southwest, sir," Wilson said.

"Signal for the pilot and call all hands."

"Aye-aye, sir."

For such a stocky man, Wilson could move swiftly. He was gone between one breath and another.

"May I come on deck, Stephen?" Julia asked.

"Yes, but hurry and stay out of the way." Then he, too, was gone.

Julia snatched up her bonnet and was already tying the ribbons when she brushed past their half-eaten meal on the table. Overhead she could hear Wilson call, "All hands, all hands, ahoy!" Instantly there was the clatter of feet on the wooden decks.

When she emerged from the companionway, the ship was seething with life. Most of the sailors were gathering around the capstan, the new hands urged on by the seasoned crew.

As soon as the way was clear, she ran up the steps to stand near Stephen on the quarterdeck.

"Heave short, Mister Wilson," he was saying as she arrived. He intended to take in all but the last few fathoms of anchor chain.

"Heave ho!" the mate bawled at the men at the capstan, who had fitted handspikes into its sockets. Calling upon the strength of their legs as well as their arms, they began to slowly revolve around the windlass.

72

"Cheerily, men!" he called. "Heave and pawl!"

Stephen watched them, his arms folded against his chest, and shook his head. "Too many damn greenhorns," he muttered.

"O'Brien, get them going with a song," Wilson yelled at the shanty man.

"Oh, Sally Brown, she's a Creole lady," O'Brien's rich baritone rang out.

"Way-oh, roll and go!" chorused a few of the men at the capstan.

"And where she lives it's cool and shady," the shanty man sang.

"Spend my money on Sally Brown," more men joined the chorus, and the windlass picked up speed.

"Oh, ten long years I courted Sally."

"Way-oh, roll and go."

"Then told me she would not marry."

"Spend my money on Sally Brown."

Now even the new hands were picking up the chorus, and Julia could hear the heavy iron chain rattling aboard as the rhythm of the song lent the men extra strength.

The pilot came aboard just as the anchor chain, still holding to the bottom on a short cable, was secured.

"Make sail, Mister Wilson," Stephen ordered when the pilot had joined them on the quarterdeck.

"Loose the sails," the mate's voice called out, and the experienced hands jumped into the rigging. Swarming up the ratlines of the three tall masts, they sprang as effortlessly as cats out onto the yards, clambering past one another to be the first, and therefore the best, man. Quickly they cast off the bunt lines and the gaskets of canvas that bound the yardarms. Then they came swinging down on deck, leaving one man on each yard to hold the bunt jigger with a simple turn around the tye. On reaching the deck, each man ran to his station at the sheets and halyards.

"All ready, for'ard?" the mate called.

"Ready for'ard," came the reply.

"All ready the main?"

"All ready the main, sir," another man answered.

The mate called to each man still in the yards in turn, and upon receiving affirmatives from all, he called, "Let go!"

Julia caught her breath as she watched the speed with which the bare yards were clothed with white cotton. The topsails were simultaneously hoisted, sheeted down, and the yards were trimmed.

Once again, under Wilson's direction, the men ran to the capstan and, straining in their revolving circle, broke the anchor free from the bottom. The cat block was hooked on and the fall was manned. Now, with a word from the mate, the shanty man sang out the first words of "Time For Us To Go," and the men, joining him, pulled with a will.

The *Crystal Star* began to move, and Julia felt goose bumps run up her arms and back as the sails began to fill. The ship swung round, pointing her bowsprit southeast on the course that would take her out of the harbor, past the rocks and shoals of the entrance and into the Roads.

With the setting of each additional sail, the ship picked up speed, and the swishing sound of the bow wave deepened and steadied as the *Crystal Star* sliced her way through the swell. Instead of a man-made thing of lumber, copper, iron, and canvas, she had become a whole, living creature, as real and as sensitive to the men who handled her as a spirited horse. She breathed.

Julia clung to the rail and her cheeks were flushed as she faced forward. The breeze rustled her bonnet strings and pressed her heavy skirts against her legs, but they went unnoticed. She was living with the ship, feeling the power of her sails, feeling the movement of each wave.

Leaving the pilot in charge, Stephen stood silently beside her and examined the ship and men under his command. He watched each sail in turn, noticing how well or poorly it set and drew, making mental notes on its modification. He critically observed the men, one by one. Some obviously knew their trade well; some were slower, but experienced; others had never shipped out before and had to be instructed in even the smallest detail by the mates and their fellows. The instruction was not always gentle, sometimes reinforced by a cuff or blow.

The crew was mixed. About half came from the Cape, two of them young boys. A few were sailors signed on at the wharf in Boston. Then there were the inevitable farm boys from inland, who had never seen a ship before. Even Tim Barnes, the youngest member of the crew, who hailed from East Dennis, knew more than they did, but the inlanders were strong and husky from farm work and seemed eager and willing. They'd settle down and soon would be walking the cross trees as nimbly as though they'd been born to it. The lure of adventure and romance which had drawn them to sea was a powerful goad, and what that didn't accomplish, the mates, with stronger action, would.

Then there was the most important factor, the *Crystal Star* herself. Being freshly built, the ship was stiff and slow, but as soon as she ran into a gale or two, she'd limber up and pick up speed. Until then, there was no telling how fast she could go.

With the coming of darkness, a full moon rose, lighting the men in the rigging, dark figures against white sails. Soon afterwards, they were in the Roads and the pilot dropped over the side into his small schooner. The sails were trimmed for the more easterly course that would take them out the channel between Long Island and Deer Island. Only those remained aboard who would be with the ship until they reached Hong Kong . . . or deserted or died first.

Hours later, looking aft from the starboard rail, Julia watched the moonlit sands of Cape Cod slip by and knew that midway, not long before the land hooked north, her home lay dreaming in the moonlight. How many months, how many years, she wondered, would it be before she smelled the marshes and the pines again, before she saw lamplight streaming from the windows of the tall white house, before she heard the sounds of the sawyers and blacksmith in the shipyard?

There was no melancholy in her thoughts. The land, the house, the yard had kept her prisoner while each ebb of the tide had called her to come, to follow. Now there was freedom in the strengthening wind, in the bow wave cleaved by the powerful ship.

She turned to smile at Stephen, to share this moment with him. He was watching her intently, his own face expressionless in the pale white light.

"You're mine now." His voice was so low that only she could hear him. "Completely mine."

She laughed. "Master of the ship and all she carries?"

"And of you."

"Oh, Stephen, don't be so serious. I'm so happy. So very happy to be here." She slipped her arm through his, sheltering from the wind behind his warm body.

He brushed her cheek lightly with the knuckles of his hand and, moving closer, looked deeply into her eyes. Then he smiled. "You really are, aren't you? No regrets?"

"None at all."

"Good. I'll see you below now."

"But I wanted to see the last of land."

"It will be hours yet. You should get some sleep."

"Not tonight! I couldn't."

"I think you can."

"I'm too excited. I feel so *alive!*"

"I know an excellent remedy for that." He put an arm around her and firmly led her from the quarterdeck. "Mister Wilson!" he called.

"Aye-aye, sir."

"Call me if she changes."

"Aye-aye, sir."

"I thought you said not till we'd cleared Race Point," Julia said as he opened the companionway door.

"That's one advantage in being captain. I can always change my mind."

During the night, the wind picked up, and when Julia went on deck the next morning to smell the brisk clean scent of salt, there was no sight of land. Only an occasional bird dipping into the white-crested sea gave sign that land lay not far behind them. With the wind on the starboard quarter and all her canvas set, the *Crystal Star* flew steadily along as though she were a great white gull, trailing her black feet in the water.

"I missed it," she said as she joined Stephen on the quarterdeck. Despite the little sleep he'd gotten, he looked as fresh as the morning. He was alert, but relaxed, having allowed the second mate to take charge.

"What did you miss?" His smile told her that he was remembering the night.

"The last sight of land."

"There was nothing to see. Land doesn't disappear suddenly like a curtain dropping on a play. It dwindles away. It's not until later you realize it's gone."

"Where are we now?"

"We're standing nor'east by east until we're well clear of the Cape. Then we'll head due east."

Julia moved a little closer to the helmsman so that she could look at the compass card, then raised her eyes to look forward at the flying jib.

"And there lies Europe," she said.

"Aye," Stephen agreed. "It's many a league, but it's there. Not that we'll see it. Come mid-Atlantic, we'll head south. Do you have a hankering to see Europe?"

Julia smiled. "Someday, perhaps. Not now. It's too close."

"Sometimes it's not as close as you might think."

"I know." Julia moved to the weather rail and leaned against it so that she could look up at the massive spread of canvas. When Stephen joined her there, she said, "I heard you get up in the night."

"Several times. I tried not to wake you."

"You didn't. Not really. I was only half awake when I felt you'd gone. Then you were beside me again. Was anything wrong?"

"No. I never sleep soundly when we're near land . . . nor when the weather's likely to change. Especially with a green crew. You'd best get used to it."

"I will. It's just . . . well, it's the first time you've left me at night since we've been married."

"Were you lonely, my lady?" The creases beside his mouth deepened as he grinned at her.

"A little."

"Think how lonely you'd be if I'd left you ashore." He leaned with his elbows back on the rail and watched the men at work.

"I know that loneliness too well."

"But not for me!" He jerked away from the rail to stare down at her, his body tense and his face suddenly angry.

"No." Julia pressed her lips together and put a tentative hand on his sleeve. If only she could recall the words she had spoken so unthinkingly. "I didn't mean to remind you, Stephen."

"Well, you have." The muscles of his square jaw tightened and he shook her hand from his arm.

"I won't again. I promise."

"But you'll think of him."

"No. He's gone. Dead for almost four years. Besides, Stephen, it wasn't the same."

"Enough the same for you to remind me that I'm not the first."
She stared out at the horizon where the empty sea met the lonely sky. "Strangely enough, you are."

"That's a lie. Does it have to be so obvious?" His voice was rough, but Julia could see the pain in his eyes when she glanced at him.

It hurt her more than his anger, and to avoid it, she looked back to the sea. "There was a girl," she said softly, "just turned sixteen, who wanted more than anything else to go to sea. She was too young to be a wife, too young for love or a man. So she married a pretty boy who said he'd soon take her to sea . . . even though she didn't know what love meant. When he died, she died. Why, I don't know. But I'm not that girl, Stephen. I'm your wife, and I know what love means." Oh, forgive me, Jason, she thought as she looked down at the deep green water that rolled steadily beneath them.

"So then you met another pretty boy who offered to take you to sea." The bitterness of his voice matched the bleakness she could see on his face.

"No," she said and wanted desperately to wipe away his anguish. "I met a man, and I found out what love really is."

"But if I hadn't promised to bring you to sea, you'd never have married me."

"Stephen, you're a man of the sea. You should understand." She raised her hand toward him, but when she saw the rejection in his eyes, she dropped it. "You know, if I'd never seen the sea before, I would have had to come . . . for you. To stay ashore without you . . . even last night, when I woke and realized you'd gone . . . then I felt the motion of the ship and I knew you were near and I could safely go back to sleep."

He looked at her for a long silent moment. She felt as though he were trying to penetrate through her eyes into her soul. Then suddenly he smiled, and it was like a shaft of sunlight finding its way through storm-tossed grey clouds. He looked years younger than he had only a second ago. When they had first met, Julia had only been amused by what she considered his calculated display of boyish charm, but for a long time now, she had found it irresistible. Her anger was drowned by the surge of love she felt for him. She smiled back.

78

He glanced up at the sky. "It's nearly noon. Time for you to take your first sights at sea, my lady. Tomaii," he shouted. "Bring up the sextants."

When the tall South Sea islander appeared with the sextants, Stephen handed hers to Julia. She caressed it for a moment before she raised it to her eye to adjust the glasses. Her father had taught her the rudiments of navigation when she was growing up, and as his parting gift to her, he had given her this sextant, which he himself had used for so many years.

As the sun reached its zenith, Julia and Stephen took their sights and called them down to Tomaii, who had returned to the cabin to stand by the chronometers. The pitch and roll of the ship, though slight, made it difficult for Julia to line up the horizon. It had certainly been much easier to do on shore.

When Stephen lowered his sextant, he grinned at her. "Well, my lady?"

She bit her lip. "I botched it."

"Well, you'll learn. Come below, and we'll see where we are."

In the saloon, Stephen checked the thermometer, then the two chronometers. After running through the equations on his slate, he unlocked the chart drawer and spread a chart out on the table. With parallel rules and divider, he plotted their latitude while Julia watched over his shoulder.

"Not a bad run," he said when he had finished. "Now let's see yours."

Julia watched as he ran through her figures, then held her breath as the parallel rules walked across the chart. Stephen pushed back his chair and laughed. "You've planked us up on the rocks at Race Point."

She felt waves of heat suffusing her face. He didn't have to laugh at her!

He was still laughing, but more gently when he saw her hurt expression. "It's not all that bad." He swung an arm around her waist and pulled her around the chair and down into his lap. "I've seen far worse from men who called themselves mates, and they've never given me half the satisfaction you do."

She trembled as his fingers opened the first button of her bodice and she felt the warmth of them on her skin. "You'll soon be accurate, my sweet. You learn fast." Then his lips descended on hers.

79

For a long while after that, she didn't care how far off her observations had been.

After Tomaii had cleared the remains of their dinner from the table in the saloon, Stephen took a large leather-bound book out of a drawer and brought it over to Julia. The words *Crystal Star* were embossed in gold on the cover.

"The mate and I are going to have our hands full with a new crew," he said as he handed the book to her. "No reason why you can't keep the log."

"I've never kept one before," she said, running her fingers over the smooth cover. She was secretly pleased that he would trust her with it.

"You kept the journals at the shipyard, and you write a fair hand. You'll have your duties on board, same as anyone else. No one gets a free ride."

Julia laughed at his mock scowl. "Aye-aye, captain, but you'll have to make allowances for an apprentice."

"A log's a log," he said and pulled up a chair next to her. "I noticed some from your father's old ships in his study. You must have read them."

"I practically knew them by heart. When I was a little girl, I used to read them and pretend that I was on the voyage, too." She smiled as she thought of those rainy afternoons when she had curled up in her father's big leather chair with a globe beside her.

"Well, then you'll have no problems," he said as he watched the wistful expression on her face and wondered what she was thinking about. So often she seemed to elude him.

She opened the book and saw Stephen's strong, bold handwriting on the first page:

April 18. Hove up anchor and underway at 6:20 PM. To Boston Light in 2 hr. 35 min. SW S WSW Moderate breezes, fine weather.

"You've already begun it," she said and was surprised at the disappointment she felt.

"Only just enough to get you started. The rest . . ." He leaned over and riffled the blank pages. "The rest are yours to fill. Every

80

day, no matter what the conditions, an entry will have to be made."

"I wonder what those pages will say." She turned a few of them as though she could read what was yet to be written.

"Little enough of any import, I hope, except for all the new records we'll set," he said briskly as he rose from his chair. "Good breezes, fair weather, and a swift voyage. I've told the mate to call all hands at six bells. I'll talk to them while the weather holds."

"Do you expect a change?"

"I hope not, but when we hit the Gulf Stream, we're going to have more than one seasick hand on board."

"Probably including me."

He gave her a quick glance. "I don't think so."

"I'm not exempt."

"Well, don't go and get seasick just to prove it." The clock struck six bells. "Come along."

When they arrived on deck, the crew was already assembled, facing aft. There was a stir, but no words were spoken as Stephen and Julia mounted the quarterdeck. Once there, Stephen spent a few moments surveying the men, searching every face as he held them in silence. When he finally spoke, his voice had a hearty ring, but it sounded false to Julia.

"Well, my lads, we're bound for China together," he began. "First, though, you'll get your feet wet on the Horn, which you won't like. Then you'll get a taste of the beautiful, dark-haired vahines in the Sandwich Isles, which you will.

"You're all Yankees, so there's no reason why you shouldn't make a good crew. Perform your duties well, and we'll get along. We're going to drive this ship and set new records, and I'll have no sogering aboard. The first man who shirks his duties and slows us down will find I mean what I say.

"I'm not an easy man, so don't think I am. Some of you may have heard a tale or two about me in the past. You can believe them." From amongst the men lined up below, there came almost imperceptibly the sound of several sharply drawn breaths. The mates searched the faces of the men, but those who didn't look puzzled remained expressionless.

Stephen's face was stony and all trace of his earlier geniality had vanished as he stared at the men for another silent moment. Then he said abruptly, "Mister Wilson, dismiss the men."

"Aye-aye, sir. Starboard watch, below."

Julia remained beside Stephen on the quarterdeck while the starboard watch trooped down to the fo'c'sle and the larboard watch returned to their duties. Soon, at four o'clock, they would change watches.

When the mates had left the quarterdeck, Julia turned to her husband. "Stephen," she said in a low voice, "what did you mean about the tales the men might have heard?"

"This is no place to discuss it," he said tersely and glanced at the helmsman who, staring stolidly forward, gave no sign that they were present.

Later, while they had supper below in the saloon, Julia brought up the subject again. "Stephen, what *are* those tales?"

He looked at her blankly for a few moments. Then he put down his knife and fork. "What I said this afternoon, I meant. I'm going to drive this ship, and any lazy loafer who doesn't do his best will pay for it. There have been times in the past when I've had to enforce discipline, and I'm not in the least reluctant to do it again. As you'll see."

"Why, some of them are barely more than children," she said, chilled by the coldness of his face.

"Children grow up fast at sea. The minute they signed the Articles, they left childhood behind them. They're not children, Julie," he said, his voice softening. "The youngest is thirteen. They're men, and that's the way I want you to consider them. They get no more consideration than any other man aboard. Understand?"

"You play a harsh captain," she said as she thought of young, towheaded Tim Barnes, whose father, a sea captain himself, had arranged for a berth for him aboard the *Crystal Star*.

"In order to be a master, you have to be firm. You know that as well as I do. Discipline is absolutely necessary on board. Where would we be if they sogered off while we rounded the Horn? Dead. We're not like the British with sailors all over the deck. We carry small crews on big ships, and every man has to know his duty and do it on the instant. We're not playing a pretty game on a pretty ship on a pretty ocean. We'll be going through some of the roughest passages a man can make. Just by coming out here, we're defying the sea, the winds, the currents. If discipline were more strictly enforced at sea, there'd be fewer widows on shore. Wilson's a good mate. I don't think we'll have many problems." He pushed back from the table.

Suddenly he found his appetite gone as he thought of the voyage ahead, of all the unknown factors that lay before them, of the possible disasters that would be his responsibility and his alone. There was no one else upon whom to put the blame if anything went wrong. He felt suffocated in the cabin. He needed to breathe the fresh sea air, to see the tall, pulling sails, to hear the creaking songs of taut halyards and shrouds. He needed the reassurance that only the ship could give him.

"I'm going on deck," he said abruptly.

"I'll come, too."

"If you wish."

She looked at him in surprise, not understanding his sudden cool withdrawal. She sat still for a moment, feeling rejected, but then she slowly got up and found her bonnet.

When she joined him on the quarterdeck, however, she found his mood had lightened. "I was just going to come for you," he said, and taking her by the elbow, he pulled her to the rail. "Look, my lady. The Gulf Stream."

She searched the sea for a moment, and then she saw, as clearly drawn as though cut by a knife, the emerald green water change to liquid indigo. The contrast was unbelievable. She drew a deep breath and clutched the rail. However, she found, as the bow entered the Stream, the contrast wasn't only in the color. The *Crystal Star* bucked like a horse that didn't want to enter the water.

The mate had men at the sheets and braces, ready to trim sail as they crossed the line and left the calm waters behind them. Julia held tightly to the rail as the ship, rolling and plunging through the white-crested, deep-blue waves, drove swiftly on.

One of the farm boys was already seasick, heaving his recently eaten dinner over the rail into the clean foam. She looked at him in surprise and then quickly away. The sight of his illness turned her stomach, but Stephen only laughed. "That'll clean him out."

As the hull soared high on the crests, then plunged deep into the troughs, Julia felt a new sense of freedom sweep over her, and she untied her bonnet with one hand while holding tightly to the rail with the other. She shook her head to give her hair to the wind, which ran long fingers through it, whipping the black curls until they streamed out behind her. She felt like one of the gulls that soared and played on the edge of a storm, riding the sudden drafts that rose and fell.

Stephen moved closer to her at the rail, and she turned to smile radiantly at him. "It's glorious!" She could taste the salt on her lips and feel the moisture of the fine driven spray on her face.

"You look like the spirit of the ship," he said, hypnotized by her vibrant beauty.

"I don't want to be a spirit," she said. "I want to be me, here, now, forever. I'm alive!" She raised her face to the strong wind that felt like her own blood coursing through her veins. The rail beneath her hands, the deck beneath her feet seemed to be as much a part of her as her arms and legs.

"It won't last forever," Stephen said, glancing up at the sky. "See those clouds?"

She followed his look to windward and saw a mass of dark grey clouds boiling up in the evening sky. The sun setting in the west gave them a malignant purplish cast. As the storm bore rapidly down upon them, she could see dark streamers trailing from the cloud bank and lightning slashing down on the empty sea.

The mate came up on the quarterdeck and said uneasily, "Captain Logan?"

"Well, what is it, Mister Wilson?" Stephen asked impatiently.

"Permission to shorten sail, sir."

"Were you on board this afternoon when I said that this ship was to be driven?"

"Yes, sir." The mate looked at him apprehensively.

Stephen's jaw became squarer and the muscles in it flickered. "We'll shorten sail when it becomes necessary and not a minute sooner."

"Aye-aye, sir." The mate turned to make his way to the deck below. Then he paused and came back to Stephen.

"It's the green hands, sir," he said, wetting his lips. "They have no experience."

"Well, this will give them a chance to gain it, won't it, Mister Wilson?" Stephen said acidly.

"Aye-aye, sir." The mate worriedly touched his cap and left them.

As she watched him go, Julia felt that some of Wilson's nervousness had rubbed off on her. She looked at Stephen. His eyes were narrowed as he considered the mate's retreating back.

"Soft! Too soft for a mate," he said between tight lips. "That man will bear watching."

"Stephen?"

"Go below, Julia," he said without looking at her.

"But . . ."

"I said, go below. Now!" His eyes commanded her with steel strength. There was no debating them.

Julia felt he half expected her to say 'aye-aye, sir' too. Instead she defiantly lifted her chin and, shaking out her hair, scowled at him. But she went below.

When he followed her to the saloon a few minutes later, he didn't look at her, but went directly to the locker that held his oilskins. As he put them on, he glanced around the cabin. "Stow everything that's lying around," he told her. "You've no business leaving bonnets and books all over the place."

She looked at the one bonnet and the one book lying on the settee, and keeping her lips tightly clamped, she went to pick them up.

Stephen watched her as he shrugged into his jacket. "After you've finished with that, go to bed."

"It's too early!" Despite her resolution not to speak to him, the words burst out.

"It's going to get late mighty fast. When I give you an order, you follow it. You're under the same discipline as every man on this ship, and I don't want any nonsense from you. I'm too busy to argue with you or give you any reasons for my orders. You'll do as I say. That's my last warning," he shot at her, and going to the door, he slammed it shut behind him.

As Julia clutched the table, she turned white with anger. Then she threw the book at the door with all her strength. "Treat me like a common sailor, will you?" she yelled at the varnished door. "I'll show you! You just wait, Stephen Logan!"

Seeing the book lying open on the deck, she felt remorse. It wasn't Sir Walter Scott's fault. She bent to pick it up just as the ship gave a great lurch. She fell in a heap on the deck, and she heard water rushing overhead. Above the roar of the wind and the crashing waves, she could faintly hear men's voices shouting, but she couldn't distinguish their words. The brass sperm-oil lamp, swinging wildly in its gimbals, cast strange racing shadows over the saloon. Julia stared at it in concern, then relaxed as she realized that it wasn't the lamp that was swinging. The lamp stood still while the ship swung around it. It made her feel dizzy. She looked away from it. Pulling herself up, she made her way into their cabin while holding on to anything at hand as she went.

Stephen was right. It had gotten late fast. She got her night-gown out and, sitting on the wide bed, took off her clothes. As she undressed, she looked out the stern window and saw dark seas rising like mountains astern of them. She remembered the mate's uneasiness and wondered how the business of shortening sail was going.

She thought of the farm boy she had seen lying seasick in the scuppers and wondered how he could ever have climbed up the ratlines and out onto the yardarms. He couldn't be over sixteen and had probably seen the sea for the first time in his life only a few days ago. He was probably more terrified than Tim Barnes and the other thirteen-year-old. Although as royal boys, they would have to climb almost a hundred and fifty feet to take in the topmost, smallest sails, the royals, they both came from seafaring families. From the cradle on, they had been told what to expect even if they were now experiencing it for the first time. If she had been a boy, her father would undoubtedly have sent her off when she was no older than they were.

She curled up under the blankets and thought of the men in the wildly pitching rigging and what it would have been like if only she had been born a boy. Like the sea-bound youths of the village, she had climbed the tallest trees on Scargo Hill when a high wind was blowing in order to get the feel of it, and she had sailed her own small dory at every opportunity. But now she realized that they had never come close to the reality of a ship beset by a storm. She didn't hold the thought long, for the *Crystal Star* was like an enormous cradle rocked by a giant hand, and she fell asleep to the sound of water crashing against the hull.

When she wakened, it was grey morning, and Stephen was asleep beside her, his head buried in her shoulder and his hand wound in her long hair. The walls of water rising behind them as they fell into the trough didn't seem quite as high as they had the night before, and she could see golden clumps of sargasso weed scattered through the indigo blue water.

She lay contentedly listening to the broken rhythm of the crashing water and Stephen's light breathing, feeling his body warm and strong, even in sleep, against hers. She remembered his anger of the evening and wondered at herself for rising to it. It wasn't she, but his responsibility for the ship and all the lives aboard her, that would always have to be his first concern. He was first and foremost the captain and only after that her husband. She smiled and fell asleep again.

It seemed only an instant, filled with dreams of climbing the wildly lurching rigging, losing her footing, plunging down past yards of billowing canvas, being caught by strong arms, when she roused enough to know the arms were Stephen's. She opened her eyes to see his tawny hair framed against the towering blue seas. He was looking down at her and smiling.

"You sleep soundly in a gale, my lady. You never stirred when I came to bed. Weren't you afraid?"

She smiled back lazily. "Mmm-mmm. Not when my favorite captain's in command."

He stroked her cheek lightly with his fingers. "So you trust me that much?"

She reached up and touched his fingers. "You have very capable hands, my love. Is everything all right?"

"No damage. Not so much as a ripped sail." He lay back on the pillow with triumph written in his smile. "And we made excellent time. I was right not to reduce sail until the last minute."

Julia looked through the stern window. When the ship reached the crest of a wave, she thought she could see lighter patches in the torn grey sky. "Are we through it?"

"The worst passed over hours ago." Stephen stretched luxuriously. "The seas will be rough a while longer, but we've a good strong wind to carry us through them. She's a good ship, Julie. Good and stout and strong."

"Did she spring any leaks?"

"Nothing serious. Only had to man the pumps a few times."

"And the foremast?"

"I've told you there's nothing wrong with it," he said impatiently. "It stood up beautifully."

While she was dressing, Stephen pulled on his oilskins, still wet from the past night, and went up on deck. Julia put on her warmest clothes, for with the storm, the weather had grown dankly chilly.

Just as Tomaii started serving breakfast, Stephen returned,

stamping his boots and noisily slamming the door behind him. He shucked off his oilskins and practically threw them at the steward.

"Take these to the galley and see if you can dry them out," he said roughly.

When they were alone, Julia asked, "What's wrong?"

"I don't know," Stephen said as he vigorously toweled off his face and hair. "She's not handling the way she should. She's as dry as can be expected. The sails are properly trimmed. All I can think is that the cargo has shifted. I have Wilson checking the holds. The mates should have told me earlier."

"Maybe they didn't want to disturb you."

"That's no reason. It's rank stupidity on Wilson's part." He pulled out a chair at the table and threw himself into it. "I'm not sure he even noticed. He mumbled something about her being a new vessel and the storm limbering her up. If that were true, she would be less, not more sluggish."

"When you signed him on, he came with good recommendations, didn't he?" Julia asked apprehensively.

"The highest. Well," he sighed, "maybe once he gets used to my way of doing things, he'll improve."

"I hope so."

"So do I!" He slammed the top of the table with his open palm. "By God, I need a good first mate. I *have* to have one. My first command! I have to prove I can handle it."

Julia's eyes opened wide. "You don't have any doubts about that, do you?"

"Not about myself," he said and his lips tightened into a flat line, "but this is an important voyage. Probably the most important I'll ever make. Everyone watches to see how a new master does the first time around."

"But you've taken command before." Trying to calm him, Julia put her hand on his sleeve.

"Only standing in for a sick captain. Never of my own ship. With a good record behind you, you can afford a bad voyage. Everybody has them. But when that one bad voyage is your first, you're finished. You never get another ship. I've seen it happen."

"Maybe if you talk to Mister Wilson . . ."

"Oh, I'll talk to him all right. I have quite a bit to say to our Mister Wilson." Stephen frowned and poured some coffee. "If he doesn't straighten out by the time we reach Rio, I'm going to put in and see if I can find a better mate. There's no one on board who's qualified."

"What about the second mate?"

"Randall? It was his watch."

"Oh."

"You may well say 'oh,' " he said grimly.

"Maybe they'll shape up."

"They damn well better."

There was a knock on the door and Kenneth Wilson entered. He held his cap in his hand, and despite the damp chill of the air, he was perspiring.

"You were right, sir. The cargo has shifted."

Stephen folded his arms, rocked back in his chair, and looked steadily at the mate for one long moment. Then he slammed the chair down on the floor and barked, "Well, get down there and restow it, Mister Wilson!"

"Yes, sir." The mate slapped his cap on his head and scuttled from the room.

Stephen picked up his cup and stared pensively into the coffee.

Julia, after watching him for a few minutes, felt that she had to say something. "It's a relief to know what the trouble is."

"No. It isn't." He looked up at her and his eyes were dark grey and weary. "Wilson should have seen that it was properly stowed before we left Boston. It should never have broken loose in a small gale. Then when it *did* break loose, he wasn't even aware it had happened," he said broodingly. After a moment, he took a gulp of scalding coffee. "It won't be easy to restow now. Let's just pray that we don't have any serious injuries as a result of his stupidity . . . and pray they get it secured before we hit rougher weather."

"You expect *more* bad weather?" She put her cup down abruptly.

"I always expect it. You're a damn fool if you don't. There are other things the men should be doing. Overhauling the rigging, checking the hull. Instead they're down in the hold with casks, maybe guns, rolling around, ready to break an arm or a leg or worse."

"You're really worried about the men?" After Stephen's attitude towards them yesterday, she wasn't sure that he cared about them any more than he would about a block or a shackle.

"Damn right, I am. We need every man on board. Can you

imagine what it's like down there with the ship pitching and rolling like this? Crates sliding all over, ready to crush a man against a bulkhead? Barrels sweeping down on him? I'd like to have Wilson flogged!"

"From the sounds of it, you intend to . . . with your tongue."

"I only hope it will do some good, but how do you beat stupidity out of a man and a few brains in? I don't know." He wearily rubbed his face with the palms of his hands.

"Don't get discouraged, Stephen. It will all work out. I'm certain it will. You're just tired with too long a night and too little sleep." She laid her hand on his arm.

"You think so? Well, you talk to your friend down there and ask her to treat us kindly."

"Stephen!" She took her hand away as though he had burned her. "I've asked you not to talk that way."

"Do you think I'll offend her?" He cocked one eyebrow.

Julia was glad to see some warmth return to his eyes, but she didn't want to be teased about the sea. As far back as she could remember, the sea had filled a major part of her life. When she had been a child, she had played joyfully with it, had taken her triumphs and her tragedies to it, and had told it of her sorrows. In those long ago days, the sea had always answered, and the voice of the sea was as distinct and clear to Julia as her own mother's voice. Perhaps clearer.

As she had grown up, her father had warned her of other people and their superstitions about sea witches, and she had learned to keep her silence in its presence unless she was absolutely certain she would not be overheard. The sea's voice still echoed in her mind in answer to her thoughts, but it, too, rarely spoke aloud anymore.

However, the gossip that she was a little strange and sea-possessed had never completely died. When Stephen had come to the Cape, he had heard of it. He had laughingly scoffed at the idea, and Julia had never disabused him. There were times, though, when he seemed to give it some sort of credence, but she did not encourage his belief. It could be especially dangerous aboard a ship, for sailors were almost always superstitious to one extent or another.

"You said you didn't believe that nonsense!" she answered sharply.

"I don't." He smiled at her contritely and took her hand in his. "I'm sorry, Julie. I guess I am a little tired and more than a little worried. I didn't mean to take it out on you."

"Why don't you get some rest now?" she asked, squeezing his hand and forgiving him with a smile.

"Not until the cargo's secure." He hauled himself up from the table. "I'm going on deck."

When Stephen returned to the saloon, he had Kenneth Wilson in tow. The mate's brown eyes, which could narrow and harden when he spoke to the men, were rounded soft with fear.

"If you'll excuse us," Stephen said to Julia, "I'd like to have a few words in private with Mister Wilson."

"Yes, of course." Julia gathered up her book and sewing. She was glad enough to escape the confrontation which was coming, though she guessed she wouldn't be able to avoid hearing some of it through her cabin door.

As soon as she had disappeared, Stephen turned on the mate.

"Well, Mister Wilson?" His voice cracked like a whip.

"The cargo's restowed with no damage, sir." The mate could feel perspiration rolling down his face, but he didn't dare take out his handkerchief to wipe it off. Not while the captain tried to turn him to stone with those cold grey eyes.

"No damage to property or no damage to the men, Mister Wilson?"

"No damage to either property or men, sir."

Stephen paced to the end of the saloon and back again. He ended up directly in front of the mate.

"You're very fortunate, aren't you, Mister Wilson?"

"Sir?" the mate said nervously.

"No damage to the men. Do you know that a man could have been killed down there? And what would that have made you, Mister Wilson?"

"I don't know, sir."

Stephen looked at him for a long moment in silence, looked at his plump face and balding head, looked at his bulky body clad in oilskins.

91

"I believe a man responsible for the death of another is commonly called a murderer, isn't that so, Mister Wilson?" The very quietness of Stephen's voice chilled the mate.

"Yes, sir."

"And no broken bones, no crushed arms or legs that must be amputated, so you can't be called a butcher, either." Stephen continued to look him up and down as though he were some order of vermin.

"No, sir."

"Not this time, Mister Wilson."

When Stephen turned and started down the saloon again, Wilson pulled out his handkerchief, but the captain whipped around just as he was about to wipe his face.

"You may not be so fortunate the next time, Mister Wilson, but there had better never be a next time. Do you understand me, Mister Wilson?"

"It wasn't my fault, sir."

"*Not your fault?*" Stephen advanced on him. "Not your fault that the cargo shifted?"

"No, sir." Kenneth Wilson wondered if the captain were going to hit him. It might be better than the cold, contained menace of his voice.

"Well, then, tell me, Mister Wilson, why *did* the cargo shift?"

"I don't know, sir."

"You don't know." The captain's words were brutally mocking. "And why don't you know? Who was in charge of seeing to it that the cargo was stowed properly before we sailed?"

"I was, sir," the mate said miserably.

"That was my impression, too, and yet you tell me you don't know why it shifted."

"It was the storm, sir."

"The storm. You call *that* a storm?"

"Yes, sir."

"Well, it wasn't, Mister Wilson." Stephen strolled to the stern window to look out at the grey sea that was growing steadily calmer. "It was a strong breeze with a little rain thrown in."

"But, sir . . ."

"Don't '*but, sir*' me!" The captain spun around and glared at

92

him. "You say you've been around the Horn three times?"

"Yes, sir."

"And you have the temerity to call what happened last night a storm?"

"Yes, sir."

"Well, it was not, sir. Not to anyone except a weak-kneed, sniveling, yellow-bellied, sogering sea slug. You're supposed to run this ship for me. The men know you were responsible for seeing to it that the cargo was securely stowed. How much respect do you think they're going to give you now? And without respect, how do you intend to enforce discipline?"

"I won't have any trouble enforcing discipline, sir."

"Oh, a real bully boy, are you?" Stephen smiled unpleasantly as he strolled down the pitching saloon towards the mate. "Handy with the belaying pin and not much else?"

"No, sir."

"Well, you have a very tight rope to walk now, Mister Wilson. I want this ship driven and I want discipline, and I don't care how you enforce it. I *would* advise you to be careful, though. Men don't welcome a bully boy when he loses the handle to his name and is sent forward to finish out the voyage amongst them as a common sailor."

"You . . . you wouldn't demote me, sir?"

"Wouldn't I? Don't push me too far, Mister Wilson. I would advise you to check that cargo and recheck it. There will be no more questioning of my judgment as there was last night in the matter of shortening sail. You will have the rigging overhauled immediately. You will check this ship from stem to stern, from quarterdeck to bilges to see what damage we may have sustained from your 'storm.' You will make *sailors* out of those men. Their performance last night was disgraceful."

"For some, it's their first voyage, sir."

"I am well aware of that, Mister Wilson, but if there's a man aboard who still looks like a landlubber next week, I will lay that fault at your doorstep."

"Yes, sir."

"And always keep in mind, Mister Wilson, that if you can't run a taut ship, then I will find someone who will."

"Yes, sir."

"You may go now. Send Mister Randall below."

"Sir, he's good as second, but he hasn't got the experience to be first mate."

"Be careful, Mister Wilson. You're questioning my judgment again."

"Yes, sir."

"You're also jumping to conclusions. Did I say I was going to replace you immediately?"

"No, sir."

"Never . . . never jump to any conclusions about me, Mister Wilson. I said you are dismissed. *Send Mister Randall below.*"

"Yes, sir."

Kenneth Wilson leapt for the door and then fumbled with the handle. He had forgotten he had the handkerchief in his hand, still unused. Once he got the door open, he hurried through and was glad to have it shut behind him. Anything was better than having those penetrating, cold grey eyes stabbing through him, freezing him. It was going to be a long voyage.

Chapter Five

1842

Until they sighted the other ship, the days settled into a routine segmented by the taking of sights, making entries in the log, tracking their course across the chart. There was sunrise and sunset, meals taken in the quiet saloon, hours spent on deck watching the waves roll off the bow. The sea, varying from hour to hour, changed her color and texture with the slant of the sun, the weight of the wind, and the clouds passing overhead. They ran into occasional squalls, but none so heavy as the first, and they, too, became part of the routine.

When there was no overcast, the nights became the most enchanted time with stars pressing close above the sea in the clear, dustless air. They watched Hercules and the Herdsmen, the Swan and the Lyre move across the sky. Orange Arcturus and bluish Vega, white Deneb and yellow Altair colored their nights before the sea magic lured them to their wide feather bed below where there were other enchantments to explore.

It was just after they had reached mid-ocean and the *Crystal Star* had begun a slow curve towards the south that two things happened. The winds became light and variable and a vessel was sighted. Eight bells in the afternoon were ringing and one watch was preparing to go off duty when the lookout sang out, "Sail ho!"

"Where away?" Wilson called to him.

"Four points off the starboard bow."

Julia, looking to windward, strained her eyes as she searched the horizon, but she could see nothing.

"Here. Take a look." Stephen handed her the telescope and pointed out the position of the other vessel. Looking through the glass, she could see a white patch as tiny as a sea bird in the distance. She lowered the telescope, and once again the sea was a vast, empty circle, devoid of any life save their own. Still she stared with longing in the direction of the invisible vessel.

"Isn't it foolish?" she said. "A little speck of sail on the horizon, and I'm as excited as though we'd sighted land."

Stephen, enjoying her delight, smiled at her. "We're all excited. It proves we're not alone in the world." He raised the telescope to his eye again. "Her course seems to lie a little east of ours. Perhaps we'll pass close enough to speak to her."

The men off watch had gathered at the weather rail or climbed into the rigging to catch sight of the stranger. When Stephen lowered the telescope, the mate raised his full black eyebrows in question.

"It's all right, Mister Wilson," Stephen said quietly. "Let them look. Just as long as none of the men on watch neglect their duty."

"Aye-aye, sir." Wilson said but he looked disapproving.

Their courses were slow in converging, and when darkness came, they had only been able to determine that she, like the *Crystal Star*, was a full rigged ship.

When the first light of false dawn appeared in the sky, they saw her dark shape a couple of miles off to starboard following a course nearly parallel to their own. As sunrise brightened her sails, Julia caught her breath. The ship looked achingly familiar, and yet, she reasoned, there must be other ships, dozens of them, with very much the same lines.

"I wonder who she is and where she's going," she said.

"We should know soon enough," Stephen said. "She's trimming her sails, heading in our direction."

Julia looked appraisingly at the other ship as she rose and fell over the waves, the copper sheathing of her bow flashing in the sun. Although she carried almost as much canvas as the *Crystal Star*, there was a little more bulge forward, and she took the waves

with less grace than did their own ship. Julia strained her eyes to
see the figurehead.

"Think we can beat her, Julie?"

"I'm sure we can," she answered absently.

"What makes you so certain?"

She looked at Stephen and saw the glint of worry that flickered
behind his air of self-confidence. She smiled at him. "We have the
better ship . . . and the better master."

He shook his head. "We don't know who her master is yet. It
could be Bob Waterman or Nat Palmer."

Julia was afraid she *did* know who her master was, but she
wasn't going to mention it to Stephen until she was sure. Instead
she said, "No one's better than you, Stephen, not even Waterman
or Palmer."

"You really think so?"

"Yes . . . of course."

With a smile that thanked her for her confidence, he raised the
telescope to his eye and studied the other ship.

"Here. Take a look." He handed the glass to her. "You can just
make him out. He looks somewhat familiar, and he's facing in our
direction, studying us. Perhaps you'll recognize him."

Her fingers were trembling slightly as she tried to steady the
telescope. And there was the figurehead! As she had half hoped,
half feared, the wooden girl was wearing a flowing blue gown, her
windswept black hair wreathed in seaweed and roses, one foot
stepping forth to rest upon a porpoise, and a whelk shell in her
hand.

There was no need to look at the captain now, but she did. His
dark blond curls were covered by a visored cap, but there was no
mistaking the shoulders bulging under his jacket, the wide lips
that always seemed on the verge of a smile, and the large jaw.
David!

When she lowered the glass, she was aware that Stephen was
staring intently at her.

"You look pale, Julia. What is it?"

"The ship. It's the *Jewel of the Seas*."

"Your ship!" There was a note of accusation in his voice.

"I only own part of her." It was ridiculous to feel defensive. Just
because her father had given the majority of shares in the *Jewel* to
herself and Jason as her dowry was no reason for Stephen to be

jealous. Jason had died before the ship was even launched. Besides, it was so long in the past.

"Then you know her captain, too?"

"Yes. It's David Baxter."

"Oh, yes. Well, he'll have to come aboard and report to you," Stephen said as he took the glass from her and raised it to his own eye. "Yes. I can see the figurehead. The *Jewel of the Seas,* but it's really a portrait of you, isn't it, Julia?"

"Yes. My father named the ship after me."

Because the airs were light, it took longer than they had predicted, but eventually they were within hailing distance. Julia glanced at Stephen, but he made no move to speak the ship. Instead the captain of the *Jewel* raised a speaking trumpet to his lips and called out.

"Ahoy the ship! What vessel is that?"

"The *Crystal Star,* ten days out of Boston. Captain Stephen Logan," her husband shouted through the trumpet the steward handed him. "We have your owner aboard."

It was only then, Julia realized, that David saw her and recognized her.

"Julia," he called and waved his cap at her. "With your permission, Captain Logan, I'd like to come aboard."

"Honored to have you," Stephen answered.

During this exchange, the ships had drawn closer together, and it wasn't long before each vessel backed her main topsails to slow her down. A long boat was lowered from the *Jewel* and his men rowed David Baxter across to the *Crystal Star.*

As he climbed over the rail, he seemed to just keep coming. Julia had forgotten what a giant of a man he was, dwarfing all others. Several inches over six feet, and he filled his clothes to the point of looking heavy, but Julia knew he wasn't. She remembered seeing him half-stripped on the beach at home. It was a sight she had never really forgotten, though in the past she had often wished she would.

He towered over Stephen as they shook hands, and when he turned to her, the triangular grey-green eyes that slanted slightly downward were filled with affectionate warmth.

"Julie, what a wonderful surprise," he said as he tried to keep his tone casual. There must be no betrayal of the emotions he'd felt when he first realized that she was near. "Never expected to find you in the middle of the Atlantic. Were you trying to intercept me, to take that voyage on the *Jewel* at last?"

She could see Stephen stiffen with David's words, and she spoke quickly. "No, David. We're just as surprised to see you as you are to see us. I'm Mrs. Logan now."

"Are you?" There seemed to be genuine pleasure in the wide smile that included them both. Neither of them guessed the jarring impact her words had on him. "Congratulations, Captain Logan. And you look right pert, Julia. Seems marriage agrees with you."

"Yes, it does," she said with her head tilted back to look up at him. "Where are you bound? What with all the excitement of launching and rigging the *Crystal Star*, I've lost track of your comings and goings, and Papa hasn't mentioned you lately."

"We're eight days out of New York bound for Hong Kong. And you?" He glanced at Stephen.

"The same destination, but we have a stop to make in the Sandwich Isles." Stephen was warming to this man he'd met two or three times before and had always thought of as a clumsy giant. Obviously, whatever his friendship with Julia, it hadn't been serious. At any rate, those rough-hewn features weren't the sort to attract her. "Won't you come below and join me in a glass of grog, Captain Baxter?"

"That I will," David said as he rubbed his hands together. "There's nothing like it for the morning chill."

They moved aft together, and the mate, after a word from Stephen, gave orders to proceed on their way. The *Jewel of the Seas* sailed a course parallel to them, the two ships keeping company.

Once below, David Baxter had to duck his head and lean his shoulders forward to avoid hitting the overhead. Julia smiled and thought he must have to spend most of his time either on deck or sitting down to be comfortable aboard any vessel.

"How's your wife?" she asked as they gathered around the table in the saloon. "What was her name? Cynthia?" Julia knew very well it was. There had been a time when she thought she would never be able to pronounce the name without feeling ill.

Although he was six years older than Julia, David had been her friend since childhood. After Jason's death, he had tried to remain her friend, but in her grief, she had rejected him as she had rejected all others. When she had finally been able to accept his friendship, she had then felt that he was trying to push it into a deeper relationship, and once again, she had held him away. He had sailed for England, and while he was gone, she had considered making the next journey with him in order to explore her feelings for him. Aunt Martha had agreed to go along as chaperone, but when he returned, it was with the news that he had married an English girl. Was it possible all that had happened only last spring?

"Yes. Cynthia," David said noncommittally. "When she writes, she says she's well, but I haven't seen her for many a month. Still refuses to come to America to live, and since the *Jewel's* trading has been in the opposite direction, I've not been to England."

"And the baby?"

David was silent for a moment as Tomaii set the glasses of grog in front of them. Finally he said in a low voice while looking down at his drink. "There is no child. Cynthia miscarried."

"I'm sorry. But your wife *is* all right?"

"Yes. 'Twas early when it happened."

"Well, there will be others."

"Aye. I suppose so."

Stephen had been silently watching them and listening to their conversation, but now he grew impatient with the gossip in which he had no part. "Are you rounding the Horn or will you try for Good Hope?" he asked.

"I've got no choice in the matter." David smiled at Stephen. He seemed relieved to dismiss the subject of his family. "It's old Cape Stiff for me, though God knows, I'd prefer Good Hope. I've got a load of supplies to deliver to Valparaiso, and they've got cargo there for me to carry to China. If you're bound for the Sandwich Isles, you'll be rounding the Horn, too."

"Yes. As you say, I have no choice in the matter."

"Good. 'Twill give us a chance to test our vessels. We seem fair well matched."

"I don't think so, Captain Baxter," Stephen said, the white lines beside his eyes crinkling in a smile. "Our ships may have come off the same ways, but the *Crystal Star* was just launched in March. How old is the *Jewel?*"

"Not old." David's grin was a challenge. "Launched in the fall of '38. Not quite four years ago. Just old enough to be seasoned."

"You'd best be careful, David," Julia warned him. "We've sharpened up the lines on the *Crystal Star.*"

"I've noticed," David said and took a sip of the warm drink. "So you're being unfaithful to the *Jewel* and betting on your new love."

"Yes," Julia answered with a lift of her chin. She wondered if David had ever known how much he'd meant to her. She wasn't sure she had ever really known herself. It made no difference. It was done. Over. She touched Stephen's hand. "I'm betting on the newer ship and my husband."

"You a gambling man?" David asked Stephen.

"Enough of one to wager ten dollars as well as the usual hat that we'll round the Horn before you do," Stephen answered with a lazy grin.

"Done," David said and put out his large, square hand. "And twenty dollars more and another hat says I'll make port in Hong Kong before you do."

Stephen narrowed his eyes as he thought about it. "That's fair enough. We each have a call to make first. We deduct days spent in port from our total time?"

"Agreed." David stretched his long legs out before him and raised his glass to Stephen.

"You've had command of the *Jewel* ever since she was launched?" Stephen asked curiously.

"Aye. Had the *Curlew* before her, but she was bark-rigged and no match for the *Jewel*. An old, tired lady."

"I've heard of the *Curlew*. How long did you have her?"

"Well, I was mate aboard her for two years. Then seven years ago, just when I'd turned twenty, old Captain James retired and the owners gave me command."

Stephen's face was courteously polite, but Julia could sense the envy that lay behind his mask. She held her breath, waiting for David to ask the obvious questions in return. For Stephen to have to admit to a man almost two years his junior that he'd had to wait until he was twenty-nine before getting his first command would be ignominious.

David, glancing down at the table, saw Julia's fingers tighten around her almost untouched glass. He'd had misgivings about seeing her again after their meeting last spring when he'd had to tell her that he was married. He had been relieved when he'd come on board to find her smiling gaily at him with no touch of the past in her deep blue eyes. So whatever it was that was upsetting her now had something to do with the present conversation. He decided to change the subject.

"You seen any of my family lately?" he asked her. "I haven't had a chance to get home since last year."

"Yes. Your parents came to our wedding. They're doing well," Julia said, but suddenly neither man was listening to her. They were listening to the cadence of the waves against the hull.

"Wind's changed," David said, getting up. "I'd best get back to my ship. Thanks for your hospitality. If I don't see you before then, I'll save a snug spot for you in the harbor at Hong Kong."

"Don't hold it too long," Stephen said as he shook hands with him. "We'll probably have come and gone long before you drop your anchor."

Once again, the *Crystal Star*'s main topsail was backed and the *Jewel of the Seas* approached them. As soon as the longboat was clear, Stephen ordered their sails filled away, and they left the *Jewel* in their wake.

"Stephen aren't you going to wait till David gets aboard for an equal start?"

"I'm racing a record as well as him. Besides he's the one who offered the challenge. Let *him* try to make up the time."

"I doubt he will," Julia said. "He doesn't have the ship."

"I know he won't. He struck me as too free and easygoing. I doubt he even knows how to drive a ship."

"I don't know," Julia said dubiously as she watched the longboat being hoisted aboard the other ship. "He's made some good voyages for us."

"And broken several records, too. I know. I've heard enough about him, but the man still doesn't live up to his image."

"Well, I'm sure you'll beat him round the Horn. After all, you beat Cousin William, and if you could do that, you could beat anyone."

"I'm glad you have such confidence in me, my lady." Stephen looked astern at the *Jewel*, now with her canvas spread full and following swiftly in their wake. He wondered how much Julia's falling in love with him had to do with his outsailing her former father-in-law that one time. He doubted that she was aware of what both William Thacher and he knew. The only reason it had ever happened was that Stephen was in temporary command of a newer, better ship.

* * *

102

For several days, they gradually opened up their lead on the *Jewel* until one morning the sun rose to show them that she had disappeared over the horizon astern of them. Stephen relaxed for the first time since they had spoken to the other ship. He began to instruct the more seasoned hands in the rudiments of navigation, for the schooling of future mates and masters was the responsibility of every captain. When they reached 35°N and 30°W, they were heading due south and the weather became perceptibly warmer.

Julia had often heard men speak of the monotony at sea, but she didn't find it so. While it was true the days faded one into the other, there was something peaceful in thinking about only one day, sometimes only one hour, at a time. The future lay so far ahead, there was no point in worrying about it. The past seemed to lie as far behind as another lifetime, pleasantly remembered, but not dwelt on. Land, with its responsibilities, was far distant, and they concerned themselves with it no more than it concerned itself with them. They lived in a world, they were the world, ruled by nature, that of man as well as that of the elements, and all their care was bound up in this one small tight planet of ship, horizon, sea, and sky.

They spent most of their days and nights together. Julia had not realized how little, when things were going well, the captain actually had to do. At sea, the mate ran the ship and crew, while the captain laid out the overall course and strategy. And, of course, he worried.

As they approached the equator, the weather became balmier, and at night, phosphorus flickered in the waves like the shattered reflections of stars. The bow wave was illuminated against the dark hull by their radiance, and the nights were never black in this star-sea-lit world. The familiar constellations, the Big Dipper and the Giraffe, fled and disappeared northward while the Peacock and the Altar appeared in the southern sky.

For breakfast, they sometimes had flying fish, crisply fried by the cook, who also, in his spare time, went fishing for the dolphin and bonito that occasionally followed in schools behind the *Crystal Star*.

One day, while noting their position on the chart, Stephen said to her, "Well, Julie, you really are a daughter of Neptune now."

"What?" she said absently as she leafed through the log book.

"We've crossed the equator." He grinned at her. "Don't you remember? When a man first crosses the line, he becomes a son of Neptune forever. I suppose he had daughters, too. He must have. He was a lusty old man."

Julia looked up from the book and laughed. "Well, if we're in his kingdom, you'd best not say 'was' and 'old.' "

"Then we'll have to appease him." Stephen's grey eyes glinted with amusement as he looked thoughtfully at her. "A sacrifice?"

"Stephen!"

"Yes," he said, and when he saw the startled look on her face, he rubbed his chin in a pretence of serious consideration. "A sacrifice. He's one of the gods who demand it. A nice young pig, perhaps, or a chicken?"

"You can't throw fresh food away like that," she said, appalled at the thought of wasting the little they had to last them until they reached the Sandwich Islands.

"I don't know why not. He gave us a good dinner last night and a fine breakfast this morning. But you're right. I don't think that would satisfy him."

He gathered up his navigational instruments and carefully put them back into their fitted rack. Then, handling them like delicate and precious jewels, he returned the precisely balanced chronometers to their velvet lined and padded case. Before he was able to remove the chart, Julia stood up and lightly traced their course across the middle of the earth with one finger.

Suddenly she felt a sharp tug on her hair from behind. She was just about to whip around when Stephen said, "Don't move."

She stood still for a moment, but when she felt her hair swing free, she turned on him to find that he was holding a knife.

"Stephen! What on earth are you doing?"

He opened his other hand to display the blue-black curl that lay on his palm.

"You cut my hair!" she said and pulled the ends around over her shoulder to see what damage he had done.

"Yes," he said soberly. "A sacrifice. One that Neptune will value more than any other I could offer. He'll understand it's one of my most treasured possessions."

"*Your* possession? It's my hair!"

He carefully laid the curl on the chart and sheathed his knife.

Then he swept her hair behind her shoulders and pulled her to him.

"My hair, my lips, my eyes, my nose," he said as he kissed each in turn. "You're mine, Julie. My most beautiful, my most cherished possession."

"I am *not* a possession!" she said, suddenly furious, and tried to push him away.

"Oh, yes, you are." His arms tightened around her. "Don't try to struggle with me. You're mine."

She knew from past experience that, when he was determined, it was impossible for her to break away from him. Why should men, just because they were stronger, think they had the right to own women? she thought angrily as she refused to respond to his caresses.

"You're still fighting me, my lady," he murmured, his lips tracing a path up the side of her neck to her cheek.

"I thought you wanted to give that curl to Neptune," she said stiffly.

"All in good time," he whispered in her ear.

She leaned her forehead against his shoulder. There might be no way for her to free herself from his embrace, but she didn't have to look at him.

"That's better, my sweet," he said as he kissed her ear. Then, holding her face cupped in one hand, he found her mouth.

Why, she wondered as he forced open her lips and the first strands of ecstasy touched her, could he always do this to her? Her body was a traitor! But even as she thought this, she could feel her breasts rising to meet him and her body joyously responding to his touch.

When he released her, his eyes were hazy with love and so luminous, she forgave him. If her kiss could please him as much as his pleased her, why should she begrudge him the happiness they shared?

"Give me your ribbon, Julia," he said softly.

"My ribbon?" But even while she asked the question, she was reaching up to untie the ribbon that bound back her hair. Then she handed it to him.

"Blue." He nodded his approval. "Neptune's favorite color when he's in one of his better moods."

"What are you going to do with it?"

"You'll see." He handed the ribbon back to her and picked the curl up from the chart. "Tie it in a bow around this."

"It's too long," she said as she understood what he wanted. "I'll cut it first."

"No. Give it all. Don't begrudge it."

After she had carefully knotted, then looped the ribbon into a bow around the lock he held between his fingers, they made their way towards the companionway, dropping their hands from each other's only when they reached the steps.

As they arrived on the quarterdeck, Stephen nodded at the mate. "Mister Wilson, you may inform the men that we have just crossed the equator at twenty-five degrees twelve seconds west."

"Aye-aye, sir," Wilson said with just the right shade of deference. "Twenty-five degrees twelve seconds west."

Stephen watched him with bemusement as the mate went forward to call out the news to the crew. Then he drew Julia aft to the stern with him.

"Do you feel more confident about Mister Wilson now, Stephen?" Julia whispered once they were out of earshot of the helmsman.

"I don't know," he said when they reached the taffrail. "I really don't know. He seems to be shaping up, but it's still a long way to Rio."

"You'll lose time if we put in." She leaned on the rail and looked out at a sea that was empty of all life save their own.

"That's something I'll have to consider," he said thoughtfully as he unbuttoned his shirt and pulled the ribbon-bound lock from its hiding place. Then he smiled and handed it to her. "Throw our offering over the stern, my lady, and ask Father Neptune to forgive my slanders."

She smiled back at him, and then leaning over the taffrail, she tossed it into the milky blue sea. The sapphire colored ribbons streaming out fluttered in the wind, then floated on the swirling water as lightly as seaweed.

"A bouquet," Stephen said quietly as he watched it in their wake. "A bouquet for Neptune from one of his daughters."

Leaning on the rail, Julia followed its progress until it was left far astern. "Pretty," she whispered when it had finally disappeared from sight. Strangely, she felt that what Stephen had offered in jest, the sea had accepted with solemnity.

"More than pretty," he said while he twined one of her long curls around his finger. "It was beautiful. You don't begrudge it, do you?"

"No." She leaned back against him. "I only hope he'll grant us fair winds in return."

"It's a gift, not payment in advance. You don't buy favors from the gods."

"I'd sacrifice another one if it would guarantee us a good voyage."

"Not until we cross the equator in the Pacific." He smoothed the black curl that was still wound around his finger. "I can't spare any more until then."

Their contemplation of the waves that flattened out in their wake was broken by a cry of "Sail ho!"

When the lookout had indicated that the sail lay astern of them, the mate handed the telescope to Stephen.

"Can't make out much yet," Stephen said as he looked through the glass, "but he seems to be following us. We'll show him our tail."

When he handed the glass to Julia, he turned to look aloft at the towering sails that stood starkly white against the blue sky. Critically he studied each in turn. Then he started snapping out orders to the mate.

The crew had very little time to celebrate the crossing of the equator, although during the dog watch they did elect one of their number King Neptune. For hours, they were kept busy trimming the sails to take advantage of every lift or knock of the wind, but still the vessel astern of them grew slowly larger.

The next morning, Stephen was still on deck with the telescope and orders. During the night, the other vessel had gained on them only imperceptibly. By mid-morning, however, she was more visible, and the wind was dying.

"I think it's the *Jewel of the Seas*, damn him," Stephen said to Julia. Then he shouted at the mate, "Mister Wilson, wet the sails."

Within minutes, every canvas bucket aboard had been lowered over the side to be filled with salt water and was being hoisted aloft to the bare-chested men who were scattered over the yards. After three weeks at sea, even the farm boys had become fairly agile while working far above the decks of the ship, but it was no easy thing to feel only the foot ropes supporting them in mid-air while they flung bucketfuls of water down on the canvas. As the hours went by, they became more adept at it, but it was steady and grueling work. When the watches changed at noon, the men who were relieved ate quickly and tumbled down into the fo'c'sle to rest in the four hours allotted to them.

Stephen, however, after he had taken the noon sights, had Tomaii bring his food on deck, but it went untouched as he paced back and forth, alternately watching the crew and sails, then glancing at the vessel astern of them. It wasn't until the first watch of the evening that he was satisfied with the distance they had opened up between themselves and the other vessel. Then he went below for the first sleep he'd had since they had sighted her the day before.

They didn't completely shake the *Jewel*, however, for later that day, the wind, faithful until then, deserted them, and they lay becalmed in a flat, oily ocean. On the horizon, there was an occasional glimpse of sails, reminding them that they were not the only ones the wind had forsaken.

The sails slatted against the spars and often had to be furled to prevent them from chafing. At the hint of a slight breeze, the men were sent aloft again to unfurl them. The *Crystal Star* was lifeless, a thing of wood, copper, and paint, as she rolled with the swell of the sea. The air was hot and stifling, and Julia looked longingly down at the water, wishing that she could go for a swim, but the occasional fin of a shark cutting through the surface made it impossible. Besides, even without the danger of sharks, she knew that Stephen would never permit it. There was no possibility of privacy, and she was the only woman on board.

During the dog watches, she watched enviously while the sailors poured buckets of salt water over each other. She didn't envy them by day, though, when she watched them go aloft with a bucket of tar and a handful of oakum to work their way down from the mastheads with only a rope tied into a bowline to support them as they tarred the rigging from the stays to the footropes, from the lifts to the shrouds. Nor would she have traded places with them when they went down on their knees to push a holystone, commonly called the seamen's Bible, across a sand strewn deck until the wood shone through as clean as though it had just been laid.

There were plenty of chances to observe the men at work as she sat listlessly under the awning Stephen had had rigged for her and fanned herself for lack of any other breeze. Although she wore the lightest dresses she owned and only one petticoat, even these clung to her skin and seemed a sticky burden. Sometimes to escape the brutal rays of the sun that not only poured down from overhead but were reflected upwards from the blue, glassy surface of the Southern Ocean, she would go below to the cabin, and after rinsing her body with only one tepid cup of fresh water, would lie naked on the bed.

At night, they stayed on deck until after midnight in the relative coolness of the darkened world. When she could no longer avoid going below, Julia once again envied the sailors, who all slept on deck with only their trousers on, curled up on a coil of rope or a hatch cover, strewn over the ship like an army of fallen soldiers.

They worked by day, though. When they weren't tarring the rigging or holystoning the deck, the mates kept them busy caulking seams, cleaning, and painting. With each catspaw of wind, the sails were reset and trimmed, for every advantage must be taken if they were ever to get through the doldrums.

Stephen was unbearable as he paced the deck, studying the blue, cloudless sky, watching the slick surface of the sea for the least ripple. He sometimes went aloft himself to stare out over the unending calm. Whenever she spoke to him, he snapped at her, and she thought it was just as well that she was too enervated to snap back. He was up and down all night, waking her each time he rose or returned to bed. His body was hot beside her, and when he took her, he did it quickly, giving her no satisfaction, only a restless yearning.

At times when she drifted in the borderline world between wakefulness and sleep where the will begins to lose control over the mind, she found her thoughts turning to David Baxter and picturing him just beyond the horizon caught between the same unrelenting sun and the same unforgiving sea. Would life aboard the *Jewel of the Seas* be identical with that aboard the *Crystal Star*? She couldn't imagine that large, unhurried man turning irritable and restive. Yet he, too, most likely kept his men hard at work and trimmed his sails at every opportunity.

On the eighth day in the doldrums, Julia stayed below after dinner in the relative coolness of the saloon while Stephen went back on deck to resume his eternal pacing. She could hear his footsteps overhead beating out a ceaseless rhythm as she went to get the logbook. Tomaii was still clearing the table when she sat down, and she watched him curiously. Going to sea had been such an exhilarating experience at first, she hadn't really paid much attention to the tall South Sea islander. Later, slipping quietly in and out of the saloon while he served them, he had become an unnoticed fixture in their lives.

After he had finished clearing the table, Tomaii brought her a fresh pot of tea and then began to wash the overhead deck light silently. Julia riffled through the pages.

For every day, there was a page, and printed in the left hand margin were the twenty-four hours. In lined columns opposite them, there was space to list the knots, fathoms, courses, winds, leeway, air temperature, and water temperature for each hour, while the right half of the page was given over to remarks, which usually had to do with the wind's force, the weather, sails that were sent down or taken up, and the number of times they had tacked if at all.

In squares at the bottom of the page, there was a final figure for the day's course, distance run, and the different reckonings of latitude and longitude, whether by dead reckoning, observation, or chronometer.

She could follow their course from the 42°21' latitude by 70°2' longitude with moderate southeast winds when they had set sail from Boston to the notation for May 1 at 24°40' by 40°23', when the winds had stayed steadily southeast by east throughout the day. Calm faint airs interspersed by calms, but the weather had been fine.

The ship's day began at noon each day, when they took their sights, and now as she summed up their findings at the bottom of the page that had begun with the ship's day of May 18, she saw that Stephen had written in his bold incisive hand below her own notations of calms and fitful breezes.

"Lord, You are trying my patience."

She smiled as she finished her entry, but then she sanded the book, closed it, and pushed it away with a sigh. The keeping of the log represented her total work since the *Crystal Star* had sailed. With the cook in undisputed charge of the galley and the steward reigning over the captain's quarters and wardrobe, there was really nothing for her to do. She had never felt so useless in her life, she thought.

How were things going at the shipyard? she wondered, and she could picture herself working with her father in the office, or out amongst the bustle that surrounded the vessels, knowing that she was contributing something. But here she sat with her hands lying idle in her lap. Home lay far behind them and, with every hour, grew more distant.

It would be months, perhaps a year, before she saw it again, and she was committed to a confining ship and the stranger Stephen had suddenly become. Here there were no friends, no family. She couldn't speak to anyone but her husband, the steward, the taciturn cook, and the mates, and even then, Stephen disapproved of her having any lengthy conversation with either Wilson or Randall. Why he should object to her talking to poor, plump Kenneth Wilson, or lanky, sandy haired Frank Randall, who was a few months younger than she was, she didn't know. She didn't agree with Stephen when he said it would ruin discipline. After all, she wasn't the captain. Only the captain's wife, and she had no power to uphold.

As she looked around the saloon, she noticed how brightly polished the steward kept the walnut paneling above the impeccably clean ivory paint of the wainscoting. No trace of salt appeared on the beveled plate glass of the stern windows, and the brass lamps gleamed in their gimbaled brackets. Despite the food and liquids the sea sometimes dumped upon the settee, the red velvet looked as new as the day it had been tacked on. She doubted that any of the maids at home would have been able to keep the room in such perfect order as Tomaii did, even in this dust-free world.

When the steward passed in front of her with a pail of water, she looked appraisingly at him. His hair was straight and black with reddish highlights, and his eyes were a melting brown that was set off by his light, creamy skin. He was well-built and always carried himself with an easy dignity.

"Where are you from, Tomaii?" she asked. "What is the name of your island?"

He carefully put down the pail and looked at her with a gleam of joy in his eyes. "The most beautiful of all, Mrs. Captain. It is Mooréa."

She was fascinated by the rich lilting flow of his voice. She wanted him to go on speaking.

"Where is that, Tomaii?"

"Very far from here. In the Pacific Ocean."

"Near the Sandwich Isles?"

"No. Far, far beyond them. It is more beautiful."

He seemed so at ease on a ship, enjoying what he was doing, whether it was serving them, washing clothes, cleaning the cabins, or climbing the rigging when all hands were called. What had his life been like on that distant island? It must have been very different. How had he been able to adapt with such grace to life aboard a ship of people so foreign to him?

"Are you ever homesick?" she asked him curiously.

"How?" He was perplexed, wanting to help her, but not understanding what she was asking.

"Do you ever think about your home and miss it and wish you were there?"

"Yes," he said. His face cleared with understanding and his strong white teeth flashed in a smile. "Many times. In the beginning . . ." He shook his head. "Very bad. Now sometimes I remember, but it is not so bad."

"Why did you ever leave it?" she asked, pushing her hot hair away from her sticky face, but not so conscious of the heat now as her interest in the steward grew.

"Oh," he shrugged. "Young boys have foolish notions. The island is small. Ships come like clouds across water. They have many good things and they chase the whales. The captain says, 'You go?' I say, 'Yes. I go.' " He shrugged again, but this time more sadly.

"And you've never been home since?"

"No," he said, and the sadness spread from his body to his face. "I try. I learn to speak as Americans do. When I hear a ship go Tahiti, I sign the Articles. They lie. They never go."

She studied him for a moment in silence. She wondered uneasily if he knew. Then she decided to tell him.

"We're not going to Tahiti, either, Tomaii," she said gently. "I hope no one told you we were."

"No," he said as he plumped up a pillow that was lying beside her on the settee. "Captain Logan does not lie. He is a good man. But I need money. He says we go Pacific. It is all right."

"And you don't know whether you'll ever be able to get home again or not." She wondered how she would feel in his place. She couldn't even begin to imagine how lost and lonely it would be.

"Oh, yes, I know," he said, and his smile was gay with

confidence again. "Someday I will go, and someday you, too, will come. I will show you high mountains with clouds of rain, many rivers of sweet water, many pretty girls. You will like."

"I'd like to go." Suddenly the heat and the monotonous rolling of the ship over the swells were less oppressive. "You've helped me, Tomaii. Thank you."

"I have helped you?" He was obviously pleased, but he was also confused.

"Yes," she said as she straightened her back and picked up the logbook with a purpose. "You *have* helped me. You've reminded me that we are going to places like your Mooréa. We're not leaving things. We're going towards them."

He still didn't understand, but he was glad to see the earlier melancholy on her face replaced by a confident smile. "You feel more better now, Mrs. Captain?"

"Yes, I feel a heap more better now. If only the wind would come."

"The wind will come," he said. "The wind always comes."

Tomaii was right. The next day, though they felt only the lightest breath of air, there was air, and the sky turned a heavy-laden grey with clouds so low they almost seemed to brush the topmost spars. As the hours passed, the sky grew blacker and blacker, and the atmosphere was so thick, it was difficult to breathe. Then the water fell.

It came, not in drops, but like a solid vertical wave, drenching them in less than a second. All available containers were brought on deck to catch the fresh water, so precious now. It spouted from the scuppers, but still the decks filled until they were knee deep. Julia, with her eyes closed and her arms well away from her body, held her face up to it, luxuriating in it as the rain washed the salt from her sticky skin and cooled her hot body.

"You'd better go below now, Julia," Stephen said, and opening her eyes, she saw him standing beside her. He was smiling for the first time in days.

"Oh, no, Stephen. I need this."

"The men need it, too. They're entitled to their bath, and they can't possibly strip while you're on deck."

"I'm just as dirty as anyone else. I need a bath, too."

"Well, you can't strip on deck. You can have one in the privacy of our cabin."

She looked below at the men who were frolicking in the water. The rain was almost like a curtain, but she could see them splashing each other with great scooping handfuls of water in the pond the deck had become, and she could hear them laughing and shouting like schoolboys. For just this moment, discipline had been relaxed. They deserved their time, and if her being on deck spoiled it in any way, she knew she had to leave.

It was still hot below, the windows and ports closed tight against the rain. Trailing water across the cabin deck, she went into the small head and opened the port. The rain was still pouring down, but there was no wind to blow it into the ship. Gratefully, she stood near the port and slowly peeled off her sopping clothes. Then she loosened her hair and wrung it out so that the fresh water trickled down her body, cleansing it, refreshing it.

The memory came, strong as though it had been yesterday, of standing on the back porch at home when she was a small child and feeling the joy of fresh water as her father washed away the beach-gathered salt and sand. She could feel the soft breeze and smell the warmth of summer spruce.

There was a knock at the door, and she opened it a crack to peer through while hiding her naked body behind it. She couldn't see anyone.

"What is it?" she asked, suddenly anxious. With everyone on deck shouting their lungs out and the heavy pounding of the rain, no one would hear her if she needed help.

"The captain says bring you water, Mrs. Captain."

She sighed with relief. It was Tomaii.

"Just leave it out there," she said.

She heard him make several trips back and forth and then he called out, "All ready," and banged the door to the saloon shut.

As soon as he had gone, she darted out and bolted the door. Then she turned to look with real appreciation at the round wooden tub half-filled with water and the two buckets and towels standing beside it. Once in the tub, she took a large sponge and squeezed the water in miniature torrents over her head and shoulders. How marvelously spendthrift, how luxuriously wasteful of the most precious commodity to be had at sea! She soaked in it for a few minutes, but even as she sat there, it was getting warmer. She fumbled for the bar of soap on the floor beside the tub, then knelt to wash her hair. Once she was satisfied that it was clean, she dipped the sponge into a bucket of water and rinsed it. It seemed to take forever to get the soap out of her hair. There was just too much of it! She should have encouraged Stephen to cut more while he was about it.

After she had wrapped a towel into a turban around her head, she soaped her body, and the soap lathered in a way it never did in salt water. She needed almost all the water in the buckets to rinse away the suds.

Just as she was rinsing off her leg, standing with the other on the floor beside the tub, the door handle rattled and then there was a loud banging.

"Who is it?" she called, quickly taking a towel and wrapping it around her body.

"Who do you think it is?" It was Stephen's voice.

"I wasn't sure," she said as she unbolted the door and let him in. "I felt a little exposed."

"You are," he said with a laugh as he shut the door behind him and whipped off her towel in one motion.

"Stephen!" she said, reaching for the towel he held behind him.

"Very pretty." He grinned at her like a sopping satyr before he gave her back the towel.

"Well, I'm clean." She wound the towel around her. "Is it still raining?"

"Not much. Just a drizzle. The men have plugged the scuppers and are practically swimming around out there."

"What fun! I'm glad you let them do it."

"If I didn't, I'd have to smell them," he said and wrinkled his nose as he began to unbutton his shirt. "Now for *my* bath."

Julia looked at the soapy water in the tub and the almost empty buckets. "I'm afraid I've used up practically all the water."

"With that cloudburst? Hardly. Tomaii's bringing more," he said, flinging his wet clothes carelessly on the deck. "He should be here any minute. You'd better go into the head until he's finished."

When the steward had come and gone, Stephen called her to come out. She found him already sitting in the wooden tub, lathering his arms and chest with vigor.

"I'd best get out some clean clothes . . . if there are any left," she said, going towards the cabin.

"Wait, my lady. Aren't you going to wash my back?"

115

"You're getting spoiled, Stephen," she said, but she went willingly to him.

"Captains deserve spoiling," he said as he handed her the sponge. Then before she could go around behind him, he grabbed the end of her covering towel and whipped it off of her again.

"Stephen! That's the second time. If you don't behave, I won't wash your back for you." She reached out for the towel, but he threw it toward the stern windows.

"I always wanted to be washed by a nude nymph," he said lasciviously, his eyes traveling appreciatively over her naked body, stopping to linger pointedly at some of his favorite spots.

"The door's not even locked. Anyone could walk in."

"They wouldn't dare, but go lock it if it'll make you feel any better."

She was all too aware of his eyes following her as she walked to the door and bolted it. When she turned, she instinctively crossed her arms in front to protect herself from his hot gaze.

"Don't do that, Julie," he said as she approached him. "You don't have anything to be ashamed of and I *am* your husband."

She smiled and dropped her hands. She couldn't understand her sudden reluctance to be seen. After all, they *had* been married for some time now. Maybe it was because she felt so clean.

As she scrubbed his back, she could feel the tense muscles relax and she enjoyed the feel of his firm flesh beneath her fingers.

"That's my darling," he sighed with his eyes half closed as she poured fresh water over his back and shoulders. When she started to hand the sponge back to him, he said, "Don't stop now."

"Don't stop what? Your back couldn't be cleaner."

"That's just my back," he said as he knelt up in the tub. "You *are* going to spoil me, aren't you?"

She looked down at him doubtfully. "You want me to wash *all* of you?"

"All of me, my handmaiden," he said, grinning at her, and suddenly he was *her* Stephen again, not the irritable, remote stranger he had been for the past few days. " 'Purge me with hyssop and I shall be clean. Wash me, and I shall be whiter than snow.' "

She smiled wickedly back at him, all thoughts of modesty now gone, and she lathered his stomach. " 'His belly is as bright ivory overlaid with sapphires,' " she quoted back at him. Then she kissed him lightly. " 'His mouth is most sweet; yea, he *is* altogether lovely.' "

"You'd better be careful," he warned her, "or you'll end up in this tub with me."

"There's not room for two."

"Do you want to try to prove it?"

"No, and you're the one who'd better be careful now," she said, laughing as she soaped him gently. "I have you at my mercy."

"Only for the moment," he said, cocking a tawny eyebrow at her.

After she had rinsed him, he stood up and stretched. "Never . . . never in my life have I enjoyed a bath so much. Here I've been washing myself all this time and never knew what talents you were hiding from me. We'll have to make a habit of it."

"Well, it won't be much of a habit unless we get more rain. I think that's the thing I miss most."

"Rain?"

"No. Fresh water. Baths. Sometimes I dream about Scargo Lake and all that lovely fresh water. I never appreciated it at home, but then I never got so hot and sticky there, either."

"You're not getting homesick?" He stepped out onto the towel she had laid on the deck for him.

"No. Not really."

"You're the one who wanted to go to sea." He looked at her face carefully when she handed him a towel.

"I do. I like it. It's just that I can't help thinking of home sometimes, wondering how everybody is, how the shipyard is doing, what they're planning to build next." She went to pick up the towel he had thrown and when she raised her head, she looked out the stern window at the flat sea that reflected grey clouds overhead. It had stopped raining.

"We haven't been gone that long," he said as he toweled himself vigorously. "Nothing will have changed."

"It's just that I feel so useless," she said and turned back to look at him. "Sometimes I wonder if they're not right when they say a ship is no place for a woman."

"You're far from useless," he said, coming to her and holding her to his still damp body. There was comfort in his strength. "The place for you is where I am, my lady. I need you."

"Do you, Stephen? Do you really?" she asked as she slipped her hands up the muscles of his arms.

117

"How can you doubt it?"

"I don't know, but sometimes lately, you haven't seemed to need me, you haven't even seemed to really want me around. I've thought about what it would be like to stand on shore and watch you sail away . . ."

"That's something you'll never do."

"I hope not . . . but will you always feel the same?"

"Julie," he said, and there was concern in the soft bluish-grey of his eyes, "I have to go up on deck and make sure that Wilson has restored some sort of discipline. But I don't want to leave you feeling like this. I'm not going to change in the way I feel about you. Why should I?"

"They say men do." She lowered her black lashes to conceal what he might read in her eyes. "Tire of a woman after a while. Get bored and want to be free to go off on their own. Find another woman in another port."

"You've been listening to a lot of old biddies who don't know what they're talking about," he said impatiently as he pulled away from her and went into their cabin to find dry clothes.

"I've heard the men talk," she said and followed him to the cabin where she leaned against the doorframe. "Sometimes in the early evening, when they're off watch, I've overheard them. They talk about the lovely vahines in the Sandwich Isles, the pretty Chinese girls in Whampoa, the high spirits of the Portuguese. I know that at least two of them are married."

"Don't you ever repeat what you hear or see once you get home!" he said sharply, turning towards her with a white shirt in his hand.

She crossed to the bed and sat down. She looked at him, looked at the muscled shoulders and powerful arms, the hair on his chest darker than that on his sun-bleached head, the slender hips that ran down to strong, straight legs.

"I won't repeat anything," she said. "What purpose would it serve? 'Twould only hurt their wives. Everyone knows a man hangs his conscience on the Horn when he goes round and picks it up again on the voyage home, but no woman wants to believe *her* husband would do such a thing. They suspect, but they don't want to know."

"Not all men are that way," Stephen said as he buttoned his shirt.

"Most, I think." Julia got up from the bed and began to search through the drawers for clean linen.

"Well, you'll see for yourself when we make port. Just don't let any of the men suspect you notice anything."

"I've already decided that I'm not even *going* to notice anything. I'm like their wives. I'd rather not know."

"That's best," he said, tucking his shirt into his pants. "But we weren't talking about the men. We were talking about us."

She shrugged and pulled a petticoat over her head.

"You were saying that I'd become bored with you," he continued. "Have you seen any signs of it yet?"

"No. Not really." She sighed and her smile was sad. "I know you've had a lot of things on your mind, what with being becalmed and all. It's just . . . just a feeling I've had about the future. Lately, I've started to have a dream at night. It's always the same. I dream you're sailing away from me, going to some other woman, never coming back. It frightens me." She looked forlorn and vulnerable.

Stephen took her gently in his arms and pulled her to the bed. Sitting next to her, he held her close as though to protect her from that unknown future and brushed her damp hair away from her face.

"I don't think you brought a crystal ball along," he said quietly. "There's only one thing you need to know about the future, and that is that I love you more each day, and I'll never stop loving you as long as I live. You're the most precious thing in the world to me." He grinned at her crookedly. "How could you bore me? You're like the sea, always changing. Calm and sunny one day. Blowing a gale the next." He lifted her chin so that she had to look into his smiling eyes. "And sometimes you rain."

Still, held in the protection of his gentle strength, she felt a sad foreboding.

Chapter Six

1842

After the rain, there were occasional breezes, but few lasted as long as an hour, and they came from every point of the compass. The next day, a ship appeared on the horizon once more, and Stephen was sure it was the *Jewel*. Slowly over the following days, she gained on them, and through the telescope they were able to confirm that David Baxter was following close on their heels.

And once more, Stephen became sleeplessly irritable, driving the men aloft to trim sails to a breeze that existed only in his imagination. Kenneth Wilson, red-faced and perspiring, his thinning hair plastered by damp heat to his scalp, became quicker with his fists or a belaying pin when the men moved too slowly to suit him. The only sounds became the thuds of his blows, the orders shouted out, the footsteps of the crew, the clucking of the hens, and the creakings of the ship. It was a silent world and every noise was magnified a hundredfold.

Then a few days later, they met the southeast trades, which scooped them up and sent them scudding southwards. As they left the *Jewel* far behind, tension eased, and during the dog watches, the men began to smile again and the music of a harmonica floated up to the quarterdeck.

A day finally came when, shortly after breakfast, they heard the lookout in the crow's nest shout, "Land ho!"

The excitement of seeing land for the first time since leaving Cape Cod in their wake many weeks ago pervaded the ship. The men who were off watch abandoned sleep and came tumbling up from the fo'c'sle to climb the rigging and stare towards the west, as though the sight of land, any land, would nourish them.

Julia knew by their reckonings that they were soon due to raise Cape St. Roque or some part of that massive, jutting shoulder of Brazil, yet she, too, felt the thrill of discovery as she raised the telescope to her eye. It was only a small patch of dusky, smoky blue lying on the horizon between the brighter sea and sky, but it was land.

"I hate to take the time for it," Stephen said beside her, "but we'd better go in and verify our position. The chronometers should be checked."

"David Baxter will have to put in, too, won't he?" Julia asked.

"He'd better or he's a damn fool."

"So we won't really lose any time to him."

"No," Stephen said as he took the glass from her and raised it to his eye. "We are *not* going to lose any time to him."

They sailed a course that would parallel the shoreline, and before noon, they were close enough to recognize the village of Pernambuco. The red-tiled roofs, the white-walled buildings and palm trees were strange to Julia's eyes. Through the telescope, she could see people going about their business, dogs and naked children playing in the streets.

"Are we going on in, Stephen?" she asked, hoping he would say yes.

"And lose time? Absolutely not. As soon as we've taken the noon sights, we're going to trim ship and get away from the coast. A storm could come up at any time, and as long as we're near shore, we're vulnerable."

Julia noticed the mate, whose attention was not on the ship, but on the shore. For all his earlier fuss and noise, he seemed dejected.

"What about Rio?" Julia asked Stephen quietly.

He looked at her narrowly, then glanced at Kenneth Wilson. "I still haven't decided," he said abruptly. "It's a long way down this coast. There's still time."

121

With the air of the fair southeast trade winds and the Brazilian current, they flew down the coast of Brazil. As they neared the latitude of Rio, Stephen often looked in the direction of the invisible land, a thoughtful, weighing question in his eyes. Wilson looked, too, his glances quick and nervous when he thought he was unobserved.

The day came when the decision must be made, and while the mate was off watch, Julia asked Stephen, "Well, what are you going to do about it? Are we going in?"

Stephen was silent for a moment, then looked up at the sails, which were filled with air, straining tautly at their lift lines. Their power could be felt in the driving hull and seen in the bow wave. He raised the glass and swept the horizon. There was no sign of any life but their own on the empty sea.

"No, I think not," he said. "There's no guarantee I'd find a better mate than Wilson, and we'd lose time. We may not be able to see him, but I have a feeling that Baxter in the *Jewel* isn't very far behind us. At times, I can almost feel him breathing down my neck."

"It's only a bet, Stephen. If you think Wilson's a liability . . . you wouldn't risk the ship for ten dollars, would you?"

"It's not just the ten dollars."

"Then what is it?"

"I am going to win." His jaw tightened, and the lines beside his mouth deepened to hardness when he spoke.

Here the South Atlantic was a busy ocean with porpoise and birds and an occasional whale blowing. A day almost never went by now without spotting a sail, sometimes several. Quite a few vessels passed close enough to exchange signals with them and Julia knew that those who were homeward bound would report seeing the *Crystal Star* and give her last known position when they arrived in port. With each vessel they overtook and passed, Stephen's assurance in his ship and in himself increased, and he drove the men harder than ever.

It was on a day of light airs that they met the brig *Flying Fish* out of Boston, commanded by Captain Frederick James, who hailed from Dennis. After exchanging signals, the two ships approached each other and hove to, while Captain James had his boat lowered.

Julia stood by Stephen as they welcomed their guest aboard. She had known Captain James almost her entire life. On his short trips home, the robust, grey-haired captain often came to visit the shipyard and sharply appraise the vessels on the ways with eyes of a cool blue northern sky.

Now, as he climbed aboard and saw Julia, his face lit up with real pleasure. "Is that really you, Julia Howard?"

"Yes, except that I'm Julia Logan now," she said as she took his hand. "My, it's good to see a face from home."

"Not half so good as it is to me. It's been a long trip. Two weeks to round the Horn," he added as he looked at Stephen.

"That sounds like good time," Stephen said politely.

"Icebergs. Shouldn't have been there this time of year, but there they were, a large field of them on the other side of the Horn."

"Where?" Stephen was instantly alert.

"I'll show you on your chart, if you've got one."

"Yes, certainly. If you'll come below, perhaps you'd join me in a glass of brandy, sir."

"Sounds good," the captain said as he followed Julia down the companionway. "Hope it's half as good as the one young David Baxter had aboard the *Jewel of the Seas*."

Stephen froze with his hand on the handle of the saloon door. "Was this recently?"

"Aye. Strange coincidence, Julia, to see your father's ship just yesterday and you today. Or are you sailing in company? Your father own the *Crystal Star*, too?"

"No," Julia said and then looked at Stephen, whose face had first paled and then flamed. "But we did meet him a while back. Last we saw of him, he was well astern."

"Oh?" Captain James raised his eyebrows, then saw how it was. He'd sailed many a race himself. "Well, no doubt you'll catch her again soon. Who does own this ship?"

"Captain Asa Crofton is the main shareholder," Stephen told him. "I have a few shares in her, myself."

"Captain Asa?" The older man chuckled. "He still alive?"

"More so than ever," Julia told him.

"He's a sharp-tongued old cuss, but I have to admit I like him. It'll take a lot to kill that old coot. Do you know anything about my family? Baxter said he hadn't been home for so long, he didn't know anything."

"Last I heard, they were all well. There was gossip that your niece Annie was thinking about getting married. I don't know how much truth there is to that, though. And your daughter Jessica had a little boy about three months ago."

"I heard about the baby, but not about Annie. Little Annie. I can't believe it. Hope I get home in time for the wedding."

Stephen was impatient with the gossip. As long as Captain James was aboard, they were losing precious time, and all the while, Baxter was up there, opening his lead. He poured a glass of brandy and handed it to Captain James. "How are you fixed for provisions, Captain?" he asked.

"To tell the truth, not too good. We've got some scurvy aboard. You got any fresh vegetables you can spare?"

"Yes. I'll have my men put some onions and potatoes in your boat. Now," he indicated the chart, "can you show me where this ice field lies?"

While the two masters were going over the chart and discussing the conditions that lay behind each and, therefore, ahead of the other, Julia got out the letter she had been working on ever since the last lot of mail had been entrusted to a homeward-bound vessel. She added a few lines and sealed it. Her family would receive a steady, though ever less frequent, flow of letters from her on the outward-bound half of the voyage, but she knew that she would hear nothing from them for many months to come.

Not long after Frederick James's visit, they crossed over the Tropic of Capricorn into variable winds that blew from every point of the compass or none at all. Squalls could come upon them from any direction, and the men were kept busy trimming, reefing, and unfurling the sails. Stephen constantly worked the ship, taking advantage of every trick the ocean could throw at them.

When they were 35°S, far at sea off Rio de la Plata, they sighted lightning flickering in the west. Then a massive black cloud came rushing out from the land. With the first weak flash of lightning, Stephen said, "Pomperos! Shorten sail, Mister Wilson, and no blasted sogering!"

In the dead calm, Julia observed both watches, driven by the curses of the mates, working desperately. She had so often heard men speak in lowered voices of the pomperos, the dreaded storms too frequently encountered in this region. Now she was seeing one for the first time. As enormous bolts of lightning blazed through the darkness of the immense cloud, momentarily filling the sky with fire, she shuddered.

Suddenly, Stephen realized she was still on deck.

"Julia, get below! Now!"

There was no disputing the urgency in his voice. She picked up her skirts and ran down into the cabin, choosing the bed as the safest spot. There was no sound in the hull beside her, and she felt a breathless expectancy as the *Crystal Star* sat motionless on the dead sea, helpless before the storm that was swiftly bearing down upon them. Then it struck like a giant hand, and Julia was slammed against the bulkhead. The ship ran before it in a bombardment of rain and hail.

The gale continued for two miserable wet, cold days, but Stephen, on one of his trips below, was exhilarated. They had sighted and overtaken David Baxter once more. Slowly the winds eased, and by the time Julia was able to go on deck again, they had left the *Jewel of the Seas* far behind them. In calmer seas, they were able to dry out and put the ship in order before they hit the Roaring Forties.

It grew steadily colder as they went southward into a winter land. They saw the Falkland Islands as a blur of blue on the horizon, and soon they sighted Staten Island off their starboard bow. That night, although they were in the region of Cape Horn, the air was light and steady. After dinner, Julia, dressed in her warmest woolens, went on deck with Stephen to see the Southern Cross and the Magellan Clouds that now blazed almost directly overhead.

Even while they watched the luminous night sky, the stars in the southwest were blotted out. Stephen took a sharp breath and said, "Cape Horn! Mister Wilson, call all hands! Julia, go below and lay out my oilskins and southwester."

Through that long night of howling winds and broken seas,

Julia could not sleep. She didn't even bother to undress, but lay fully clothed with her cloak wrapped around her under all the blankets and quilts they owned. And still the cold penetrated into her very bones with a searing pain. The *Crystal Star* felt like a wooden chip hurled from wave to wave. There was the crash of seas breaking on the deck, but the only voices she could hear were the winds shrieking through the rigging like lost, demented souls escaped from hell.

And if she found it unbearable below, what of the men on deck? Those at the leeward halyards would be inundated in the icy waves that leaped aboard with such fury. They would be in constant danger of being swept overboard if the sea outmatched their strength. Yet were they any worse off than those aloft, who pummeled at frozen canvas with bare hands while riding that tall pendulum which could whip through a terrifying arc and swing them well over a hundred feet in less than a minute? A lost hand hold, a foot that slipped from the foot rope and they would be plunged forever into the coldest grave a man could find.

Each time she heard the roar of water on deck, she thought of Stephen and had visions of his being swept away, of being pierced by a piece of flying timber, of being hit by a wind-freed block. And her heart would stop.

There seemed no letup to the fury of the storm, and when the ship screamed in agony, she felt as though she were alone in a battered, crewless vessel. It wasn't until Stephen came below to warm himself with a glass of hot grog that she was reassured that there was any life aboard other than her own.

"How is it?" she asked him. She had to shout to make herself heard.

He shrugged. "It's Cape Horn. Sleet, hail, rain, and snow. High seas and a bad head wind." He leaned back in the chair and closed his eyes for a moment, his oilskins dripping water on the deck.

"I've heard it was bad, but I never expected this."

"This isn't bad," he shouted and grabbed at the bed boards to steady himself when the ship gave a sudden lurch. "Only normal. It can get far worse."

"Than this!" As she hung on to her bed, she wondered how it possibly could. She wondered, too, about the sanity of any man who, having once experienced it, would ever try to round the Horn again.

"Yes. We're hove to until we get the royal yards down and the sails reefed. Then I think we can beat a little to windward."

"You're going to fight it?"

"Well, I'm not going to turn tail and run. This is what we set out to do, and this is what we're doing."

"How's Wilson?"

"Doing better than I expected. He's white as a sheet, but aside from that, he's showing no signs of fear. He's pushing the men hard, and they're working well for him."

"Good. How's the ship holding up?"

"Fine. It's what you built her for, isn't it?" He drained the last of the hot liquid with one gulp.

"Maybe Papa did, but *I* certainly didn't."

"Damned right, he did. He knows the Horn." He sighed and rose from his chair. "Better get back on deck."

Through two sleepless nights and a day, the gale raged, but suddenly on the second morning, the wind died, and they were surrounded by a fog so dense the bow couldn't be seen from the quarterdeck. There was little rest on board, for the waves still ran high and tossed the powerless ship amongst them. The sails thundered and the booms and yards clattered until they were secured.

Then the wind returned.

On the fourth day, the sun shone bright and clear, and though they still fought heavy head winds and high seas, Stephen let Julia come on deck to get some fresh air for a few moments. There was brilliance not only from the sparkling sea, but from the thick ice that glittered on the stays and shrouds. She shut her eyes as she came out of the companionway onto the sanded deck to shield them from the sharp, dazzling, almost painful vision.

When she opened her eyes, she gasped at the sharpness of the cold air as she stared, fascinated. "The *Crystal Star!*"

"What?" Stephen looked at her as though the storm had left her witless.

"She looks like her name. A crystal star. How beautiful."

"It's not beautiful. It's damned dangerous," Stephen said, impatient with her wide-eyed innocence. "There's too much weight aloft. The crew have been busy chipping it off, but the fog and spray keep coating everything with ice."

127

"That doesn't make it any less beautiful."

"So's a mountain lion."

To ease her eyes, Julia turned and gazed over the taffrail. Far astern of them, there was another sparkling object. A ship.

She looked at Stephen. "Is that . . .?"

"Yes. He's following close. Been there for days."

"Do you think he'll catch up with us?"

"*No!*" Stephen walked across the rolling deck away from her and went to speak to the mate.

In a few minutes, he was back and put a steadying arm around her. "I'm taking you below. We're in for it again." He nodded at the blackening horizon.

Ten days after sighting Staten Island, they were clear of Cape Horn, and Stephen was in high good spirits. Not only had they come undamaged through the passage, but he had also won his hat and the ten dollar bet. Now he was confident that there would be another twenty for him when it came time to collect his winnings from David Baxter in Hong Kong. He hummed a tune beneath his breath as he set a course that would keep them well clear of the coast of Patagonia as well as of the icefields Captain James had charted for him.

The southerly winds of the Roaring Forties, now their ally, swept them northward towards the equator. Not long after they passed Robinson Crusoe's island of Juan Fernandez off the coast of Chile, they picked up the strong southeast trades that sent the Pacific rolling in great, powerful swells. The *Crystal Star* slowly recovered from the battering the Horn had given her as the crew worked from sunrise until the first dog watch. Spars were greased, rigging was overhauled and tarred, and chafed or torn sails were mended. The smells of paint and tar, which even the fair winds could not completely diffuse, were familiar, comforting smells to Julia. They reminded her of the shipyard.

Everything went well, their progress swift and steady, until they reached the equator. It was here, when they felt secure in the knowledge that the Sandwich Islands lay not too many days ahead of them, that they met the typhoon.

The barometer had been dropping all night, and at daybreak,

the sky, though clear, had a heavy grey look as did the very air around them. Lookouts were posted with a stern warning to watch for any sign of a storm from any direction.

It was too hot and muggy to stay below, the wind was dying, and the ship wallowed in the swell. Julia wandered the quarterdeck as she tried to stay out of the way of the officers and sailors. The men were swarming up and down the ratlines, out on the bowsprit, manning the capstan as they shortened sail in preparation of what they knew must come.

Then they saw it far over the sea. The wind. Almost immediately after it was sighted, they could hear it roaring as it bore down upon them. Julia had only just enough time to get to the cabin before it struck. The deck and overhead became the walls, and the walls were her deck and overhead. Everything tilted at a crazy angle.

She was thrown onto the dresser and into a momentary darkness before the ship shuddered and righted itself. Even rounding Cape Horn, Julia had not heard this madness of wind and sea, the shrieking protests of the *Crystal Star* as her canvas was torn and shredded, her wood wrenched loose from her fastenings, smashed and splintered. They were paying now in full for all those long, rolling, halcyon days of the South Pacific.

She lay on the deck and wondered. If they abandoned ship, would they remember her? Would they have time to come for her? Should she leave the cabin? Get close to the companionway, where she could hear if they called? Was there anyone left *to* call? How could any man stand against that chaos of wind and water? The decks must be swept clean. And Stephen? Dear God, what of Stephen? She had to get to him!

Then panic overwhelmed her. On her hands and knees, she clawed her way across the pitching deck, grabbing at anything solid. Just before she reached the door, a drawer shot out and struck her in the ribs, then seemed to take on a life of its own as it slid away from her only to strike her again on the knee. She went down with a gasp, but in terror, she dragged herself forward with her hands clutching the raised door sill and managed to pull herself over it into the saloon. She shrieked when her knee scraped over the sill, but her fear was so strong, she hardly noticed the pain or her reaction to it.

Once she was in the saloon, she couldn't find anything to grasp in the lurching darkness, and she was rolled back and forth until she slammed up against a chair that was lashed to the table. One of its legs jabbed at her ribs close to where the drawer had struck her, and she held tight to the chair as she fought the blackness that threatened to overcome her. Inch by inch, she fought her way to the door that led to the passageway. Holding onto the handle, she pulled herself up on her good knee and tried to open the door, but it refused to budge.

Then another gigantic blast of wind and waves knocked the ship almost flat. The door flew open and slammed her against the bulkhead. Water poured into the room.

Oh, my God! she thought. We're sinking. The ship's a coffin. I've built my own coffin. I've got to get out!

Fumbling desperately, she found the hook and managed to latch the door open. Then, with her fingers tightly curled around its edge, she pulled herself onward. With a violent, sudden motion, the ship righted herself, and Julia slid down the wooden panels of the door while the fittings ripped at her skin and clothing. She could hear more clearly now the roaring sea as it swept across the decks. Then came a sound like ten lightning bolts striking at once. Another wave-impacted lurch of the ship knocked her against the opposite bulkhead, and all was dark.

When Julia awakened, she was in bed and the sheets clung damply to her skin. She wondered why Amelia hadn't changed them. Each shallow breath she drew was an agony that lanced her side and every part of her body felt like a separate piece of pain. Opening her eyes, she saw water-reflected sunlight dazzling bright on the ivory walls of the cabin. She turned her head on the pillow and found it hurt unbearably, but before she closed her eyes, she could see the floor. It was strewn with debris. Clothing, books, broken glass, and furniture lay everywhere. Then she remembered where she was, remembered the storm, remembered the terror. And Stephen? What of Stephen? But she wasn't able to hold the thought long.

Later, through a long dark tunnel, she heard a voice calling her name. She groped towards it and tried to find the light. Finally, she was able to open her eyes. Stephen was leaning over her, stroking her hair away from her forehead. It was a Stephen she hardly knew. His usually clean-shaven face was covered with dark stubble. His grey eyes were weary and bloodshot. New lines were etched on his forehead and beside his mouth.

"Julie. Thank God!" he said softly when she opened her eyes.

"Stephen?" She knew it was him and yet the fact that he was alive, that he could have survived such unrelenting fury, was difficult to grasp.

"I'm here, my lady." He took her hand between both of his.

"What . . .?" A pain in her side caught her as she tried to speak.

"We're in bad shape, but we'll make it."

"How . . . bad?"

"I'll tell you later." He brushed her fingers with his lips and then laid her hand back on the bed before he rose. When he returned a minute later, he carried a bowl and a biscuit. "The cook made you some broth."

"This happened before," she said groggily.

"No, it didn't." He put the bowl on the built-in bureau and tenderly propped her up with pillows.

"My head!" It felt as though it would explode and she gasped for breath but that only brought more pain.

"I know. I don't want to hurt you, sweetheart, but you have to eat." He watched her with concern. "Rest a minute."

When she opened her eyes again, he was sitting on the bed beside her with the bowl in his hand. Immediately he lifted the biscuit out of the bowl and held it to her lips, and she found that she actually enjoyed the salty, beef-drenched flavor of the sea bread. How could she hurt so much and still be ravenous? Bit by bit, he fed her until the last of the biscuit and the broth were gone. Then he gave her a glass of water. It was tepid and stale tasting, but it slaked the thirst the salt had produced.

As he took the glass from her, she asked again, "How bad?"

He put the glass on the bureau, then turned to search her drained white face. It was difficult to judge whether she had the strength for the truth. Then he could see the fear growing in her eyes, and he nodded.

"All right." He sat wearily down on the bed beside her and took her hand. As he spoke, he looked out the porthole above the bed at the long rolling waves that were now peacefully blue. "The foremast went first. Whether it was flawed as you thought or whether it would have gone anyway, I don't know. It took part of the bowsprit and most of the other masts and rigging with it."

131

"Did you salvage anything? Enough for a jury rig?"

"A little. Enough to get some sail on a couple of short spars."

"And?"

"Julie, it can wait until you're stronger."

"No. I have to know!" It was difficult to concentrate on his words through the pressure in her head, but she would only be able to rest once she knew how hopeful or how helpless their situation was. "If you won't tell me, I'll be imagining all kinds of things."

His mouth twisted in a bitter smile and he looked down at her. "All right, Julie. The rudder was smashed, but we've managed a poor substitute. Most of the rails have been carried away. All of the livestock lost. We have only one undamaged longboat left and one that's broken but might float. Most of the spare spars and yards are gone. We've been blown far off course. Our only hope is to run before the wind and pray that we'll find a friendly island. There are hundreds of them to the south of us, but not all of them are friendly. If the weather favors us, we should make it."

"And if it doesn't," she whispered.

He closed his eyes and shook his head. Then he opened them again, and she could see the anguish written there. "It's the end. We'd be helpless in the face of another typhoon."

Julia thought about it for a moment, thought about the reports she had heard all her life. Missing at sea. An unexplained disappearance. So this was what happened to those vessels. This was what their families, their wives and sweethearts never knew down through the long, aching years. No. It mustn't happen to them.

"What about the men?" she asked.

Stephen couldn't look at her. He got up and went to stare sightlessly out of the stern window. His voice was flat and toneless. "We lost three, including the second mate."

"Frank Randall." She thought about that shy, sandy-haired man, who was younger than she and now would be forever young. "Who else?"

"Jim Greene and Andrew Hope."

"Oh." Both farmboys, this was their first voyage . . . and their last. "What about the royal boys?"

"One with a twisted ankle and the other with a broken leg," he said dully. "They'll be all right. Tim's already hobbling around, and Jake should be able to handle some light work in another day or two. At any rate, there's no need to send them up to tend the royals . . . not for some time to come."

"And the others? Was anyone else hurt?"

"Oh, yes." His shoulders shook and she wondered if he was crying. Stephen? No. He didn't know how to cry. But when he spoke again, his voice was so choked, she thought he must be. "Almost everyone was injured to one extent or another. Five of them seriously, including Tim and the first mate."

"Wilson!" She jerked up, and it felt as though she'd banged her head against the overhead. She had to lie down again. This was serious. Without a first or a second mate, they were really in trouble. Stephen could not run the ship without officers. "How seriously is Wilson hurt?"

"A broken arm, but he's able to stand watch."

"Thank God for that. The ship so smashed, men killed. Was any of it his fault?"

"No. Not this time. The way he fought to save men . . . . He may even make a master someday." He returned to sit beside her, and she could see that he was running the thin line of exhaustion. "It's the sea's fault. The wretched, bloody, filthy, perishing sea."

"We're so short-handed! I wish I could help."

Stephen laughed bitterly. "What could *you* do?" Then he compressed his lips. "I'm sorry, Julie. It's just that I'm so tired. My God, you don't know how worried I've been over you. I could lose the ship, lose all my men, but not you. Never you."

She tried to smile despite the awful pain that almost blinded her. "Well, you're not about to lose me. I'll be all right."

"All right? When I examined you, I couldn't tell where one bruise began and another left off." He lightly stroked her cheek. "I've bound your ribs. I think a couple of them are broken. And your right knee's swollen. But it's your head I'm really worried about. Somehow you hit it . . . badly. Before we left home, your father told me about the hurricane, the tree, the whole thing."

"He didn't!" She closed her eyes. Perhaps that would help. "What did he tell you? That I was crazy?"

She could feel his warm hand cover hers. "It was for your own good, Julie," he said quietly.

"The two of you discussing me . . . behind my back."

"He was worried that it might happen again. He wanted me to know only so that I could take care of you."

"Men!" She opened her eyes to see if he were looking at her

with the pity she had once known too well and loathed, but there was only love mixed with worry on his face.

"Men who love you and want to protect you. Is that so bad?"

"I don't need any . . ."

"You don't?" One eyebrow shot up and he smiled at her. "Next time, I'm going to lash you to the bed just as I lashed myself to what was left of the mizzen mast. I'll never know how you managed to get into so much trouble. You should have been safe and snug below."

"I was afraid," she admitted in a whisper.

"I know. We all were. Rest now." He gave her hand a final squeeze and rose from the bed. "Get back your strength. We may need you yet."

"Stephen?"

"Yes?" He turned when he was halfway to the door and looked back at her.

"Are you all right?"

"Just bloody tired."

"Part of my fear, Stephen, it was for you. I was terrified that you'd gone . . ."

"Well, you're not going to lose me that easily, either," he said with what was only an imitation of his normal, lighthearted grin.

"Can't you get some rest?"

"I will soon. Go to sleep."

By the time they sighted the first islands, Julia, despite a continuing headache and a pain that occasionally caught her in the ribs when she reached for something, was on deck to see them. First, their sheltering clouds, looking like islands themselves, would appear on the horizon. Then a few sea birds would fly out and circle the ship. Occasionally they lit on the makeshift rigging. Some of the islands were barren coral atolls with only a few lonely, tattered palms springing from their sandy surface. Others, rising green and purple from shores of black or pale yellow beaches, were lushly volcanic, but their lagoons were reef locked and barred the entry of a large ship.

Tomaii, invaluable in his knowledge of this exotic world, piloted them past island after island, but he always refused to put in. One, he would say, had no safe harbor. Another was populated by cannibals.

134

The sight of land so near and yet forbidden was unbearable. The crew looked longingly at coconut palms and banana trees as they slid by. Kenneth Wilson, who had grown thinner on their short rations and who still carried his arm in a sling, suggested that they anchor offshore and send in a party for fresh food and wood, but Stephen only shook his head. Another storm would wipe them out, and here in this coral world, it would be triply dangerous.

He was determined to push on to Tahiti as Tomaii had advised. There he knew he would find missionaries with medicines for the sick and injured. Supplies should be more plentiful and the task of repairing a ship, easier. He pored over his incomplete charts and tried to remember all he had heard and read about the islands. Phrases by Bougainville, Cook, and Forster flickered through his mind, and he tried to profit by their experience.

By the time they finally sighted the clouds that signaled the twin islands of Tahiti and Mooréa, scurvy had made inroads into the crew, and only a few men were able bodied enough to carry on with their duties.

Finally the islands themselves hove into view, first as blue shadows beneath their white clouds; then as tall mountains, their peaks buried in fleece. Sun and shadow chased across the varicolored green of rippling hills and black ravines. White cascading waterfalls flashed in the sunlight.

Julia, her headache forgotten, stood on the quarterdeck and stared at the incredible beauty that each moment became ever more visible. Because of their reduced crew, Stephen worked the ship with his men while Tomaii both steered and navigated.

The tall Polynesian glanced at Julia and smiled at her obvious wonder.

"You like?"

"It's beautiful, Tomaii," she breathed.

"Over there." He nodded proudly to starboard. "Mooréa. My home."

"I've heard tales about these islands from men who've been here, but no one could ever truly describe them. Words won't do it."

"Words!" He shrugged. "It is."

"Yes," she said as she watched a passing cloud turn a ravine from dark purple to jade green. "It certainly is."

"Soon you come my home."

"You said that once before at the beginning of the voyage."

"Yes." Then he shouted his intentions to Stephen and rapidly spun the wheel to larboard.

Julia looked speculatively at Tomaii. Always tall and proud, he had acquired a new regality with his approach to home. "We hadn't planned on putting in here," she said thoughtfully, "and yet you told me I was coming. Did you know this would happen, Tomaii?"

Glancing at the broken rails, the shattered masts, he shook his head. "Not this!" Then he turned his attention to the water and swung the ship to larboard.

She wanted to question him further, but his face was closed to her as he concentrated on their passage through the strait. Still, as she watched a whale spouting in the distance, she could not help wondering about him. The South Seas were his seas. There was a strange coincidence that he, who so yearned for home, was now here. Accidently? She pushed the question away. It *was* coincidence. It had to be. Besides, she wanted to concentrate all of her thoughts on this lush new world.

As they entered a pass in the reef, a flock of outrigger canoes, filled with laughing natives and piled high with coconuts, flowers, breadfruit, and bananas, raced out from shore and surrounded the derelict ship. Stephen, seeing their approach, left the crew and came aft.

"Tell them to stay clear until we've anchored, Tomaii," he ordered.

They passed by a frigate whose stern gallery rested on the uplifted hands of two enormous caryatides. *"La Reine Blanche,"* Julia read her name aloud. "She looks like a naval vessel."

"She is," Stephen said. "A *French* warship and one of the most murderous in design. I wonder what the devil she's doing here. Last I heard, the British had control of these islands."

"Do you think it means trouble?"

"I don't know what it means, but we have no choice. We have to put in. We'll anchor over near those whalers. Three of them are flying the American ensign and one the British. They may not smell very pleasant, but it'll be more appetizing than gunpowder."

As soon as the anchor was down, the canoes closed in on the *Crystal Star.*

"Tell them one boat at a time!" Stephen shouted at Tomaii, but it was too late. Already the natives were swarming up the sides of the ship with bunches of bananas and ropes of coconuts, baskets woven from palm leaves and strings of fish.

"Mister Wilson! Keep an eye on them. Station the men around the ship. No one's to go below!"

"They are friends!" Tomaii was insulted. "Bring gifts. Not steal!"

"They'll take every damn scrap of metal they can lay their hands on, and you know it, Tomaii. Tell them that we have iron goods and later we'll trade, but not if so much as one nail disappears before we open shop."

The steward nodded in agreement and went forward to meet his countrymen. The light-skinned natives were pressing around the sailors, offering them the bounty of their land. There was no bargaining. They handed the food to the crew simply as a gift. They were like genial hosts who laughingly welcomed some long-awaited guests. When Tomaii joined them, they joyfully hugged and patted him while they bombarded him with questions and jokes.

Julia, watching them, marveled at their fluid grace and hand-some features. She was surprised to see an occasional pair of blue eyes. Each man wore a bright flower tucked behind one ear, and they threw necklaces of delicately woven garlands over the shoulders of the crew. The heavy fragrance soon permeated the ship.

Tomaii, who had taken off his shirt and decked himself out with flower leis, made his way aft. Two natives followed him. Taking off one of his gardenia necklaces, he dropped it over Julia's head, then another over Stephen's.

"A chief." He gestured to the tall, handsomely heavy man who had accompanied him.

"Good." Stephen bowed slightly. "I'm honored to meet you. Is the queen well?"

Julia started to listen to their conversation, but she was distracted by a flicker of movement in the water to starboard. There was gay feminine laughter, and flower-crowned heads with dark hair streaming out behind them appeared. Graceful bare arms cut the surface of the water. Lines were lowered over the sides, and the girls, their lovely, lithe, naked bodies glistening in the sun, climbed gracefully up them. Each girl carried a square of cloth in her hand, and as soon as she stepped over the broken rail, she whipped it open and draped it around herself, making a dress out of a simple piece of fabric. They blossomed like the flowers they wore.

"Why didn't they come out in the canoes?" Julia asked Tomaii.

He shook his head. "Tabu. Men only. Women swim."

"That's not fair."

He shrugged. "Tabu," he repeated.

"Well, I don't intend to swim ashore without a stitch of clothing on," she said, but she envied the native girls their freedom and lack of self-consciousness.

As she watched the crew enthusiastically welcoming the girls, there was another hail from the water, but this time the accent was unmistakably Yankee.

"Put down the ladder, Mister Wilson," Stephen ordered. Then he muttered to Julia, "We've got to get these natives off the ship."

"Oh, let them stay. Look at all the food they've brought us, and I must say it's nice to see smiling faces again."

"We're not here to entertain the natives. We're here to repair the ship. The sooner, the better." He moved to the starboard side to greet the man who swung up onto deck.

"Looks like ye've run into a bit of trouble," the lanky redhead said. "Captain Peter Snow of the whaler *Black Swallow*, New Bedford."

"Captain Stephen Logan," he said as they shook hands. "My wife, Mrs. Logan. Ran into a bit of a gale."

"Looks more like a hurrycane." Peter Snow glanced around the deck. "Pleased to meet ye, ma'am. First white woman outside of those damned missionaries I've seen in many a day."

"How do you do, Captain Snow." Julia wasn't sure she liked the way he looked her up and down, but then, as he had said, he hadn't seen a white woman for quite a while.

"Ye've more than your share of company," Peter Snow said and nodded at the natives. "Want me to clear the decks for ye?"

"I can handle my own ship, Captain Snow," Stephen said in a voice that would warn off any man.

"No offense, no offense." The whaling captain smiled easily above his beard which, like his hair, was roughly cut and

138

uncombed. "It's just that I've picked up a bit of their lingo. Nice people. I like 'em, but ye've got to be strict with 'em. Else they'll be settin' up housekeeping on your decks."

"I'm always willing to learn, Captain." Stephen relaxed and gestured toward the foredeck. "If you would be so kind?"

Ambling forward, Peter Snow flapped his hands as though he were shooing a flock of chickens before him. He shouted good-naturedly as he went. Although the sounds he made bore a certain resemblance to the native speech, it was harsh and sharp-cornered when he spoke it. Julia wondered how they understood him.

Understand him they did, though, for they were cheerfully slipping over the sides, the men into the outriggers, the girls into the water. Whatever the captain was saying, it certainly didn't seem to offend them. Yet Julia felt badly at the ship's lack of hospitality, especially when she saw the mounds of food they had left behind them.

"They'll be back," Captain Snow said as he rejoined them. "Ye'll never be rid of 'em completely, but if ye'll heed my advice, don't let more than a few on at a time. Watch your crew, too. They'll smuggle girls on if they can get away with it. Once they get shore leave, men sometimes get notions. Tend to disappear. Lot of desertions here."

"So I've heard." Stephen watched the mate, who was trying to restore discipline amongst the men. It was an almost impossible task with men so weary of the sea as these were. "Seems wiser to let the natives come on board than to allow the men on land, but I'm afraid we'll have to put ashore in order to make repairs. How's the local situation? I see the French are here in force." He nodded at the frigate.

"Aye. They're taking over. Been quite a flap about it. Admiral Du Petit-Thouars sailed in here the end of last month. Said the French was taking possession if the Tahitians didn't come up with ten thousand Spanish dollars within twenty-four hours." Peter Snow shrugged. "Queen Pomare, now, and a lot of the people are agin it, but what can they do? The queen's been writing to England for years, tryin' to get protection. All she ever got was promises."

"Is it safe ashore?" Stephen glanced at Julia.

"Safe as ever. Seems it's all settled. Jacques Moerenhout's been

139

appointed *Commisioner Royal,* and Pomare acts like she's not goin' to stir up any trouble, least not for a while. Long as you don't take sides, they'll give you no problems."

"How about a drop of rum?" Stephen asked him.

"Sounds good."

Stephen looked around the ship for Tomaii to serve the liquor. Although most of the men still wore their leis, they were back at work, but there was no sign of the steward.

"Did you see where Tomaii went?" he asked Julia.

She shook her head. "Maybe he's below. Now that he's no longer needed to work the ship, he most likely thought he should go back to being steward."

"Maybe," Stephen said, suddenly grim, as he led the way aft with Julia and Captain Snow following him.

As they walked through the passageway below, he threw open every door, but there was no sign of Tomaii. After searching through the cabins adjoining the saloon, he returned to find that Julia had brought out the polished case that held the decanters. Peter Snow had made himself comfortable on the settee and was watching Julia.

"This Tomaii. Native to these parts?" the whaling captain was asking.

"Yes," Julia answered as she put the case on the table and turned to fetch the glasses. "His home is on Mooréa."

"Then over the side I'd say." Peter Snow fingered the newly red scar that ran from his eye to his jaw. "Ye got him here, and that's the last ye'll see of him."

"Oh, no," Julia protested. "I'm certain he'll be back. He even invited me to visit his family. I can't think he'd break his word."

"One smell of frangipani and they revert. Turn back into savages. Not that they're ever much *but* savages."

"That's not true!" Julia snapped as she thought of the many kindnesses of the steward. "You think of them as savages because that's the way you treat them. Throwing them off the ship when they brought us food and flowers! Do you call that civilized? You'd never be so inhospitable to guests back home."

"Julia, you're the one who's being inhospitable now!" Stephen said sharply. "Captain Snow is our guest, an *invited* guest, and you're attacking him. Sir, I apologize for my wife's behavior." He turned to the red-haired Yankee and poured rum into the glasses

140

Julia had put on the table while he pointedly ignored her.

"No need, no need." The captain's smile revealed that several teeth were missing. "Mrs. Logan's most likely right."

"How do things stand ashore?" Stephen changed the subject. "Any men capable of helping us with repairs? Any ship chandlers around?"

"Ye're in luck there. Tahiti's opening up. More traders every year. Some white men . . . likely deserters, but who knows . . . have set up doing repair work, trained a few natives if ye can get them to work. Got carpenters, joiners, even a few blacksmiths. Be as big as Oahu soon." He emptied his glass in one long swallow. As soon as he put it on the table, Stephen refilled it.

"I'm glad to hear that," Stephen said as he put the stopper back into the decanter. "What about crew? I lost three men in the gale, one died later, and I'm not too certain whether a couple of others will pull through or not."

"Well, there ye'll not do as well . . . unless you can come up with some deserter who's got tired of sittin' on his backside. Maybe ye can talk some of the natives into it. I don't know. Where ye bound?"

"The Sandwich Isles first. Then China."

"Well, if 'twas me, I'd take aboard some natives as far as Oahu. Pay 'em off there and get meself some white men."

Stephen nodded. "Sounds like good advice." Then he added more grimly, "I may need a new steward, too, now that damned Kanaka's gone."

Chapter Seven

1842

Tomaii reappeared on the third day. Julia had been sitting with Megan Fairfield on the Fairfields' wide verandah in the shade cast by a palm-leaf roof that rustled pleasantly in the breeze. Some small sound caught her attention and she looked up to see Tomaii strolling around the corner of the house.

"Tomaii!" she said in amazement. "Where have you been?"

"Go see family," he said simply and waved his hand towards the strait that separated the two islands. His English seemed to have lapsed upon his contact with his homeland.

"Captain Logan's very upset. He thinks you've deserted."

"No." Tomaii crossed his arms and stood proudly beside the steps. "Go get help. Get men to work on ship."

"Won't you ask the gentleman to come up and sit down?" Megan Fairfield interrupted.

"I'm sorry. Megan, this is Tomaii, our steward and my friend. Tomaii, this is Mrs. Fairfield. We're staying with her and the Reverend Fairfield while we're here."

The tall Polynesian nodded, then came up onto the verandah and squatted on his heels near Julia. He was wearing only a long skirt that was painted in shades of brown and black upon a background of white. Around his neck, there was a garland of flowers, and behind his right ear, he had tucked a pink hibiscus. There was something so exotic about his appearance, it was difficult to relate him to the steward who had served them for so many months and had brought them safely to Tahiti.

"How did you know where to find us?" Julia finally asked.

"Everyone know," he said simply.

"Were you able to get some men to help us?"

He nodded.

"Well, you'd best let me talk to Captain Logan before he sees you. He'd probably clap you in irons or something for deserting."

Tomaii nodded again. "I know. I watch until he leave house. Then I come."

"How many men can you get?" Julia knew that, despite Captain Snow's reassurance, Stephen was having a difficult time in finding labor.

"Maybe ten, twelve. Maybe more."

"Well, that would certainly help." Julia frowned as she thought for a moment. "Can you come back tomorrow at this same time, Tomaii?"

He rose and nodded. "I come," he said solemnly as he looked down at her. Then he was gone into a grove of palmettos and banana trees.

"I don't know how Stephen's going to take this," Julia said after Tomaii had disappeared.

"He'd better be thankful to have some men. It's rather difficult to find workers around here." Megan Fairfield took another stitch in the shirt she was making for her husband.

"He should, but you never know with Stephen," Julia said doubtfully. Looking out over the lagoon that swam with blues and greens and whites in the morning sunlight, she could see the splash of tan bodies and two outriggers setting out for the reef. She wondered if she would ever understand her husband.

"I like your Tomaii," Megan interrupted her thoughts.

"Yes. You know, on the voyage, he was just about my only friend. Least he was the only one I could really talk to. Stephen didn't approve of my conversing with the officers . . . or anyone else."

Megan looked down at the sewing in her lap and the fair brows above her black eyes met in a frown. "I don't know whether it's worse to have a jealous husband or an indifferent one."

143

"Surely George isn't indifferent!" Julia said in amazement. How could any man be indifferent to lovely Megan with her neatly coiled silver hair, her slender body, and her quiet ways?

"Perhaps that was a poor choice of words. Preoccupied? I don't know, Julie." Her lip trembled a little as she looked out over the lagoon. "I get so lonely sometimes. I can't talk to the other women here, the missionary wives. I feel much closer to the Tahitians, but they wouldn't understand, either. You're the first person I've met since I've been here that I've felt any . . . any kinship with."

"I know. It's strange," Julia said thoughtfully. "To become such good friends in just three days. I never really had any at home. My sister Amelia, maybe, but she's four years younger. Very different from me. And my sister Sarah is closer to me in age, but she's more different still. I could never call Sarah a friend."

"I had four sisters." Megan smiled, but it was a rather sad smile. "We had a lovely time together."

"Where are you from, Megan?" Julia looked curiously at this dainty young woman who seemed so out of place in a mission.

"Maryland. Not far from Annapolis. We had a beautiful place out in the country." Megan's black eyes were glowing now as she spoke. "Lots of parties. Guests would come and stay for weeks."

"You miss it, don't you?"

"Very much."

"But it's so beautiful here!" Julia got up and went to the railing in order to have a better view of the lagoon. "I don't think I could ever get tired of the trees and the flowers, the mountains and the streams. I love the way the clouds veil the mountains, the warmth, the showers. I love the people, their grace, their laughter. I even love their funny leaf hats. It's paradise!"

"It was before *we* came," Megan said, and there was a bitterness in her voice that Julia could not believe Megan possessed. "The white man, the serpent, tempting the Polynesians to eat of the fruit of knowledge. 'For God doth know that in the day ye eat thereof, then your eyes shall be opened; and ye shall be as gods, knowing good and evil.' "

"Why, Megan!" Julia turned and leaned against the rail to stare at her friend. Megan's face was stony and her eyes were looking far beyond the trees at which she stared.

"They didn't know there *was* evil, not our kind," Megan continued. "They were happy and healthy. They lived long lives together, loving each other, and then they died. That didn't bother them very much because they knew they'd go to heaven, and heaven could only be another Tahiti where they could fish and swim and make love. What was evil about that?"

"Why nothing, I suppose," Julia said. She really didn't know what to make of this sudden outburst from a woman who had been so quiet and self-contained.

"We brought them diseases and knowledge, Julie, and those diseases are killing them off, and that knowledge is destroying them."

"But they worshipped idols! Surely you and George are doing good by bringing them the word of God," Julia protested.

"Maybe their idols were aspects of God."

"And they had horrible wars."

Megan laughed and the bitterness that had been in her voice became a part of the laugh. "Not nearly so horrible as ours. One man or two might be killed. Then the war was over."

"Megan." Julia came back to sit beside her friend and lightly touched her hand. "Does George know how you feel?"

"No!" Megan looked alarmed. "I wouldn't dare let him even guess. Oh, Julie," she said and clutched Julia's hand, "I should never have been a missionary's wife. The God I know and the God George serves seem to be two different people. I just can't believe in his."

Julia could see how deep Megan's distress went. "How do you stand it?"

"Sometimes I don't think I can." She released Julia's hand and picked up the shirt, but she didn't sew. "I try to help them when they're sick with a white man's disease, though that's pretty hopeless. They usually die. But I can't preach to them about a vengeful God. When they ask me, I tell them He loves them. They're His children. I know when they go up in the hills to dance the old dances. George would be furious if he knew that they actually tell me and that I don't tell him. They tell me lots of things." While she had been speaking, her voice had grown softer and a dreamy look had come across her face. Now she glanced sharply at Julia. "I *can* trust you, can't I, Julie?"

"Yes, of course you can." Julia smiled. "If you want to know the truth, I can't believe in a vengeful God, either."

"I knew you'd understand. Would you like to go up in the hills with me today? It's not far. I'm going to visit an old lady. George thoroughly approves of my charity visits."

"I'd love to," Julia said and then she looked suspiciously at her friend. "What's really up there, Megan?"

"You'll see." Megan smiled secretly, then put away her sewing and rose from her chair. "It will soon be time for dinner. Is Stephen going to join us?"

"Yes. He said he'd be back about noon."

After the meal had been cleared away and the two men had left on their separate duties, Megan gathered a few items of clothing and some food into two baskets, a black Bible riding ostentatiously on top of one of them. She called to the two young maids to join them.

They set out through tunnels of green over a winding, well-worn path. The dampness in the air brought out the fragrance of a thousand flowers, and once they were well out of sight of the shore, Megan plucked two hibiscus and handed the red one to Julia. "Wear it behind your left ear. That means you're married." She tucked the pink one into her own fair hair.

They left the path and wandered through a tangle of foliage. Julia felt completely lost, but Megan and the two girls seemed to know exactly where they were going. They circled a boulder, and when they came out on top, Julia caught her breath. Here, one of the many mountain streams formed a pool of blue crystal in the volcanic rock. The maids put their baskets down, and Megan took off her bonnet and began taking pins out of her hair, letting it flow like cascading silver over her shoulders.

"What are you doing?" Julia asked in astonishment. Megan, always so proper, was beginning to look a little wanton.

"Coming from Cape Cod, you can surely swim, can't you, Julia?"

"Yes. Of course."

"This is my own private pool, at least for the moment." She was unbuttoning her dress.

"Aren't you afraid someone will see you?"

"These people aren't peeping toms. They see nothing sinful or strange about the body God gave you. And no white man knows his way here."

Both of the maids had stripped off their clothing and now they dove together into the deep water.

"Come on, Julie." Megan's black eyes sparkled. "Don't be a

prude." She stepped out of her pantalettes and stood un-ashamedly small and slender like an ivory figurine.

"Oh, I'm not," Julia said as she took down her hair, "but if Stephen finds out, he'll kill me."

Megan laughed and dived into the pool, her white body arching and her silver hair flashing in the sun before she neatly entered the water. Julia hastily threw off her clothes and dived into the pool to join them. The depths were deliciously cool after the hot day.

Megan was watching her as she surfaced through the sun-warmed upper layer of water. "Don't worry about Stephen. If George finds out, he'll *surely* kill me." She swam toward Julia, her wet hair streaming out behind her like a water nymph. "So we'll go together."

Julia turned to float on her back and let the sun warm and caress her body. The two Tahitian girls and Megan, laughing and chattering, were playing a game of water tag, the palm trees clattered overhead, and a waterfall roared far up the mountain. An occasional bird ventured near to investigate and discuss the matter. Peace, Julia thought. There really is peace. She didn't want to go back to the house, to the ship, to all the problems that life involved. She wanted to float here forever until she became a part of the water itself.

Megan splashed her with a wet hand. "You're it." Darting like a fish, she swam away. Julia laughed and, plunging under the water, followed her.

Later as they sat upon the rock and let the sun dry their naked bodies, Julia asked, "Do you come here often?"

"Every chance I get. I've lived on this island for three years, but it wasn't until two years ago Faia showed me this pool. We've been coming here ever since."

"And George never suspects?" Julia watched the native girls weaving garlands out of flowers they had picked.

"Not yet, anyway. I'd know about it if he did. He's so occupied with other things, he really doesn't pay much attention to what I do. Besides, before the afternoon's over, we'll visit a few people who will be delighted to tell George how good I was to come and see them. My time's accounted for."

"But what if something happens and he needs you? What if he goes looking for you and can't find you?"

"At the first house, they'll tell him I was there. They'll keep him on some pretext or other and send a messenger to me. They all know where I am."

"Megan!" Julia laughed. "You're a terrible missionary. Swimming naked, encouraging the people to lie. The next thing you know, you'll be taking part in their heathen dances."

"I would if they'd ask me." Her smile sparkled with mischief as she rubbed her hair dry with a piece of calico. "Wouldn't you?"

"I don't know. I don't know enough about Tahiti, and Stephen keeps closer track of me than George does of you." She sighed. "This has been such a perfect day, but I won't dare come with you again. If Stephen finds out, he might let it slip when he was talking to George. 'Twould only spoil your pleasure, too."

"Why, Julie!" Megan said with mock severity. "How could your husband ever suspect such a thing when you've gone to call on the sick with a proper missionary's wife?"

"I don't know." Julia picked her dress up from the black boulder. "Sometimes I think he reads my mind."

"Your face more likely. You show too much what you feel. Even I sometimes know what you're thinking, and I haven't known you as long as Stephen has."

"Maybe I do, but I'm not very good at concealing my feelings."

"Well, I'll tell you a secret," Megan said as she coiled her hair into a bun, which she secured to the back of her head. "In order to make other people believe in you when you're playing a role, you have to almost believe in it yourself."

"And that's what you do?"

"Sometimes." Megan picked a few flowers out of Faia's lap and began to weave them together. "I can't let George crush me. A lot of missionary wives die young, way too young, and I don't intend to be one of them. I try to hide the way I feel, but I can't always go around with a pious face. I don't find the strength in God that George does. I wasn't brought up that way. I want to laugh and be young. When I see the people singing and dancing, I want to sing and dance, too. Sometimes I think George was born old."

"How did you ever happen to marry him?" Julia picked up one of the small white gardenias that the Polynesians called tiare and inhaled its heady fragrance.

"Oh, Julie, I don't know. He was so tall and handsome and shining with that lofty brow of his and that golden hair, and he

148

was so dedicated. He looked so strong and noble when he spoke in church."

"You met him in church?"

"Where else?" Megan smiled. "No, that's not really true. The first time I ever saw him, he was preaching at St. Anne's, telling about the poor heathens and their great need. I met him a few days later when Papa asked him to dinner. He was so charming and eloquent, so different from my other beaux. I fell madly in love with him. Now I don't know whether I really fell in love with him or with the romantic idea of going to live with him in some fascinating heathen land where I could do so much good. I think I rather fancied I'd turn into some sort of ministering angel." She gaily placed the crown of flowers she had woven on top of Julia's braids. "But I didn't and here I am."

"Yet whenever he's near, you seem so devoted to him." Julia smiled back at her friend and then leaned over to see her flower-crowned face in the water.

"That's part of the role I play. No. That's not really true." Megan pulled on her coarse black stockings as she thought about it. "I guess I really do still love him . . . in a way. Perhaps I'm trying to catch his attention. Make him really see me. If only once he'd pay me a compliment. But George doesn't believe in vanity. He thinks I'm vain enough already."

Julia lay back on the black boulder and looked up through the tall palms at the blue sky with its soft fleeting clouds. "Well, you have a right to be vain. You're beautiful, Megan."

Megan glanced sharply at Julia, then away. "Do you really think so?" she asked wistfully.

"Of course I do," Julia said emphatically. "It's not a matter of thinking. You just are."

"You know, at home, people were always telling me how pretty I was. I became so used to it, I didn't really hear them." She gave a wry smile and shook her head sadly. "Now I'm fishing for compliments."

Julia rolled over on her stomach and propped her chin in her hands so that she could better look at her friend. As Megan sat toying with the flowers, she looked like a lost child. "Have you ever thought of going home?" she asked.

"Ten times a day, but I won't." Megan threw a flower into the pool. "If I did, I'd never come back. And then I'd never be able to hold up my head again. Everyone would find out I'd run away. My family, my friends, they tried to stop me from marrying him. They'd never let me forget that they'd warned me. So here I'll live and here I'll die."

"Megan." Julia reached out and touched her small hand.

"It's all right, Julie." Megan flashed her a smile. "I can bear it here in Tahiti. The people are so wonderful. Every time I start feeling sorry for myself, I just remember that George could have been sent to the African jungle or something horrible like that. Your being here helps."

"I wish we could stay a long time."

"Well, you're here now, and it's going to be a while before your ship's ready to sail, so let's make the best of it. Are you ready? We'd better go visit Mama Omemema."

When Megan and Julia and the two basket-laden girls entered the clearing, they found a small and bent, white-haired old lady sitting in the shade of a breadfruit tree beside an open-walled house. As soon as she saw them, she waved her hands, and the children, who had surrounded her, scattered.

"Ianora!" she called to them.

"Ianora, Mama Omemema," Megan said and went on to speak the lilting musical speech of Tahiti as though it were her own language. Julia listened in amazement. At home, Megan spoke English with only a few Tahitian words thrown in.

The old lady nodded and answered her at great length. When she had finished, Megan turned to Julia and said, "I've told Mama all about you, and she says she is very pleased that you have come to visit her. She says she expected you. Shake hands with her, and then we'll go and sit in her house for a little while."

"I'm *very* pleased to meet you, Mrs. Omemema," Julia said as she took the dry, brittle fingers in hers.

Omemema answered her with a one-toothed grin and a warm deluge of words.

Once they were in the small house, Megan and the old lady began a long, earnest conversation. Since she couldn't understand the language, Julia took the opportunity to look at her surroundings. All but one of the walls of woven matting were rolled up, and

150

there were mats on the wooden floor. A few carved bowls sat in one corner, but otherwise the floor was bare. Bundles of cloth and woven baskets hung from the rafters, and Julia guessed that they must contain the family's possessions. Like the Tahitians themselves, the house was scrupulously clean, yet warm and graceful. The pillars that supported the roof were carved. Julia wondered if they portrayed the overthrown gods or perhaps members of the family. While she was speculating about them, a young girl of about twelve entered and shyly offered them coconut milk in wooden cups and a bowl of chopped coconut meat.

After Megan had taken a sip of the milk, she turned to Julia. "I don't know how you feel about it, but Mama Omemema is somewhat famous as a seer. She's told me some things about you. Do you want to hear them?"

"Only if they're good."

"They are . . . so far."

"Then I'd like to hear them." Julia picked a piece of the coconut from the bowl and popped it into her mouth.

"She says you are the favorite daughter of a powerful chief and that you also come from a land that has risen from the sea as has this island. When you were born, it was spoken that you would come to Tahiti and that you would return someday. When you do, it will be of great importance to me."

"Good. I'd hate to leave here and think I was never coming back."

The old woman interrupted and said something. Her words were accompanied by intricately graceful gestures.

Megan listened, then nodded and turned once more to Julia. "She says that we're both favored children of the water gods, and so we shall always be friends. I am the child of the rivers and streams," she translated as Omemema continued, "running steadily through light and shadow on the surface but strong and dark in the depths. You are the child of deeper, open waters, happy beneath the shining sun and a fair breeze, but driven by the winds, tormented by storms until you become something very different."

"Well, that doesn't sound very good," Julia said. "Maybe she'd better not go on."

Megan listened to the old woman's continuing speech. "It's really not bad, Julia. She says that as the rivers run to the sea and mingle in friendship, so do we meet, accepting each other as part of one another. As clouds rise together from the sea to fall upon the mountain streams, so will our thoughts and lives touch and meet, separate, and meet again time after time."

Julia studied the old woman's wrinkled face. Her brown eyes were young and yet eternally ageless in their knowledge. She hesitated, then asked, "What about the future? Does she know what will happen to me?"

Megan questioned Omemema and then shook her head. "She says she cannot tell you. You should not know. Only by living through it unforeseen will you fully understand it. She *can* tell you that you will have much joy and just as much sorrow, and sometimes they will come to you together. You will have bitter enemies, but for every one of your enemies, you will have at least two friends who love you deeply. You will live a long, long life, but you will die many small deaths before the big one."

Julia shivered. It was a lot of gibberish really. An old native woman in a primitive hut in a heathen land. The voice went on.

"She says you do not want to believe her, but it is true. You have already died once." Megan looked at her curiously.

"Megan, I don't think I want to stay."

The old woman patted Julia's arm with her frail hand and smiled at her while she spoke.

Megan nodded and said, "She understands, but she says you will want to return to see her. She will welcome you when you do."

Julia rose and leaned over to thank the old lady, whose smile widened to show her one tooth. Her eyes were warm and sympathetic.

Once out in the sunlight, Julia felt better. The maids, who had been gossiping and eating oranges under a mimosa tree with some girls of their own age, joined them. Accompanied by a laughing troop of naked children, they followed a path that led diagonally up the hillside.

"Megan, do you believe in that sort of thing?"

"I don't know." Megan reached up to capture a lavender butterfly. She opened her hand and, though its feelers moved in the slight afternoon breeze, it seemed content to stay. Then she raised her palm to show it a streak of sunlight. Glowing like a jewel, it fluttered its wings for a moment, and then it flew away. "I suppose I shouldn't believe in it, but she's foreseen a lot of things."

"Maybe she just knows people, understands them."

152

"Probably," Megan said lightly. "She's never too specific."

Still it worried Julia. "What has she told you about your future?"

"I've never asked. I don't want to know. Now is what I care about, and she's given me a lot of good advice. Mostly, though, we talk about other people."

That evening after supper, Reverend Fairfield was called away to attend a dying woman, and Megan went with him. Stephen and Julia moved out onto the verandah to enjoy the cool evening breeze. In silence, they watched the setting sun light the clouds that hung over Mooréa as it turned them from golden fleece patched with azure to tangerine, pink, and scarlet against the ever-changing, mingling blues and greens of the peacock sky.

"It's a fantasy," Julia breathed, "too beautiful to really exist. There's a magic in Mooréa as though a wizard had cast an enchanted spell over it. If you tried to reach it, it would vanish, and there would be nothing but coral reefs and the sea. I feel as though everyone who lives there must be happy. No sadness, no tears, no death. Just sun-filled days and misty nights, laughter and love. Everyone is beautiful and every child is free."

Stephen tilted his chair back and, drawing on his long cigar, let the smoke trickle slowly into the fragrant air. "It's where that devil Tomaii is."

"On, no!" Her hand went to her mouth. "I meant to tell you. He came here today."

"Here!" Stephen brought his chair down with a thud. "What was he doing here?"

"He wanted to talk to you. He went home and brought some men back with him to help repair the ship. Ten or twelve or so. So you see he didn't really desert."

"He damn well did desert, disappearing like that the minute we'd anchored. When he left, he had no intention of coming back. Now that he's had second thoughts, he's brought a peace offering. What if I don't want ten or twelve men?"

"Don't you?"

"Yes, I do," he conceded. He got up and went to the railing, where he flicked the ashes off of his cigar. "I'm having a hard time rounding up what we need. They know they've got me over a barrel. I've got to have material and men, and they're trying to rob me blind. I've almost reached the point of paying their prices.

Every day we sit here is a day lost, and Baxter is surer to win that twenty dollars."

"Can't you count the time we spend here as time in port?"

"I suppose I could, but we've still lost time . . . a lot of time. Where can I find Tomaii?"

"He said he'd come back tomorrow morning." Julia rose and went to stand at the railing beside Stephen. The light was rapidly leaving the sky, and she wanted to catch one last glimpse of the lagoon before it vanished into total darkness.

"Then I'll wait for him. What did you do this afternoon?"

"Megan took me to visit an old woman and a couple of sick people." Julia tried to sound casual.

"Where do they live?" Stephen flicked the ashes from his cigar again and looked at her intently.

"Not far. Up there." She pointed to the hills that lay behind the house.

He frowned as he studied the hills. "I don't like the idea of two women wandering around alone up there. No telling what might happen."

"We're a lot safer there than we would be in some parts of Boston," Julia protested. "Besides the two maids went with us."

"A lot of protection they offer! They'd run like a couple of scared rabbits if anything happened. You have to realize, Julia, that not so far in the past these people were cannibals."

"Nonsense!" She tossed her head. "Megan explained that to me. They only ate their enemies and then only if their enemies were brave. Anyway, I'm safe as long as I'm with Megan. They love her."

"A pack of lazy beggars. They'd rob you of anything you have."

"Well, I don't have much for them to rob. I really think you misjudge them, Stephen. They're very generous. They just don't have our sense of ownership. And they're not lazy. At least you don't see them lying around in the shade of a tree the way some of these white men do."

"That may be so, but I still don't like you wandering around like that. I'll talk to the Reverend about it. Not that his advice is worth much. His wife could be carried off by headhunters, and he wouldn't notice it for days."

Julia stared out into the darkness. With the setting of the sun, the wind had died, and only small rustlings could be heard in the brush. As she leaned on the railing she thought about George Fairfield. Finally she said, "He's a rather cold man, but I'm sure he cares about her."

"Does he? I hadn't noticed. A beautiful woman like that, and he lets her run around wherever she pleases as though she were one of those dried-up excuses for wives the other missionaries have."

"They're good women. It's a hard life for them."

"You call this hard?" He laughed. "A nice house, servants. You're the one that keeps calling it a paradise." He tossed his cigar over the railing, and it arced red until it disappeared into a stand of palmettos. "Let's go to bed early tonight while they're still gone. Everytime the bed creaks, I feel as though the good Reverend were listening and counting each one with a disapproving frown."

Julia laughed. "I know. I've thought that sometimes, too. Still, he may be more of a man than you give him credit for."

"Maybe, but don't you try to find out." He put an arm around her and pulled her close. "Mmmm. You feel so fresh and clean. What's that smell?"

"Coconut oil. I put it on my hair after I washed it today. George won't let Megan use it, but Faia gave me some. It's good for your hair, and I thought you might like it."

"I do," he said and began to pull the tortoise shell pins from her hair.

Within the week, Stephen, with Tomaii's help, had rounded up enough men and supplies to start work in earnest on the battered ship. Julia's days were varied. Sometimes she went with Stephen to watch the progress on the *Crystal Star*. Sometimes she stayed home or went visiting . . . and swimming . . . with Megan. When she wakened in the morning, she never knew what the day would bring.

So much depended upon Stephen's ever-changing mood. One day, he would insist that she accompany him. The next, he might forbid her to go near the ship. Although he valued her knowledge and the experience she had gained while working with her father, he resented the looks the natives as well as the white men cast her way.

The man who now infuriated Stephen above all others was Peter Snow. Whenever Julia was with him, the lanky, red-haired whaling captain was sure to show up early and spend the day loitering around the beach while he offered unsolicited advice. When Julia stayed with Megan, Captain Snow was rarely present, and Stephen guessed that he spent his time with the native girl it was rumored he had taken for a temporary wife. Upon closely questioning Julia, Stephen was reassured that she never caught sight of him except while she was near the ship or in church.

On Sunday, the man had stood irritatingly close to Julia and himself. Throughout the service, he had watched her and completely ignored the Reverend Fairfield. His attentions were so obvious, Stephen wondered if, for some obscure reason, Snow weren't trying to bedevil him.

Julia could hardly escape being aware of him and his close scrutiny, either. Whenever he was near, she was careful to stay close to Stephen. All of her life, she had been accustomed to men's flattering attention, but the looks Peter Snow gave her had an ugly quality. She privately wondered whether it was his life in the South Seas that had stripped the veneer away from his eyes and permitted the lust to show through so clearly or whether it had always been his nature. Whatever the cause, she didn't like it. Although he was invariably polite, she was afraid of him.

One morning when Stephen and George Fairfield had left the house, Julia asked Megan, "Are we going up to the pool today?"

Megan looked up from the clothes she was folding. "Julia," she said hesitantly and her black eyes were filled with uncertainty, "I don't know how to tell you this, but I learned something from Faia last night. She's heard that Stephen has hired a man to follow you."

"He wouldn't!"

"I don't know. Maybe it's just gossip, but she knows him. He's a big, powerful man from Mooréa. I think he's one of Tomaii's cousins."

"I'm going down to the ship right this minute and ask Stephen! He has no right to do such a thing!" Julia's blue eyes were blazing as she snatched up her bonnet.

"Wait, Julie." Megan put a hand on her arm. "Maybe it's just gossip. Why don't we make sure before you talk to Stephen?"

"But to have me followed! Watched! It's incredible."

"Faia thinks he's supposed to be your bodyguard. It has something to do with that redheaded whaling captain."

"But he never so much as gave me a hint!' Julia threw her bonnet down on the table. "This is out and out spying!"

"Well . . ." Megan folded another sheet while she thought out what she was going to say. How could she phrase it without further upsetting Julia? "If you accuse him of spying, won't he think there's some reason why you don't want to be watched? That you're hiding something?"

Julia stared at her for a moment. Then she understood. "The pool," she said slowly.

"Yes, and if he finds out, he might tell George."

Julia sank down into a chair and sighed. "You're right. I can't spoil it for you. You have few enough pleasures as it is, and you'll be here long after I'm gone. I'll miss it, though," she added wistfully.

Understanding what the pool and its freedom meant to Julia, Megan smiled at her. "Well, let's go anyway. Perhaps we can lose him before we get there."

"No. I won't take the chance." She stared out through the open door at a thicket of banana trees that shone bright green in the sunlight. "Oh, Megan, I feel as though I was in a cage. Wherever I go, whatever I do, Stephen's there. Here, for the first time since we've been married, I've felt free. Now the bars of the cage have been lowered again. Damn Peter Snow!"

After handing the maid the pile of folded laundry, Megan sat down across the table from Julia. "Perhaps Captain Snow will sail soon. Then Stephen will relax."

"He says not. He sends his ship out with the mate in command while they look for whales, but he stays close to shore."

Megan rested her chin on the palm of her hand and looked thoughtfully at Julia. "What do you think of him?"

"Snow? I don't like him." Julia shivered though the day was warm. "He's . . . he's dangerous. There's nothing he's ever done that I can put my finger on, but I'm very uncomfortable when he's around."

"Then perhaps Stephen's right in trying to protect you."

"Oh, he probably is," Julia said wearily, "but the least he could have done is to tell me about it."

"Maybe he didn't want to upset you," Megan suggested.

"Most likely you're right, but sometimes he's just too blasted *over*-protective," Julia said almost bitterly.

157

"Julie, you asked me a question once." Megan, with her chin still on her hand, stared concernedly at Julia. "Now I'll ask you. Why did you marry him?"

Julia laughed and the bitterness was gone. "It's very simple. I love him. I really do. I love him desperately. I love the feel of his hair under my fingers. I love to watch the blue come into his grey eyes. His wide brow. His laughter. I love to see him standing on the quarterdeck, master under God." Then she added more soberly. "It's just his jealousy that comes between us. He sees every other man as a threat. Even my poor dead Jason."

"Jason?" Megan cocked her head to one side.

"My first husband," Julia said quietly. "He died at sea."

"You've never mentioned him before. I'm sorry." Megan could see that there was a cloud of pain in Julia's eyes. "Was that why you were so upset when Omemema said that you had died once?"

"Yes."

"I really am sorry, Julie."

Julia sighed and then shrugged. "It was a long time ago. But what Stephen doesn't understand is that the love I had for Jason, the sorrow I felt when he died, only makes me value Stephen's love the more. I know how quickly a man can die, how long the grief lasts. I don't think I could stand to go through it again. If Stephen's ship goes down, I'll go with him. It's easier than being left behind."

Megan reached across the table and took both of Julia's hands in hers. "Julie, you feel too much! You care too deeply. I've noticed it before."

"I know." Julia gave her a wry smile and pressed her hands. "I think I'd like to go back and see Omemema again. Could we go today?"

"No. She's not there. She's gone away to visit one of her daughters on the other side of the island. But she left something for you." Megan squeezed Julia's hands once more, then rose and went into her bedroom. When she returned, she handed Julia a smooth black pebble that was in the shape of an egg and had one thin thread of white spiraling around it. "She said if you asked for her, I was to give you this and tell you to hold it when you're troubled."

Julia looked at the small stone. "What is it? It looks like an ordinary pebble to me. Does it have some special significance?"

Megan shrugged. "None that I know of, but don't tell George I gave it to you. He'd say I've been trafficking with the devil."

As Julia closed her fingers around it, the pebble felt smooth and cool as though it had just been picked up from a riverbed. "It doesn't feel like an instrument of the devil."

"Perhaps I shouldn't have given it to you." Megan's voice was troubled and her eyes worried. "Perhaps I should never have taken you to see her."

"It's all right, Megan. I know there's nothing evil in it. It's just a pebble I could have picked up anywhere. There's no need for me to explain it to anybody."

Work on the *Crystal Star* progressed smoothly and more rapidly than Stephen had forecast. One Sunday evening after the sun had set, he and Julia once again sat alone on the verandah and watched the phosphorus surf on the reef and the stars that could be glimpsed through the branches overhead. In the nearby church, the natives were singing familiar hymns in their strange language.

"Another week or ten days will see us finished. In two weeks time, we should be back at sea." Stephen stretched contentedly.

"So soon?" Julia asked pensively. "I've enjoyed it here."

"Well, I haven't!" Though it was difficult to see the expression on his face by starlight, the irritation in his voice was clear. "Trying to get these people to work is like shoveling sand against the tide. When they show up, there's no one better, but you never know when they'll decide it's a good day for fishing. We've lost time . . . far too much time . . . here. We'd have been in China now but for that blasted storm."

"It's the money that's worrying you, isn't it?"

"Damned right it is. Don't forget Captain Asa told us not to come home until the *Crystal Star* has paid for herself. If we go north to the Sandwich Isles now, we'll lose more time, and I'm not even sure the sea otter will still be waiting for us. I have half a mind to sail directly for China."

Julia smoothed the flounces of her rose voile dress uneasily. "But what will we do with the cargo that was bound for Oahu?"

"I've already sold off most of it for twice the profit I would have made there. It shouldn't be difficult to unload the rest for a very good sum."

"And the otter? We'll need it to help pay for the tea, won't we?"

"No. I've looked into that. I can get a load of sugar, pearl shell, and coconut oil here that would sell quite well in China, I think."

"Then maybe the storm was a bit of luck?" she said as she tried to cheer him up. When Stephen was in this kind of brooding mood, it was difficult.

"No." He rose and began to pace up and down the verandah. "All this work is eating into the profit. Materials, workmen, crew. Every time I turn around, someone else has his hand out. I could probably hire some Tahitians to sail with us if we were going to Oahu, but I don't think I could convince them to go to Hong Kong. If I decide to sail direct for China, I don't know where I'll find the crew." He paused to pull out his second cigar of the evening, which was unusual for Stephen.

"You can't find any Americans or Europeans who'd like to sign the Articles?"

"There's no hope of that. I've even asked some of the scum, but no one will leave Tahiti. The only solution I can come up with is to tell the natives that I'm bound for Oahu, load up with Tahitian goods, and sail straight for Hong Kong. I can't see any other way to clear a profit and get a crew at the same time."

Julia instinctively glanced around to see who might have overheard him. In the darkness, it was difficult to tell, but all she could hear were the normal rustlings of night. Still, she lowered her voice when she spoke. "Besides being dishonest, isn't that taking a big risk?"

"You mean a mutiny?" He paused in his pacing long enough to stare down at her, and by starlight she could see the muscles in his shoulders tensing under the linen of his shirt.

She looked down at her hands and realized that she was nervously pressing pleats into her thin dress. "Yes," she said quietly.

"I'm not worried about a mutiny. The crew's loyal. At least, none of them has tried to run off yet. If there's any discontent amongst the new hands, they'll back me up. Besides the Tahitians won't be able to navigate once we get away from the islands, so they'd never attempt to take over the ship."

"I guess there's safety in that, isn't there?" she said as she thought of all the tales of attempted mutinies she had heard from her father and his cronies. Sometimes the attempts were successful.

"A lot of safety . . . as long as we're out of sight of land, of course." He went to the rail and stared off into the darkness.

"Incidentally, that reminds me," he continued in a lighter vein. "There's a vessel named after you in the harbor."

"The Jewel of the Seas?" Julia brightened at the thought of seeing David Baxter. "Was she hit by the typhoon, too?"

"No. Our luck isn't that good. Or should I say *my* luck?" He leaned against the railing and raised an eyebrow as he looked at her. "Since you own most of the *Jewel*, it wouldn't be good luck for you if she were damaged, would it?"

"No. But I would like to see you win your wager. If it's not the *Jewel*, then what is my namesake?"

Stephen laughed. "Not a very flattering one, I'm afraid. I wouldn't claim her if I were you. A small whaler out of Sydney, and a more slatternly-looking one, I've never seen. Her rigging is all slack and bleached nearly white. Her hull and spars are a dingy black from lack of paint or care. I can't say I blame her crew for being demoralized."

"Do you think you could hire a few of them?" Julia asked hopefully. "Maybe some are one-voyage men."

"No. I doubt I would if I could. They're whalers, not merchant sailors . . . won't know the meaning of discipline. Besides they're in the Calabooza Beretane charged with attempted mutiny."

"Mutiny! Was anyone killed?"

"Nothing like that. They just refuse to sail on the *Julia* anymore. I did look into the crew, though. I heard of one who caught my interest. A fellow named Melville. I sailed with a good second mate named Harry Melville several years ago. Thought I might take a chance on him, but this fellow's first name is Herman."

"That's a pity. You could use a good second."

Before Stephen could reply, there was the sound of someone crashing through the brush. Then one of the crewmen burst into the clearing.

"Fire, Captain," he said panting when he reached the verandah. "Fire aboard the *Crystal Star.*"

"Oh, my God!" Without a second's hesitation, Stephen vaulted over the railing.

"Wait for me!" Julia knocked over her chair as she sprang out of it. "I'm coming, too."

"No! You stay here," Stephen shouted over his shoulder. "Don't come near the ship." Running down the path, he disappeared around the bend.

161

Chapter Eight

1842

Julia stood indecisively on the steps. Should she follow him or not? It was the *Crystal Star* that was on fire. Her ship! Yet Stephen would most likely be angry if she appeared, and he had enough to worry about.

She made up her mind and ran down to the beach. Maybe she could see something in the distance. But when she arrived, there was nothing, not even a glow in the sky. She hoped that meant the fire was small.

Wandering aimlessly over the coarse sand and watching the phosphorus foam at the water's edge, she thought of the day the keel was laid, the hours and weeks and months of her growth. She remembered that glorious day when they had sailed from Boston. The cabin and saloon were her home. She *had* to do something to help the *Crystal Star*! Then the sound of singing, which surged up once more, caught her attention. The church! There were people there. A lot of them. People who could help fight the fire.

Keeping her attention on the ground, she quickly picked her way up the dark path towards the church. A tall shadow quietly detached itself from the others and stepped out onto the path in front of her.

"Well, Miss Julie, I wondered how long ye'd keep me waiting." She froze as her heart turned over and the blood rushed to her head. She recognized the harsh voice of Peter Snow.

"Get out of my way, Captain. I have to get to the church," she said with a calmness she didn't feel.

"Gettin' religion all of a sudden, are ye?" He grabbed her arm and barred the way.

"I'm going to get people to help fight the fire, which is what *you'd* be doing if you had any decency." Her voice was ridged with ice as she tried to shake him off. "Let go of my arm!"

"They've plenty of help. This is the chance we've been waiting for, sweetheart. Yer husband's safe down there, and so is that bloody savage he's had followin' ye around." His arm closed around her waist, and as he crushed her to him, she could smell liquor on his fetid breath.

"*Let me go!*" She could feel her heart battering at her ribs and panic rising in her as she struggled to break loose, but his thin arms were like bands of iron.

"Ye don't have to pretend with me, sweetheart. Ye know ye want it as much as I do." He bent his head towards her, and she struck at his face with her free hand.

"I want nothing from you, you filthy whaler," she shouted and tried to claw at his face. "In one second, I'm going to start screaming."

He laughed and held her tighter. "Scream away. There's none to hear ye."

Kicking at him with both her legs and pummeling at him with her fist, she yelled as loudly as she could, "*Help! Help! Stephen! Someone! Help me!*" But as she fought for breath in his tight embrace, each word grew fainter. Only in nightmares had she ever fought so hard to be heard.

He clamped his hand over her mouth, and his voice became ugly with anger. "I tell ye, there's none to help ye. Ye've put on yer act. Now be quiet."

As he dragged her away from the path into a grove of banana trees, she realized that he fully intended to hurt her. How much? she thought desperately. The vision of his filthy body, his foul breath mingling with hers gave her new strength, and she flailed at him, biting and kicking, but she couldn't break away.

Then he was trying to force her down onto the ground and she

163

was able to get her back against a palm tree. If only she could get one knee free, she knew where to kick him. A fight had broken out at the shipyard once, and she knew what a blow to that one spot could do. If only she could raise her knee just enough, but he was crushing her to him. She was finding it harder and harder to breathe, and she could feel herself growing weaker.

"Take your hands off my wife, Snow!" Stephen!

She gave one last push and jumped free as the man turned to swing at her husband. He missed and fell, and Stephen was on top of him, choking him, hitting him, but Snow shook him off. They rolled over the ground, thrashing in the underbrush. Their blows came faster and faster.

Julia found a long, heavy stick and approached their entwined bodies. But how could she hit Peter Snow without touching Stephen? She hovered over them as she watched for her chance. Then suddenly one form relaxed and lay still.

Stephen rose panting, his coat ripped and his pants torn. "Did he hurt you, Julie?"

"No. No, I don't think so." She leaned back against a tree and found that she was trembling as she rubbed her sore arm.

"Are you sure? If he did, I'll kill him." His knife flashed in the dim starlight.

"No, he didn't! Put it away!" Julia recoiled at the sight of the deadly instrument.

Stephen nodded and sheathed his knife as he came towards her, but he said grimly. "He'll pay for this yet. That was only the first installment."

"Oh, Stephen." She threw herself into his arms, and his strength, his protection, surrounded her. How could she ever have said that he was overprotective? She needed him so badly. Then she felt a wet warmth on her face where it touched his. She put up her hand to his cheek and her fingers came away sticky with blood. "You're hurt!"

"No, I'm all right." He let his lips graze her forehead, and then he guided her back to the path.

When they reached it, she suddenly fell apart. Shaking and sobbing uncontrollably, she huddled in his arms. He let her cry for a moment while he stroked her back.

Then he said, "Julie, control yourself. I want to get you away before he comes to. My guns are in the house."

The shock of his words, the thought of the man's regaining consciousness and pursuing them before they reached safety, was enough to sober her. She tried to match her steps to Stephen's as he hurried her along.

When they reached the house, the church was emptying and the Fairfields were on their way home. As soon as she saw her guests, Megan ran up to them. "What on earth happened?"

"Snow set fire to a couple of my boats and then came skulking over here to attack my wife," Stephen said in a voice filled with venom.

"I'm thankful it wasn't one of the natives," George Fairfield said in his solemnly ponderous way.

"Oh, Julie, how awful," Megan said. "Did he hurt you?"

"No," Julia said and then she remembered. "Stephen! The ship?"

"Two longboats gutted. Aside from a little charring, the ship itself is undamaged."

"Thank heavens." Her legs were trembling so, she sank down on the steps.

"Julia, get up!" Stephen said and reached down to help her.

"I don't think I can." She leaned her head against the rail. Her legs had brought her this far, but they refused to carry her any farther.

"Let her sit here, Captain Logan," George Fairfield said with anxious compassion. "She's had a shock. Megan, fix her some tea."

"No. I want to get her into the house. That man's still out there."

"He wouldn't dare bring violence to *this* house." The Reverend Fairfield was suddenly impressive as he lifted his golden head with righteous assurance.

"This house or any other he put his mind to. Come on, Julia." Stephen pulled her up until she was half standing. Then he scooped her up and carried her up the steps and into the house. In their bedroom, he laid her on the bed. Then he went directly to his sea chest, unlocked it, and brought out a pair of pistols. After he had loaded them, he rammed them into his belt.

Alarmed, Julia raised herself on one weak elbow. "Stephen, you're not going to kill him!"

"Not tonight. Not unless he tries to come in here," he said tersely. Crossing the room, he sat down in a rattan chair with his back to the wall and laid one gun on his lap, his right hand touching the grip. From where he sat, he could see the open door and windows.

Julia closed her eyes. Outside every noise sounded like a footstep, and she could imagine the whaling captain prowling through the bushes that surrounded the house. When she opened her eyes quickly to reassure herself that Stephen was still there, she saw that he was watching her.

"Do you think he'll try to come?" she asked tensely.

"There's no telling. No sane man would, but no sane man would have set a fire and then attacked a helpless woman, either." His eyes traveled from the door to the windows and back again. With his torn shirt and dirt-smeared face, he looked fully as wild as the whaler. "I almost wish he would come. I'd like to get a shot at that son of a bitch."

"Your cheek. We should do something about it," she said as she looked at the dark streak on his grimly set face. With an effort, she sat up on the bed.

"Stay where you are!" he snapped out the order. Then with his left hand, he explored his cheek. "It can't be much, just a scratch. At any rate, it's stopped bleeding. Wrap yourself up in a blanket. If he sees you like that, nothing's going to stop him."

Julia looked down at her dress and, for the first time, realized that, in her struggles with Snow, he had managed to rip the front of it. When she saw her exposed breast and thought of the Reverend Fairfield seeing her like this, she blushed with embarrassment. She only hoped he was too far above worldly things to have noticed.

Just then, Megan and Faia came through the open door with a basin of water and some towels. When she saw Stephen's guns, Megan hesitated.

"I thought you'd want to get washed up," she said quietly.

"Mrs. Fairfield," Stephen said slowly, "you and your maid had better get out. Until we know where Snow is, it would be wise if you stayed away from us."

Megan put the towels on a nearby table and motioned for Faia to do the same with the basin. Then after a glance at Julia, she looked directly at Stephen. "I'll bring some tea. You may not want it, but Julia needs it."

"We both need it." Stephen tried to smile at her, but it was a failure. "And I'd appreciate it if you'd lace it with rum or brandy."

"I'm sorry, but we don't have any spirits in the house. The Reverend has never permitted it."

"Then bring the tea."

As soon as they had gone, he ducked down and went to his sea chest. After rummaging in it with one hand while he continued to watch the windows, he brought up a small bottle.

"Here's some rum," he said as he handed it to Julia. "Put some in our tea when it comes."

Drinking tea flavored with rum, they sat in a silence that grew more tense with each long minute. Any noise was sufficient for Stephen to raise his gun and point it at a window. Over an hour had passed before the Reverend Fairfield knocked on the frame of the door and entered the room.

"I've just received word," he said. "They have Snow locked up in the calabooza."

"That's efficient." Stephen laid the gun carefully aside, then got up and stretched.

"He went stumbling back into town saying you'd attacked him. I'd already sent word to the police of what happened. So when he appeared, they were ready for him." From the look George Fairfield gave them both, Julia had the feeling that he was thinking that none of this would have happened if they'd attended the church service.

"Thank you, Reverend," Stephen said. "Now there's only one question. How strong is that calabooza? It won't be easy to hold a man like Snow."

They held Snow for three days. On the fourth, the jailer didn't secure the lock on the split log that served for leg chains carefully enough, and he escaped. On the sixth, his body was found near a village eight miles away. No effort was made to determine the cause of his death. His body, exposed for two days to nature and the pigs that ran wild on the island, was mangled and torn almost beyond recognition. Julia noticed that now, when she went down to the ship with Stephen, the men carefully avoided looking at her.

She saw the question hidden in Megan's eyes as well as in George Fairfield's. What had been paradise became a place of unspoken speculation and ugly suspicion. She was relieved when Stephen announced that they would sail on Saturday, and she saw equal relief on the Fairfields' faces.

Stephen demanded and got two of the *Black Swallow*'s boats in restitution for the ones Peter Snow had destroyed. Despite his prejudice against whalers, he was also able to quietly hire away four of Snow's best seamen. They mistrusted their former mate, who was now the captain of the *Black Swallow*. With these men and two Tahitians who expressed a willingness to ship out for Hong Kong, the crew was complete, and Stephen decided to sail directly for China.

On Friday morning, Megan sat on Julia's bed and watched her pack the sea chests. "I'll miss you," she said sadly.

"I'll miss you, too," Julia said as she carefully laid a piece of tapa cloth next to a long shell necklace. It was difficult to meet Megan's eyes. "But it's best for us to go now."

"Yes, it's best. I'm sorry that it had to end this way."

"Well." Julia straightened up and pushed the damp tendrils away from her face. "It can't be helped."

"I'll never forget you." Megan picked up Julia's heavy silk shawl from the bed beside her and smoothed it into a square.

"I'll be back." Julia smiled at her reassuringly. "Remember what Omemema told us? She said I'd be back. Said we'd meet and separate many times."

"I wish I could believe her." Megan's black eyes were wistful.

"Then believe *me*," Julia said briskly. "Stephen is already talking about Tahiti's being a better market than Oahu. If there's a profit to be made, he'll make it. He'll be back and I'll be with him."

Megan got up and began to wander around the room. She picked up one article after another, but without really seeing them, she put them down. She glanced uneasily at Julia who was bending over the chest, and then away again. Knowing that Julia might take offense at what she wanted to say, she hesitated, and yet she was worried about her friend and felt she had to warn her. When she finally blurted out the words, she was painfully embarrassed by them.

168

"He troubles me, Julie. I'm afraid for you."

"Afraid because of *Stephen?*" Julia straightened up and stared at Megan with incredulous blue eyes.

"Yes," Megan said in a very quiet voice.

"That's silly," Julia laughed. "Stephen would never hurt me. Believe me, Megan, I don't know what happened, and I don't want to know, but if he had anything to do with Snow's death, then he only did it to protect me."

"I never said he did!" Megan dropped the brush she had just picked up.

"No, nor has anyone else dared to suggest it." Julia went to the window to look out at the lagoon she so loved and which she would see for the last time the next day. "But I see the suspicion in their eyes."

"When you come back, it will all be forgotten, Julie."

"Will it?" Julia turned to look at her friend whose hair glowed like filigreed silver in the early morning sunlight. "I hope so. It's been so beautiful here, and meeting you, knowing you . . . that's something very special. On hot days in the doldrums, I'll remember your crystal pool and think of you swimming in it. Maybe when we come back, you'll be teaching your baby how to swim there."

"You guessed?" Megan's face became almost as radiant as her hair.

Julia smiled at her. "Yes."

"I . . . I wasn't sure, but I was going to tell you anyway before you left."

"Write and let me know what happens." Julia went to Megan and took her hands. "You know how to get in touch with me."

"I will. Maybe you'll return before he's born." Megan's black eyes glowed with excitement. "Then you'll have to be his godmother."

Julia laughed and released Megan's hands. "A fine godmother I'd make! You'd do better with one of the missionary wives."

"Well, maybe you can be his fairy godmother." Megan's smile was full of elfin mischief. "Every child needs one of those, too. Seriously, Julie, if anything happens to me, will you take him with you? Take him back to my family in Maryland?"

"Megan, nothing will happen to you."

"Julie, please promise me. I couldn't bear to think of my child being left alone with George. He can't love a human being. He can only love God."

Julia looked carefully at Megan, and she could see a fear in her eyes. Was it a premonition? Shivering slightly, she hoped not. "I'll promise that *if* I can, I'll take him home for you," she said seriously. "Might be I'd have to fight both George and Stephen, but I'll try."

Megan sighed with a relief that showed how deep her fear had been. "That's good enough for me. I think you always get what you want, Julie."

"Yes, but not necessarily the way I want it. My father used to say, 'Be careful what you ask for. You may get it.' " She closed the lid of her sea chest and moved to Stephen's. "At any rate, this is an awfully morbid conversation for such a beautiful day. My last day in Tahiti. Can't we take a picnic and go a little way up into the hills? I'm almost finished, and Stephen said he wouldn't be back till evening. Didn't I hear George say the same thing?"

They sailed at dawn, just as the sun, rising above the mountain peaks, turned the trailing edges of the low-lying clouds into scarlet and golden rose. Standing at the taffrail, looking back at the slumbering town of Papeete and the shadowed hills of black and green, Julia managed to hold back her tears until they could no longer be seen by those who watched from land. Stephen, glancing at her, saw them trickling silently down her face, but he said nothing.

When they came to the deep blue-water pass in the multicolored reef, she turned and looked forward. Across the strait lay Mooréa. The sun was high enough now to pick out the blue-green shadows of its ravines and the high white spray that flung itself in a protective barrier around the island.

"We never did get to Mooréa," she said. "I wanted to visit Tomaii's family, and now it's too late. I wonder if he's watching us."

"I'm sure he is," Stephen said gently.

"I think I was right. It is a magic island. It's not for us."

"We'll go there next time. Without a ship to repair, we'll have time to explore. I'll take you to all the bays and inlets we've never seen. We'll go to Point Venus, to Tahiti-Iti. We'll go to Mooréa, all the places we had no time for."

"Will you, Stephen?"

"Yes, I will." He moved to the rail beside her, and though he did not touch her, she could feel his warmth and strength.

During the outward voyage, past the islands of the mid-Pacific, fighting northward through the variables of Capricorn, Stephen remained more even-tempered than she had ever seen him before. It seemed that the injuries she had suffered during the typhoon and the attack upon her by Peter Snow made him place a higher value on her company, and there was more laughter in their days.

As far as the ship went, however, he had not changed. Through every freak of weather, through every changing condition of the sea, he drove the *Crystal Star* onward under her cloud of canvas. They passed rapidly from the South to the North Pacific. As they approached the Ladrone Islands, Stephen had the mates drill the men in the use of cannon whenever the weather permitted. Those who were not assigned to the larger guns were issued muskets, which were returned at the end of every practice session and locked away. Much of their time was spent in making cartridges.

For once, Julia was allowed to participate in the activities of the crew. As they neared the pirate-infested waters, Stephen instructed her first in the use of a pistol, then in that of a rifle, pointing out the art and peculiarities of each. Standing side by side with the seamen, she aimed at the same objects and vied with them for the best shot. Nothing that flew or floated near the *Crystal Star* was safe from their barrage.

Fortunately their marksmanship was not put to the ultimate test, for they sailed safely on through the Philippine Sea. They sighted a few junks and many smaller craft, but none approached them. The American and European vessels they met reported that all was quiet ahead.

After they had passed between Luzon and Formosa, the sea became calm and the winds disappeared. Stephen ordered that the lookouts be doubled. The South China Sea, reflecting sampans and junks like a mirror, was broken only by the leaping of a fish, the dive of a water bird or the long oars of a native craft dipping silently into the water.

Where Julia found beauty here, and fascination in watching the daily lives of the native families on their boats, Stephen found only anxiety and irritation. The enchanting, exotic sound of reed flutes floating across the still water at night would drive him to pacing the quarterdeck until dawn.

Any one of those innocent looking boats . . . or all of them . . . could be pirates. When any approached too closely, he ordered them off. If they persisted, he reinforced his words with a warning shot or two. Finally at dawn on the third day, a light favoring breeze sprang up, and every sail was finely set to take advantage of it.

As they approached Hong Kong, they met an ever-increasing number of junks and sampans with mats for sails or cotton dyed a rusty red from pig's blood. Navigation became more hazardous as the huge rock islands, rising straight from the sea, littered their course with treacherous irregularity, and no one aboard the *Crystal Star* had ever been to the newly-founded colony. Then they saw, very long and low upon the sea, a land that had no attendant clouds.

"Kowloon," Stephen announced with satisfaction. Then he handed Julia the telescope and pointed forward. "Look carefully over there. You'll see Hong Kong. The Fragrant Harbor."

Julia's hand was steady as she took the glass, but she felt her stomach flutter with excited anticipation. China! At last. After a lifetime of stories of this most exotic of forbidden lands, she was finally here. She remembered her father stroking his small amber Buddha with his fingers and the lost dream that had been in his eyes.

True, this wasn't Canton, but an island that had been settled only a little over a year ago. Still, it was China!

She spent the morning watching that low blue mist on the horizon turn into variegated green mountains that rose steeply from the coast.

As they neared Lei Yue Mun pass at the eastern end of the island, the crescendo of water traffic built up. Now there were not only junks and lorchas to contend with, but hundreds of smaller craft that scuttled everywhere. The tall and towering rock islands became fewer until they were left behind, but in their place more and more smaller ones appeared, some so minuscule they were almost invisible. Stephen ordered the number of lookouts in the rigging doubled.

Off the starboard bow, the immediate high hills of the mainland rose brownish grey and starkly barren from the shore. The land seemed as inhospitable as its rulers, who had for so many centuries refused admittance to any *fan kwae*, or foreign devils, as the Chinese called the white man.

When the people in the smaller boats saw the *Crystal Star* come hurtling into the channel with all her sails set and straining forward against the lines, they quickly propelled their craft towards the shores of the pass, which was only a few hundred feet wide.

Once they were through the channel, one cloud-draped mountain, towering hundreds of feet above the others on the island, suddenly appeared. Only a few bare spots were visible in the lush green vegetation that covered it. Though the sun was shining bright upon the mountain, Julia felt it was shrouded in mystery and intrigue. However, the presence of armed British frigates and brigs as well as merchantmen flying the ensigns of many nations, which they found as they entered the calmer waters of the enormous harbor, swept away any impression of mystery the island might hold. Still she suspected there must be intrigue. At least she hoped so. What would China be without intrigue?

Surely the mandarins must still exert their wiles as they fed their greed. While they publicly bowed to the orders of the Emperor and carried out his edicts, money quietly passed into their hands would purchase an often circuitous route around the ruler's commands. Many a mandarin had suffered a long and painful death as a result of his manipulations, but when discovered, most managed to shift the blame onto lesser functionaries, who died in their stead.

Julia remembered tales told of those who sailed the China Coast in their small, fleet-winged opium clippers. When they arrived at their destination, usually a small outlying island, the mandarin's junks would be lying in wait for them. After a public explanation of the clipper having suffered a long and arduous journey due to foul winds and adverse currents, the mandarin would soberly pull out of his boot a long red document, an Imperial Edict. It was made quite clear that no barbarian ship was allowed to wander at will through the Middle Kingdom, and under no circumstances would one be allowed to trade. However, the Son of Heaven was not so cruel that he would forbid those in distress from obtaining food and other necessities. It ended with a stern injunction that, when the vessel was so supplied, it must depart at once.

When the document had been read and returned safely to the mandarin's boot, he would rise. His servants would return to his barge, while he would go below at the captain's invitation. Once below, all pretence would be dropped and business negotiations would begin. The captain would inform the mandarin how many chests of opium he planned to deliver to his district. The mandarin would declare the amount of cumsha he required from each chest. After a few more glasses of wine and a cigar or two, the mandarin would make his departure. The next day, several smaller junks would sail out from the mainland and take delivery of the opium with no further official interference.

The cumsha always handed upwards, which dwindled as it passed through each pair of hands, represented a major expense to the shipowners, but the profit was still large enough to allow for it, and so the Americans and Europeans continued to trade in China.

However, the craftiness of thieves could become an unexpectedly burdensome expense. Although long boats with guards prowled the Whampoa anchorage by night, daylight could reveal that a vessel had been stripped of several sheets of copper. Floating with the current and hidden under a broken basket or drifting log, the thieves would approach their victim. Once they had tied themselves and their camouflage to the vessel by a rope made of coconut fiber, they would calmly pry the copper off the bottom and then float off again with their plunder.

She remembered, too, the tales of pirates so daring, they would attack a vessel if she dared anchor in a calm in Macao Roads in plain sight of but out of reach of the shore batteries of the Portuguese.

There were people who mysteriously disappeared and just as mysteriously appeared again with tales so strange, they were not credible. A servant would turn up after several months with a hand missing and yet speak of a mother who had been dying. A cook would be returned to the doorstep of a factory in Canton with his own hatchet buried deep in his chest. Though no words of explanation were ever given, the warnings were clear enough.

"Well, I may have beaten him around the Horn, but I don't think there's any doubt as to who won the race to Hong Kong," Stephen said, interrupting her thoughts. He nodded at the western side of the crowded anchorage.

Julia followed his glance. Yes. There was the *Jewel of the Seas*, gleaming with a fresh coat of black paint. What could she say? That she was glad to see her ship safe at Hong Kong? That she was looking forward to seeing David Baxter again? That she was sorry Stephen had lost his wager?

Stephen evidently didn't notice her silence, however, for he continued, "I'm surprised he's still here. I'd have thought he would have loaded and been on his way home by now. It must mean that there's no tea available for shipment."

"Oh, I hope so. Then we'll still have a chance of being the first ship home," she said and thought of the additional profit that would bring. Idly she glanced around the harbor to see if she recognized any of the other vessels. Then she grabbed Stephen's arm. "Look who else is here!" She pointed to the east of the *Jewel.*

"The *Belle of Canton!* Well, I'll be damned." Stephen took off his visored cap and smoothed back his hair. "Last time I saw Will Thacher, he swore he'd never bring her around either the Horn or the Cape of Good Hope again. Said the *Belle* was too old."

Julia thought of the man who had been not only Jason's father but was her mother's first cousin as well, and she laughed. "I reckon he just plain couldn't resist it. He placed an order with Papa for a new ship, but Cousin William never could stay put. Even the Atlantic's too confining for him."

"I suppose so," Stephen answered absently. All of his concentration was now focused upon the job of finding a safe anchorage where they would swing clear of the other vessels.

Once the anchor had been lowered through the murky green water, a pattern emerged in the random traffic as a number of boats converged upon them. Some were sculled by one long sweeping oar. Some were rowed by two or more. There were even a couple of sampans sailing directly toward them.

Julia was a little alarmed when she saw the scowls on some of the people's faces as the boats bumped against each other and heard the angry intensity of their voices as they not only shouted at the ship but quarrelled amongst themselves.

"Stephen! They're not pirates, are they?"

"With the British Navy present? Hardly." Then he shouted at the mate, "Mister Wilson, keep them off!"

"Well, what do they want? They don't have any food." Julia still felt a little nervous. These people were nothing like the gay food-and-flowerladen natives of Tahiti. "They don't seem to be selling anything."

"Nothing but their fair young bodies." Stephen gave her a wicked grin.

"I don't believe you. You're just trying to make me believe China is more evil than it really is."

"Am I? Then why do you think there are so many girls in those boats?"

"There do seem to be a few," she admitted, "but look at all the old women they have with them for chaperones. And see how many men and children there are in some of those boats." She went to the rail to get a closer view of the upturned faces of the water people who were crowding around them in great noise and confusion. "I can't make out what they're saying."

Stephen joined her. "They're speaking Pidgin. You'll pick it up quickly. Now take that man down there." He gestured at a sampan just a few feet away from the *Crystal Star*. Its owner was a wizened man whose bright eyes barely peered out of his wrinkles. There were also two women aboard, one old and one young, and three children. All except the children were dressed in black trousers and padded jackets. Brown reed coolie hats covered their heads. "He's asking for our garbage."

"Not really!"

"Yes. And that one." He nodded at a smaller sampan that seemed filled to overflowing with one old woman and five young and pretty girls, who were all smiling enticingly. "That one wants to do our laundry. The girls are slaves she bought and trained when they were quite young." He twisted one corner of his mouth wryly. "They perform other services than just laundry. Amongst their many talents, they have an absolute genius for knowing exactly which day is pay day on every ship in the harbor, and their number and affection increases accordingly."

176

Her attention was caught by a lithe, robust girl with hair as black as Julia's own. A single long braid tied with a red ribbon swung below her waist as she sculled a small boat toward them. Her skin was a light yellowish brown and her complexion was translucently clean and glowing with good health. Her black almond eyes were sparkling with merriment.

"Hi-yah! Missee! Wantchee go ashore?" she shouted when she noticed Julia watching her.

Julia shook her head but smiled at the girl. "What about her?" she asked Stephen.

"Oh, she's a free agent. A Tanka girl. One of the water people. She was probably born on a boat. It's where she makes her living, and it's where she'll probably die."

"She seems happy."

"The Tanka girls usually are, just as they're usually quite pretty. They're the local transportation system. For just a few cents, they'll take you wherever you want to go or run errands for you. You have to be careful, though. They'll smile at you and overcharge at every opportunity."

"They're more virtuous than the laundry girls then?"

Stephen smiled at her and Julia thought there was a reminiscent quality to his grey eyes. "If they're married, they're quite respectable. Before that, they're available. They're not slaves like the laundry girls, though. If they don't own their own boats, they may be working for the owner, but they're free in all other ways."

"Ahoy, the *Crystal Star!*" There was no mistaking that booming voice and Julia looked forward to see Cousin William, big, bluff and hearty as ever, standing in the bow of a boat being swept toward them by another Tanka girl.

"Ahoy!" she called back, and picking up her skirts, she rushed down to the midships section of the maindeck, where the men were already lowering the ladder.

He had hardly set foot on deck before he swept her into his arms and she could smell the mingled scents of salt, tobacco, and leather that had meant Cousin William to her ever since she had been a young girl. He gave her a hearty kiss on the cheek and his silver-gold whiskers tickled her nose. When he held her away from him, she could see that there was a suspicion of moisture in his green eyes.

177

"Well, Julie, I've been waitin' for you. What in tarnation took you so long gettin' here?"

"Oh, Cousin William! How *good* to see you." She gave him another hug. "We ran into a typhoon and ended up in Tahiti."

"Tahiti!" His eyebrows shot up. "I thought you was headed for the Sandwich Isles."

"We were, but we were pretty badly damaged. We barely managed to limp into Tahiti."

"That bad?" William frowned and looked at Stephen, who had been standing back and smiling at this greeting. He, too, was fond of the big, burly captain, who had helped him obtain his command of the *Crystal Star*.

"Yes, sir," Stephen said. "It was very bad. In the years I've spent at sea, I've never seen a storm like it . . . and I hope I never do again."

"Well, if it was anything like the one they had here in Hong Kong a year ago July, then you're lucky to have survived it. From what they tell me, nine vessels were lost right here in the harbor. Four were driven ashore but were able to get off afterwards, ten were totally dismasted, eleven lost their bowsprits or a mast or two, and two lost their rudders. Several others had damage to their hulls. That's to say nothing about the junks, Tanka boats, and Chinese cargo boats. Hundreds, maybe thousands, of people killed. Never were able to make an accurate count."

"How horrible," Julia said and shuddered when she remembered the violence they had undergone in their own typhoon. "Still I think you'd be better off here than going through it at sea." She looked up at the mountains that guarded the harbor.

"Don't know 'bout that. Vessels broke loose of their moorings and were chargin' round the harbor out of control. And the land was no more safe than the water. All the houses and the bazaar were blown down. The hospital and temporary barracks were totally demolished. Still, I'm glad to see you've survived in good order." William Thacher looked around the decks at the patched rails and then up at the three tall masts and spars that were poor substitutes for the strong and true ones with which they had begun the voyage.

"More or less," Stephen said with a wry smile.

Once they were below in the saloon to have an anchor-down

drink, Stephen turned to William Thacher and asked anxiously, "How's the tea situation?"

"None's come down for a couple of months, so you're none too late, even if you was off beachcombin' in the Societies. I'd advise you to get right to work on it, though. What kind of cargo did you bring?"

When Stephen had told him, he nodded his head. "Aye. You'll have a good market for all that. The Tahitian goods will most likely gain you as much profit as the sea otter would. Best firm to deal with is Russell and Company, though it'll pay you to talk to the other factories. As for the tea, you'll have to carry it for an American firm. Least as long as the British hold to their damned Navigation Act. Hong Kong's considered British territory even if it is called a free port."

"I also have some opium, sir," Stephen said casually as he stirred the rum and water together. He knew that, in New England, a prejudice against opium trading had begun to spring up and he didn't know how Will Thacher felt about it. However, he did know that he could trust the man. "I've a notion to go up the East Coast with it. I hear the smugglers are operating more openly since the British armada is here to offer protection from pirates."

"Opium, is it?" William Thacher shook his head. "I used to trade in it. Thought the only real danger was to those of us who carried it. Now I've come to believe there are more dangers to the user than we once thought. Still, if you've got it, you'll have to sell it."

"Well, I'm not going to dump it overboard, not after the trouble I went through to obtain it."

"No. Well, the East Coast's still not what I'd call safe. The Chinese signed a treaty with the British at Nanking at the end of August. Admitted they were beaten and declared five ports open to the world. Canton, Amoy, Ningpo, Shanghai, and Foochow. Also the British get to keep Hong Kong. But I don't trust either side. There've been lulls all through the Opium War. Just long enough to get the tea crop out. They swear the war's over now, but I don't put too much stock in it. If it starts up again, the navy will be running up the rivers. Then the pirates will be out in full force again."

"There *is* the chance to make the best profit by dealing with the

179

smugglers, though," Stephen said thoughtfully.

William shook his head. "I wouldn't take Julie up there. That's certain. If you want to risk it, leave her here with me. She'll be welcome on board the *Belle* anytime."

Stephen frowned. "I'll think about it."

"No, Stephen," Julia interrupted. "If you're going up the East Coast, *I'm* going with you."

"You'll do what I think best," Stephen said sharply.

"In this case, I'll do what *I* think best," she flashed at him. "I am *not* going to become a widow in Hong Kong harbor."

"Stubborn," Cousin William laughed. "Thought you could handle her, Logan, but it appears you're no better than the rest of us when it comes to Julie. Never seen anyone yet who could head her in, not even when she was a young girl."

"Cousin William," Julia said indignantly. "I am *not* stubborn. It's just that I know what's best in this case."

"Didn't you always? But you've heard the old saying. When all others survive, it's the captain's wife who meets with disaster. Borne out just recently. In the typhoon last year, the *Prince George* was smashed to matchsticks. All hands survived, but the captain's wife drowned."

"That's a lot of nonsense. The poor woman probably didn't know how to swim."

"There's not that much swimming you can do in a typhoon. It's luck . . . or joss as they call it here."

"Well, I feel very lucky . . . or is it jossy? If the *Crystal Star* goes up the East Coast, I go with her, and that's final. At any rate, can't we sell the opium here?"

"It's certain you can. May not get as much for it, but it's better than losing your ship . . . and maybe your life." Cousin William rose and began to inspect the saloon's fittings. "If you do plan on going up the coast, I wouldn't spread the word around that you carry opium, though. The pirates have their contacts, plenty of them, here in Hong Kong, and they'll just be laying in wait for you if they know you're sailing with it aboard."

Stephen frowned. "I'll have to give it some thought."

"There's not much time if you want to be rid of it and ready to sail with the first tea you can get," William warned him.

"I know. However, if I do go up the coast, Julia is not going with me." When he saw her start to speak, he added, "You'll enjoy your cousin's company for a change, Julia, and I am *not* going to risk your life."

"You were risking my life when you brought me to sea," Julia lifted her chin and stared at him coldly. "Pirates can't be much worse than a typhoon."

"Much worse," Stephen said levelly. Then he turned to William. "We can talk about it once I come to a decision. Is there a good place for us to stay ashore while we're here?"

William shook his head. "Wouldn't advise it. Last year, they had malaria so bad, it wiped out a good many people on shore. Didn't seem to bother those who stayed aboard their ships at night. Something wrong with the night air on that island. There's been one plague after the other. Guess it's all right by day."

Chapter Nine

1842

That afternoon, while Stephen was ashore, Julia watched the activity in the harbor. She thought it strange that David Baxter hadn't come to pay a call on them. There were men moving about on the decks of the *Jewel*, and one towered over all others. It had to be David. Raising the spyglass to her eye, she focused upon him.

It was true. There, lounging against the rail and staring in her direction, was David Baxter. She waved to him and he briefly waved back, but then he turned away and went to speak to a man. Without looking in her direction again, he went below.

As she lowered the glass, Julia was puzzled and a little hurt. It was a deliberate snub. That wasn't like David. What could be wrong? Well, she decided, she might as well find out.

Just then, she saw the same Tanka girl who had caught her attention earlier in the day. At least, she thought it was the same girl. The wide, conical hat she wore now shaded her face, but the dusty dark blue trousers and jacket looked the same. Julia beckoned to her, and the girl, leaning heavily on her oar, swiftly sculled to the side of the *Crystal Star*. After questioning Wilson about the amount to pay for her passage, Julia went down the gangway.

"Hi-yah, missee! Wantchee go ashore?" the girl greeted her as she had that morning.

While Julia had watched the craft that spun around them, she had tried to absorb some of the Pidgin they spoke and now, as she settled herself in the rather grimy boat, she decided to try it out.

"No go ashore. Go shipee." She pointed at the *Jewel.*

The girl smiled at her, and her teeth were strong and white. "Shipee can do-ah, missee." She paused for a moment in mid-stroke and pointed to her chest. "Nien-si my."

Julia smiled back at her. "Missee Logan my."

The girl nodded and continued her vigorous rhythm on the sculling oar. "Missee Loh-gan. Wantchee go shipee, wantchee go ashore, go boat-ah my. Werry bad more boat-ah. Werry good boat-ah my."

Julia looked at the boat. Although it was quite small, there was matting arched over the center portion, forming a cabin. It must be tiny, barely large enough for this tall girl to stretch out in.

"You live boat-ah?" she asked the girl.

"All time live boat-ah," the girl agreed. Then she turned to laugh gaily at the owner of the sampan with which she had nearly collided. He was waving his fists and shouting at her in anger, but Nien-si's answer, though lengthy, seemed to be lighthearted enough. In fact, she seemed to enjoy the game of dashing up to other craft as though she were going to cut them in half, only to swerve away at the last moment. Julia wasn't sure she had chosen the safest conveyance in the harbor, but it did add an element of adventure to what might have been a rather dull ride.

As they approached the gangway, Julia called out, "Ahoy, *Jewel of the Seas.*" She paid the girl, who seemed happy enough with the fare Wilson had indicated, and without waiting for an answer from the ship, Julia mounted the gangway.

At the top, she found several sailors waiting to help her aboard. She recognized a few faces from home.

"Permission to come on board?" she said and smiled at their amazement.

"The owner always has permission to come aboard," David said in a voice that was at once soft and yet able to carry over the noise of the harbor. As he materialized out of the companionway, his shoulders seemed to fill the small opening.

He looked at Julia as he came slowly forward to greet her, and his heart plummeted for a second and then continued its regular beat. There she was with the curling wisps of black tendrils framing her forehead, the wide sapphire eyes he could never forget, smiling mischievously at him like the truant schoolgirl he had once known. The dream he had once had of seeing her here was now a reality. He had filled so many hours watching that figurehead rising above the seas, leading the way across oceans, and had longed for the girl herself, not the carved portrait that was only a constant reminder. Now she was finally on the deck of the *Jewel*. When Stephen Logan didn't follow her, he looked over the side and saw the Tanka girl in her boat.

"What are you doing riding around with Tanka girls?" The hint of a frown could only slightly diminish his broad smile. "Your first day in Hong Kong, too. Why didn't your husband order a longboat for you, and where *is* your husband?"

Julia laughed at his consternation. He didn't seem to know quite what to do with her. "He's ashore talking to Russell and Company. Said I'd only find it dull. What I did find dull was the waiting. I'm finally in China, and all I can do is look at it. I'm dying to go ashore, but Stephen said I wasn't to go alone. He didn't say anything about my going visiting, though. I've been expecting you to come see us for hours. Since you didn't, I decided to come to you. So here I am!"

He smiled at her and it was the old, easy smile of their childhood. "And the Tanka girl?"

"That was fun. Seems I've already got a friend in Hong Kong. Her name's Nien-si."

"I know what her name is," he said as he led the way aft. "She'll cheat any greenhorn she can get her hands on. How much did she charge you?"

Julia told him and he nodded. "Fair enough. She must sense a kindred spirit."

"*Kindred spirit?*" She whirled on him. "I do not go around cheating people, David Baxter!"

"I know." He grinned at her. "But you're both a little wild. I've seen Nien-si at work in the harbor, and I can remember you skinning by anything that floated in that dory of yours when you were younger."

Julia laughed. "I suppose I did." Then with a mischievous twinkle in her eyes, she added, "Still do when I get the chance."

"I don't doubt it. Well, now you're here, why don't you come below and have some tea?"

"I will." She looked around the decks. The sails were neatly furled and the rigging well coated with tar. Everything was trim and clean. "I see *you* didn't run into any trouble on the way over."

"No." He gestured for her to precede him down the companionway. "I've been concerned about you, Julie. Expected to see the *Crystal Star* long before this. Were you held up in Oahu or . . ."

"Or." She turned to face him just as she entered the doorway to the saloon. "If you were all that concerned, why didn't you come and see us as soon as we anchored? Cousin William did. I thought you had a few more manners than you've shown, David."

"It was the bet," he said earnestly, and now that he was no longer smiling, she could see the sun wrinkles beside his eyes. "Didn't want to greet you with my palm held out. Since I didn't know the circumstances, I thought 'twould be best to wait till I got word."

"What nonsense!" She swept into the saloon and sat down in the nearest chair. "Nobody would've thought you'd come to collect."

"Maybe." He gave orders to the steward for tea, then sat down in a chair opposite her. "What did happen to you?"

By the time Julia had told him about the typhoon and their stay in Tahiti, the steward had served the tea and disappeared.

David shook his head. "Your husband must be a master of the first cut to have come through that. When I saw her through the glass, the *Crystal Star* did seem a little worse for wear, but I'd no idea you'd encountered anything like that. Well, Julie," he said as he stretched his long legs out before him and leaned back in his chair, "you still got an appetite for the sea?"

"As long as I never have to go through that again." She stirred her tea, then looked up at him through her long black lashes. "Course, it gives me a few sea stories of my own to tell now. I won't have to follow you around, begging for them, the way I did when I was a little girl."

He looked at her for a moment, and the rim of blue around his grey-green eyes seemed to have grown darker and wider. " 'Twasn't all that long ago you were asking me to tell you a few."

"I know, David," she said softly. Glancing around the cabin, she tried to find some means to change the conversation. She saw a row of wooden figures on a shelf above the settee. Rising, she went to them and picked up a delicately carved flying fish. "Did you get these here?"

"No." David sat slouched with his legs half filling the width of the saloon and watched her every movement with a quiet concentration. "I carved them."

"You did?" She examined the dainty thing in every detail. "I didn't know you could do anything like this."

"Neither did I till I became master of the *Curlew*. Never was much of a reader, and there's not much else to do. Would you like that?" He nodded at the fish in her hand.

"I'd love it. But it's the prettiest thing you've done. I can't accept it. You should take it home to your wife."

"My wife isn't at home," he said ironically.

"Well, I mean in England. Don't you consider where she is your home . . . at least partly?"

"No. Not really."

"David, I'm sorry about your child, but you shouldn't blame Cynthia. It's not her fault. No woman wants to lose her child."

"She *says* she lost it." There was a note of bitterness in his voice which just was not like David at all. Julia looked at him closely, and she could see that beneath the dark blond curls, his face, which had always been so open and easygoing, had new lines of pain.

"Don't you believe her, David?"

"No." He was staring at her intently. "I don't believe there ever was going to be a child."

"David, don't be bitter. You've told me what a lovely girl she is. And she's your wife."

"I didn't lose a child, Julia." His triangular eyes never left her face while he spoke. "I lost you."

"Oh, no, David." She clutched the flying fish and she could feel the sharp angles of the figure digging into her hand. "You never had me. It's true I love you, but not that way. Never that way. It's just as I've always loved you. As a brother, as a dear friend." Liar, she added to herself.

He straightened up a little, pulled his teacup to him and looked into it. Then he took a sip and was surprised to find that it was cold. "I saw a strange sight in the Atlantic . . . somewhere near the equator," he said. "One of my men fished it out."

"Oh?" Julia returned to her seat and put the flying fish carefully on the table in front of her. "What was it?"

"Looked like one of your curls bound in blue ribbon."

"Did you keep it, David?"

"No. I thought you must have a reason. I threw it back."

"I'm glad you did. It wasn't meant for you."

"Who was it for?"

"Neptune." She tried to make her smile light and gay. "Who else?"

"Your one true love."

"No, David." She couldn't continue to smile. "My husband is my one true love."

"Well, that's as it should be." He straightened up briskly. "Would you care for more tea?"

"No. I'd best be getting back to the *Crystal Star*." She couldn't remember ever having felt so uncomfortable with David, not even when he had been encouraging her to sail aboard the *Jewel* with him a couple of years ago. Was it such a short time?

"I'll have a longboat lowered for you."

"Don't bother." She pushed back her chair and rose from the table. "I'd rather go with Nien-si. She's probably not far."

"Julie." He rose and blocked her way. "It's not safe to go wandering around by yourself. You're not in Cape Cod Bay nor in Boston Harbor, neither, for that matter. There are very real dangers all around us . . . even if you won't acknowledge them."

"Oh," she shrugged. "I'm not worried about Nien-si. She looks strong enough to take care of herself and me, too. I think she and I are going to be real friends."

"You just don't understand China, Julia." For once David sounded impatient. "Nien-si may be your friend, but she's bound to have greater loyalties elsewhere. If they force her to choose, she'll side with them. Else life could be too dangerous for her. I'll take you back to your ship."

Just as they were coming out of the companionway into the golden sunlight of late afternoon, they heard a hail.

"Ahoy, *Jewel of the Seas!*" It was Stephen and he didn't sound very happy.

Nor did he appear to be happy as he came up the gangway. Ignoring Julia, he looked directly at David. "Permission to come aboard?" he asked coldly.

"Of course, Captain Logan." David had his hand held out in greeting even before Stephen had stepped on deck. "I'm delighted to see you. Julia and I were just having a cup of tea and talking over old times."

"My mate told me she had come here," he said as he shook hands with David. "Could we go below, Captain Baxter, and settle our wager?"

"Of course, of course. As I recollect I owe you ten dollars and a hat. Will you join me in a cup of tea or perhaps a glass of brandy?"

Stephen nodded and pushed aft. Julia looked at David for a moment. He raised his eyebrows in question. All that she could do was shrug and follow her husband.

As soon as they arrived below, Stephen went directly to the table and began pulling money out of his pocket. He counted out ten one-dollar bills. "The difference between our wager for the Horn and the one for Hong Kong. The hat will have to come later," he said curtly as he laid the last bill with great deliberation on top of the pile.

"There's no rush." David brought a decanter of brandy and glasses to the table. "We've yet to figure it up. The wager exempted time spent in port."

Julia sat down. She didn't know what was going to happen between the two men. It appeared that neither one of them was in a particularly pleasant mood, though David tried to act the part, and she didn't feel like standing through it. She suddenly felt very tired and wished that she was safe in her cabin on board the *Crystal Star*. Why did men have to make such a pother of things? Would Jason have been the same if he'd lived? If he hadn't insisted upon making that short but disastrous second voyage after they were married?

She looked around the saloon. This was the room she had planned with such care for it was to have been their home, Jason's and hers. But Jason had never lived to see it. The ship swung as the tide turned and sunlight came streaming through the aft windows. It had the mellowness of things past, and just as Jason was in the past, so it seemed was this moment. The two men, herself, the rich paneling, the crystal decanter, the cries of the Chinese boatmen, all captured in an unending moment in the spiderweb of time.

"I don't believe it's in much doubt." Stephen shattered the moment and life went on. "Time in port means time necessary to unload and ship cargo. Much of our time was spent in repairs."

"Not my definition at all." David raised his glass and drank. "Time in port means time not spent at sea. In view of the typhoon, I think we ought to call off the second half of our wager altogether. It wasn't a fair race."

"Typhoons are part of the vagaries of sailing the Pacific. Our risk was equal. The wager stands."

"Why not let it stand on the homeward voyage? We can settle in Boston . . . or on the Cape as you wish."

Stephen picked up the money and looked at it thoughtfully. Then he flung it back on the table. "Take it and be damned, Captain Baxter. Come on, Julia, I want to talk to you . . . aboard the *Crystal Star*." He grabbed her hand and pulled her up from the chair.

David followed them to the gangway, but in view of Logan's cold anger, there seemed nothing more that he could say. With his hands in his pockets, he watched them pull away. Thoughtfully he followed the progress of their longboat until they had boarded the *Crystal Star*.

When he returned to the saloon, he saw the flying fish lying on the table where Julia had left it. He picked it up and stroked it with fingers that looked too large and clumsy to have fashioned such a delicate thing. Then he carefully put it back with the rest of his collection.

Once Julia and Stephen were in the saloon of their own ship again, she could see that his earlier anger had been light compared to the fury that now showed in his face. His eyes had the greyness of early morning light on a flat clouded sea, and the muscles in his jaw were hard and tense.

"Well? What do you have to say for yourself?"

"What do you mean what do *I* have to say for *myself*?" She pushed the wisps of hair back from her face as she readied herself for battle. "*I* didn't come stalking onto someone else's boat, throwing my money in their faces. *I* didn't absolutely ignore my wife when she was someone else's guest."

"You had no right to go aboard that ship without me, without a chaperone of any sort."

"And what do you think was happening, Stephen?" She squared her shoulders and drew herself up to her full height. "Do you take me for one of your laundry girls? David Baxter is an old and respected friend of my family, and he's master of *my* ship, as you seem to enjoy reminding me. There's absolutely no difference in my going to pay a call on him than there would be if I called on Cousin William."

"No difference except twenty years or so," he said between his teeth, "and I've never heard you mention that Baxter was a relative. When I went ashore, I told you to stay on board. The minute my back was turned, you were wandering around the harbor with some strange Tanka woman. Not the best company in the world. God knows what kind of trouble you could have gotten into."

"You did *not* tell me to stay aboard. You told me not to go ashore, and I didn't. Furthermore, you're the one who told me the Tanka women were the local transportation system. You said absolutely nothing about them being dangerous. I've seen all sorts of people being ferried about by them, including a couple of women."

"Chinese women."

"No. White women."

"Then the husbands of those women are damn fools."

"Be that as it may, Stephen, I am *not* going to sit on this ship as though I was a prisoner the whole time we're in China." She lifted her chin and looked through her lashes at him. Then she picked up her skirts and walked airily to the window, from which she could watch the seething water life below.

He followed her and whirled her around by the shoulders to face him. "You'll do as I say. You seem to be forgetting that I'm captain of this ship and your husband as well."

"If you think it's so dangerous," she said as she shook his hand away from her shoulder, "you'll arrange some transportation for me and an escort as well."

"*You're* giving orders aboard now?"

"I'm not giving orders. I'm simply telling you what you will do. I did not sail halfway around the world, endure loneliness and typhoons, just to view China from the decks of a ship."

"You'll see China, but I had business ashore today. Despite what you may think, we did not make this trip for your pleasure. We came to do business and make money. That is the first consideration. Whatever time we can spare from that can be spent in

190

exploring the local color, but we will *not* sacrifice profit to your curiosity."

Julia glared at him, then saw that the worst of his anger seemed to have expended itself. She turned back to look out the window. "What did you find out ashore?" Her voice was cold but not cutting.

"We're moving in to the jetty to begin unloading part of our cargo tomorrow. Unless the goods were badly damaged during the voyage, we should make a reasonable profit."

"Only *part* of our cargo?" She whipped around to look at him. He had gone to the liquor chest and was fiddling with the square-bottomed decanters.

"Yes. There's the possibility that some prices will rise during the next few days, and I need to keep it aboard for ballast when we go up the coast to sell the opium."

She leaned back against the windowframe and watched him. "You're not really going to sell it yourself?"

"Damn right I am. I intend to make every penny I can."

"Even at the expense of your life?" she asked dryly. Then when he cocked an eyebrow at her and she noticed that the wayward lock of hair had fallen over his forehead, he became inexpressibly dear to her. She *couldn't* lose him. Going to him, she laid a hand on his sleeve. "Oh, Stephen, please don't do it. I really don't think I could bear the waiting and wondering."

The smile he gave her was very tight. "You won't have to wait and wonder. You're coming with me."

"But you said . . ."

"That was this morning. Your escapade this afternoon has made me change my mind. If I were to leave you alone with Will Thacher, you'd be looking for trouble the minute I sailed. He admits *he* can't control you. You'll be safer where I can keep an eye on you, even if we do run into pirates." And safer from David Baxter, too, he thought.

Early the next morning when the mist was still rising from the water and the peaks of Hong Kong were veiled in haze left over from dawn, two large sampans appeared. Each had a single tattered fore-and-aft sail, whose patches ranged from a rusty red to a pink-tinged white. While one man aboard each boat used a long oar for a rudder, the women and children squatted on the decks and ate their breakfast. It was fascinating to watch them agilely dip their chopsticks in and out of the wooden bowls they held cupped in their hands. One round-faced little girl gave the remainder of the food from her bowl to a family of pigs that were penned just forward of the cabin.

Julia wondered how the entire family could sleep in that small shelter formed by thin rattan mats laid over arches of bamboo. They did look warm, though, she thought. Their black jackets were torn and dirty, but they were well-padded against the early morning chill.

By the time the sampans had come alongside the *Crystal Star,* all eating utensils had disappeared into the cabins, and aside from the infants who were hung on their mothers' backs, each person aboard was ready to cast lines and receive them from the ship. Though everything was done amidst a sing-song shouting, it was done efficiently, and as soon as the anchor was up, the sampans were towing the *Crystal Star* towards Hong Kong.

As they approached the island, Julia watched it grow larger. It was incredible that the busy port, which had been sparsely settled by a few fishermen and pirates until the British had raised their flag on Possession Point on January 26, 1841, could now be the focus of such teeming activity. Not only was the harbor filled with vessels of every description, but on the narrow stretch of land between the water and the steep mountains, she could see hundreds of houses, a stone barracks, warehouses, wharves, and jetties. Despite plagues and typhoons, the British had dug themselves into Hong Kong with a determined tenacity. They had found the greatest known offshore harbor in the Orient, and they intended to keep it.

She wrinkled her nose as they drew closer to land. Not only were the signs of civilization here. The smells were, too. After months spent at sea, the odor of garbage mixed with spices and the sickly sweet smell of opium assaulted her senses. She decided that she would have to take a perfumed handkerchief with her when she went ashore.

By the time they reached the stone wharf in front of Russell and Company's factory, as the warehouse was called, Queen's Road was bustling with activity. There were English, Portuguese and Americans in their wool frock coats, trousers, and tall top hats.

Occasionally she saw a white woman in a full-skirted, slightly bustled dress. Julia was glad that, amongst the dresses she'd had made in Boston, she had bowed to the latest fashion and had ordered a few with the bustle, which she thought was ridiculous, and had added twenty new petticoats to her wardrobe.

Then there were the Chinese. She had heard people say that they looked alike, but they didn't to her. They ranged in height from men as tall as Cousin William to women as tiny and dainty as dolls. Some had skin as white as alabaster, some as dark as walnut, and in between there seemed to be every shade of brown and yellow imaginable.

And the clothes they wore! She caught occasional glimpses of men in long silk robes with carefully tended queues down their backs and women in embroidered silk tunics and trousers, whose hair styles ranged from elaborate coiffures to free-swinging falls bound up in back by a piece of embroidered cloth. For the most part, however, the people were shabbily dressed in clothes like the sampan people or in rags. There were beggars with outstretched hands and hawkers with baskets slung on poles they carried across their shoulders.

Yet beggars or merchants, Europeans or Chinese, they all seemed to be buoyed with optimism. The air was as filled with it as it was with the sounds of the thousands of hammers and axes that rang out from new buildings that were surrounded by bamboo scaffoldings. Though the Tanka people had lived here for centuries to be followed by the Hokla and the Hakka, it was filled with the newness of opportunity, of fortunes to be made. Hong Kong. Fragrant Harbor. The first free port of China.

Once ashore, Stephen guided Julia to the enormous three-story stone building that was the factory. Even in the few steps it took to reach it, they were surrounded by beggars of all ages, some with festering sores, some with horrible mutilations. As Stephen rushed her through the crowd, she could see missing arms, legs, and eyes conspicuously displayed by their owners, and she was torn between the desire to help them and revulsion at the sight of them.

"Come on, Julie," Stephen said as he pulled her up the steps of the factory. "Don't waste time or pity on them. They bring it on themselves."

"What do you mean?"

"I mean they purposely mutilate themselves . . . or their parents do . . . so that they can make a living begging."

"How could anyone do that!" She felt dirtied by the people who had pressed around her and was glad to reach the sanctuary of the portico.

"As I said, to make a living."

One of the huge teak doors, which was carved in a complex design of dragons, eagles, flowers, and ships, swung open, and a fair-skinned Chinese man dressed in a long blue cotton robe stood bowing and smiling before them.

"Masser. Missee," he greeted them. "Wantchee see Cap'n Lloyd-ah?"

"Wantchee see Cap'n Lloyd-ah chop chop, savvy?" Stephen said as he handed his felt top hat to the servant.

"Come-ah chop chop, never mind." After a few more bows, the man scurried through a doorway to their left.

Julia looked around at the Indian rugs that covered the polished stone floors and at the marble walls that bore a few intricately woven tapestries. On each side of the front doors, there was an enormous blue and white porcelain jardiniere, half as tall as Julia. Furniture of carved teak painted black was placed at pleasing intervals, and on an occasional table there was a solitary enameled bowl or an exquisite ivory carving. The building couldn't be over a year old, and yet it had the solidity of long tradition.

"Stephen, I can't believe this! I'd always heard the factories in Canton were large, but I never realized that anything could be this grand. How many rooms does it have?"

He smiled at the almost childlike wonder in her eyes as she looked around the room. "If it's anything like the American factory in Canton, I would say hundreds. Beyond this, there are probably courtyards surrounded by counting rooms, offices, and storerooms. The living quarters will be on the next two floors. I'm surprised they felt the need to build anything this large in Hong Kong, though. In Canton, everyone . . . a hundred Chinese servants, half that number of Portuguese clerks, a few Americans, and a handful of visitors . . . had to live in the one building. There was no other place for them. But here, where they can build, I would think most would prefer to live in their own homes."

A door to their left opened and the man who came through was tall and thin to the point of emaciation. His shoulders stooped forward under his green wool frock coat, and there was the seaman's cap line on his forehead, which the sun had imprinted and time could never erase. His dark hair was thinning on top, but he made up for it with a beard that came just below his chin while leaving his slightly yellow face clean-shaven.

"I'm sorry if I kept you waiting," Mitchell Lloyd said as he approached them. "We're still in a bit of confusion what with all the construction going on."

"Not at all." Stephen inclined his head in a slight bow. "Julia, may I present Captain Lloyd? My wife, Mrs. Logan."

"I'm very pleased to meet you, ma'am. Perhaps you would be more comfortable upstairs while Captain Logan and I conduct our business." He gestured at the marble stairs that swept upward in two directions. "There's another lady, Mrs. Kirkwood, and two of her children waiting while Captain Kirkwood is occupied. Then you'll dine with us, of course?"

"Thank you," Julia said, but she felt disappointed. She had wanted to see how business was done in China.

The parlor in the suite upstairs was luxurious, however, and Mrs. Kirkwood herself was an experience. Small and bright-eyed with grey hair that had once been red and skin that had seen too much of sea, salt, and the Orient, Mary Kirkwood was a fund of information and very fond of imparting it.

"Come sit down beside me, dearie, and let's get acquainted, seeing as how we probably have a few hours to be friends." She patted the embroidered silk of the sofa. "Now, Nance, you watch Hamilton for a while. Don't let him fall out of that window," she addressed a girl in her middle teens, whose strawberry hair fell down to her shoulders in ringlets.

"Yes, Mum," Nance said and went to hold her small brother by the jacket as he leaned out of the wide-silled window to watch the activity on the road and wharves below.

"Children can be a problem out here, especially boys," Mary Kirkwood said to Julia. "His amah's gone home to visit her family on the mainland. I couldn't make out whether it's a matter of sickness or death, but off she went. Heaven knows when she'll get back."

"You sound as though you'd been here a while." Julia was amused by the sparkling briskness of the older woman. Her brown eyes danced behind her steel-rimmed spectacles, and she looked as though she would be at home anywhere in the world.

"Land, yes. Fifteen years now." Mrs. Kirkwood picked up her needlepoint and took a stitch. "Captain made one voyage without me after we were married, but I said, if he was going to the Indies, then so was I. England was no place for me without him."

"But you can't have been in Hong Kong very long," Julia said as she watched an older Chinese man set a carved red lacquer tray of cookies with a cup and pot of tea on a nearby table.

"Aye. From the beginning. First we had to live aboard ship in the harbor, but soon as we could we built a snug little house in Happy Valley. I liked that house, I did, but the air there was no good. Hamilton! That's enough cookies. You'll spoil your dinner. Now go look out the window so you can tell me if anything exciting happens." She watched for a moment until her son had left the table with the cookies and had returned to his post at the window. Then she returned to her needlepoint. "As I was saying, the air in Happy Valley was no good. I lost a little girl, midway between Nance and Hamilton, to malaria, and I said to Captain, 'We're going back on board ship. I'm not risking any more of my children's lives to the plague.' "

"Would you like some tea?" Julia interrupted, even though she felt that it was the older woman's place to make the offer. Still she didn't think that Mary Kirkwood would stop talking long enough to do so.

"Yes, dearie, that I would. Nance, you pour some tea for yourself and Hamilton after Mrs. Logan has finished. Don't drink the water out here, dearie. That nice Mr. Lloyd did and look at him. It does something to your guts. Well, as I was saying, we abandoned that house in Happy Valley and built another just like it in Queen's Town. Night air's better there. Guess we built in too much of a hurry, though. A typhoon come along last summer and blew it down. Lucky we had a cellar so we didn't get blown away along with the house."

"What an awful time you've had," Julia said as she handed a cup of tea to Mrs. Kirkwood. "Are you living in the factory now?"

"Oh, no. We just come to meet you and have dinner with you and your husband after the men finish doing business. We've rebuilt the house and we're settled, least when we're ashore we are, and after all these years the *White Hawk's* just like home to me when we're afloat. I won't let Captain leave us behind when he makes the run to India for the opium, though, I won't."

"You've had to build three houses in less than two years, and yet you seem to like Hong Kong," Julia said in amazement.

"That I do," Mary Kirkwood said emphatically. "Better than Macao by a long shot. Didn't see as much of Captain then as I like. They didn't allow white women in the settlement at Canton, and when he went up to the factory there, that's where he'd have to leave us. Macao. It's a nice settled place and the Portuguese are nice people, too, but it was lonely when all the men went up to Canton for six months at a time. I'm glad to be on British soil again, too. Though it took us long enough to make it British."

"Then you've been here all through the Opium Wars?"

"Been through them and lived through them. Nance! Watch Hamilton," she said as her son's feet left the ground. He did look as though he were going to crawl right through the window. "Can't say I liked the wars, though. May not even be over yet, but we'll hold on. The Chinese may think they're the mightiest nation on earth. They call China the Middle Kingdom because they think it's the center of the earth, but they have no idea what the rest of the world is like. Course, we don't know what China is like, either. Haven't been many white men allowed in beyond the settlement in Canton. Just a small strip of land between the Pearl River and the walls of the city. Once in a while, a sailor used to try to sneak in, but it's a rare one who ever made it out alive to tell the tale. Used to come out in pieces, though, all cut up. It's enough to make your blood run cold to hear tell about it."

"Now there are to be five free ports," Julia said thoughtfully as she looked out the open window at the mainland. "I wonder if they'll let white women visit them."

"Who knows the ways of the heathen Chinese?" Mrs. Kirkwood shrugged. "They say one thing and do another. It's not going to be their way much longer, though. I can tell you that. Not while the British Navy is here to back up our words with guns."

Chapter Ten

1842

Dinner was served in a long dining room, where fires were lit in the large marble fireplaces at each end of the room. There were scrolls upon the walls as well as paintings of ships in the harbor of Hong Kong, and carved teak screens stood in front of the tall windows. A few thick pastel rugs lay upon the black lacquered floor. Besides the Kirkwoods and Julia, fifteen American men sat down at the damask-covered table. They included visiting captains as well as members of the firm itself.

After a sumptuous meal of smoked salmon, fresh fish, and roast lamb that was served with pickled carrots and cabbage, boiled potatoes, and fresh fruit, Julia found herself restless and longed to escape the hot stuffiness of the room and the sound of too many voices. She realized that, aboard ship, she had become accustomed to fresh air and solitude. When Stephen suggested that they take a stroll along Queen's Road, she accepted immediately.

They paused in the portico to watch crates being swung out of the hatches of the *Crystal Star* under Mister Wilson's direction, and then they plunged into the street that, though wide, seemed too narrow for the rickshaws, sedan chairs, and seething life that filled it. Although the beggars were still noticeable amongst the crowd, none approached them.

"What did you do, Stephen?" she asked as she lifted a scented handkerchief to her nose. "Threaten to turn your guns on the beggars?"

"No." He took her arm and held her close beside him as they began to walk up the road. "Captain Lloyd arranged for me to make a payment to the King of Beggars so they'd leave us alone."

"The King of Beggars! Oh, no! I don't believe it." She picked her way carefully along the rough rock surface of the road.

"It's true. They have their own guild, and my payment will be distributed amongst them." He paused to let a pair of rickshaws hurry by and grinned at her. "Paid off the King of Thieves, too."

"You didn't!"

"I did."

"So now we won't be robbed, I suppose," she said dryly.

"At least not by professionals, though there are amateurs arriving by the boatload from the mainland every day."

"What about the King of Pirates, then? Can't we pay him off, too, so he'll leave us alone when we go up the coast?"

"No." He frowned. "That isn't done. A lot of them *are* organized, but not all. The only payment they understand is gunfire."

"Stephen, I wish you wouldn't insist on going up the coast. Mrs. Kirkwood says her husband does it, but he has an opium clipper. I think somehow the English are better at opium smuggling than we are. Americans have never practiced it on a very large scale, and we just don't have the skill. I feel nervy about this whole venture."

"Your crystal ball again, my lady?" He repressed a smile.

"No. There is something wrong, though. I can just feel it."

"I wouldn't worry. It's the very fact that Americans haven't done much smuggling of opium that gives us a factor of safety. After all, *we* weren't involved in the Opium War. While they barred other nations from Canton, Russell and Company was allowed to keep its factory open."

"Still . . ."

"The pirates aren't going to suspect us, Julie. At any rate, Captain Lloyd has arranged for a man to go with us to guide us to a rendezvous. There's a certain island up the coast where we can make contact." He stopped in front of a walled house and lowered his voice. "You didn't mention our plans to Mrs. Kirkwood, I hope."

"No, of course I didn't. She was just telling me how trade was carried out here. Anyway, what would have been the harm if I had? She's a good soul."

"A good soul that doesn't know when to stop talking. Don't trust anyone out here, Julia. Someone is always listening."

"Behind that wall?" She raised an eyebrow and nodded at the house.

He narrowed his eyes as he looked at the stone wall. "There could be. Look, there's an ivory carver's shop. You'll be interested in that."

And though she *was* interested in watching the men who sat in the open-fronted shack that was made partly from mud and partly from boards, she found it hard to dismiss the trip up the coast. She did, however, try to concentrate on the deft hands that chipped and smoothed the ivory into the most delicate and intricate statues and landscapes. After all, this was one of the things she had come so far to see.

The sound of giggles and the words *"fan kwae"* made Julia turn to see a black lacquered sedan chair, whose red silk curtains were parted slightly by a small jeweled hand. She had just a moment to glimpse the blur of a small white face and black eyes before the curtain was pulled shut. The eight coolies who carried the sedan chair immediately began to trot forward.

"What was that all about?" she asked Stephen, who was watching the sedan chair speculatively.

"Curiosity. Probably a couple of concubines, maybe even wives. The sort of women you won't see on the streets. You've probably given them enough to gossip about for days. Hong Kong's come a long way if the richer Chinese have brought their families over."

"But concubines aren't really family, are they?"

"They most certainly are. They may not have the prestige of the first wife, but legally they are part of the family until they die. If the first wife doesn't produce a son, then one of theirs could become the next ruler of the family." He nodded at the ivories displayed in the shop. "Do you see anything you fancy?"

"Everything." She smiled at him. "I don't want to make a choice today. I just want to *see*."

"Then perhaps we'll find something to see up here." He turned into a dusty, unpaved lane that twisted between fine houses with red tile roofs and open-fronted shops, where tradesmen squatted behind wares that were often spread upon a piece of cloth. There was soapstone, incense, ginseng and herbs, tobacco, dried and fresh vegetables, and delicacies that drew flies.

Finally, when they had lost sight of Queen's Road, Stephen stopped in front of an open-air shop that seemed more prosperous than many. There were five men kneeling in front of small flat stones. One held a slender bamboo stick, which he whirled with incredible speed between his palms. Another rapidly moved a small bow back and forth so that its string spun a thin metal rod so fast it didn't appear to be moving at all. The other three each concentrated upon something they appeared to be rubbing with a paste.

The man with the bow paused and looked up when Julia and Stephen stopped in front of the shop. Laying down his bow and metal rod with meticulous care, he bowed low to them and then silently got up and went to the rear of the shop. He returned with a white silk cloth which he laid out on a thin wooden board. Upon this, he laid one by one the jades he lifted from the shelves of a square wooden box.

The colors of the jade ranged from the purest white to the darkest, murky green, but it was the clear, almost translucent bluish greens that caught Julia's eye. She lightly stroked one smooth stone and found it cool and hard to her touch.

The shopman smiled and nodded approval. Then he searched through his chest once more. Pushing some of the lesser stones aside, he laid a bracelet in the center of the cloth. Julia caught her breath when she saw it and her hand reached for it even before the wish had formulated in her mind. She held it up against her wrist in the sunlight, and she could see that each intricately wrought panel displayed a Chinese god. The figures and their backgrounds were sculpted in relief, but the lines within their faces, the folds of their clothing, the outlines of hills and trees were accented by the markings that lay within the stones themselves. As she turned her wrist, it became obvious that the entire bracelet had been cut from a single piece of jade for the circular links that held the panels together were from the same stone.

While she admired it, she was aware that Stephen was dickering with the shopman, but she was too entranced with the jade to really listen. She knew that it was too expensive. It was the most exquisite work in jade she had ever seen.

"Well, Julia, it's yours if you want it," Stephen said.

"How much?"

"Never ask the cost of a gift."

"I can't accept it, Stephen." Reluctantly she laid the bracelet back upon the white silk. "We'll come back another day and find something else."

"If you want it, I want you to have it." Below his top hat, his grey eyes were touched with the blue of tenderness. "I never did give you a proper wedding gift. I wanted to wait until we were in China so that I could find something very special. We're here now."

She looked at him, then back at the bracelet. She had never wanted a piece of jewelry so much before. Yet if he was willing to risk so much for the profit that might be made by going up the coast, she couldn't allow him to squander it.

"Not unless you tell me how much, Stephen."

"Fifty dollars."

"Oh, no. That's too much." It was half of one month's salary for him.

"It's a bargain." He was suddenly impatient. "If you don't want it, I'll buy it anyway. I know what it will fetch in Boston."

"Yes. I'm sure you'll make a good profit on it," she agreed. Yet she would have preferred to leave it here on this side street in Hong Kong than to have it taken home where she might see another woman wearing it. That's ridiculous, she told herself as she waited for Stephen to pay the man.

"Can we go farther up this road?" she asked when he had put the parcel, carefully wrapped in rice paper, into the pocket of his frock coat. Perhaps there would be another bracelet, of neither so grand nor so beautiful a jade, that they could afford.

"I don't know where it goes. It would be better if we returned to Queen's Road. We can get a rickshaw there."

But when they reached Queen's Road, they found their way blocked by a laughing crowd that surrounded a juggler. He was tossing plates, bowls, and sticks around in the air so fast they seemed to form a solid circle. Nearby there was a man playing a flute in a high piercing song. There seemed to be no way through the close-packed throng.

"How are you enjoying Hong Kong, Mrs. Logan?" Mitchell Lloyd materialized at her elbow.

"Very much, thank you," she said politely. "How did you get through all these people?"

"Oh, it's not difficult. Just push. The Chinese are usually good-natured about it."

"And when they're not?"

"I wouldn't worry about that if I were you. All you have to do is smile at them, and they'll forgive you anything."

Stephen had been listening nonchalantly while they spoke, but now his mouth tightened. "We were just about to look for a rickshaw to take us to Tai Ping Shan."

Mitchell Lloyd stopped smiling. "I don't think it's very wise to take Mrs. Logan there," he said quietly.

"Why not? My wife wants to see China, and surely Tai Ping Shan is more like the real China than Queen's Road is."

"What are you talking about?" Julia asked.

"The native settlement," Captain Lloyd said. "We have very little control there, and since the British will not allow a mandarin to rule the Chinese here on Hong Kong, unpleasantness sometimes occurs."

"Yet you've just pointed out how good-natured the Chinese are," Stephen persisted. "I wouldn't think we would find any trouble on a sunny afternoon."

"As long as you insist, allow me to send for my own rickshaws." There were lines of worry on his emaciated face. "At least you'll be assured reliable guides who speak Pidgin." He motioned to a boy dressed in clean blue cotton, who had been standing nearby with his eye half on the juggler and half on the Americans, and he spoke to him in a low voice.

"That's very kind of you, Captain Lloyd," Julia said. "I hope we're not putting you to any trouble."

"No. None at all." He pulled out a gold watch from an inner pocket and looked at it. "You mustn't stay over an hour, though. Darkness comes with amazing swiftness here, and you should be back at the factory well before sunset."

The rickshaw boys kept an even pace with one another as they trotted first along Queen's Road and then up winding dusty lanes carved out of thin-soiled rock. Here the streets were less noisy, and Stephen had only to raise his voice a little for Julia to hear him as he pointed out the houses and ramshackle hovels, the opium dens with their adjoining gambling rooms, the apothecary shops, wine shops, and tailors. In even the meanest, most temporary huts, there would be a flowering plant in a pot or a bird singing in a bamboo cage. Children involved in the games of childhood stopped to stare at the *fan kwae* as they went by. Girls with their younger sisters or brothers hung from their backs were so small Julia wondered how they managed to bear the weight. There was the sound of gongs, cymbals, and flutes in the background, and in an occasional quiet lull, the click of Mah-Jongg tiles could be heard. And always above them were the steep mountains of Hong Kong.

So fascinated were they by the sights and sounds of the native quarter, they didn't notice that, just a little behind them, there was another rickshaw, which kept a steady pace with theirs. Although the day was sunny, the hood was raised and shadowed the occupant's face.

And there was another sight that would have distracted Julia from anything behind. She had begun to grow accustomed to the garbage heaps with dead dogs or cats lying on them, but now they passed a small building, and there were dead men and women lying on the steps.

"Stephen!" she gasped in horror.

"Don't look," he said. "It's the poor. They can't afford to bury their dead, so they leave them at a temple for the gods to look after."

"It doesn't look to me as though the gods are doing a very good job of it," she said as she tried to fight nausea.

"Well, someone will look after them . . . eventually. You'd do well to get used to seeing the dead. They're not always below ground here. When we used to go up the Pearl River, we'd see them by the dozen floating downstream."

"No one ever told me about this side of China."

"I don't suppose they would."

"Stephen, let's go back," she said as they approached an intersection.

"Feeling nervy again?"

"Yes, I am."

"Well, you wanted to see China, and . . ."

Suddenly three coolies dressed in streaked blue cotton darted out. One of them knocked down the man who was pulling Julia's rickshaw, and the other two grasped the handles and charged through the crowd, knocking people down as they went.

"Stephen!" Julia screamed once, then held onto the seat of the rickshaw as it bounced over the ruts of the road. The people along the street became a blur of startled faces, and yet no one did anything.

The sound of drums, gongs, and cymbals became louder. People were singing in high nasal tones, whether in sorrow or joy, she couldn't tell. Then at a sudden turn in the road, they ran into a procession of white-garbed people, who were carrying scarlet banners. Some were tearing at their clothes and shrieking. The procession slowed down the two pullers, and Julia saw that this was her moment. She took a deep breath and leaped over the side of the rickshaw.

Landing in the midst of spectators, they broke her fall before she hit the ground. She was slightly stunned for a moment as many hands reached out for her and helped her up. A woman was brushing the dust from her dress and muttering, "Ay-yah, missee, missee," when Stephen appeared around the bend in his rickshaw. There was another one close behind him.

Even before his rickshaw had stopped, he jumped down and pulled her away from the hands that held her. His face was strained, and the color had drained away from under his tan.

"Are you all right, Julie? What happened?"

"Yes, I think I'm all right." She was shivering, and his arm felt strong and comforting around her. Safe, she thought. "I don't know what happened. You saw as much as I did."

"Captain Logan, I'm right sorry this happened." The craggy, red face of the man who stepped out of the other rickshaw was full of embarrassed apology. One eye was covered with a patch, but the other was sky blue and abashed. His muscles bulged under the rather shabby frock coat he wore.

"You?" Stephen looked at the man in amazement. He had never seen him before.

"Yes, sir. Cap'n Lloyd sent me to look after you. Don't seem I did too good a job. Fred Gill's my name. Used to be mate for Cap'n Lloyd till they shot my leg out from under me." There was a stiffness to his gait which neither Julia nor Stephen had noticed before. Looking down, they saw the wooden leg.

"Then perhaps you can tell me what this is all about," Stephen said, angry now that he was reassured that Julia was safe.

"That's something we'll most likely never know," Fred Gill said and shrugged. "Could be they thought to kidnap Mrs. Logan and hold her for ransom. Chinese been making money that way for centuries."

"You mean someone plotted to do this? How could anyone have known we'd come here? It was a spur of the moment decision."

"Most likely so was theirs. Saw their chance and grabbed it. Could be they was just trying to scare us into staying out of Tai Ping Shan. Keep us from meddling into their wicked doings."

"Well, whatever it is, we'd do well to get back to the ship," Stephen said. "The only problem is that we're missing a rickshaw."

"Mrs. Logan can take mine," Fred Gill was saying when they saw Julia's puller dragging her rickshaw toward them. "Bad man leave-ah," the man said glumly as he stopped in front of them. "Man very, very, very bad." One side of his face was bruised and he kept his head bowed in shame.

"Did you get a good look at them, Mrs. Logan?" Fred Gill asked.

"I doubt I'd ever recognize them again. They had those hats on. Wasn't much of their faces to be seen."

"Don't matter. Even if you could remember, they'll most likely take care to stay hidden till you sail."

"I think they just disappeared into that procession . . . whatever it was."

"A funeral." Fred Gill nodded. "Good thing for you it come along."

"Yes, wasn't it," Julia agreed as she let him help her into the rickshaw. "I'm glad that at least some of them bury their dead." She nodded at her coolie. "It wasn't this man's fault. I want you to make that clear to Captain Lloyd."

"Aye. Nothing in China is nobody's fault."

When they returned to Queen's Road, Julia was glad to see that they had finished unloading for the day so that she was able to go below immediately to her cabin to bathe and change her clothes.

My, she thought as she washed her face, you can't say my first day in China hasn't been eventful. I'd be just as happy if things would settle down and stay quiet for the rest of our stay. I've had more than enough excitement for one voyage. Yet there was something in the music of the waves as they hit the hull that made her uneasy.

The next days were uneventful as they unloaded cargo and then returned to the anchorage to wait. Occasionally she saw Nien-si in the harbor and they waved to each other, but Julia traveled in the safety of a longboat as Stephen demanded. She visited the Kirkwoods and met other families who had made their home in the new colony. It was only a temporary home, they all agreed. As soon as their futures were assured, they planned to return to their real homes, whether they lay in America or in England. They seemed content, however. Only a few spoke of leaving their husbands and returning to their native land alone or with their children.

Stephen often took her on the shopping expeditions he made to round out the cargo that would be primarily tea and silk. He was interested in the occasional finds he would make of rare porcelain bowls and jars, bronze trays, sandalwood fans, wooden and ivory carvings, as well as jewelry of jade, rubies, and pearls set in gold and silver. He spent most of his time, however, at the factories and their warehouses, where he selected sets of china and other items from the stores of the China traders.

Then one late afternoon, he came aboard and told Julia they would sail that night. Shortly after sunset, he sent a longboat ashore and when it returned, Fred Gill was in it. The sailors, who had been instructed with fierce threats by Mister Wilson, made sail and weighed anchor in near silence. All lights on board were extinguished, and the moon rose red and full to guide them as they entered the channel between the island and the mainland.

Standing by the taffrail in order to be out of the way of the men on the quarterdeck, Julia watched the moon to starboard and the land to port. Kowloon, she thought. Kowloon, China, which I may see but never enter, and the red of the moon seemed to spill blood on the land. She shivered and clutched her shawl more closely around her shoulders.

The water was fully lit by the moon, but in its rising it cast strange shadows from the rock islands that littered the sea. It altered all perspective and more than once she caught her breath as they slid by an almost submerged rock that was seen only as it appeared in their wake. The sampans and fishing junks, some lit by paper lanterns, rocked on the calm night sea. All was quiet except for the hiss of the bow wave and the flutter of a sail that had momentarily lost the breeze.

It was a long night, and though Stephen urged her to go below to sleep, Julia could not, for the tension on board pervaded even the empty main cabin. She felt safer out in the open with her rifle on the deck beside her, and she thought of the open gun ports and behind them the cold cannon which could so quickly become hot.

She watched the men, Stephen, Fred Gill and the helmsman, whose faces were colorless, almost expressionless, in the cold white light. The sailors on the main deck and in the ratlines were shadows without shadows.

The sky in the east was just beginning to show the palest of greys when Fred Gill pointed to a tall rock island that rose from the sea to twice the height of their masts. "That's it," he said. "There's a cove on the other side where they'll be waiting."

Stephen nodded and gave Wilson quiet orders to change course.

When they rounded the far side of the island, there was an enormous junk, with eyes painted on its bows, waiting for them. Julia sighed with relief. Soon, soon, they would be rid of the opium.

"Steer away! Steer away!" Fred Gill in his panic snatched the wheel from the helmsman's hands and swiftly turned it.

Stephen, without waiting for an explanation, called out the orders that sent some men running to tack the sails and others below to their battle stations. With the keys in his hand, Mister Wilson ran below to open the locker that held the muskets and rifles.

The junk had been waiting for them, however, and even before the last man had taken his weapon up into the ratlines, they had begun the chase.

"It was a sampan supposed to meet us," Fred Gill said as he relinquished the wheel to the helmsman.

Stephen nodded. Then he noticed that Julia was still on deck. "Go below, get your pistols, and stay there. Bolt the door," he ordered her sharply.

She wanted to rebel, but the urgency of his voice left no room for argument. Without a word, she scooped up her rifle and went swiftly below. She had just dropped the bar on the door when there was a loud boom, and the ship shivered. The *Crystal Star* had fired her first shot.

After that, the noise came without ceasing. She sat with the pistols on her lap, the rifle propped against her chair, and her hands to her ears. When there was a loud crash forward, however, she took them away and started up. The *Crystal Star* had been hit. Her ship! Where? How much damage? She put the pistols carefully on the table and began to pace the cabin floor. How *could* she stay below?

She looked out the stern windows and could see no sign of the junk. That meant it was alongside. Then the ship shuddered in a long agonized shriek, and she could hear men yelling in high screams. It wasn't human. It sounded as though banshees had come rising out of hell. There was nothing for it. She *couldn't* stay below. Not now. Everyone would be needed if they were to save the ship.

She grabbed her weapons and unbarred the door. While still standing on the steps, she peered out of the companionway. The deck was a tangle of lines and sails. And men! Two were lying like broken dolls. They couldn't be! They couldn't be! Worst of all were the filthy, black-garbed men who poured over the port side of the *Crystal Star*. The shrieks they made as they came were unbelievable, unbearable.

A great cold anger swept through Julia. It left no room for fear. Her hand was calm and steady, and with one small part of her mind, she wondered at the coldness that was within her as she loaded and fired. None of the pirates seemed to notice her in the shadow of the companionway so intent were they on the men on deck.

When no more seemed to be coming from the junk, whose grappling irons still held her fast to the *Crystal Star*, Stephen jumped down from the quarterdeck, where he and his men had dispatched all who approached it. With his ammunition gone, he had appropriated the fighting iron from one of the pirates, and swinging the cruel long links and ball above his head, he aimed at a tall thin Chinese, who came at him with a knife. He had just smashed the man to the deck when someone cried hoarsely, "Sail ho!"

Then they saw what they had been too occupied to notice

before. Bearing down on them was a steamship, its paddle wheels beating the water to a froth and black smoke pouring from her funnel. In the distance were two full-rigged ships with all sails set and straining in the morning breeze.

Stephen, as he glanced up to see the ships, saw Julia, too. "Damn it! Get below!" he shouted.

His attention was too much on her, and he didn't notice the man coming up behind him with a sword, but Julia saw him. Raising her gun, she aimed and fired at the pirate. When he fell to the deck, Julia smiled sweetly at her husband. "In a minute, Stephen."

As she loaded her gun, she continued to smile. Now the coldness was underlaid with exhilaration. There was no need to take another shot, however, for the pirates, now realizing that the steamship *Nemesis* was headed in their direction, scrambled over the side to the junk and loosed the few grappling irons that still held the vessels together.

The junk had sustained too much damage, however, and the men aboard the *Crystal Star* were just beginning to care for their fallen comrades when the *Nemesis* overhauled the junk. After a heavy bombardment of shells and rockets from the steamship, the native vessel caught fire. Then there was a great explosion. Flame and smoke shot up into the sky, and the screams of the pirates were only faintly heard over the roar of the fire.

"Damn it, Julia," Stephen said from beside her as she watched the charred remnants of the junk sink into the sea. "When I tell you to stay below, you'll damned well stay below from now on."

"I didn't really come on deck." The exhilaration was ebbing and there was only a bone-tiredness to replace it as she looked around at the blood-stained sails, the dead men, and the wounded. "I was in the companionway."

"But you weren't safe behind a barred door," he said grimly. "How long were you there?"

"I don't know. A while." Then she added in a flash of anger, "I'm not completely useless, Stephen. I'm not one of your sweet Boston girls and you damn well know it . . . and did before you married me. You're the one who taught me how to use those weapons. If you didn't mean for me to use them, why did you bother?"

"For *self*-protection," he said between his teeth.

"Which is exactly what I used them for. If those creatures had gotten below, a bar on a door wasn't going to stop them." The anger died and she was even more tired than before. "How much damage to the hull?"

"One hole well above the waterline. We put more into them," he said and nodded at the water now littered with debris, "but the damn things won't sink. Mister Wilson," he called to the mate, "have the wounded brought to the main cabin."

"Can I help?" Julia asked.

"Yes. That is *one* thing you may do . . . if you've the stomach for it."

"I have the stomach for it." The smudges under her eyes made them seem a deeper indigo than ever, but the look she gave him was cool and steady.

The long table in the saloon was turned into an operating table, where Stephen and Mister Wilson tried to staunch major wounds and remove the bullets that had lodged in flesh while Julia and Fred Gill inspected and cleansed the lesser damage of men only lightly grazed. When she heard the screams of the men and realized how many of them were only boys, a great sadness swept through her. All for the sake of profit? But that was the way of the sea, she told herself sternly, and the way of trade. Besides, although there were several seriously injured, none that she knew of had died. That reminded her of the pirate dead lying on the decks, and she realized how bravely and how well these boys had fought. Still . . .

"I thought everything was arranged," she said to Fred Gill as she poured brandy on a flesh wound on a boy's leg. "I thought there wasn't supposed to be any danger."

"I don't know." He shook his craggy head, but she couldn't see his good eye. In profile, only his eye patch showed. "I don't know, ma'am. All's I can say is *supposed* to be safe is the closest we can come to a guarantee out here. Someone we trusted betrayed us. That's all I can say."

"But Captain Logan said that all your contacts were with men you'd used and trusted before."

"They were. Somebody loyal to us yesterday wasn't loyal today." He poured a glass of rum and handed it to a blond boy who had been only lightly cut on one arm, but who was shaking and staring about him in bewilderment. "Here, lad, drink up. Then get back to your duties."

They were so absorbed in the wounded that they weren't aware they had been boarded until two men stood in the doorway. One was a British naval officer, resplendent in the gold that adorned his blue uniform. The other wore a pale blue frock coat cut in the latest fashion. His shirt, vest, and cravat, however, seemed more severe and plain.

"Captain Logan?" the naval officer said.

"Yes?" Stephen looked up impatiently. "I thank you, sir, for your assistance, but can't the formalities wait? As you can see, I'm busy just now." He bent anxiously once again over the man on the table.

"I think we can help you. This is Doctor Mansfield. Perhaps he could take charge for you for a while."

"Well, thank God for that." Stephen left his patient and held out his hand to the officer. Only when the man did not take it did Stephen look down and realize that his hand was streaked with blood. "The medicine chest is over there," he said to the doctor. "Bandages there. We have quite a few wounded. I don't know how seriously. That man," he nodded at the sailor lying on the table, "has an arm you might see to. I hope you can save it. I can't."

Already the doctor had taken off his coat, rolled up his sleeves, and was bending over the man. After inspecting the wound, he nodded, "It's quite possible. I'll see what I can do."

"Meanwhile, perhaps we could go on deck to discuss the situation," the officer said. "Sorry. I haven't introduced myself. I'm Captain Bennington of Her Majesty's Ship *Nemesis.*"

"Captain Bennington." Stephen nodded, then went to rinse his hands. As he was drying them on a soiled towel, he looked at Julia. "You'd better come on deck, too. There's not much more that you can do here."

Julia looked at the men who sprawled in chairs or lay on the floor. "I'd best stay here," she said doubtfully.

"No. This is no place for you. Come along."

The air on deck was fresh and clean after the stench of blood and vomit in the cabin, but the sight of the royal and topgallant masts and yards that lay on deck together with their bloodied sails was depressing. As she gazed at it, Julia realized how very tired she was. She was surprised when she looked up to see how relatively untouched the rest of the rigging and sails were.

Stephen and Captain Bennington had gone up to the quarterdeck, and a few sailors were clearing away the rubble. No dead or injured pirates remained on deck, though she remembered they were there when she went below, and she vaguely wondered what had happened to them. She really didn't care, she thought, as she sat down on a hatch cover and buried her face in her hands.

After a few minutes, she remembered seeing two full-rigged ships following the *Nemesis,* and she took her face from her hands to look for them. They were close. Close enough to recognize the *Jewel of the Seas* and the *Belle of Canton.* David and Cousin William! She felt comforted. It would be so good to throw herself into Cousin William's burly arms and cry out this whole long night and morning, but she knew she wouldn't.

Chapter Eleven

1842

The *Jewel of the Seas* was the first to reach them. No sooner had her sails begun to luff than a longboat was lowered over her side and men swung into it. They rowed directly across the ruffled water, which was filled with planks and bodies, to the *Crystal Star*.

When David Baxter stepped aboard, he was followed by a figure in a blue padded jacket and trousers. Nien-si! Julia realized with a start. It was amazing enough to see David and Cousin William appear out of the blue just when they most needed help, but the Tanka girl . . . what could she possibly be doing here? Julia stood up to greet them.

"Julia . . ." David came to her with his arms held out as though he would take her into them. Then he stopped short and just looked at her. Her green dress was torn and blood-smeared. Her arms and hands were dirty, and there was a streak of blood mixed with the grime on her pale face.

He touched her cheek lightly with one finger. "It's not yours?"

"What?" She looked at him bewildered. Her brain must be befuddled, she thought, from tiredness.

"Blood." The concern in his grey-green eyes gave lie to the mouth that always seemed on the verge of a smile.

She touched her cheek and felt the streaked stiffness. "Oh, no. Not mine."

"Were you hurt at all?"

"No, not at all," she said dully and sat down on the hatch cover again. "How did you know . . .?"

"It was Nien-si." He nodded at the Tanka girl, who stood beside him. "She overheard a conversation. Heard some pirates planned to attack you and where. Then she remembered you'd come out to the *Jewel* that first day and figured we were friends. Last night, after she saw you leave, she slipped aboard the *Jewel* and told me the whole story. I sent word to Captain Thacher and then notified the British Navy."

"Then you came after us."

"Yes. We came." He looked around the deck. The sailors who had rowed him over were helping the crew of the *Crystal Star* as they tried to disentangle sheets and lines. "Looks as though we might have been too late if it wasn't for the *Nemesis*, though. Got under way after we did, but she got here first."

Julia looked at the steamship as it slowly paddled in a circle of the area. It was ugly. The black paint showed streaks of rust on her long, lean hull. She was slab-sided and she trailed soot behind her.

"I never did like steam," she said wearily, "but I guess it does have some uses."

"Aye. The Chinese call her the devil-devil-ship. Without her, the Opium War might well still be going on."

"And we might all be dead."

"Aye." David looked at her steadily for a moment, then roused himself. "Best I go up and talk to your husband and Captain Bennington."

"Yes," Julia said dully. "Best you do." Before I do something foolish, she thought. It would be so good to have those steady solid arms around her, to comfort her as he had in her childhood.

She watched him as he mounted the quarterdeck, and then she turned to Nien-si. It was hard to think of the little Pidgin she had learned. It was hard to think of anything.

"Sittee you please?" She patted the hatch cover beside her.

Nien-si took off her large coolie hat and nodded. She sat down a little distance from Julia and studied her. "Missee no hurtee?"

Julia shook·her head. "No, hurtee. No, Nien-si, have many hurtee. Nien-si come-ah, no hurtee. Many, many thankee." How

215

in Pidgin could she possibly express her appreciation to the girl?

However, Nien-si seemed to understand. Her strong teeth flashed and her oblique black eyes sparkled in a smile.

"Missee Loh-gan friend-ah my. Many, many man makee missee much, much bad; dead-ah makee. Missee friend-ah go quick-quick my."

"Nien-si, Missee Chinee talk-ah no good-ah." She reached over and touched the girl's strong golden hand. "I'll have to tell you in my own language. Maybe you'll understand. Even if we spoke the same language, I doubt I could ever tell you how much I owe you, how thankful I am to you. I wish there was something I could give you, something I could do for you."

Whether it was her gestures, her face, or her tone of voice, Nien-si's intelligent eyes seemed to comprehend what Julia was saying. She reached over and patted Julia's knee.

"No thankee, no thankee. Missee friend-ah my. No more ship boat-ah go, Missee. Nien-si boat-ah go all time. Savvy, Missee? Friend-ah my, Missee?"

"Of course, Nien-si. Nien-si friend-ah my very, very good. Very, very, very good." She was trying to think of some practical way in which she could express her appreciation. Could she give the Tanka girl money, or would that insult her? Perhaps a gift? But what would Nien-si want? She seemed so whole and carefree as she was.

Her thoughts were interrupted by a booming shout from the rail.

"Well, mermaid, I've seen you in some strange situations, but never thought to see you in one the likes of this. You always did manage to find trouble, didn't you?"

Julia looked up to see William Thacher climbing aboard. He was trying to look his old hearty self, but he didn't really look anything but worried.

"I'm all right, Cousin William," she answered the question in his eyes. "And I'm not the one who gets into trouble. Everyone said I was looking for it when I went riding with Nien-si, but without her, we'd be in worse shape than we're in now."

"That's true." He bowed to the Tanka girl. "Very, very many thankee, Nien-si."

The Chinese girl just smiled at him, got up, kowtowed once, and then went to the rail in order to leave Julia alone with the captain.

William Thacher looked at Julia for a moment. When she didn't rise, he sat down beside her and pulled her into his arms. For the first time since they had sailed the evening before, Julia felt that she could relax. Now she was safe.

"If Ben could see you now," he chuckled.

She thought of her father and all the tales of his youth he had told her. "Guess he wouldn't be surprised," she said. "From what I hear tell, he's been in spots just as squeezed."

"Well, you look just about squeezed out. I'm takin' you aboard the *Belle*, where you can sleep without all this commotion."

"No!" She straightened up. "I can't leave the *Crystal Star*."

"Can as far as Hong Kong. For once, Miss Julia, I'm the one givin' orders and you're the one that's goin' to follow them."

"Stephen won't permit it."

"Stephen damn well will permit it . . . less he wants a report of his bad judgment to get back to your father and Captain Asa." He pulled her head back against his shoulder and stroked her hair.

"It wasn't bad judgment," Julia murmured. "Someone betrayed us. You and Papa . . . and I bet Captain Asa, too . . . have all done things like this."

"We didn't take a woman along when we did it, though."

Despite her weariness, she laughed. "That's just 'cause you didn't have me along."

He laughed with her. "That's true. That *is* a mitigatin' circumstance and one your father and Captain Asa will most likely take into consideration. Nonetheless, you'll do what I say. We'll sail in company back to Hong Kong, so nothin' will happen to your husband or your ship. I'll put a few of my crew aboard to help out and I don't doubt Baxter will do the same."

Julia thought of water and cleanliness and a nice soft, quiet bed. There would be no peace in her own, she knew, not with the saloon turned into a hospital ward. They would probably use her bed for one or two of the wounded, anyway. She knew Stephen wouldn't sleep till they were back in Hong Kong harbor. Besides, it was so comforting just being with Cousin William.

"You'll have to ask Stephen," she said. She could already feel sleep stealing through her.

"I'll not ask. I'll tell him." He pulled her away from him and watched her until he saw that she was able to sit alone. "You hold on a few more minutes. Then I'll get you aboard the *Belle* and you can just fall down and sleep."

It was a while before he returned, and when he did, Stephen

came with him. There was a dark stubble on his face, and his eyes were red from lack of sleep. However, there was command in his stride. There was no question as to who was master of this ship and who were the guests.

Yet his voice was gentle when he spoke. "Julie, you go aboard the *Belle* with Captain Thacher. We're going to wait a few more hours to see if the sampan shows up for the opium. Captain Bennington says he can't officially condone it, so the *Nemesis* is leaving."

"Doubt they'll be far away, though," William Thacher said.

"I doubt it, too," Stephen agreed. "They'll want to sink all the pirates they can lay their hands on. However, we can't count on it."

"But you can't stay out here alone in this condition," Julia said. It hurt her neck looking up at the two men. Tired as she was, she stood up. It was easier.

"We won't be alone." Stephen put an arm around her when he saw that she was beginning to sway. "Both Captain Thacher and Captain Baxter have agreed to stay with us. I don't think any pirates would care to attack three armed merchant ships at once."

"You've got to sleep, Stephen." She knew he must be as tired as she was. Tireder. "And what about the wounded men?"

"Julia," his smile was crooked as he held her closer to him, "you're not to worry. I can stay awake for days if need be, and the wounded have been cared for by Doctor Mansfield. No one is going to die, and they're as well off aboard as they would be in the hospital ashore. Better if what I've heard is true."

Now that he was near, she didn't want to leave him, especially with the opium matter still unsettled. "But what if a storm comes up?" she asked. "With that hole in our side. . . ."

"No storm that bad will come up," William Thacher said, "not at this time of year. Summer's the season for typhoons. Come along, Julie."

Once she was in bed in Cousin William's comfortable cabin, however, Julia found that sleep was impossible. The events of the night and the morning kept repeating themselves in unsequential scenes in her mind. The blood-chilling shrieks of the pirates mingled with the screams of the wounded in the saloon. The first sighting of the war junk was superimposed upon the picture of the pirates pouring over the side of the *Crystal Star*. Then she would see the sword raised against Stephen's back, and her heart would stop as it had not at that awful moment.

The most difficult thing of all was to comprehend her own reactions to the battle. It was as though someone else had stood in her place and done the things she had never thought she could do. Another Julia? No, she could never be so cold and calm. And yet the thought of it gave her strength. She knew that she would never be afraid again. Something would happen inside her mind, her body, that would not allow her to be afraid.

The thought quieted her, and though she did not realize she was falling asleep, she slept.

When she wakened, a rising sun was shining in her eyes, and water sang sweetly against the stillness of the hull. She knew they were at anchor. Was it possible that an afternoon and a night had passed without her knowing it? What had happened in that time?

She threw back the quilts and nearly fell as she jumped out of bed. She had forgotten she was wearing one of Cousin William's voluminous nightshirts, and it hung well below her feet. When she thought of putting on the dirty, blood-stained clothes she had tossed on the chest at the foot of the bed the day before, she wrinkled her nose in disgust. Still there was no help for it. Everything else she owned was on board the *Crystal Star*.

Hitching the nightshirt up, she went to the washstand and gave her face a quick wash and smoothed her hair. As the sleeve of the nightshirt fell back from her hand, she stared at the mirror. On her wrist was the carved jade bracelet she had so wanted. Stephen! Remembering how tenderly he had looked at her that day, she suddenly wanted him. She had to be sure that he was safe.

Quickly she went to the chest, and there, spread across it, was a pink dress he had chosen for her in Boston, and underneath it were fresh petticoats, stockings, and underclothing. He *was* safe. No one but Stephen would have known what clothes of hers to bring.

Then she was aware of men's voices murmuring in the saloon. She dressed as hastily as she could and opened the cabin door.

Cousin William and Stephen, sitting at the table, were talking together in low voices. Before them were plates of sausages, fresh fish, potatoes, bread, and a large pot of tea. At the sight and smell of food, Julia realized how starved she was.

As she entered the room, the two men stood up and Stephen came to her. He was freshly shaved and his hair neatly groomed.

219

From the electrically vital way he moved and from the gleam of blue in his grey eyes when he smiled at her, the past day might never have been.

"Oh, Stephen!" She realized how, even in her sleep, she had been concerned for his safety.

"My lady," he said with a mock bow, "you look somewhat better than the last time I saw you." Then he put an arm around her and led her to the table.

"So do you." She smiled back at him. Even to be parted from him for an afternoon and night was too long. "You brought my clothes."

"The ones you were wearing weren't fit for anything but the fire," he said, but his eyes were saying other things.

William Thacher, after watching them for a moment, took one last sip of his tea and rose. "Got to be gettin' on deck," he said as he picked up his weathered cap.

"Oh, don't go, Cousin William," Julia said, aware that she had been rude. "I haven't thanked you yet for . . . for everything."

"Time enough to thank me later," he said gruffly. "Got a few things need checkin' on."

As soon as he had gone, Stephen took her into his arms and in his kiss there was ecstasy and elation. "I missed you, my lady," he said as he stared into her eyes.

"Oh, I missed *you*, Stephen," she sighed and her hunger was forgotten. "The bracelet. . . ."

"It was always yours, didn't you know that?"

"I wanted it, but it was so expensive."

"You refused it when I offered it to you out of love. Now you have to take it, my lady." His eyes glimmered with amusement. "There's a law in China that says, if you save someone's life, you're responsible for them as long as you live. So you see, you're responsible for making me happy. If you don't accept the bracelet, you'll make me most unhappy."

She looked down at the bracelet and bit her lip. "There wouldn't have been any need to save your life if I hadn't been there. It was my fault. I distracted you. If you hadn't been looking at me, you would have been paying more attention to what was going on."

"Who knows? We're both alive and well, and that's what counts." He kissed her on the cheek and then pulled out a chair for her. "Go ahead and eat. As your cousin says, there's time enough for other things later."

220

"How are the men?" she asked as she piled sausages, fish, and bread onto her plate.

Stephen sat down opposite her and poured a cup of tea for her and another one for himself. A sharp line appeared between his brows when he spoke. "Still alive. If gangrene doesn't set in, we'll take them all home again. We put the most serious cases ashore. The hospital here isn't as bad as I thought. At least it's new and clean."

"Some of those wounds looked pretty bad," she said doubtfully as she cut up a piece of fish.

"A few will carry reminders of the day for the rest of their lives," he admitted, "but thanks to Doctor Mansfield, no limbs were lost."

"I slept so long. So much must have happened."

"You were sleeping soundly." He smiled again. "I was tempted to forget this wasn't my ship. I almost crawled into bed with you."

"You should have."

"With William Thacher on the other side of the door?" He lifted an eyebrow and grinned at her cockily. "Not likely."

She smiled at him secretly as she chewed a piece of fish. Then she asked, "What about the opium?"

"We sold it for a tidy profit." Satisfaction smoothed out the lines in his face. "A lot more than we expected. Of course, some of the extra will have to go for repairing the ship and to pay for the men's care, and there's ammunition to be replaced. Yet we sold the opium for six times its worth in Boston."

"That is a lot," Julia said thoughtfully as she broke off a piece of bread. "I suppose it makes the gamble worth while."

"On my investment alone, it will mean almost twenty-five hundred dollars clear profit. It'll mean a lot more than that to the shareholders." With his finger, he drew lines upon the table as though he were figuring up the gains. "And once we turn the profit at this end into tea and silk and China goods, who knows how rich we'll be. It's more than likely the ship *will* pay for herself with this voyage."

"And you're a shareholder as well as master." Julia smiled at him, happy for him that he was able to prove himself in his first command. "Ever since Boston, I've thought that opium was more trouble than it was worth, but seems I'm wrong."

"You may not be so wrong at that. I'm not sure I'll ever carry it again. It cost us time. The tea should be coming down soon. We'll have to move fast to sell the rest of our cargo and get the ship ready to sail for home. I want the *Crystal Star* to be the first ship into New York with the fresh tea."

"We will be, Stephen," she said and emphatically bit into a piece of sausage.

He leaned back in his chair and smiled at her. "Well, if that's what your crystal ball says. It foretold the evil. I only hope it can foretell the good as well."

"My crystal ball is a ship and a man. I know them both quite well by now."

"Yes, she's a lovely ship," Stephen said. "The sailors swear she has a happy soul and practically sails herself. They say no other ship would have survived the typhoon. Do you know, despite everything, I don't think there's a one that wouldn't sign on for another voyage."

"A good captain, too." Julia had cleaned her plate, but she was still hungry. She eyed the platters on the table speculatively. Then she thought about the Tanka girl. "We should do something for Nien-si, Stephen. Without her, we might not have come through it."

"We'd probably have come through it, but the cost would have been high. A lot of men alive today would have been dead but for her."

"Do you think she'd be insulted if we gave her money?" Julia helped herself to more sausage. It was getting cold, but her hunger did not allow for dainty distinctions.

"Insulted!" He threw back his head and laughed. "I would think not. You don't make much money ferrying passengers around the harbor."

"Yet I don't think she did it with thought of payment."

"No, I'm sure she didn't. She seems genuinely fond of you. I don't understand it. You only took that one ride with her, didn't you?"

"Yes, that's all. We always wave to each other, though." In the midst of pouring a cup of tea, she looked up at him with a gamin smile. "David Baxter says we're kindred souls. He says we're both reckless with boats."

"Well, that's a side of you I never saw," Stephen said dryly. "Nevertheless, she risked a lot to get help to us. She returned to Hong Kong with us aboard the *Crystal Star*, and I had a chance to talk to her. I found out she doesn't own that sampan. She works for a rich man who owns several of them and she has to turn over all the money she makes to him. He gives her just enough to exist."

"But she works so hard. That doesn't seem fair."

"That's the system, but I agree with you. I told her to find a sampan that's for sale and that I'd buy it for her."

"Oh, Stephen!" Julia rose and threw her arms around his neck. "That's wonderful."

He grinned as he put an arm around her and pulled her close to him for a moment. Then he pushed her away. "Go on and eat now."

"What about the ship?" Julia resumed her seat as the steward brought in a fresh pot of tea. "How much damage was done?"

"Not as much as it seemed at first. A couple of yards and topmasts broken, some sails shot up and torn. Easily remedied."

"But that hole?"

"We managed a temporary patch while we were waiting for the sampan to show up. As soon as we've unloaded the rest of the cargo, we'll have permanent repairs made."

She reached across the table and touched his hand. "You're not planning any more adventures, are you, Stephen? Just some nice, normal trading and then home?"

"Oh, I don't know." He squeezed her hand and gave her a lazy grin. "Since you're so handy with a gun, my lady, I might arrange a little more practice on the way home. I wouldn't want your talent to go to waste."

"Stephen!" She looked at him warningly.

"No," he said more seriously, "I don't plan anything, but until we're out of the South China Sea, there's no guarantee it won't happen again."

"We won't be carrying opium."

"They don't care what we're carrying. They'll take anything they can get their hands on. We'll probably set sail at the same time as others, however, so I don't think they'll be quite so bold."

"Well, I can use some peace and quiet for a spell." She took a long, satisfying sip of the hot, sweet tea.

When they went aboard the *Crystal Star*, there were only the second mate and one man on watch. The rest were below sleeping or in the hospital. As soon as they were on deck, Stephen dismissed from duty the men who had rowed the longboat. Julia was glad that he did. They seemed exhausted.

The ship was surprisingly tidy. Though it would take a long time to bleach out the stains on the deck, the wood had been scrubbed, and the lines were all neatly in place.

The mountains, the wooded and the barren, rose as serenely as ever. A nearby sampan was fishing with cormorants, who had rings tied around their necks to prevent them from swallowing the fish they caught for their master. Singsong voices, the squeals of pigs, the crowings of an occasional rooster, and the laughter of children rang out over the water. Julia caught sight of Nien-si ferrying two sailors ashore from a Dutch ship and waved to her. All seemed as peaceful as Hong Kong Harbor could ever be.

The *Nemesis* was quietly anchored near the British warships and transports. No smoke rose from her fat, squat funnel. It was hard to believe what a formidable fighting ship she could be.

Stephen saw her looking at the steamship. "There's the future, Julie. If they're able to get one of those out here, then they'll go everywhere."

"Those!" Julia scoffed. "Never. They were lucky to get her here. They say she only draws six feet, sometimes five. Six hundred and thirty tons, one hundred eighty-four feet long! May be all right for coastal waters, but give her a good storm at sea, and she'll turn turtle and sink like a rock."

Stephen glanced at Julia, then rubbed his chin and looked again at the steamship. "She has speed, though. Got to us before the *Jewel* or the *Belle* when they had a head start. Think what that speed will mean crossing oceans."

"They can't do it." Julia pushed back her tumbled hair that had not had a good brushing for a couple of days. "They're always having to put in for more wood or coal. Makes them expensive as well as impractical. Besides, from the records.I've seen, they may do all right when the wind's ahead, but when it's abaft of abeam, almost any square-rigger can outdistance them."

His eyes never leaving the iron ship, he shook his head. "She's got two masts for sail as well."

Julia shrugged and made a wry face. "All they're good for is to set canvas on fire."

"Look at her, Julie. Really look at her. Don't close your mind against steam. The *Nemesis* was meant for a special job, but there are others, and each one that's built will be an improvement on the last. Your father would do well to think about building them."

"Never! They can't replace a good, well-rigged sailing ship. The

224

smell alone would ruin any cargo of tea they tried to carry . . . even if they could get it there in time to keep it from going stale."

"I didn't say they were pretty, but if they can out-trade us, then they'll take over the sea."

"Maybe, but that day won't come for another century. There will always be those who prefer sail." She turned her back on the iron monster and looked at the graceful sailing vessels that lay to larboard.

The next day, they moved again into the wharf in front of the factory, and the remainder of their cargo was unloaded. While the ship was being repaired, her bottom scraped, and the holds painted white in preparation for the cargo of delicate tea, Julia and Stephen stayed at a guest room in the factory. It was a pleasant room with a black teak four-poster bed, which was draped with a fine mesh cloth, but she didn't find it as comfortable as their cabins aboard the *Crystal Star*.

Although Julia enjoyed inspecting the silks and china, the screens and porcelain in the warehouses, she found herself growing restless with life ashore. She wondered at herself for Stephen tried to entertain her. He took her to watch the horse races at the Jockey Club and for walks up into the hills, from which the view was marvelous. Often she went to have tea with the Kirkwoods and other ladies when Stephen was involved in business that excluded her. There was more companionship here in Hong Kong than she'd had for months, and yet she longed to be back aboard the *Crystal Star*. She had grown used to the privacy and solitude that were hers on board ship, and here ashore, there was no time or place she could really call her own.

One afternoon when they returned from the races, she found a bamboo cage with a cricket inside. She had seen children and vendors in the streets carrying them, but she never thought she would find one on a table in her room. Without pausing to take off her bonnet, she went to look at it and found there was a note attached. The handwriting was rough and uneven, but she was able to decipher it.

> To a gallant lady.
> With my greatest esteem.
> Fred Gill

225

She handed the note to Stephen who had come up behind her and was looking over her shoulder.

"Why on earth would he send me a cricket?" she asked. "Why would *anyone* send me a cricket?"

Stephen smiled as he read the note and then looked at the cage. "It's a nice gift, well meant. He probably sent it as an apology."

Julia took off her bonnet and tossed it on a chair. "The man has nothing to apologize for."

"He's been a little upset since the pirate attack. He seems to feel you think it was due to his carelessness." Stephen ran his finger over the delicate bars of the cage.

"That's ridiculous. I merely asked him why it had happened." She moved restlessly around the room, setting things straight that were already straight. "Besides what am I supposed to do with a cricket aboard ship?"

"If you feed him greens, he'll sing for you," Stephen said as he watched her. "It's a pet, just as a dog or a cat might be."

"But in a cage?"

"How else would you keep him?" He rubbed his chin with one finger. He didn't understand why Julia was upset.

"I don't know." As she picked up her bonnet to put it away, she had another thought. "What will happen when we run out of fresh greens?"

"He'll die, of course."

"That's terrible."

"Well, perhaps you can give him to your friend Nien-si when we sail."

Julia brightened at the thought of the Tanka girl. She hadn't seen her since they had come ashore to live. "Has she found a sampan yet?"

"Yes." Stephen went to the table that held the decanters and glasses. He poured a brandy for himself and a glass of sherry for Julia. As he handed it to her, he said, "I meant to tell you about that earlier. She came to see me this morning. I gave her the money."

"That's good. At least *she* won't be in a cage anymore."

After a night of the caged cricket's song, Julia made up her mind that she was not going to keep him nor would she give him to Nien-si. Instead she took him to the Kirkwoods', where Hamilton immediately opened the cage and released him in the flowering gardens of the moon-gated house. As she saw the small creature spring away to freedom, Julia smiled.

Once the ship was repaired and the holds painted, they moved back aboard the *Crystal Star*. The harbor was emptier now, for many of the merchant vessels had gone up the Pearl River to the Whampoa anchorage. It was rumored that tea would soon be available at Canton, and everyone was anxious to be on hand when it arrived. The *Belle* and the *Jewel* had gone, but Stephen was determined not to leave in ballast. While he was ashore trying to find a cargo for Whampoa, Julia often stayed aboard the ship. Here she could watch the life of China without having to cope with the dirt and dust of the land.

Sampans, junks, and lorchas, all with their eyes painted on their bows and lucky inscriptions lettered upon them, were constantly coming and going. There was always something interesting to watch since all phases of family life occurred with little or no privacy. The one boat that she missed, however, was Nien-si's. After looking for her for several days, she mentioned it to Stephen just as he was preparing to go ashore for a morning appointment.

"Have you seen Nien-si?" she asked him. "I've wanted to see her new sampan, but we've been aboard three days, and I haven't been able to spot it."

Stephen removed his top hat, smoothed back his hair before he replaced it, and glanced around at the busy life of the harbor. His face was turned away from her when he said abruptly, "Don't look for her anymore."

"Why not? Has she gone ashore to live?" That seemed incredible. From what she had heard, the water people didn't care for land and some never touched their foot to earth from the moment they were born until the moment they died.

"No." Stephen gripped the rail, and Julia could see that his knuckles were white. "She's not coming back, Julie."

Fear mixed with anxiety, but more fear than anxiety, made her clutch her own wrist very tight. "What is it? Something's happened. You know what it is. Her new sampan . . ."

"Her sampan was found smashed to pieces," Stephen said, and his voice was hoarse as he continued to stare out at the water.

"And Nien-si?" She could hardly bear to ask the question, but it must be asked.

"They say she's dead." Stephen couldn't tell her the brutal details of the Tanka girl's murder.

"Because of us! It's true, isn't it? She died because she saved us."

"Not necessarily. There could have been other reasons."

Julia looked at him steadily, and when he refused to meet her eyes, she knew that there could only have been one reason.

"I suppose so," she said. She felt a little numb. The morning, which had been so beautiful, was no longer beautiful.

Stephen looked at her then and saw how pale her face was and how large her indigo eyes looked against its whiteness. Wishing that he could shelter her from the world, he put an arm around her and held her close. "Don't take it so hard, Julie. This is China."

"Yes." She could feel the tears starting to well up, and for some reason, she didn't want him to see her cry. This was a private grief. "You'd better go," she said. "You'll be late for your appointment."

He stroked her cheek and studied her face. "Are you going to be all right, Julie?"

"Yes," she said thickly. "I'll be all right."

He hesitated for a moment, but then he thought of his appointment. A few days ago a badly damaged ship had arrived, and although she had been slated to carry her cargo on to Whampoa, she had had to unload it immediately. There might be something in it for him, and he couldn't afford to be late for the meeting.

"All right, Julie, I'll go, but I'll try not to be too long." Despite the fact that there were sailors nearby holystoning the deck, he lightly brushed her cheek with his lips.

When Stephen was in the longboat, Julia waved to him and he waved back, but as soon as he was gone, she ran below to their cabin. Flinging herself upon the bed, she buried her face into the pillow and burst into long sobs that shook and tore her body. "Nien-si," she cried, "Nien-si." And she couldn't forget the Tanka girl as she had first seen her. So lithe, so free, with her almond eyes sparkling, the long braid so gaily tied up with a piece of red ribbon. She could hear again her words. "Hi-yah! Missee! Want-chee go ashore?" And later, when they had sat side by side on the hatch cover, "Friend-ah my, Missee?"

"Oh, yes," she sobbed, "I was your friend, Nien-si, but little good it did you. You saved my life, but in knowing me, you died."

Later as she dried her eyes and washed her face, she thought of the old Tahitian woman, Omemema, and knew that this was another of her small deaths. China would never be the same for her. Behind that exotic mask, she would always sense the wanton cruelty that could snuff out so gay and young a life.

Stephen found the damaged ship had a cargo of cotton that he could carry up to Whampoa, and he was content, for the freight rates the shipper was willing to pay for it were above the average. Julia was glad to leave, too, for now when she looked at the harbor, she saw the emptiness of it without the Tanka girl laughing and sculling her sampan from vessel to vessel.

The morning after the last bales of cotton were jammed into the holds and made secure on deck under tarpaulins, the *Crystal Star* set sail for Whampoa. The men who had been wounded in the pirate attack had all recovered enough to sail with them, though some were still not able to carry out all their duties. Stephen hired three Chinese to supplement the crew for the short voyage, and a pilot came aboard just before the anchor was raised.

Julia, despite her disenchantment with China, found her spirits rising as they glided toward the western channel. As they passed Mount Victoria, she wondered if she would ever see it or the island it guarded again.

Once they had passed Lantao Island and started up the Canton River, she watched the larger islands they passed, and their names, the familiar ones of childhood, sang through her mind. Sawchow Island. Toang Koo. Lintin Island, which had been the base for the opium trade for many years before Hong Kong was settled. The river was so broad here, she could not see the other side, but to starboard, they passed Fansiak, Mah-chow, Ty-shan, Suichan.

The water traffic had thinned out once they left Hong Kong, but now as they made their way up the broad waterway, there were more and more boats to be seen. When they entered the narrower confines of the Pearl River, they found craft of every imaginable sort surrounding them, making navigation around the sandbars and the small islands difficult.

Julia, however, was happy that they had to pass so close to land, for now she was able to see a side of China she had never seen before. There were willow trees along the shore and, beyond them, fruit trees, fields, and rice paddies. Men and women were working there with their bullocks and oxen. Children at play along the riverbanks smiled and waved at the ship as they sailed by. Pagodas could be seen on high hills, and there was smoke arising from the tiny villages. Hong Kong, with its arid soil, had none of this. It seemed a tight, cloistered island of evil when compared with these small fields that rolled inland in an endless patchwork of green.

Yet when they entered the Bocca Tigris and Stephen pointed out the shell-torn Bogue Forts on the islands of Chuenpee to starboard and Tycocktow to larboard, she was reminded of how recently the Opium War had been raging. It was here only a year ago January that the British Expeditionary Force had, with the aid of the *Nemesis,* fought to clear the way to Canton.

When at last they came to the Whampoa anchorage ten miles south of Canton, they found over forty merchant vessels from the Western world, their masts making a black forest against the green high hills of Whampoa Island. Eighteen of them were American. The rest flew the flags of Britain, Denmark, Portugal, Holland, and France. As Julia thought of the ones they had left behind in Hong Kong Harbor, she realized that this must be the largest foreign fleet ever assembled in Chinese waters.

It was peaceful now with the floating villages bordering the shores and the constant water activity that was so like Hong Kong. Yet less than two years ago, battles had been fought in this river. Long and bloody battles between the British Expeditionary Forces and the Chinese mandarins.

Stephen, with his driving energy, hired a lorcha at sunrise the next day to take him up to the Settlement at Canton. When he returned, he was followed by several lighters, and immediately the work of unloading the cargo of cotton was begun.

It took several days, but no sooner had the holds been emptied of cotton than the chests of tea began to arrive. Though they were sealed tightly in cedar lined boxes, the fragrance of tea began to fill the ship. There were days when more than a thousand chests of Hyson, Congou, and Souchong tea arrived. On other days there was less, but there would be boxes of ammunition, bags of rice, and barrels of flour, meat, and vegetables.

In the evenings, Stephen and Julia would visit the other ships in the anchorage, often dining aboard them, and they were visited in return by the captains and their wives, although there were few women in the fleet. Julia enjoyed this social life more than she had the one ashore in Hong Kong. Because the tea was finally available and they would all soon be sailing for home, there was a festive air here that she had not found in the colony.

During the day, she watched the mandarins' barges, something she had not seen in Hong Kong. Their approach was heralded by the beating of gongs, which warned lesser craft to make way for them, and *all* other craft were lesser in the eyes of the mandarins. With scarlet pennants flying and rows of oarsmen in fine livery, they made their way importantly down the river. In a roofed area that was protected in good weather only by posts or screens of intricately carved teak, the mandarin would sit at his ease on piles of silk cushions or on a carved chair that was like a throne. Never on the streets or on the waters of China had Julia seen clothing like theirs. Their embroidered robes and hats glowed like jewels when the sunlight caught them. Occasionally she would catch a flash of long fingernails encased in silver as they smoked their waterpipes or sipped delicately from priceless cups. While an attendant waved a sandalwood fan, they gazed upon the river with the boredom of ownership, for only the Emperor could gainsay their very complete power.

She didn't have long to enjoy it, however, for within two weeks after they had begun to load tea, the hatches were battened down. Pigs, sheep, a cow, and coops of chickens were brought aboard to live on the main deck. The rigging, which had been overhauled before they left Hong Kong, was overhauled once more, and then, on a morning of fair wind, they sailed down the Pearl River homeward bound. The *Jewel of the Seas* and the *Belle of Canton* also weighed their anchors and followed close behind them.

The race back around the Horn had begun. Stephen and David had once more made a wager. William Thacher, claiming that the *Belle* was too old to bet on, had not. Still he would try to outtack and outsail them all the way to America. No East India captain worthy of his name could resist the challenge of another vessel before him.

As she leaned on the taffrail and watched the sails of the other ships blossom upon their yards and masts, Julia remembered how, when she was a child, she had stood on the highest dunes to see just such ships as these. Though she was now twenty-two, the magic was still there. She took a deep breath and could smell the spices and sandalwood and the land that smelled like no other land. The dreams of her childhood had been fulfilled, but they were still there. The world was large, and as yet, she had seen only a small portion of it. She smiled as she thought of the voyages ahead and the years to come. This was her home, this ship, and she was content that it was so. It was where she belonged.

Chapter Twelve

1844

Over a year had passed since that record-breaking passage when Stephen, bringing the *Crystal Star* from Whampoa to New York in eighty-five days and six hours, had made good his promise to Captain Asa that the ship would pay for herself on her first voyage. Then the next passage home from China had brought them to New York in the startling time of seventy-eight days, and Stephen had found himself proclaimed a hero by the press. Whether he walked the streets of New York or the roads of the Cape, people pointed him out to one another, and he was frequently stopped by those who wanted to shake the hand of the man who had whittled down the distance between China and America to almost eleven weeks. There was little time for him to enjoy his fame, however, for after two weeks at home, they were once again bound round the Horn for Tahiti and Hong Kong.

With this third voyage, Julia found that time had begun to segment itself into latitudes rather than weeks and into voyages rather than months. The *Crystal Star* had become more a home to her than the house where she had been raised, and the worries of the land had become trivial when matched with those of the sea.

They had sailed through every vagary that wind and water

could provide, and her health had remained radiant. The ills of the land came aboard only with an occasional sailor, and the clean breezes of the ocean soon swept them away. Scurvy rarely touched them for Stephen believed strongly in carrying large quantities of potatoes and onions. Whenever it was available, fruit was always aboard.

She was surprised, therefore, when in August the first queasiness of seasickness attacked her. Two airless days in the stifling heat of the doldrums had sent her up on deck shortly after sunrise to sit beneath the awning. The morning air seemed momentarily cool after the claustrophobic closeness of the cabin, but the effect was soon dispelled. The slatting of sails that were set to catch the nonexistent breeze and the useless rolling of the swells that ran beneath the turquoise mirror of the sea grated on her nerves.

She scanned the luminous sky anxiously for one of the strange black curtains that traveled over the water. The deluge they brought gave a relief that lasted only a little longer than the rain itself before the unrelenting sun drew the water back into the sky, leaving the ship and her people as parched as ever. Still, even a momentary relief was better than none at all. But in that sky that arched over the circular horizon, there was nothing, not even the smallest cloud to lend its reflection to the miles of gleaming pale blue sea.

Julia's light muslin dress clung to her in salt stickiness, and the bodice seemed so tight, it was difficult to breathe the scorchingly hot air. She had cast aside her corsets several days ago, but even so, she was wearing one of her looser dresses, and it should have fit comfortably without their aid. However, none of her clothes seemed to fit properly anymore. Most likely it was a lack of exercise, and she sighed as she thought of the brisk walks she normally took around the deck. Not today. Not unless they were favored by a breeze.

The one thing she could do today, though, was to let out a dress or two. There was no point in being unnecessarily uncomfortable, and it would give her something to think about instead of constantly yearning for the release the trade winds would bring. At the moment, even sewing seemed an enormous task. She didn't feel as though she had the energy to push a needle through the lightest fabric, and the thought of extra material across her lap made her feel hotter. Well, perhaps after breakfast she would feel more up to it.

However, when Charles, a dark-skinned native of the West Indies and their new steward, appeared on deck with fried fish, eggs, potatoes, and rolls, she found that the sight, and especially the smell, of food was repugnant. How she could have put on weight was more than she could fathom. In the last few days, she'd had little appetite for it. Still, she told herself, I must eat if I'm to have any energy at all.

Two bites of fish and one sip of coffee were all that was needed. Gagging on them, she pushed the small table quickly away from her and ran for the rail.

The first spasms had barely subsided before Stephen was at her side. His hand was hot and damp as he held her forehead, but his strength and support were reassuring.

"Don't fight it," he urged her. "Let it all go."

Once more and it was over. Feeling completely drained, she clung to the rail. What little energy she'd had was now completely gone.

Stephen called to the steward for a glass of water and had her rinse her mouth. Yet she could still taste the acid. As he pulled out his handkerchief and wiped her face with what water remained in the glass, Julia thought longingly of her clean, dry bed at home and the cool breeze that would be coming through the tall windows.

"Are you going to be all right?" Stephen asked as he watched her anxiously.

"Yes. I think so." Her stomach felt nothing but empty, yet she didn't want to move away from the solid support of the rail. "Just give me a few minutes."

"You'd better sit down," he said firmly and pulled her away from the rail. She leaned her weight against him as he led her to the chair, and the helmsman took his eyes off the sails long enough to glance at her anxiously.

As Stephen helped her sit down, he examined her face carefully. All of her usually vivid color had gone, and her tan skin looked sallow. Even her eyes seemed a paler blue.

"It's not like you to get seasick. You never have before." His voice betrayed his mounting concern.

"No." She really felt too tired to speak. "Maybe it was the fish."

"I don't think so. The cook caught it fresh this morning, and you didn't eat enough to make any difference anyway," he said as

234

he glanced at her plate. "You'd better go below and lie down for a while."

"Oh, no. It's so hot . . ." She leaned back in the chair and closed her eyes.

"A dose might help. I'll get out the medicine chest."

"No!" Her eyes flew open. The last thing she wanted was to be dosed. "I'm all right now. As long as I don't have to eat. Oh, if only the wind would come. Or it would rain. Something! I'd be all right then."

"I wonder." Stephen leaned back against the pin rail that ran around the mizzen mast and continued to search her face as though he would find the answer there.

His scrutiny made Julia uneasy. She felt she had to offer some excuse. "It's just the heat and this eternal rolling that's made me seasick."

"I doubt you're seasick, but I don't know what else it could be. None of the men have been sick, so you couldn't have caught anything from them."

"Well, don't worry about it, Stephen," she said irritably. "I'm all right now. Just leave me alone."

"Is there anything you want?"

"Yes. For you to stop fussing about me."

"All right," he said calmly. For all his impatience with the doldrums, he refused to be stung. And he *was* worried about her. The nearest doctor was hundreds of miles away, far beyond this cruel circle of sea and sky. "Make sure you stay out of the sun."

"The last thing I want to do is to sit in the sun. Now stop fussing."

He nodded and returned to his usual occupation of scanning the sea and sails for the slightest hint of air, but all morning his eyes kept returning to Julia, where she sat pale and listless. The only time he had seen her ill before was when they'd been battered by the typhoon on their first voyage. Meanwhile, she'd lived at sea for over two years, and nothing had ever seemed to faze her.

Julia was aware that he was watching her, but she pretended not to notice it. What made her uneasy were the curious glances she caught from the officers and men. If it wasn't so hot, she would go below. Finally, in irritable defense, she sent Charles to her cabin to fetch her sewing basket and one of her lighter dresses. She didn't feel like fitting it now, but at least she could rip out the seams. If the men saw her doing something, *anything*, maybe they'd forget about this morning's incident. Why, she thought, did it have to happen in front of practically the entire ship's company? Why not in the privacy of her cabin?

By eleven o'clock, she had finished with the dress and the sun was blasting down its full power. The sight of a whale sounding off the starboard quarter made her long for water. She decided to go below and rinse off with salt water. It would help for a while if not for long, and she couldn't be any saltier than she felt now. Then she could lie down and rest. She hadn't slept well the night before, and she needed something to sustain her through the long day that seemed to stretch interminably before her.

She was standing in their cabin, dripping water on the bare boards, when Stephen entered the room. He paused in the doorway, and his eyes scanned her naked body as though he were searching for some sign of disease. The impersonal, almost clinical, way that he looked at her, with none of his usual appreciation or desire, irritated her further. She put her hands on her hips and stared back at him.

"Have you seen enough?" she asked.

"I think so," he said calmly.

Julia lay down and, closing her eyes, tried to ignore him. When he didn't go away, she opened them again. "Well?" she said. "What is it?"

"I think I know what's wrong." Incredibly enough, he was actually beginning to smile.

"Well, don't keep me in suspense, Stephen. You might share your secret with me."

"I think you're going to have a child."

The words came so bluntly, so unexpectedly. Julia gasped, then sat up and stared at him. It was true, she hadn't had her period for a while. Days at sea slipped so imperceptibly one into another that she'd lost track. And after two years of a very active marriage, she had begun to give up hope. When they'd last been home, her mother had blamed her failure to conceive on the sea. She had said that the constant motion of the ship made some women barren.

So be it, Julia had thought at the time. Though she had longed for a child, Stephen's child, she would not and could not give up the sea, the ship, and her husband for the remote possibility that she would conceive during his short shore leaves. Other women did, she knew, but then other women started their babies at sea, too.

She looked down at her body, then stroked her hands over her damp skin. It was hard to tell without a mirror, but her breasts and waist did seem to be larger while her arms and legs remained the same. She dubiously ran her hand across her stomach. Was it really plumper?

Stephen sat down on the bed beside her and gently laid his hand on her bare skin. Bemused wonder softened his face as he gazed at the spot where his child might lie. His eyes traveled slowly up her body to rest upon her breasts, and they were more voluptuously beautiful than he had ever seen them. He briefly touched his lips to each nipple with a love that verged on reverence.

As he lifted his face, Julia pushed herself up on her elbows, and she could feel the weight of her breasts. Excitement began to rise within her.

"Do you think I am, Stephen? Do you really think I am?"

"I'm fairly sure," he said as he noticed a new softness to her face, a delicacy to her skin. It reminded him of the glow of a peach that has reached the perfection of its ripeness. Then he grinned in his happiness. "I am well acquainted with the territory, you know."

"And you're glad?" A hint of anxiety touched her growing smile.

"Glad?" He shook his head in amusement and delight. "I'm exultant, lyrical, joyful, jubilant, and enraptured." Then he took her in his arms to hold her, to protect her, to support her with his strength. While he brushed his lips across her moist forehead, he murmured, "Oh, Julie, I'm so very glad."

Despite the heat, she clung to him, and their common joy united to enfold the child. Neither noticed the sweat that drenched them nor the stifling air of the motionless cabin.

"We *will* have princes and princesses in our castle, after all," she said as the child who had been unimagined an hour earlier began to assume reality.

"Did you ever doubt it?"

"Yes. Sometimes."

"Just remember that, in Ombedia, all things are possible. For a few, a little patience is required. That's all."

"Yes." She looked at him and realized with a quiet elation that a new dimension had been added to the love she already felt for him. He was not only her husband, her captain, her lover, but now he was the father of her child. Their child.

"It will be a happy child," he said and there was a wistfulness behind his confidence. "With all the love and protection we can give him."

"Aye, we'll make him happy." Knowing that Stephen was thinking of his own lonely childhood, she kissed him briefly, and they smiled their joy into each other's eyes for a few quiet moments. "I'm so glad that he'll be born at sea."

"Well, that's another matter," he said quietly. "You'll have to go ashore, of course."

"I will not!" She drew away from him and sat back on her knees.

"You most certainly will," he said, still smiling.

"I was born at sea and that's where my child will be born." Already she was beginning to square her shoulders as she gave him a long, steady look.

"No." His eyes were smoky with tenderness, but his chin was set. "Julia, you've been at sea long enough to know what can happen. What if, when your time comes, we're caught in a gale? Who would help you if we ran into a hurricane or a typhoon? I couldn't. The ship would have to be my first concern."

Julia felt strength returning with her determination. "Then we'll just have to get someone. I *am not* going ashore."

"A sea-going midwife? You'll have a hard time finding one." Stephen laughed and then cupped her chin in the palm of his hand. "Come, Julie, don't be foolish about this."

"Aunt Martha will come if I ask her." Julia's eyes sparkled as she began to make her plans.

"And what will your mother do without her?" Stephen asked more seriously as he realized just how determined Julia was to have her way in this matter.

"Amelia's there. You know that. As soon as Michael went to sea, Amelia moved back home."

"And Amelia has two children of her own to care for . . . or will have soon."

"Well, there's Sarah . . ." Julia said with less certainty.

"You know as well as I do that all Sarah cares about is herself . . . and that spoiled son of hers. She wouldn't lift a finger to help anyone." Stephen rose impatiently and paced to the stern window, where he stared out at the slick surface of the milky blue sea.

"Maybe she's changed," Julia said, though she knew her argument was growing weaker.

"Sarah will never change, especially not to help you."

"I suppose not." Julia lay back again with a sigh. "I'd rather have Aunt Martha than anyone else. Still, if she can't come, I'll find someone. I have the whole world to choose from."

Stephen turned and looked at her, and the fear that was rising in him showed itself as anger in the flickers of the muscles of his jaw. He couldn't lose Julia. He could afford to lose anything else, but not Julia. Too many times he had put her life in jeopardy, but he had sworn he never would again. Especially not now. This time he would have to be firm with her. He strode to the side of the bed and stared down at her with his sternest air of command.

"Julia, you are going to have that child ashore. You'll go home as soon as we reach New York, and that's where you'll stay. You'll have Aunt Martha there to help you when you need her and a good midwife . . . and Doctor Willett, too, if it's necessary."

"Stephen, do you remember our wedding day?" she asked softly.

He looked at her with suspicion. He knew she was trying to outmaneuver him, but what tack was she trying now? "Of course, I remember our wedding day. It took long enough to get you to the altar. You don't think I'm likely to forget it, do you?"

"I'm not talking about the altar. I'm talking about later that day. It was aboard the *Crystal Star*, in the saloon. You said, 'From now on, where I go, you go, too.' That was just as much a promise as any of the vows you made at the altar."

"No, Julia. I will not risk your life."

"It's my life."

Suddenly the anger was gone from his fear. She looked so lovely, so vulnerable lying there. He sat down on the bed beside her and spread her heavy hair across the pillow away from her damp face. "It's not your life, my lady," he said gently. "It's mine . . . and our child's."

Once Stephen had left her and she was alone again, Julia lay back against the damp pillow, the heat forgotten in her continuing excitement. A child! Was it really possible? She tried to think back. She could remember her period coming just as they arrived in

New York after their last voyage. The packet from New York to South Yarmouth hadn't been bad, but traveling on to East Dennis by stagecoach had been quite uncomfortable.

Since then?

No. There had been nothing since then.

She started counting on her fingers and suddenly she smiled. Let Stephen rage all he would. Their child would be born at sea.

Stephen had fingers, too, but his memory was less clear than Julia's on a matter that concerned her more than it did him. When he questioned her about it, she smiled and shrugged. How could she remember? Until it was impossible to transfer her to a homeward bound vessel, she was determined that he shouldn't realize the truth. By the time they reached the South China Sea, however, it had become obvious to Stephen that it would be a close race home. Too close.

The day before they reached Hong Kong, Julia, leaning on the windward rail, was enjoying the now familiar sights of fishing sampans and junks bobbing on the ruffled waters among the rock islands when Stephen joined her.

He was silent for a moment as he, too, watched the native craft. Then he said, "I've come to a decision, Julia."

"Oh?" Julia had a very strong premonition that the decision had something to do with her and she wasn't so sure she wanted to hear about it.

"I'm going to put you ashore in Hong Kong. You can stay there until the child is born. When you've recovered your strength, you can sail on the next vessel that leaves for America."

Julia straightened up and, with her chin held high, looked at him coldly and calmly. "You will do nothing of the sort," she said.

Stephen's eyes narrowed and his lips tightened into a thin line. "Julia, I've spent over two years telling you that *I* am master of this ship, and you will follow my orders."

"You can only order me aboard *this* ship," she said. "There'd be nothing to prevent me from taking passage home immediately after you leave, and nothing *will* prevent me. If you won't take me, then I'll be on board the very next vessel that sails."

He pointedly let his eyes wander over her body. Then he smiled grimly. "No one would take you in that condition."

"Wouldn't they?" She raised her arched brows. "Cousin William will be arriving soon in his new ship, and if he won't take me, then David Baxter will. He'll have no choice. I'm still part-owner of the *Jewel of the Seas.*"

"Owner or no, he won't take the chance. If anything happened to you aboard the *Jewel,* your father would strip him of command and see to it that David Baxter was never given another vessel."

"Nonsense. Nothing can possibly happen to me at sea. But Hong Kong . . ." She looked in the direction of that still unseen land. "You really intend to leave me there to bear my child in the midst of malaria, cholera, and all the other plagues that swarm on that island?"

Stephen remained silent, and she could see, by the stony set of his jaw, that he was not going to argue any further with her.

"And where do you plan to have me stay?" she asked bitingly. "In one of those filthy hovels in Tai Ping Shan?"

"No," he said and his voice was cold. "Don't be overly dramatic. I'm sure Mrs. Kirkwood would be glad to have you."

"I'm sure Mrs. Kirkwood would *not* be glad to have me. Her house isn't all that large. Besides, she's always going off to Calcutta with 'Captain.' "

"Then one of the other ladies. They're so bored with one another, they'll be glad to have someone new to liven things up."

"I warn you, Stephen. I'm not going to stay."

"And I'll warn you. If you don't do just as I say, I'll never take you to sea with me again."

"That I don't believe."

"Believe it or not, as you will. I mean what I say." He called to the steward for his sextant and left her abruptly.

Two days after they had landed, Julia was in the Kirkwoods' garden. Nance had married a young naval officer and had gone to live in England, and Hamilton was as usual tagging along after his father. The garden, with its view of the busy harbor and the distant grey-brown hills of Kowloon, was restful. The December sun shone brightly on the richly variegated chrysanthemums that surrounded the small pool, and young willows, turning gold with winter, swayed in the light breeze. Julia was grateful that her hostess had not asked any other guests for tea.

Mary Kirkwood was sympathetic as she listened to Julia's tale, but when she had finished, she said, "I'm not so sure your husband isn't right, dearie. A ship's no place to bring a child into the world. There's danger enough in childbirth without adding the risk of the sea."

"But I *know* I'll be all right," Julia said.

"And the child?" For once the soft brown eyes did not sparkle behind their spectacles.

"He'll be all right, too." Julia picked up a small cake and then put it down again. "I don't know how to explain it. I feel safer . . . more at home . . . at sea than I do on land."

Mary Kirkwood shook her head, and the sun glinted on the russet hairs that shone amongst the white. "It's only natural for you to want to be with your husband. Lord knows, I can understand that. I've stuck close by Captain all my life, I have, but when the wee ones were on the way, I come ashore. Can't say it was easy to part with him. What must be done must be done, though."

"Oh, I hoped *you'd* understand me," Julia said impatiently as she wiped her fingers on a small wisp of a napkin. "Thought you'd help me convince Stephen that there's no danger."

"No. That I can't do. Not in good conscience. There is danger. Why, Kate Potter lost her twin babies right here in Hong Kong harbor during a storm just last fall. Her husband couldn't leave the deck, and there was none below to help her." A reminiscent sadness crossed her face, but it was only a passing cloud, for almost immediately she was smiling warmly at Julia. "I'd like you to stay with us, though. You can have Nance's room. It's been right lonely without her, and I'll enjoy having you about the house."

"Oh, Mary, it's kind of you, but I just can't. And please don't tell Stephen you've invited me. If he found out, I know he'd insist I stay in Hong Kong."

"Sounds to me as though he's already made up his mind."

"He thinks he has, but I'm going to change it. I don't know how, but some way . . ."

Mary Kirkwood looked at her young friend. She saw the slender shoulders thrown back despite the weight of her swollen breasts, the firm chin that was almost too strong for a woman, the red lips that pressed together, and she sighed. Julia Logan didn't seem to understand that there was a way for a woman to get what she wanted, the soft and gentle way. Instead of using smiles and sighs and tears, Julia met the world head on. That was all right for a man, but it just wouldn't do for a woman. She wondered about

Julia's mother. Hadn't she taught her daughter anything?

"Well," she said finally. "I'll see what I can do to help you."

"Oh, would you?" The sapphire-eyed smile that Julia flashed at her was dazzling. With that smile, Julia should be able to get anything she wanted from her husband, Mary Kirkwood thought, but then Stephen Logan was a strange young man. No, not strange, she corrected herself. It was just that, like so many masters, he kept his thoughts to himself.

"There's a young American woman here," Mary Kirkwood said thoughtfully, "name of Rose Doane. Don't know whether you've seen her or not."

"No, I don't think so," Julia said politely. She was too involved in her own problem to be interested in Mary Kirkwood's never-ending gossip at the moment.

"She come out as a servant with the Lewises two years ago. Don't think she's been much good to them, but they feel responsible for her. Seems she met some English sailor not long after they got here and married him. Of course, he couldn't support her, and a few days after they wed, he signed on board a vessel bound for Calcutta. Nothing's been heard from him since aside from the rumor that he already had a wife tucked away somewhere. Some say India, some say England."

"Oh, the poor girl," Julia said, her sympathy aroused in spite of herself.

"Worse than that." Mary Kirkwood did enjoy a bit of gossip. "She had a child. The Lewises wanted to send the pair of them home, but Rose wouldn't go. Kept saying that her husband was coming back. Then the child died, and I think she gave up hope. Drifts around like a ghost now, she does."

"She should go to England and look for her husband," Julia said emphatically.

"How? She hasn't a cent. The Lewises are willing to pay her passage home, but they can't support her while she roams all over England. It's most likely he's not there, anyway. Could be she's willing to go back to America now."

"She sounds right spineless to me," Julia said, dismissing this tale of a woman she had never met.

"Well, why don't you take a look at her before you make up your mind?" Mary Kirkwood's face was all innocence as she poured another cup of tea for her guest.

"Make up my mind?" Julia sat up straight. "About what?"

"Why taking her back with you, of course. If your husband thought you'd have another woman aboard to help you through your time, might be he'd reconsider?"

"He might," Julia said slowly. "He just might. And if he doesn't, maybe I'll take her with me on the very next ship that sails after he does."

"Don't do that, dearie," Mary Kirkwood said quickly, shocked that Julia would consider such a thing.

"I will if I want to."

"No, no. Your husband doesn't appear to me a man easily crossed."

"Well, be that as it may, the first thing to do is meet this Rose Doane. If I like her and if she wants to go home, then I'll tackle Stephen."

When Julia met Rose Doane at the Kirkwoods' the next afternoon, she was not impressed. The woman was only twenty-three, younger than Julia herself, but she seemed years older. Her sallow skin did not improve the pinched look of her face, and lifeless wisps of straw-colored hair straggled out from under her bonnet.

"This is Mrs. Logan, just as I told you, Rose," Mary Kirkwood said as she pulled the woman forward onto the terrace.

Julia got up from the comfortable cushions of the black teak chair where she had been sitting and held out her hand. "Hello, Rose."

The woman, without looking up at Julia, bobbed her head and lightly brushed her hand, then nervously moved back a step.

"Sit down, Rose," Mary Kirkwood said kindly.

It seemed a great effort for the woman to speak, and there was a harsh quality to her voice when she did manage to murmur, "Yes, ma'am."

"So you think you'd like to go home," Julia said although she had already decided against the woman.

"I'd do anything to get away from here, ma'am."

"But at one time you didn't want to go?"

"I've . . . changed my mind."

"Many vessels sail from Hong Kong. I'm sure you won't have any trouble finding passage." Julia felt sorry for the woman, but she felt she'd be more of a liability than a help. Also she didn't think that she wanted to spend three months with her as a constant companion.

"I thought . . . if I could find a job for the trip, then I'd have my passage money when I got back to New York. Something to get me started."

"I'm sure you'll find a way, Rose, but I'm afraid I can't take you. You see, I'll need someone who can help me when my time comes. I doubt you've had much experience along that line."

"Oh, yes, ma'am." For the first time, the woman raised her eyes and looked directly at Julia. Her eyes were startling. They slanted above her thin cheekbones almost like a Chinese and they were a strange topaz yellow. Cat's eyes, Julia thought.

"I were the oldest of nine, ma'am," Rose continued. "My mum, she depended on me when her time come."

"You don't look very strong, Rose," Julia said gently.

"But I am. Ask Mrs. Lewis," Rose pleaded. "I were sick for a while, had the malaria, but I'm stronger now. If I can jest get away from this heathen place . . ." She cast her eyes down again. "You'll see. Jest give me the chance."

"Well, I'll have to talk it over with Captain Logan, but I don't want to give you any false hopes. He's most particular."

"Yes, ma'am." The woman seemed to shrink into her own thin frame. Her disappointment was obvious.

Julia mentioned her meeting with Rose Doane to Stephen, but perhaps because of her own lack of enthusiasm, he remained adamant in his determination to leave her in Hong Kong. Meanwhile, Julia continued to search for someone else. If she found just the right person, she knew she could make Stephen change his mind. Perhaps she could persuade a Chinese woman to make the voyage.

Then one day, when they had been there a little less than two weeks, the *Jewel of the Seas* arrived in Hong Kong. Stephen had gone ashore to make arrangements for careening the *Crystal Star* on the beach in order to have her bottom scraped, and Julia was packing a few things to take ashore when David Baxter appeared on board.

Julia had seen the *Jewel* sail into the harbor earlier in the day, and she had waved across the water to David. Now as she looked up from the trunk, she was startled to see his large body filling the doorway of the main cabin. She hadn't expected a visit from him so soon.

"Julia," he said and there was the catch in his voice that he could never control when he first saw her after a long separation.

"David, how are you?" Julia flew to him and, taking both his large hands in hers, reached up on tiptoe to give him a light kiss on the cheek. Then, as always, they stood back from each other, searching to see what changes had occurred in the past months.

He did look older, she thought, though perhaps that was only because his normally unruly dark blond curls were cut shorter and combed more neatly. Or perhaps it was the effect of the longer side whiskers that slightly narrowed his too large jaw. His grey-green eyes were still warm, however, and his wide mouth still seemed about to smile even though, at the moment, he was serious.

It was an effort for David to conceal the shock he'd felt when he saw the slight bulge beneath her dress. He hadn't been prepared for this. Of course, it had to happen. He had once briefly glimpsed the depths of Julia's passion, and he had occasionally wondered at the childless marriage. Yet now that it had happened, the blow was no softer.

Julia saw his glance stray over her and heard his sudden intake of breath, but she thought it was only in surprise.

"Isn't it wonderful, David?" she said, sure that he would be happy for her. "Now when I go home, I won't get all those questions from Mama and all those sidelong looks from everyone else."

Suddenly embarrassed, he looked down at the cap he was idly turning in his hands. "Is that the only reason why you're glad?" he asked. "To still the clacking tongues?"

"No, of course not. I'm glad because it will be my baby . . . and Stephen's. We're going to make a real sailor of him between the two of us. But come sit down." She touched him lightly on the arm as she became aware of how uncomfortable he must be having to stoop under the low overhead. "I'll just call the steward to bring us some tea. Unless you'd care for something stronger?"

"No. Tea will do." David still felt stunned, but he managed to walk casually across the cabin and find a chair.

When Julia returned, she sat down across from him. "Oh, David, I just can't tell you how happy I am to see you," she said, her face glowing with happiness.

"You're . . . feeling well?" he asked. He found it very difficult to talk about the child.

"Oh, I'm fine. I was sick for a couple of days at first, but from then on, I've felt marvelous."

"You look . . . marvelous." He managed to smile.

They were silent while the steward brought in the tea, but as soon as he had gone, Julia said, "I do have one problem, though."

"What is it?" He stiffened with concern. If anything should happen to Julia. . . . "Can I help?"

"Well, if worst comes to worst, I hope you will." Julia poured the tea and handed him a cup heavily flavored with milk and sugar as she knew he liked it. "Stephen wants to put me ashore when he sails for home."

"Ashore!" Some of his tea spilled into his saucer. "Here in Hong Kong?"

"Yes."

"He's going to go off and leave you alone in your condition?" David was dumbfounded.

"He says he'd be risking my life if he took me to sea." There was a wistful sadness in her voice as well as on her face. It was a look that David remembered in the small child she had once been.

"But *he's* going off?" He pushed his tea aside and, leaning both elbows on the table, he stared at her intently.

"Yes. Well, I can understand that." There was something in David's triangular eyes that made Julia want to defend her husband. "He'll have to get the cargo aboard and sail for home as soon as possible if there's to be any profit out of the voyage. He just refuses to understand that I must go, too."

"How soon, Julia?"

"The baby? About three months, I think."

Never taking his eyes from her, David leaned back in the chair and folded his arms across his broad chest. "He's right, you know. About your not going, I mean. But seems to me, he could find a qualified master to take the ship home for him. He can't go off and leave you in a strange place with no family to look after you. The diseases, typhoons, cutthroats, robbers. . . ."

"Oh, David." She reached her hand to him across the table and he took it. "Don't disappoint me. I've been counting on you. I thought that, if he wouldn't take me home, you would."

He shook his head. "No, Julia."

She snatched her hand away and lifted her chin at him. "It's my ship."

"But I'm her master," he said firmly.

"You really *do* disappoint me. You're the one person in the world I thought I could always count on."

"You can. If your husband's dullard enough to go off and leave you, I'll send the *Jewel* home under another master and stay here in Hong Kong with you."

"Oh, no! You can't do that."

"Yes, I can," he said calmly. "I've got a good mate. He's ready for his master's papers."

"But David. . . ." The shock of what he was proposing darkened the blue of her eyes until they seemed to verge on black. "That would be scandalous."

"Scandalous or no, you need someone here with you."

Impatiently she pushed her chair away from the table and swirled to the stern window. When she looked back, he was still sitting there. She could tell, just from the way he was watching her, that both his body and his mind were as immovable as a giant boulder.

"Well, I won't let you do it," she said. "Either you'll take me in the *Jewel* or you'll sail without me, one. But you are not going to stay here. Think of your wife."

"I think about her just about as much as she thinks about me," he said shortly. "You think 'twouldn't cause gossip if I took you home in the *Jewel?*"

"She's my ship."

"We've already been through that."

Hoping the tea would give her strength, Julia returned to the table and sat down. With the first sip, she found it was cold. She made a face, but drank a little more.

"I've found a woman to go with me," she said quietly. "She's had experience with babies. She'd be a chaperone, and we wouldn't be any trouble to you."

"You're already a trouble to me."

"Well, I needn't be!" Julia slammed her cup down. "Just forget it, David. Forget all about me. I'm no responsibility of yours. I can do just fine without you."

"Can you, Julia?"

"Yes, I can!"

He picked up his cup and drank, but he didn't notice whether the tea was hot or cold. She was his responsibility whether she liked it or not, whether he liked it or not. For some intangible reason, it had always been so.

"Do you really think I can go off and leave you here in China with no one to protect you?"

"I have friends. They'll let me stay with them." she said coldly. She wondered at herself. How had she suddenly gotten on the other side of the argument she'd had so many times with her husband? "But don't tell Stephen," she added hastily. "I want him to take me home and he *is* going to take me home."

"Why this sudden urge to go home? Seems to me all you've ever wanted to do before was go to sea."

"It's not a matter of going home. I want my child to be born at sea."

"Why?"

"Because the sea looks after her own."

"Rubbish!"

"It is not rubbish."

He raised one eyebrow at her skeptically, but said nothing.

"Well, if neither you nor Stephen will take me, there's always Cousin William."

"He won't take you, either."

"Don't be too sure of that, David. When we sailed from New York, his new ship, *Neptune's Dragon,* was being rigged. He won't be far behind us."

David pulled out his watch and looked at it. "Well, I have an appointment ashore. Let me know what your husband decides. I'll make my plans accordingly."

"No."

David shrugged and, after rising to his feet, he dropped a quick kiss on the top of her head. "Remember you appointed me your brother a long time ago . . . when you were a child."

Chapter Thirteen

1844–1845

While the necessary work of careening the ship and scraping her bottom, scrubbing and painting the holds went on, Julia and Stephen once more moved into Russell and Company's factory. There had been a steady drizzle ever since they'd left the ship, and the cold leaked under the cracks of doors and through the ill-fitted windows. The thought of spending the winter in this climate depressed Julia as much as the weather did, and she longed for Cousin William's arrival. He was her last hope.

Finally there was a day when a warm wind blew the weather clear, and Julia was able to fling open the tall windows to air out the damp room. Her spirits picked up while she dressed for the walk she and Mary Kirkwood had planned. She was even humming to herself as she took one last look out the window to enjoy the sunlight on the water and on the grey hills of Kowloon.

While she watched, a full-rigged ship came clipping through the channel. She was larger than the *Crystal Star*, and with all but her skysails set and drawing, she was a beautiful sight. As the ship grew closer and her sails were furled in quick succession, Julia could see the long hollow bow, the low freeboard, and the tall, raking masts. There could be no doubt about it. She must be

Neptune's Dragon! And how like Cousin William to enter the crowded harbor with such a flourish and drop anchor with such perfect aplomb.

Julia felt like leaning out the window and clapping. Instead she sent a passing servant with a message to Mary Kirkwood. There would be no walk today.

When she reached the stone wharf, Julia commandeered one of Russell and Company's boats and had herself rowed out to the ship. If she'd had any doubts as to the ship's identity before, there were none when she saw the enormous dragon, whose tail trailed down the long hollow bow. The golden figurehead was so beautifully carved, it almost seemed to breathe fire.

The ship was a confusion of sailors when Julia boarded, but William Thacher was at the rail to meet her.

"Well, mermaid," he said as he hugged her with his usual exuberance. "Looks like I might have broken another record coming out. They can't say I'm gettin' too old for it now. All I needed was a fresh ship under my feet."

"Why, no one ever doubted that, Cousin William," Julia said as she planted a kiss on his bearded cheek. "Just don't forget she's a Howard-built ship."

William chuckled as he held her away from him and looked down at her. The jonquil yellow dress was cut full, but the wind off the water pressed the light muslin close against her body. "Seems like ships aren't the only things the Howards are buildin' nowadays."

"Well, Sarah and Amelia beat me to it, but I'll catch up," she said lightly, but then she saw the fleeting sadness in his green eyes and knew he was thinking about the child she and Jason had never had. The child who would have been his grandchild as this one was not. Yet she and Jason had had so little time together. She lightly touched his arm and her smile told him that she understood.

"Wouldn't be in any hurry catchin' up if I was you," he said gruffly. "Just concentrate on gettin' this one properly launched."

"I intend to." Then the old sadness was swept away as she thought of the purpose of their meeting. "But you've got to help me."

He shook his head, still withdrawn into his silent thoughts. "Now launching ships is one thing. Launching babies is another. Can't say I've had any experience along that line."

251

"You don't have to have any experience. All you have to do is take me home with you."

William Thacher pulled on his beard and studied Julia carefully. He, too, forgot his lost son as he considered the girl who was still like a daughter to him. There was something desperate about her appeal. No, not desperate. Demanding. Something was wrong and he was going to get to the bottom of it. "Why aren't you goin' home on the *Crystal Star*? You and young Logan got troubles?"

"Yes!" Then she saw the painful concern in his eyes and she quickly corrected herself. "No, not exactly. It's just that he wants to leave me here in Hong Kong till after the baby's born."

"I see." William looked across the water at the teeming island, where houses and buildings were crawling their way into every nook and cranny the steep mountains allowed. "Well, Julie, it makes a certain amount of sense. I hear your mother had a hard time of it when Amelia was born at sea."

"I'm not my mother," she said firmly.

"Those things run in the family."

"I don't believe it. Mama wasn't all that well even before Amelia was born. Papa says that, after they lost Nathaniel, Mama was never the same. And she didn't have any trouble when *I* was born."

"As I recall, you was born in the middle of summer when the North Atlantic was quiet as a mill pond. That's different from goin' round the Cape and up into a northern winter."

"Well, when my son's born, it's going to be quiet as a mill pond, too," she said proudly.

"You been talkin' to the sea again?" he asked skeptically.

"Let's not go into that, Cousin William. I know you don't believe me. You never did. All you ever did was tease me about it."

"Be that as it may, I see you've got it all figured out. The sea's goin' to settle down and sit nice and quiet just for you, and you're goin' to have a son."

"Yes! I don't care what you think. The sea won't be any problem, but I'm concentrating on a boy." She smiled as she thought of that son of hers running free over the decks, fishing with the cook, climbing the ratlines, growing up in the fresh sea air. "Men can do just as they please, while women . . ." She made a wry face and shrugged.

"Seems to me you've been doin' pretty much what you pleased

all your life," he said as he pretended to watch the sailors who were removing the chafing gear.

"Well, I'm not doing what I please now!" She pushed the curls that had escaped from her bonnet away from her face with an impatient hand. "Least I won't if Stephen has his way. That's what's so infuriating. If I was a man, no one would stop me."

"If you was a man, you wouldn't be in the same perdicament."

"Cousin William!" The look in her deep blue eyes was almost a threat. "Are you going to help me or not?"

"That's your husband's place, Julie," he said gently.

"You helped me once before."

" 'Twas only because you and Jason was goin' to land in a heap of trouble if I didn't."

"I may land in a heap of trouble now."

William pulled out his pipe and looked at it as though it would tell him how to handle Julia and her latest daft notion. He remembered too well that autumn when, in the newly awakened passion of her youth, Julia had been determined to defy her father and run off with Jason. Too young to consider what the results of their actions could be, they had laid no practical plans.

The future had seemed inconsequential to them when balanced against their need to be together in the few short weeks they would have before Jason sailed as first mate aboard the *Katy Saunders*. William often shuddered when he thought of what might have happened if he himself had not stepped in and found a Boston preacher who could be persuaded to marry them without her father's consent. Well, it had all worked out in the end, but it had been a difficult and lonely life for her till Ben broke down and took her back.

Despite the ominously familiar determination he saw in her eyes, William deliberately filled his pipe and lit it before he spoke.

"You was sixteen then. You're twenty-four now by my reckoning. Haven't you learned anything in the past eight years?"

"Well, if you won't help me, I guess I'll have to let David Baxter be the one." She turned away from him abruptly and, going to the rail, looked across the harbor at the *Jewel of the Seas*.

"David Baxter?" William frowned as he followed her to the rail and saw the direction of her eyes. "I thought that young man had more sense. The *Jewel*'s gettin' old. No place for a child to be born. He really say he'd take you to sea in her?"

"Well . . ." Julia trailed her fingers along the polished rail. "Not exactly. But he did say he'd stay here in Hong Kong with me till after the child comes and then he'll take me home."

William Thacher felt as though he'd had the wind knocked out of him by a rogue wave. "So that's the way the wind blows," he said half under his breath.

"The wind isn't blowing any way except home as far as I'm concerned." Julia hit the rail with her fist.

"Well, that does put a different complexion on things," he said softly. Then suddenly his voice became one of command. "Julie, come below to the saloon. I want to have a talk with you."

"We're talking now." She stubbornly refused to look at him.

"I mean in private."

She glanced back over her shoulder and saw that there was no one near them. "This is as private as we need unless you intend to start shouting at me."

"When did I ever shout at you?" William was a patient man, but Julia and her father were the only two people he had ever known who could truly exasperate him. It made him wonder why he was so fond of them.

"You never did." She turned and looked up at him with eyes that said pretty soon she was going to cry. "Cousin William, you told me once that, whenever I wanted something, all I had to do was ask. This is the first time since then that I've asked, and you're turning me down."

"Hold on now. I've hardly got the anchor down and you come aboard with another one of your hare-brained schemes and expect me to play along with you. Give me time to think this out. Maybe if I have a talk with young Logan, he'll reconsider."

"Then you don't think there's anything wrong with me going to sea now."

"I didn't say that. I just said I'd talk to him. There's other factors to be considered."

"What other factors?"

"You . . . for one."

Julia never knew what William Thacher said to her husband to make him change his mind, but after an evening spent on board *Neptune's Dragon,* Stephen returned to their room at the factory and told her that she could sail with him on the *Crystal Star.* The abruptness of his announcement and the coolness that followed for several days made Julia decide not to question him. All that was important was that she was going. Her child *would* be born at sea, and he would love it as much as she did.

From William Thacher, she could get nothing but a rather taciturn, "Well, You're gettin' your way again, Julia. Be satisfied with that." He saw no point in telling her that, once confronted with David Baxter's plans, Stephen was not hard to convince. William still felt that she was taking an unnecessary risk, but he knew Julia well enough to know that, whatever the obstacles, she would find a way. It was better when her time came for her to be aboard her husband's ship and under his care than in some dubious vessel amongst strangers. The one thing he did know was that, if she said she wasn't going to stay in Hong Kong, she would not stay in Hong Kong.

When the *Crystal Star* sailed out of Lyemoon Pass, Rose Doane was aboard, and as soon as they hit the slightly rougher waters of the South China Sea, she was in bed with the worst case of seasickness Julia had ever seen. She stayed there for a week, and Julia, with the healthy person's intolerance for an illness she had never known, was filled with impatience. She concealed it from Stephen, however, for he had taken a dislike to Rose the minute he laid eyes on her.

Each time Julia went on deck after checking on Rose, Stephen would greet her with a dry, "Well, how's *your nurse* doing?" And each time, Julia would reply, "Better."

She didn't tell him how much effort it caused her to enter the woman's cabin and bathe her face. The heavy fetid odor in the small cabin made Julia herself feel ill.

Charles, the steward, seeing Julia come white-faced and gagging from Rose's cabin on the third day out, was shocked. He took her arm and helped her into the saloon. Then he watched her with concern until she had downed the glass of water he brought.

"Miz Logan," he said as he took the glass from her, "you got no business going in that woman's room. You got to think of your baby."

"If I don't tend to her, who will?" Julia said wearily. "I'm the only other woman aboard."

"I will."

"Oh, Charles, I can't ask you to do that. It's not right. You've got enough on your hands, looking after Captain Logan and me."

"You and the Captain don't make much work. What I want is to see that woman well enough to look after you when your time comes. There's enough muttering from the men about her. If she's not going to help you, then I don't know what they'll be saying."

"Muttering? What do they have to mutter about? They've hardly seen her."

"You know sailors. They're always saying that any woman aboard besides the captain's wife is bad luck. They'll put up with her because of you. They think a lot of you. But if she don't get up on her feet and *do* something . . ." He shook his head.

"I suppose they'll blame everything that goes wrong on her."

"They're already doing that."

"Then they'll just have to mutter!" Julia snapped. "There's not much else they can do about it."

"No, but you'd better let me take care of Miz Doane. I'll get her on her feet."

Julia looked at his kind face thoughtfully. It wasn't proper for a man who wasn't related to a woman to take care of her, but proper be damned. She was sick and tired of waiting hand and foot on Rose Doane.

"All right, Charles. See what you can do."

Whatever Charles did, it was the right thing. A few days later, when the air was light and baffling, Rose staggered up on deck and sank weakly into a chair. The sight of her did not improve Stephen's temper, and Julia could understand his prejudice. The woman sat like a piece of limp, tired seaweed that had been flung aboard by a careless wave. She rarely raised her yellow eyes to look at anyone and never spoke unless it was absolutely necessary. Even then it was only a few words. A yes and a no seemed to be the extent of her vocabulary. The least she could do was tend to her hair, Julia thought irritably. It looked as though she hadn't combed it since the moment she'd stepped aboard.

Julia, trying to interest her in the life of the sea, would point out a ring dove that landed on the main yard, the men's sport as they tried to catch a shark that had been circling the ship, the school of rainbow-hued dolphins that followed them, the antics of the pet monkey one of the men had brought aboard. Rose would glance up, murmur "yes ma'am" in a harsh voice, and look down at her hands or feet again. Julia could only sigh. It was going to be a long trip.

Off the coast of Borneo, Rose roused herself enough to realize the danger of the waters, and she watched with terror the hundreds of miles of jagged islands, reefs, and shoals through which they passed. Whenever the wind blew suddenly out of a different quarter or the ship was swept through a boiling current, she covered her face with both her hands as though she had caught the last sight of life.

There was no way to reassure her that the Malay proas, whose naked inhabitants wore only a cloth around their heads and waists and who displayed pointed teeth stained black with betel nut, were no danger unless the ship hit a shoal or was becalmed. When the crew practiced their gunnery, as much to impress the natives as to sharpen their aim, Rose, with her hands to her ears, fled below.

By the time they reached Gaspar Island with its high verdant hills and low hanging clouds, Stephen's patience finally reached its end. It was not long after sunrise when they sighted the island, and Rose was still asleep below. Julia, after a hot equatorial night, had risen early to enjoy the freshness of the day, and she found Stephen there before her. He was pacing the deck, paying little attention to the island, which Julia thought was one of the prettiest in the area.

Julia had just seated herself near the companionway and opened her sandalwood fan when Stephen stopped just in front of her. He was glowering.

"This has gone on long enough," he said.

"*What* has gone on long enough, Stephen? It's too early for mysteries."

"This charade. This woman whose wages I am paying and who is doing nothing but sogering, screaming, and whining. I will not have her aboard my ship any longer."

"Well, what do you plan to do about it?" She looked at the island. From across the water, she could hear the jungle morning cacophony of birds and screaming monkeys. "Put her ashore to fend for herself amongst the headhunters?"

"No. For God's sake, Julia," he said impatiently. "It's only a few days until we reach Anjier. She can go ashore there."

"And what is she going to do in Java?" She was really in no mood for a debate before breakfast, she thought as she fanned herself. "Stephen, I know she's a trial, but Anjier is no place to leave a white woman. The Intendant is practically the only one with a really decent house, and I doubt he'd be willing to take her in. Aside from that, there's nothing but dirty roads and those squalid bamboo shacks."

He whipped off his cap and wiped his face with his sleeve. She could see by the lines in his face how tired he was. He'd had little sleep since they had left Hong Kong nor would he until they had cleared the Straits of Sunda.

"She hasn't been aboard two weeks yet," he said, "and I'm expected to put up with her for eleven or more?"

"I don't know what else we can do." Julia worked her fan more briskly for, although the sails were drawing, the light air was directly astern. There was no breeze to be felt on deck. "We've taken her on, and if we want to make a fast voyage, there's no place between here and New York to leave her."

"I'd like to put her under the mate. He'd soon knock that nonsense out of her."

"Well, she didn't sign the Articles, Stephen."

He slapped his cap back on and abruptly left her to pace the deck again. After a few minutes, he returned.

"There are bound to be other vessels at Anjier. I'll pay her passage home in one of them."

"And what are you going to say when they ask you why you don't want her aboard the *Crystal Star?*"

"Someone'll take her if I offer them enough money."

"Stephen, I know she isn't much help now, but I may need her yet. I'll feel better for having her with me when the child is born."

"What . . . seasick, weeping and wailing, fainting for all we know. That woman's going to be more hindrance than help."

"No. I think she'll be all right when the time comes. She's just settling down to shipboard life. And remember, she's had a hard time the last few years."

"Hard! I'd like to show her what's hard."

"Stephen, I need her."

Stephen paced over to the helmsman, looked at the compass, and paced back to her again.

"I have half a mind to put you *both* on another ship, one with some women aboard."

"You know you're not going to do that."

"No, I'm not. But devil take her, what am I going to do with her?"

"I'll have a talk with her," Julia said soothingly. "Maybe she'll straighten out."

"She damn well better."

When Rose came on deck an hour later, she scuttled past Stephen and went to sit beside Julia, who had had her chair moved so that the awning would shield her from the hot morning sun. The woman was so near she prevented some of the air from reaching Julia, and Julia was just about to ask her to move when she realized that the woman was almost crouching beside her as though seeking protection.

Seeing that Julia was looking at her strangely, Rose nervously licked her dry lips and said in a whisper, "Ma'am, please don't let the captain put me ashore."

"What gives you the idea I will, Rose?"

"I overheard what the captain were saying this morning, ma'am. I didn't mean to eavesdrop, I didn't, but I were jest coming up when I heard him say my name. I couldn't help but listen, ma'am. Really I couldn't."

Julia glanced over at Stephen. Despite his earlier concern, he was oblivious of the two women now. The intensity of his attention was directed on the ship and the boiling, white-foamed reefs of the Straits of Gaspar.

"You know, Rose, the captain is justified in what he was saying," Julia said quietly. "You haven't been any use to us at all. If he decides to put you off, there's not much I can do to stop him. He's master of the ship. You're the only one who can help yourself."

"Me, ma'am?" Her yellow eyes, wide with fear, seemed to tilt up more than ever. "If you won't help, there's no hope for me."

"Well, you can begin by finishing that mending I gave you two days ago," Julia said briskly. "And have some faith in the captain. He's not going to run us aground or let us be taken by pirates. I've been sailing with him for over two years. Do you think I'd still be aboard if there was anything to be afraid of?"

"I been told you was almost taken by pirates oncet."

"But we weren't, and we won't be."

"I can't help it if I'm skeered, ma'am." Rose's harsh voice had that wheedling tone that annoyed Julia more than any other.

"The only way to stop being scared is to stop acting scared."

"That's easy enough for you to say, ma'am. I doubt you've ever been skeered in your life."

"I've been scared plenty of times," Julia said impatiently, "but I don't hide my eyes and run. I take a good, long look at what I'm scared of and then it goes away."

"What?" The woman's straw eyebrows shot up. "The thing you're skeered of?"

"No, but I'm not scared of it anymore. I'd advise you to try the same thing."

"Well, I'll try, ma'am." Rose sniffled as though she were going to cry.

"Then go below and get that sewing and finish it today. I have more mending I want you to do tomorrow. Then there's washing and ironing to be done." Julia looked distastefully at the woman's soiled dress. "And I'd start by washing that dress if I was you."

"They don't give us much water."

"If there isn't enough fresh water for washing clothes in, use salt water. For heaven's sake, whatever did you do on the voyage out?"

"I don't remember, ma'am. I were sick most of the trip."

"Well, you're not going to be sick anymore this trip." Not if I have anything to say about it, Julia thought to herself.

By the end of the day, when they had reached the island of Banka with its hills and valleys shadowed by the late afternoon sun, Rose had finished the assigned mending and had changed into a fresh dress. Even her sallow face looked cleaner and her hair was more neatly combed than Julia had seen it since they'd left Hong Kong. The sight of the long, lonely marshes of Sumatra, where the trees sometimes hung blackly over the water's edge, made Rose shiver despite the heat, but she looked at it with a determination that gave Julia hope.

There was a relaxation on board as they sailed down the Java Sea, well out of sight of land. Although it was hot, they had a favoring breeze, and everyone hoped for a fast passage home. When they anchored in Anjier Roads to report their passage in the Register of Ships at the Intendant's house, Rose clung to Julia's side. However, she forgot to be frightened of the Malay proas and watched with fascination as the small, black-skinned men called out the virtues of the bananas, coconuts, oranges, mats, monkeys, parakeets, pineapples, hats, Malacca canes, turtles, yams, sweet potatoes, fowls, eggs, rice, birds, peppers, Java sparrows, and shells that filled their boats. As the baskets of fresh food began to fill the decks, she seemed almost happy, but when the longboats set out with their casks in search of water, she would glance nervously at Stephen as though she were waiting to be ordered ashore or into one of the vessels lying at anchor in the Roads.

Stephen, for his part, simply avoided looking at her. He had decided to treat her as though she didn't exist. If he glanced in her direction, his eyes seemed to go through her. If she spoke, which was rare, he didn't hear.

As they set out from Anjier for the Straits of Sunda, Julia decided to relax and forget the whole situation. It would do her baby no good for her to be caught between an agitated woman on the one side and the cold, impatient man on the other. It would be far better for her child if she enjoyed watching Java with its towering blue peaks and the land that ran down to huge groves of coconuts and plantains along the shore. There were the rice terraces that alternated with the red kina plantations, yellow tamarinds and green kananga flowers. The off-shore breeze was filled with the scent of flowers, cinnamon, and cloves. This might well be their last close contact with land until they reached home, and she intended to relish it.

Once they were well into the Straits, the character of the shoreline changed. Rocky bluffs and points rose dramatically from the water, and the land was covered with a green forest so thick it looked almost impenetrable. And yet the little proas still followed them.

Although she understood the dangers of the Straits and could still shudder if she remembered all the tales of piracy, murder, and worse which had happened in these waters, Julia had decided long ago that until and unless the worst happened, she would try to concentrate upon the beauty of the world around her.

The mosquitoes that swarmed out from shore at night were more difficult to ignore, and the cheesecloth with which she draped her bed in defense against them made the nights even hotter, but she knew that they, like the land, would soon be left far behind.

Yet even when they had broken out into the Indian Ocean and left towering Java Head, Bowers' Island, and Clapp's Island far behind, Rose continued in the nocturnal habits she had begun in the heat. It seemed strange to Julia for she had noticed that the woman became more agitated as night came on. She concluded that Rose must find comfort in the closeness of the animals in the

261

shed and pens and coops that comprised their floating barnyard.

For the livestock on the main deck was the one thing that Rose finally did take an interest in. When the ducks were let out of their coops for a stroll on deck and a swim in a tub filled with salt water, she rose from her chair to watch them. When the pigs were let out for their exercise and were chased by the sailors who tried to recapture them, she laughed. As they drew farther away from land, Rose would go down on the main deck to feed the cow a few wisps of straw and to pat the lambs.

Watching Rose with the animals, Julia realized how little she knew about this uncommunicative woman.

"Were you raised on a farm, Rose?" she asked one day.

"No'm. My uncle, my mother's brother he were, he had a small place in the country. You couldn't rightly call it a farm, but it were nice." Her thin lips softened in a smile. "We went to visit him once when I were a little girl. But . . . he died." Her smile faded and her face closed once more.

"He must have had some animals. You seem right fond of them."

"No'm. Not many. They were there, though." The woman's face lit up as she spoke of them. "All around in fields and in people's yards. All kinds of critters. I liked them. Better than people, they were."

Julia examined the woman's face. Her complexion had improved as the sun tanned away the sallowness of her skin and the fresh sea air brought color to her cheeks. With her close-set features that seemed too small for her face, she would never be pretty, but her hair, bleached to a lighter shade, made her eyes seem golden.

"Maybe when you get home, you'll be able to find a place in the country," Julia suggested.

"Maybe. There's not many jobs to be had there, though." Rose lapsed into a dejected silence. Julia found her moods trying. She sometimes seemed to cast a pall on the very air she breathed.

Julia picked up her book and had just found her place when the woman spoke again.

"Ma'am?" she said timidly.

"Yes, Rose." Julia put down her book with a sigh.

"You was raised in the country, wasn't you? That's where your home is?"

"Well, I don't know that you'd exactly call it country. There's a

262

few farms around, but the soil's too poor for them to pay well. Most people go to sea or work in the shipyard or the saltworks."

"But there are critters there?"

"Yes." Julia smiled. "There are some critters around."

"Do you think . . ." Rose paused and rubbed her hands against her skirt. The effort to talk almost seemed too much for her.

"Well, what is it, Rose?"

"Do you think, ma'am, that I could find a job there? If you was to put in a word for me . . ."

"I don't think so, Rose," Julia said gently. The last thing she wanted was to be saddled with this woman, and she couldn't ask anyone else to take her in. That was certain.

"But I'd do anything, ma'am," she pleaded, and her yellow eyes opened so wide they seemed to fill her face.

"I'm sorry, Rose, but it's as you said. There aren't many jobs to be had, and those there are go to people we've known all our lives. You'd do better in the city . . . amongst people you know."

"There's not many I know. Not any more." She took a stitch in the chemise she was mending, then looked at the waves that were running low and free. "Oh, I should never have gone to China. My mum warned me."

"Why *did* you go to China?" Julia asked. Rose certainly didn't seem the adventurous sort.

"I don't know, ma'am. I heard the Lewises were looking for someone. And there were a man I knew . . . but he were married. It seemed like it might be a good idea to go away. I should have stood home, I should."

"Well, you're on your way home now. That should give you something to look forward to." Julia felt her son stir within her and she shifted in her chair to a more comfortable position. She wished everyone were as content as she felt at this moment.

"Won't be the same, ma'am." Rose shook her head. "I'm older now, I am. A married woman with no husband to show for it."

"He'll likely turn up some day," Julia said lazily.

"But how will he find me?" Her yellow eyes were hopeless and helpless.

"He's a sailor, isn't he?"

"Yes'm."

"Well, he'll likely go back to Hong Kong someday. If you send the Lewises your address, they'll give it to him. Why, he might even come to New York and find you."

"I think he must be dead." Rose bent over her sewing and mumbled more to herself than to Julia. "Otherwise he would of come back . . . or wrote me. Course he can't write, but he could of sent word, couldn't he?"

"I don't know, Rose. It's hard to tell. Sometimes men show up years after everyone's given them up for lost. Did you ever write to his family in England to find out if they'd heard from him?"

"He didn't have no family, ma'am. He were an orphan. Least that's what he told me. Said he'd went to sea when he were a lad and never had no home. Said I'd be his home." A few tears started down her face, and she wiped them away with the chemise.

Julia sighed. She wanted to sit quietly in the pleasant warmth, watch the sails and the shadows cast by the waves, and dream about her child. Yet she, too, had known the sorrow of a man lost and she couldn't withhold whatever help she might give.

"What about the ship he sailed on when he left Hong Kong? Did you ask the captain about him?"

"I asked the mate, ma'am, but he weren't no help. Said Tom took his money and jest disappeared when they got to Calcutta. How can a man jest disappear, ma'am?"

"A thousand ways, I guess," Julia said. "Maybe he signed on board another vessel. A lot of masters don't ask questions. If they need a hand, they take him. If they're short, they're thankful to get a seaman."

"Guess he could be anywhere in the world now," Rose said and her voice quivered. "Said he hadn't been back to England for twenty years. It's not right, ma'am, that a man can go off and leave a woman that way and her with no way to find him."

"No, it's not right, Rose, but it's the way of the sea. Sailors make poor husbands."

"Guess you're right, ma'am. It's different with you and the captain, but most of them seem to be more wed to the sea than they be to any woman, they do."

Julia looked down at the deck where the men were hard at work. The sailmaker was busy mending sails. The carpenter was making a new grating to replace one that had been washed overboard in a squall. The rest of the crew were variously employed in the rigging, greasing the masts, oiling the yard trusses and steering gear, and cleaning the brass work. There were no idle hands, and all was silence except for the singing sails and rigging, the long swish of the waves against the ship, and the

264

murmur of voices on the quarterdeck. Though the men worked hard, there was peace.

"Some of them are wed to it," Julia agreed.

"I don't see why." Rose shook her head. "It's not the easiest life I ever seed. You couldn't pay me enough to be a sailor, you couldn't. It's not worth all the money in the world. Once I get off this ship, I'll never go to sea again."

"Well, to some of them, it's home. Like your Tom, it's the only home they know."

"And you, ma'am? Why do you go to sea? You don't have to. You could have a nice cozy house, I'm sure, with all the comforts."

Julia smiled at her. How could she explain to this woman who looked upon the sea as an alien and malignant thing?

"A woman should be at her husband's side," she said simply.

"But most women don't follow their husbands to sea, they don't. It's no place for a woman." Clearly Rose thought that Julia was slightly deranged.

"Well, it's my place," Julia said firmly and picked up her book again.

It was only a few days later, while they were still in the southeast tradewinds of the Indian Ocean, that the fights began. The first one was an explosion that shattered the peaceful evening hours of the dogwatch.

After battling an early morning gale that had lasted well into the afternoon, the sailors off watch felt that they had earned their leisure. Some gathered in small groups to smoke their evening pipes and gossip. A few solitaries, thinking of things known only to themselves, leaned on the rail to watch the red and gold clouds that reflected the sun as it set into a quiet sea. Two of the boys were playing with a monkey they had picked up from a proa at Anjier.

Suddenly, near the cowshed, there were shouts and curses as two men closed on each other. There was the flash of a knife, and Wilson was down from the quarterdeck as though he had flown there. Ignoring the knife, he grabbed a belaying pin and knocked the two men apart. Instantly the rest of the crew was there. Some held one man, known only as Swede. Others held an Englishman called Lojo.

265

"Bring those men aft," Stephen called from the quarterdeck and waited calmly until they were on the main deck below him.

"I've told you men that I'll have no fighting aboard my ship," he said coldly. "If it's punishment you want, you need only apply to me. I'll be glad to oblige you. Now what started it?"

The big-boned Swede shook his blond head and looked down at the deck. "I don't know, Cap'n."

"Well?" Stephen looked at the wiry, black-haired Lojo.

Lojo held himself straight and stared back at Stephen. "That damn Swede started it, Cap'n."

"That ain't true!" Swede started to lunge for Lojo, but was pulled back by two of his shipmates.

"I didn't ask *who* started it," Stephen said in a voice that would have cut through an iron anchor chain. "I asked *what* started it."

Swede, who was still held by his friends, merely shook his shaggy head again and stared at the deck.

Lojo cleared his throat and his black eyes shiftily searched the faces on the quarterdeck one by one as though he would find the answer or his salvation there. Julia noticed that he spent longest on the face beside her own. Rose's.

"Well?" Stephen's voice cracked out.

"It wasn't nothin', Cap'n," Lojo said. Then as Stephen stared at him, the cockiness drained from the man and he too lowered his eyes.

"Then don't let it happen again. Five stripes for each man in the morning," Stephen directed the mate. Then he looked at the culprits coldly and thoughtfully. "Next time it will be ten and the time after that it will be fifteen. So I would advise you men to think very carefully before you attack anyone again. Now go below until your watch is called."

Almost everyone on board except the helmsman and the mate stood as though frozen until the two men had disappeared down the forward hatch. Then the mate called out, "All right. Back to your stations, men."

The ship appeared as it had before, but now the men who gathered in small groups had lost their lazy air, and the solitaries looked tensely toward the forecastle instead of at the sunset. Stephen went below and sent first for the officers and then for the men one by one.

Julia slowly considered the way Lojo's eyes had lingered on Rose. She studied the woman, who was demurely stitching away,

266

and thought that her face looked rather flushed and self-satisfied.

"Do you know anything about that fight, Rose?" Julia asked her sharply.

"Me, ma'am?" Rose's eyes opened with innocent surprise. "How should I know anything about it?"

"Do you know those men?"

"I've only spoken to them when I were down with the critters." The flush had drained from Rose's face and her hands moved nervously in her lap. "That were all right, weren't it, ma'am?"

"I think that, from now on, you'd best stay away from the main deck unless I'm with you."

"Oh, ma'am, please don't say I can't go down to the critters. I won't talk to the men no more. I promise. But the critters know I'm coming. They'll miss me if I don't come."

"All right." Julia wondered if she were doing the right thing. Perhaps she should discuss her suspicions with Stephen. Yet Stephen had enough antipathy towards Rose. There was no point in unnecessarily aggravating it. "But see to it that you don't speak to the men anymore."

"I won't, ma'am."

The next morning, when the floggings were to take place, Julia left the quarterdeck to hide in the safety of her cabin. Even though she knew they were necessary for discipline, she had never been able to harden herself to the punishments inflicted on the men.

Rose, however, stayed on deck, and when Julia returned, she found the woman even more flushed than she had been the night before, and there was an excited glitter in her yellow eyes. The sight of Rose's feverish face bothered Julia more than the thought of the floggings had. She didn't understand the revulsion it brought, but she tried to ignore the woman for the rest of the day.

After that, fights broke out with increased frequency amongst the members of the crew. In stormy weather, there was no trouble, but Julia found herself dreading those serene days, which had once given her the greatest joy she had ever experienced.

Stephen and the mates tried to get to the bottom of the problem, but none of the men involved would speak no matter what their punishments were. Stephen was completely puzzled. He had never seen this situation arise at sea before. There had been occasional grudge fights, but now any member of the crew, except for the royal boys, seemed a likely participant.

As for Rose, Julia watched her carefully, but true to her word, she did not speak to the sailors when she went to pet the animals. The most she ever did was nod stiffly at them, and she handled herself with the greatest circumspection. Julia felt a little guilty about her suspicions. Rose was hardly a likely woman to raise trouble amongst men. She was simply too unattractive.

Julia never looked forward to rounding the Cape of Good Hope, but now the gales, the calms, the white squalls all seemed a blessing. The men were kept too busy tacking ship, clearing the vessel of the havoc a storm could wreak, furling and unfurling sails to act out their antagonisms.

Once they had rounded the Cape, there would be an occasional outburst, but too many of the men had felt the wrong end of a rope to be inclined to go very far. Still there was a tension aboard that could not seem to settle itself.

The southeast trades were carrying them rapidly through the South Atlantic and they had passed St. Helena a week before when Julia felt the first hard pains. When they awakened her, she could see the moon streaming through the cabin windows and she heard six bells striking. Three o'clock in the morning. Stephen, enjoying a peaceful night, lay sleeping soundly beside her. She hated to wake him for soon they would be in the variables and he would have little rest. But when the pains came again, she nudged him.

"Stephen!" she whispered.

He was instantly awake as he always was with the slightest shift of wind.

"Is it now?" he asked and his voice was gentle with concern.

"I think so. It's beginning anyway."

"Do you want me to get that woman?" He still refused to mention Rose by name.

"I don't know. I'd rather wait till the last minute. She flutters so."

"She'd better come now," he said firmly. Already he was slipping into his trousers. "That's what she's being paid for."

"I suppose."

Stephen glanced out the window as he pulled on his shirt. "Thank God, it's a quiet night."

"I told you it would be." Julia tried to smile through the pain that tore at her once again.

Stephen bent to kiss her lightly. "I'll be right back," he said reassuringly.

While Julia lay there waiting, she heard a woman's sudden screams and a man shouting. Rose! Stephen! What in creation was going on? Panting, she managed to sit up and slip her legs over the edge of the bed. As she paused to catch her breath, Stephen burst through their cabin door, dragging Rose, still in her nightgown, behind him.

"Get in there and get to work," he told her roughly.

"Stephen, in heaven's name," Julia said, aghast at Stephen's treatment of the woman. "Let her get dressed first. There's time enough for that."

Rose broke away from Stephen's grasp and threw herself on the floor beside the bed. She clutched Julia's knees.

"Save me, ma'am. Save me," she shrieked.

"You're the one that's supposed to be saving me." She looked from Rose up at Stephen. "What in the holy hell is going on here?"

"That one doesn't have to get dressed," Stephen said. "She doesn't give a damn who sees her in her nightgown. It was Swede she had in her bed this time. I'd be willing to wager it's been every member of the crew at other times. This bitch is the explanation for the fights we've been having."

"Rose!" Julia wasn't really as shocked as she sounded. The woman's flushes of excitement whenever there was a flogging, her nocturnal wanderings. By day, her actions might be above reproach, but at night? Evidently the critters that so comforted Rose weren't just the four-footed or feathered variety. She realized now that the suspicions she'd had at first had never really been banished from her mind, but for a long time, all she had really wanted to think about was her child.

Rose was still babbling hysterically and holding tight to Julia's knees. It was the last thing she wanted held at the moment. In her pain and exasperation, Julia reached down and slapped Rose as hard as she could.

"Get up off that floor and get dressed. The child's coming at any minute, and if you don't behave, I'll have you thrown to the sharks."

When Rose continued to blubber, Stephen jerked her up by the armpits and shoved her at the door. "You heard what your mistress said. Clean yourself and call the steward to get what's needed."

Then he gently lifted Julia's legs and eased her back onto the bed. She closed her eyes for a moment as the pain took her and when she opened them, she saw that Stephen was grinning down at her.

"I don't think it's very funny," she said.

"I do. Not your pain and not that scene. I'm sure you could have done without it. It was what you said about the sharks."

"I shouldn't have said that."

"No." He was laughing now. "It's exactly what you should have said. Don't you remember that first day we met? I promised to clothe you in silks and satins and allow you to feed prisoners to your pet sharks."

Julia smiled. It came back. The surge of overpowering love for him, for the young man who had been looking for a master's berth, for the experienced captain who now looked down at her with an equal love in his eyes. Rose didn't matter. Nothing else mattered.

"That's when we were going to be pirates," she whispered.

"Yes, my lady." He gave her his hand to clutch when the pain came again.

"But now you're sorry I'm here, aren't you?"

"No," he said. "I couldn't have left you behind. I realize that now. The only thing I regret is that we couldn't have found someone a little more suitable to come with us."

"I'm sorry for that, Stephen."

"Well, just because she's a whore doesn't mean that she can't do the job at hand."

At nine in the morning, just as they were crossing the equator, there were the first small cries, and Stephen, who had been pacing the saloon instead of the quarterdeck, came bounding into the cabin. Rose handed him his daughter.

In the wonder of the tiny girl, all Stephen's anger with Rose was gone. The miniature fingers that clutched his, the little red face screwed up and screaming her resentment at entering the world only enchanted him. This was his child. His very own.

"I'm sorry, Stephen," Julia whispered.

"Julie, love. Are you all right?" He laid the baby on the bed beside her and searched her face which was so unnaturally white.

"I think so. Tired. I'm sorry it's not a boy."

"A boy?" He smiled the smile that would make him forever young and smoothed the damp tendrils of black hair away from her forehead. "I never said I wanted a boy. You're the one who insisted that it would be, and I thought you were in the best position to know. I wanted a girl . . . like you."

"Really?"

"Yes, really."

"Are you going to give her a plank for her sharks, too?"

"Absolutely, but not until she's wearing silks and satins and is old enough to know how to use it. You'll have to give her lessons."

"Who knows? I just might do that." As she fell asleep, there was a smile on her lips.

Chapter Fourteen

1848

On looking back, Julia sometimes thought those years were the best years, the happiest years. The years before Clara had been born. She and Stephen had had all of life before them, the world had been theirs to explore, and the *Crystal Star* had lived up to her promise and had placed Stephen's name amongst the top masters.

She could never pin down exactly when the troubles started, those small irritations that gradually grew into barriers over which neither she nor Stephen could find the oneness that had been theirs. Had it been the baby's crying that kept Stephen from his much needed sleep? Had it been his resentment of the time she spent with the child, time which had once belonged solely to him?

The jealousy had always been there. She had recognized it from the earliest days of their marriage and had tried to guard against it. But jealous of his own child? No, it couldn't be. He adored Clara.

And when had he begun to drink so heavily? Although, as far as the crew was concerned, he ran a temperance ship, he himself had always enjoyed a rum or brandy. During those first few years of life, Clara had so often been ill. There had been colic, and each new tooth had been a chore. If that hadn't been bad enough, every time they touched shore, she caught something new. Julia hadn't consciously realized how more and more often she had seen Stephen pour himself a drink nor had she noted how swiftly the decanters' contents dwindled and had to be refilled by the steward.

Megan was the first to call her attention to it. It was that awful summer when they had touched at Tahiti on their way to China and found that Megan was desperate.

There had been no hint of the tragedy on shore as they approached the channel between Mooréa and Tahiti. The clouds still flickered their peaceful shadows over the green and violet mountains, the streams still sparkled down the valleys, the water still shone in its endless and sometimes deadly variety of blues and greens and whites. The well-fed native pilot who came aboard to guide them into the harbor was smiling as brightly as the sun.

Julia held Clara up so that she could see the beauty of the islands and told her stories of Tomaii, of Aunt Megan, Uncle George, and little Frederick. When the child began to squirm, Julia gave her a kiss on her pale gold hair and handed her over to her nurse, Becky. Free now of any thoughts but her own, Julia let that mixture of languorous pleasure and excited anticipation, which only Tahiti and Mooréa could evoke, wash over her. She was content to savor each moment even while she wondered if Megan had gotten word that the *Crystal Star* had arrived.

The harbor seemed strangely empty. There were only one French barque and two American whalers swinging at anchor. As they neared the shore, the outriggers that raced to meet them were more numerous than ever, but the town of Papeete seemed unusually quiet.

Stephen, who was always able to think on two or three levels at once, assessed the situation even as he critically watched John Pratt supervise the anchoring. Now that Kenneth Wilson had command of his own vessel, they had a new first mate on this voyage.

"I don't think we'll be here long," Stephen said to Julia. "Unless something unusual has drawn everyone out to sea, the trade's gone." He pushed his cap back and shook his head. "We haven't sighted a vessel for the past few days, either."

"But what will we do with the cargo?" Julia asked as she thought of the lumber, the cotton, the iron goods that filled the holds.

Stephen shrugged. "Sell what we can here and sail for the Sandwich Isles or push on direct for Shanghai or Hong Kong. The China treaty ports can probably use what we have. If the situation is as bad as it appears on the surface, we'll get under way tomorrow morning or the morning after." He hit his right fist against his left palm. "Damn! After last year, I should have known better than to return."

"But it wasn't so bad last year, Stephen." Julia was distressed at the thought of such a short stay with Megan. "We sold all the cargo then and took on what we needed for China."

"Yes and took twice as long to do it as we ever have before. The profit wasn't there, either. Not what it should have been. I saw the signs. I hoped it was only temporary, but I should have known that, with the French in control and driving the missionaries out, it was only going to get worse." He shook his head again as he thought of the lost time, the lower profits this voyage would bring.

"But Megan said it wasn't too bad. The French took over some of the native chapels and turned them into national property, and the government appropriated a couple of the missionaries' houses, but that was all."

"That was all then," Stephen said grimly. "That was a year ago."

"A year . . . yes. Oh, I hope Megan and her family are all right."

"I don't doubt they are. Or else they've gone on to greener pastures. I'm sure the good Reverend Fairfield has planned everything to his advantage. At any rate, we'll know soon enough."

"Then this is our last time, Stephen?" She looked at the islands she so loved. It was miserable to think that she might never see them again.

"Most likely, at least for the near future. If the political picture changes, then there's the possibility we'll return." He put an arm lightly around her shoulders for he knew how she felt. He, too, had been touched by the magical beauty that seemed to shimmer in the very air of the South Pacific islands. "I wouldn't count on it, though. It takes a long time to build up trade. Without the missionaries to make them work, these people won't, and they'll have nothing to offer."

"Then perhaps it's going back," Julia said thoughtfully as she remembered the ancient tales Megan had told her.

"Back? Back to what?" He looked at her strangely.

"Back to the old days when the people were themselves and not the missionaries' property."

"For God's sake, Julia, we're talking about trade."

"I know, but there will always be trade somewhere. How I'll miss these islands, though."

"And Megan." Despite his anxiety over what he would find ashore, he smiled at her.

"Yes, and Megan. Stephen, I'm suddenly right worried about her. How soon do you think I can go ashore?"

He looked at the garlanded natives who were already swinging up the ropes the sailors had let down for them. "It won't be long now," he said.

When she rounded the bend of the coral road and saw the house, Julia knew that she had reason to worry about Megan. The plaited coconut frond roof had obviously not been replaced for some time. The steps to the verandah were sagging and looked dangerously riddled with termites. The paint was streaked and faded. She entered the clearing in front of the house and felt that there was no point in going farther. No one was there.

She stood a few minutes and thought of the laughter and happiness she and Megan had shared on that verandah, the confidences they had exchanged inside the house. It was too sad. She turned away and had almost reached the road when she heard her name called. She turned around and couldn't believe what she saw framed in the black doorway. This disheveled woman with her hair streaming down like a pale curtain around her torn dress couldn't be Megan. Not neat, quicksilver Megan.

"Megan?" she said hesitantly without approaching the house.

"Julie, you've come! You've come!"

Megan ran down the steps, careless of their rotting danger, and soon was crying in Julia's arms.

"I knew you'd come, I knew you'd come," she sobbed. "Every day, I've gone down to the beach and waited for you."

"I'm here, Megan. It's all right." It's all right now." Julia held her friend close and let her cry. For the moment, she wasn't even curious about the cause of Megan's tears. She only wanted to comfort her, to give her strength.

It seemed to work, for after a while, Megan's sobs subsided, and she pulled a little away from Julia so that she could wipe her face on her sleeve.

Julia gave her a handkerchief and put an arm around her still slender back. "Come on, Megan. Come on, love. We'll go in the house and talk about it."

Megan stiffened. "I never want to go into that house again."

"It's all right now. I'm with you. I won't let anything hurt you," Julia said soothingly and pulled her friend along.

The inside of the house was almost as bad as the outside. Although it seemed stripped of its few ornaments, dust lay everywhere, and the coverings of the chairs were dirty and tattered. In one year, Julia thought. That this could happen in one year!

She settled Megan down on the sofa and sat down beside her. "Do you want to tell me about it, Megan?"

"Yes," Megan sniffled. "Yes, but I don't know where to start."

"From the beginning?"

"But where was the beginning?" There was a bewildered, almost dazed, look in Megan's black eyes. "That's what I don't know."

"Then just start anywhere."

"Freddy's gone. My little boy. My angel."

"Gone? Gone where?"

"Dead."

"Oh!" Julia was shocked. That laughing golden child. He had always been so healthy compared with her own daughter Clara. "How, Megan?"

"It was a stone fish." Megan's words came tumbling out. "George wouldn't let him play with the native children, and none of the missionaries' children had been able to come visit for a couple of days. There're not many left now, anyway. So George took him down to the beach. He said he'd watch him for me, but instead he sat down under a tree and started to read his Bible. You know George. He didn't like to waste a minute. When Freddy screamed, George ran down to the water to get him and brought him home, but by then it was too late. The spines were still in his foot. We tried to get them out. We did everything possible. But it was too late. The poison . . . Oh, Julie, it was awful." The little control she had been able to gain now broke, and her sobs were louder than ever.

"I know, I know." Julia held her again and wondered how many tears Megan's delicate body could hold. A mother's tears? How would she feel if Clara. . . . Her heart took a plunge and she hugged Megan closer to her.

As Megan's sobs came more slowly, she said, "Oh, Julie, I'm so glad you've come. I've been so alone."

"Alone? Where's George?"

"He's gone, too. Dead." And Megan's voice was dead.

"George, too?"

"Yes. He . . . he killed himself."

"Oh, no!"

"Yes. I found him . . . hanging from the rafters . . . in there." Megan shuddered as she pointed at her bedroom.

"Oh, Megan. Why?"

"Because of Freddy . . . and because we were going to have to leave. He'd been despondent for a long time. Wouldn't have any work done on the house, because he didn't want the French to have the benefit. Said all his work had been for nothing . . . that his life had been for nothing. Then the day after Freddy's funeral, I came back from walking beside the water . . . to find him."

"Oh, Megan, it's so awful. I can't believe it. George wasn't much of a man for laughter, but he seemed strong. Strong enough to take things and go on."

"No. George was never strong. That's something I learned over the years."

"But you, Megan . . . how long have you been like this . . . alone."

"I don't know. I've lost track of time." Again she looked bewildered. "It happened in February."

"It's July now, Megan," Julia gently reminded her.

"Is it? Yes, of course it is. You're here. I've kept saying Julia will be here in July. Over and over again I've been saying it, like a rhyme. If I said it long enough, then I knew I could go on until July."

"And your friends? What about the other missionaries?"

"They tried. They're good people, Julie. They tried. But something happened to me after I found George. Those people . . ." Megan twisted the soaking handkerchief as though she would tear it. "They kept telling me it was part of God's plan. God's plan . . . to take my darling Freddy? To have George do something so awful? I guess I wasn't right in my mind. I told them they could keep their God and His plans and leave me alone. After a while, they did."

"They should have arranged passage home for you."

"They tried that, too, but I told them I was waiting for you." She gripped Julia's hand convulsively. "I told them, 'Julia will come for me in July.' "

"Oh, Megan, I'm here now. I'll take you home."

"Will you, Julie? Will you really take me home?" The pleading look in the eyes beneath those fair brows was that of a small child.

"Of course, I will. What about your native friends?"

"They bring me food, water, but I have no money to pay them for anything."

"And Mama Omemema?"

"She's dead. Dead, too. Even before Freddy."

"Well, she was an old lady," Julia said gently.

"Yes. She told me she was going. She looked fine, just the way she always did. She told me hard things would happen to me. Hard for me to understand. And they did. But she also told me that you would come for me. She told me to wait for you. She said that, after you came, everything would be all right. The next day, she was dead."

"And she was right, Megan. Everything will be all right now. We can't take you home right away, you know. We have to go to China first. It'll be months before you get home."

"I know, but I want to go with you."

"You will." Julia found it hard to reassure Megan with a smile, yet somehow she managed it.

"I don't have any money for my passage, but my father will pay you when we get home."

"Oh, Megan, you don't have to pay for your passage. Not on the *Crystal Star*. You know that. But have you written to your family?"

"No. Not yet. I was waiting." The creases between Megan's brows deepened and she sighed. "It would only have worried them. There wasn't much they could have done before you got here."

"Well, let's get your things packed," Julia said briskly. "Stephen says we'll only be here for a day or two."

"They're packed. In there." She pointed at the bedroom. "I had everything packed by the first of July so I'd be ready for you."

"Then let's get you washed up and into a fresh dress."

"They're all packed." Megan sat on as though she didn't have the strength to rise.

"Well, we'll just unpack one. You can't go aboard looking like that."

"Do I look so terrible, Julia?"

"Yes. You look perfectly dreadful."

With Julia's words, Megan looked as though she were going to cry again.

"It's nothing that can't be remedied." Julie smiled at her. "Why don't we go up to your private pool and bathe?" Perhaps that would cheer Megan up.

"No. I don't want any more memories."

"Then let's get you fixed up here, and we'll go directly to the ship. We'll send some men to get your things."

While Julia helped Megan wash her hair, she thought of Stephen's words of the morning. If this had happened next year, there would have been no Julia in July. She caught her breath as she realized how nearly there had been none this year. And Megan seemed so helpless. Why, when Megan had helped so many, was there none to help her when she needed it? There was, she reminded herself. There was one, and thank God, this was not next year.

When they boarded the *Crystal Star*, Stephen was still ashore. Knowing what he thought of anyone who gave orders on his ship, Julia hesitated for a moment, but then she told the mate to send some men for Megan's trunks. If the natives knew that Megan had deserted the house, they might think she no longer wanted the few possessions that remained to her.

Stephen returned in the same longboat that carried Megan's belongings, and Julia could see just by the set of his shoulders and the way his cap was pulled down low over his forehead that his mood was not particularly pleasant. She turned quickly to her friend, whose plain muslin dress hung in loose folds on her too thin body, but at least it was clean and her hair was now drawn into a neat chignon at the nape of her neck.

"Megan, you'd best go below while I talk to Stephen."

"Julie," Megan said hesitantly, almost imploringly, "I'm not going to cause any trouble, am I?"

"No, Megan," Julia said as gently as she could. "You're not going to cause any trouble, but I do want to talk to Stephen privately."

After Megan had gone, Julia set her shoulders, ready for the battle that might be coming, but she went forward to meet him on the main deck and tried to smile as he came aboard.

"Did you find a good cargo?" she asked, hoping that would distract him.

"No, damn it, I did not find a good cargo. Nothing but oranges and pearl shells. I want to talk to you on the quarterdeck. Now!" he said harshly and led the way aft to that deserted territory.

Following him, she wondered how full-scale this explosion was going to be.

"So you're giving orders again?" He turned on her as she mounted the last step.

She paused, put her hand lightly on the rail beside her, and said softly, "I only wanted to make sure they didn't steal her things."

"And now, you're not only giving orders. You're taking passengers aboard without consulting me first." He folded his arms across his chest and his eyes were cold.

She, too, folded her arms and leaned back against the rail, but still she answered in a quiet voice. " 'Tis only one passenger, Stephen."

"You think I'm going to abet that woman in running off from her husband and child?" he asked, not in the least appeased by the mildness of her reply.

"They're gone, Stephen." Then she told him how she had found Megan and what had happened in the past few months.

Stephen softened with the telling, but at the end, he shook his head. "There are other ships, Julia. She's not going on this one."

Julia looked pointedly around the harbor. One of the whalers had sailed away that morning. The one that remained was deserted except for two men who slouched near the bow. The French barque was trim but silent. The life of the lagoon belonged to the laughing men in native outriggers, who were coming in from fishing near the reef, and to the swimmers near the shore.

"What other ships, Stephen? No American vessels but whalers have put in here for months, and it might be years before *they* sail for home. We can't just leave her here. She needs us."

"You mean she needs you." He looked up at the hills with their wandering clouds and watched the shadows ripple every shade of green across them. Then he shook his head again. "There are already enough people on this ship who need you, and your first responsibility is to your family. Julia, I am not going to sail around the world with a ship full of women."

"Please try to understand," she pleaded with him. "She's a friend. She's destitute, lost, and terribly lonely. She saw her child die in agony, and her description of the way she found George hanging from the ceiling of her bedroom . . ." She shuddered. "It's horrible. If I was in the same situation, wouldn't you want someone to help me, Stephen?"

"You wouldn't be in the same situation. You'd never find me hanging from your bedroom ceiling . . . or from anything else, for that matter."

"Stephen?"

"All right, Julie," he said with resignation. "You get your way again . . . as usual. I'll take her. At least, until we can make other arrangements. But just remember, this is not a passenger vessel. I'll find room for her, but there'll be no catering to her whims. You'll explain the strictures of life aboard a cargo ship to her and see that she abides by the rules."

"I promise she won't be any trouble," Julia said earnestly.

"See that she isn't," he said gruffly. Without another word, he abruptly turned and went down to the main deck, where he began giving orders to the mate about Megan's trunks and about the cargo he had procured.

Julia sighed as she watched him go and hoped that it was only his frustration about business conditions in Tahiti that was making him so unreasonable about Megan. He so often showed a generosity of spirit that surprised her, but his moods were unpredictable. Well, maybe once they put to sea, he'd cheer up and see things differently. She glanced for a moment across the strait at Mooréa, which was gleaming like a multicolored jewel in the luminous late morning sunlight, before she went below to check on Clara and to get Megan settled in.

However, instead of improving, the atmosphere aboard began to deteriorate almost from the moment they sailed. They were only a few days out when Stephen began to complain to Julia about women's chatter on the quarterdeck despite the fact that Megan usually preferred to remain below, away from the questions she occasionally imagined she saw in the eyes of some of the men. Then he began to accuse Julia of neglecting Clara in favor of Megan, which wasn't true.

It was only when he began to mutter about their lack of privacy that Julia began to understand the true cause of his discontent. Megan, in her grief, was the least obtrusive of persons, but she could hardly remain constantly in the close confines of her cabin, and of course, she joined them for meals in the saloon, but then so did Clara and Becky. Stephen was resigned to the claims Clara made upon her, but he chafed at yet another person absorbing her attention and time.

He began to sleep by day as they rolled across the long easy swells of the dark blue Pacific. Then he stopped eating with them and had his meals served at odd times, which kept the cook and steward constantly off balance. By night, he would pace the quarterdeck and prowl the entire ship as he looked for any fault or slight neglect by the crew. The officers and men suffered from his anger.

As she lay in her bed, where Stephen had rarely joined her since they had left Tahiti, Julia could sometimes hear the clink of decanter meeting glass. Several times she had gotten up and tried to join him in his nocturnal musings, but his anger had turned cold, and he refused to discuss anything with her. There was nothing to do but retreat.

Megan, ever sensitive to the slightest change in other people's moods, could not avoid noticing that things were terribly wrong. She took the blame on herself and was as miserable as Julia.

One day while Becky was putting Clara to bed for her nap, Megan approached Julia on the subject. It was a fair afternoon of spouting whales and rainbows. The watch on deck went silently about their work, and without Stephen's presence, there was a relaxed peace.

"Julie," Megan said without preamble. "I think I'd better leave the *Crystal Star* when we reach Hong Kong."

Julia lowered the book she had been trying to read without success ever since they'd left Tahiti. "Megan, that's ridiculous. What could you possibly do in Hong Kong?"

"Perhaps I could find a place as a governess . . . even a maid. I could make enough to pay my passage home on another ship." There was a look of hopelessness in her black eyes.

"That's out of the question," Julia said firmly. "It would take you forever to make enough, even if you could find a position."

"Then . . . then do you think you could persuade some captain you know to take me home with the assurance that my family will reimburse him for my expenses?"

Julia thought about it for a moment. It was tempting. There was bound to be someone in the China clipper fleet who would be kind enough to take Megan with him. Then Stephen would settle down. As long as Megan remained aboard, Julia felt that it was going to be a *very* long and tedious voyage home. Yet Megan was still so vulnerable. Although her face had begun to fill out and the lines of strain had begun to disappear, her expression too often was one of despair.

"No, Megan," she said briskly. "I said *we'd* take you home and we will."

Megan sighed and looked even sadder. "I really think I'd rather find another way, Julie. I know Stephen was opposed to my coming, and I'm afraid he's taking it out on you."

"Nonsense. It's only that he's disappointed about the cargo in Tahiti. Just wait and see. If there's a good profit to be had in Hong Kong, he'll cheer up."

"Is he always like this when things don't go his way? I mean . . . drinking all night and sleeping all day?"

"Stephen doesn't drink that much!" Julia protested.

Megan bit her lip and stared out at the waves. Then she resolutely looked back at Julia. "I noticed today, when you were both taking sights, his hands were shaking. He couldn't seem to keep the sextant steady. It's happened before."

"Are you sure, Megan?" Julia frowned. "Seems unlikely. If his hands weren't steady, he wouldn't be able to take the sights, but his findings always agree with mine . . . and *my* hands aren't shaking."

"Julie." Megan took a deep breath. "You're so busy taking the sights yourself, you don't have the time to see it. But I've noticed, he always calls them out *after* you do."

"Are you sure, Megan?"

"Yes. I'm quite sure."

That frightened Julia. She was certain Megan wouldn't lie. And if it was true, it meant that she alone was navigating the ship. Pratt did take the sights, too, but he had only recently been promoted to first mate. If his findings were different, it was assumed that he was wrong. Pratt's findings were usually very close to hers, though, Julia reassured herself.

She looked out across the ocean whose deep blue was broken only by the white-capped waves. There was no other sail, no land in this water world. Her sextant suddenly seemed a very fragile instrument to guide them across it. With her complete unquestioning faith in Stephen and his abilities, she had never fully realized what a dangerously invisible line they followed across this empty expanse.

And she thought of her child sleeping peacefully below in her little bunk.

Suddenly, she jumped up from her deck chair.

"If you'll excuse me, Megan, there's something I want to check on."

"But about Hong Kong, Julie . . ."

"Later, Megan," Julia said impatiently. "We'll talk about it when we get there."

"But if Stephen thought I was going to leave the ship then, it might improve things *before* we get there."

"I don't want to talk about it now." Julia swept by Megan's outstretched hand. "I have to go."

Once below, Julia spread out the chart. Their noon position was marked on it, and glancing back over the last few days, it seemed a reasonable position, and the speed estimates they'd made by heaving the log line had only seemed to verify it. She got out the logbook and read it carefully while she checked the charted position for each day. Yet one mistake could send them miles off course.

She closed her eyes, and while thinking of their position, she tried to feel the sea. She could hear it all around her, the whispers, the laughter of the waves. And then she felt reassured. Their course *was* correct. It was something she would never dare mention to anyone, but the sea had never yet played her false.

After that day, she observed Stephen cautiously so that he would not suspect he was being watched. What Megan had said was true. His hands *did* sometimes shake when he took the sights and at other times, too. She noticed the worried look on the steward's face when he filled the decanters. There was the stiff drink Stephen would take upon rising from his late afternoon sleep.

Finally she came to the conclusion that her friend was right. Megan would have to leave them when they reached Hong Kong. Julia would choose a ship for her, the right ship captained by a kind man. And the sooner she talked to Megan about it and told Stephen their plan, the better.

It was a few days before Julia could find the time and opportunity to broach the subject with Megan. First they ran into a series of squalls, and Megan, who was not the best sailor in the world, took to her bed. Then Clara fell ill again with one of her mysterious fevers, and as always, Julia found it hard to stay away from her child's side despite the capable presence of Becky.

When Megan appeared in the doorway of Clara's cabin and asked Julia if she could speak to her, Julia's only emotion was one of exasperation. She felt torn three ways . . . or more.

There was the worry over Stephen that never left her now. There was Clara, hot and crying in her little bed. Julia often wondered if the child would live to grow up. So many of the tombstones in the graveyard at home were small. There was Megan standing in the doorway with the imploring look that made Julia feel like a traitor to even consider abandoning her to another vessel. And finally there was the ship.

Julia was never alone anymore. There was always someone at her side, and the responsibilities seemed to continue to mount up until she felt their weight was more than she could endure. She longed for those early days of marriage when she had had only Stephen and the sea for her companions. She longed for those quiet hours of solitude.

"Can't it wait, Megan?" she said, trying not to let her impatience show. "Clara's so sick. These fevers she gets really fret me."

"Please, Julie. Just five minutes." She was not just imploring now, but frightened.

"All right." Julia rose from her knees and found that she was stiff. "I guess I could do with a cup of tea. Let's go into the saloon."

Once there, Julia leaned her head back against the settee. It felt so good to sit down and relax, if just for a little while. She hadn't known how tired she was, how tight her muscles were. But she couldn't relax, she realized. There was Megan.

"You look tired, Julie." Megan's voice was soft with concern.

"I am, but I'll get some rest as soon as Clara's better."

"I wish you'd let me do more for her."

" 'Tisn't that much to be done. Besides I wanted you to rest and get your strength back after . . ." Julia paused. It was difficult to remind Megan of the past. Her friend never spoke of it anymore. There was only the pain that never completely disappeared from her black eyes.

285

"After Tahiti," Megan finished the sentence for her.

"Yes." Julia took a sip of the hot tea the steward served. It almost scalded her mouth, but she could feel the heat flowing through her body, strengthening her. She took a deep breath and looked at Megan. "What did you want to talk about?"

"Well . . ." Megan stirred her tea nervously. When she looked up at Julia, the fright was back in her eyes. "I'm going to have a child."

Julia sat up with a snap. "You are! And you haven't known it before? That's incredible. George . . . It was February, wasn't it?"

"It wasn't George." Megan buried her face in her hands.

"Oh." Julia stared at her friend and remembered her state of mind when she'd found her in Tahiti. Had she been so far out of her senses that she had let some sailor or deserter take advantage of her? "That does make a problem, doesn't it?"

"Yes, I'm afraid it does." Megan dropped her hands from her face, but her voice was little more than a whisper.

"Well, it's not all that bad, Megan. You'll just have to bend the truth a little when you get home. Simply tell your family that George died later than he did. After all, you can't hurt him anymore."

"There are records."

"Say the records are wrong. No one's going to go all the way to Tahiti to find out."

When Megan didn't reply, Julia asked, "Megan, what else can you do?"

Megan's eyes seemed to grow larger as she stared hopelessly at Julia. "Even if they believed me . . . about George, I mean . . . it still wouldn't do any good."

"Well, why ever not? You've told me about your family. How loving they are. It's certain they'll love your child as well." Julia drank her tea, secure in her belief that Megan was building problems where there were none.

"Julie . . . the father . . ."

"He can't be all that bad."

"He's Tahitian," Megan blurted out and buried her face in her hands again to stifle the sobs she could not control.

"Oh!" Please, no more, Julia thought. No more worries. She rose and, putting her arm around Megan, pulled her close to her side.

"The baby . . ." Megan gasped. "Both George and I are fair."

There was such terror in the tear-stained face Megan turned up to her, Julia hugged her tighter and said soothingly, "Your family will still love the child, Megan. They may be angry with you for a while, but I'm certain, if you tell them how awful it was, they'll understand."

Megan shook her head and blotted her face with a plain cotton handkerchief. Then she blew her nose. "They might understand a lot of things, Julie, but not that. Never that."

"Are you sure?" Julia looked searchingly at Megan's face where misery mingled with fear.

"I'm sure. Oh, God, Julie, I don't know what to do. Some dark nights, I've thought of jumping overboard. There doesn't seem to be any other solution."

"Nonsense!" Julia said as she patted Megan's shoulder. "Don't ever say anything like that ever again. Don't you dare even think it. There's always a solution. Something will come up."

"I'm afraid not this time. I don't know how I could have been so foolish." Megan wiped her face again and then stirred the tea she hadn't tasted. "I was so lonely. The nights were so long and the moon would shine down on the water. There was the smell of flowers everywhere and laughter. I was so lonely. I wanted to share in the laughter."

"I know, Megan." Julia patted her shoulder once more and then went to sit down across the table from her. "Drink your tea. 'Twill make you feel better."

Obediently, Megan drained the cup before she spoke again.

"I'm glad you don't condemn me, Julie. I think you're the only person in the world . . ."

"Of course, I don't condemn you. There's a lot of people who won't condemn you."

"Who, Julie?" Megan pleaded. "Tell me who?"

Julia thought about it for a moment while she busied herself with pouring more tea. Megan was right. It was going to be a difficult thing.

"I know one person who won't condemn you," she said firmly. "My father. You'll go home with me, and you can stay with my family."

"Your father." Megan's chin quivered. "But what about your mother and sisters?"

287

"I don't know about Sarah. I reckon she'd condemn anyone for just about anything, but not Amelia. You'll love Amelia, Megan, and she'll love you. And then there's Aunt Martha. She'll take good care of you."

"Who's Aunt Martha?" Megan was beginning to become interested despite herself. "Your mother's sister or your father's?"

"Neither. She's not really related to us." Seeing Megan's interest, Julia thought of distracting her with some tales of home, but there was really no time for it. She had to get back to Clara. "Aunt Martha came to stay with us when I was very sick once, and she's been there ever since. I guess you could call her our housekeeper, but she's much more than that. We think of her as family. She thinks she is, too. She spends her life telling every last one of us what to do, and we all love her for it. Mama's never been very well, you see."

"But if your mother's not well . . ." Megan's face threatened to crumple again.

"Oh, I doubt Mama will notice one way or the other what color the baby is. She's right fond of babies. You should see her with Amelia's. And it's a big house. Plenty of room for you."

"Julie, I've never met any of your family." Megan rubbed her eyes with the back of her hand, and drawing a deep breath, she looked more resolutely at Julia. "I can't impose on them. Perhaps if I could just borrow some money from you . . . I'll pay it back someday . . . and I could find a little place far away from anyone who knows me. Then after the baby's born, I can go to work."

"Oh, Megan," Julia said impatiently. "What can you do? I'd be glad to lend you some money . . . or give it to you . . . but wherever you go, there'll be people, and wherever there are people, there'll be talk. It's best to be amongst people we know are decent and good."

Megan looked down at her cup and twisted her handkerchief in her lap. "Perhaps decent and good people aren't exactly the kind who would welcome me most now. The missionaries . . . they were decent and good, but . . ."

"Megan, I'm talking about people who are decent and good the way you are."

"Am I, Julie?" Megan's black eyes were wide with doubt and guilt. "Am I anymore?"

"Of course, you are." Julia smiled at her friend, loving her.

"You can't change that anymore than you can change the color of your eyes."

"Well, if you were going to be there, Julie . . . but you won't be, will you? You'll be going back to sea."

"I'll be there for a while. Long enough to get you settled." But I will return to the sea, Julia thought, and it won't be easy for you. She hurt for her friend who had been through so much hurt and now this, but she could do no more for her. Stephen came first. He had to come first.

But how could she tell Megan that she wanted her to go home in another vessel now? How could she even think of sending her home in another vessel? She had to think, and she couldn't think while Megan was sitting there with her pain.

Julia patted Megan's hand. "It will all work out, you'll see. I have to get back to Clara now."

Chapter Fifteen

1848

That night, when Julia went to bed, she was unable to sleep. The problems seemed to do nothing but increase, and there was no time by day for her to think about them, much less solve them. After two hours of tossing the bed sheets and unwinding them from around herself, she got up and went into the saloon. She knew Stephen was on deck, for she had heard his footsteps overhead, and she wanted to sit quietly in the lamplight. In the dark, her thoughts had begun to circle dizzily with no head and no tail.

Almost automatically she looked at the decanters and loathed the sight of them. Yet a sherry would taste good. Even if it didn't help her straighten out her thoughts, it might relax her tired muscles enough to sleep.

When Stephen came below, he found her sitting in her negligee on the settee with a glass in her hand. He glanced at her quizzically but said nothing. Instead he poured himself a brandy and comfortably settled himself in a chair opposite her. They looked at each other in silence for a long time. It was like one of her strange dreams, Julia thought, where nothing began and nothing ended and there was only an unbreakable emptiness.

Finally it was Stephen who spoke.

"So you've decided to join me in my evil habits, my lady?"

"I don't know, Stephen," she said dully. "Have I?"

He took a long, slow sip from his glass.

"Or have you come to castigate me?" he asked. "I've seen you watching me."

"No, Stephen." She felt unutterably weary. "That's the last thing in the world I want to do."

He rubbed his chin and looked at her thoughtfully.

"Well? You were obviously sitting here waiting to talk to me. What do you want to talk about?"

"I wasn't really. I just wanted to think."

"About me?"

"Partly. About Clara, too, but mostly Megan."

"Megan!" He shoved at his chair and stood up. "It's always mostly Megan now, isn't it, Julia?"

"You know that's not true," she snapped. For a moment, she'd hoped that she *could* talk to him, but now she saw it was impossible.

"Isn't it?" He glared down at her. "She's draining you. You look exhausted."

"Well, thank you. I didn't realize you even saw me anymore. And I have a right to be exhausted. Clara's been quite sick, you know. Or didn't you know . . . or care?"

Now she had his complete attention and he sat down again. "You told me she was ailing, but *quite* sick? How sick do you mean, Julia?"

She shrugged. "How can I tell you what none of the doctors can? It's the same thing over and over again. She runs a fever and cries. She won't eat."

He studied his glass as he thought about his daughter. Then he took another sip before he spoke. "I think we'd better plan on putting Clara ashore when we get home. Your mother and Aunt Martha always make such a fuss about her, they'll be glad to have her."

"No!" Julia said vehemently. "The sea's healthier than the land."

"For some." He picked up his glass and swished it like some miniature sea. "Not for all."

"Are you trying to get rid of us, Stephen?" she blazed at him.

"I said nothing about you both going ashore," he said coldly. His eyes were fixed on her so intently, she couldn't avoid seeing how bloodshot they were. By contrast, the irises seemed almost color-less. "Your family can take care of Clara. Your place is with me."

"Stephen! Clara's *our* child. We can't go off and leave her. Not even with my family. They're practically strangers to her." The idea was so horrifying, she didn't know how he could even consider it.

"I'm only thinking of my daughter's health," he said and watched for her reaction.

"So am I!" Really, Stephen could aggravate her beyond bounds. "It might help if you'd spend a little time with her."

"So now you're going to blame me for her illness."

"No, but it might cheer her up. She misses you."

"And whose fault is that?"

"If you want to make it my fault, you'll make it my fault. There was nothing else I could do about Megan, Stephen. Surely by now, you must realize that." Then she could no longer bear to have Stephen, who was so dear to her, looking at her as though she was a stranger. Her decision was made for her. "Megan has agreed to go ashore or take passage on another vessel when we reach Hong Kong."

"Whose idea was that?" He watched her suspiciously.

"Actually, it was Megan's. At first, I didn't think it was a particularly good idea. I still don't, specially now, but I can't live this way. All I want anymore is peace."

"Peace. It's a lovely word, isn't it?" Stephen inhaled the fumes from his brandy and then looked sharply at her. "Why do you say specially now? What's so special about now?"

"Oh, Stephen. She's with child." Suddenly the cares, the worries, the exhaustion of the voyage caught up with her, and she began to cry. She pressed her lips together and closed her eyes very tight in an effort to stop the tears, but they came cascading down her face.

Stephen watched her for a moment. Then he got up and went to the decanters. Once he had poured more sherry into her glass, he handed it to her.

"Drink it," he ordered. "I've found it's a very effective medica-tion for tears."

Julia took a sip, but then put the glass down on the table. It was no help. She rose blindly from the settee and groped her way towards her cabin. Before she had taken two steps, Stephen was there. His arms were around her, protecting her as they had so often in the past. He pulled her back to the settee and held her until at last her tears subsided.

"Tell me about it," he said quietly.

And then her words came pouring out as fast as her tears had. Stephen looked very sober when she had finished.

"You can't take on the troubles of the world single-handed, Julia."

"Megan's not the world. She's my friend. She . . . they were both good to us whenever we stayed in Tahiti."

"They were paid to be."

"That's not fair."

"No, it's not." He pulled her head to his shoulder and kissed her on the forehead. "The fact still remains that you're making promises on other people's behalf to Megan. Are you sure your family will welcome her?"

"I . . . I don't know. I hope they will."

"Perhaps you should have talked to them before you made the offer."

"How can I talk to them?" She straightened up and stared at him. "They're half a world away."

"You could have waited until you got home," he said quietly.

"I couldn't, Stephen. She was so frightened. She needed some reassurance. I was afraid of what she might try to do."

"Then you could have talked it over with me before you made any hasty decisions," he said and held her tightly until she once more relaxed against him. "I'm not half a world away."

"Sometimes it seems as though you are. I haven't been able to talk to you for so long."

"I suppose that's true. Well, I'm here now."

"Will you stay, Stephen?" She tilted her head to look up into his eyes.

"I'll stay, my lady." He kissed the tip of her nose and then he grinned. "If I don't, you'll most likely make any number of rash promises you can't fulfill." More soberly, he added, "And if you keep on like this, you're going to exhaust yourself beyond recovery. The first thing we have to do is solve the problem of Megan."

"Yes." Suddenly it did seem impossible to send Megan to her family. How could she have been so sure they would accept her?

"I don't want you to abandon her," he said with greater gentleness than she had heard in his voice since they had sailed from Tahiti. "She's going to need your friendship . . . and mine, too. She doesn't seem to have any other, and evidently she's incapable of looking after herself."

"Thank you, Stephen."

"But I don't want her on the *Crystal Star* when we sail for home. We'll have to make other arrangements for her."

"I suppose that's best," Julia said, so thankful to hear the warmth, the generosity in his voice, so thankful to be in his arms again. "But what'll we do when she gets home? I can't understand it, but she's positive her family won't accept the child."

"No." He reached across the table and picked up his brandy glass. He looked at it for a moment, then put it down without drinking from it. "You've never been in the South, but I don't think they will accept the child."

"Then what can we do?" There really seemed no solution to the problem of Megan.

"Well, the first possibility is the one you've already mentioned. See if your father will take her in . . . at least temporarily. She could make herself useful around the house. I'm sure Aunt Martha will find plenty to keep her busy."

"And if he won't?" she asked and yet she couldn't believe Papa wouldn't give Megan shelter. Like most deep sea captains, he had very few prejudices and a great deal of compassion.

"Perhaps Amelia?" Stephen had always been fond of Julia's youngest sister and respected her cheerful strength.

"Her house is too small. With three children, she hardly has room to turn around, and when Michael's home from sea, it's impossible." Julia thought about the winding sand roads with their houses that lay between the hills and the shore. Somewhere there must be a haven for Megan. "I wish we had a house of our own. Then we'd be sure she had somewhere to go."

"There's never been any need for one," he reminded her.

"No." She looked around the saloon whose shadows shrank and lengthened with the swinging of the sperm oil lamp. "This has always been home enough for me . . . till now."

"It still is," he said and drew his lips across her forehead.

"Yes."

"Julia, you're so tired you can hardly move. Go to bed now."

294

"I don't know if I can sleep. Not till we've decided what to do about Megan."

"Things often have a way of solving themselves. We'll find something."

"And we have to get her passage on a good vessel."

"We will. Come to bed." He pulled her up and, half carrying her, led her into their cabin.

She lay down and closed her eyes. Then she was aware that Stephen was still in the cabin. By the light of the newly risen moon that flickered off the water, she could see that he was taking off his shirt.

"Are you coming to bed, too?" she asked.

"It's my bed," he said.

There was a favoring wind on her quarter, and the *Crystal Star* slid smoothly down the long Pacific waves and up them again. With each swoop of the ship, the moon blinked off and on like a giant lighthouse in the starlit dusk of the cabin. The sea played a lyrical song against the hull, and Julia nestled in her husband's arms.

As their bodies fitted together in the comforting, familiar pattern born of the multitudinous nights of a marriage, Julia sighed contentedly and heard Stephen's sigh echo her own. The feel of his breath upon her cheek, her breath upon his throat. The steady pulsing of each heart upon the other's flesh. The silky feel of skin that caressed skin. All these contributed to the soothing drowsiness of two who had so often been one. More effective than alcohol, more compelling than laudanum, sleep came to them as they rested in the regained safety of each other's arms.

As they slept, the barometer fell, and in the morning, they watched the dark grey sea build up ever higher under clouds that grew with every hour. The wind veered to north-northeast, and while Stephen had the men aloft sending down the royal yards and studding sail booms, Julia went below to make sure that Clara, Becky, and Megan were secure in their cabins. After checking to see that the lockers and doors were tightly fastened, she went to stand just outside the companionway.

In the light that was dark and yet translucent, she could see that all hands were employed in taking down the topmasts. It was a difficult enough job under any circumstances. With the cross sea

295

that slammed against the sides of the hull, it seemed almost impossible. Yet under the mates' directions, it was soon done and the masts lashed on deck.

Then Julia heard the roar that she had heard but a few times in her life and those times far too many. Typhoon! She scrambled down the companionway steps and ran for her cabin. She lashed herself into her bed and waited. Even above the screaming of the wind, she could hear Clara crying, but there was nothing she could do for her now. Nothing. Then it hit. The ship was slammed on her side . . . farther . . . farther . . . farther . . . and then. Yes. With a shudder, the *Crystal Star* began to right herself. Julia let out the long breath she hadn't realized she had been holding.

For three days, they held on with the wind sounding like one continuous clap of thunder that never ceased. In moments when they were driven before the wind under bare poles, there was a calm that was only relative, and Julia would try to make her way through a ship that was tumbled by a confused sea into the steward's pantry and then in to see that Clara and Becky and Megan were all right. Only Becky showed any interest in the food and water Julia brought, and Julia was thankful for the Cape-bred girl whose father and brothers were all fishermen and used to the sea. Clara was all right as long as Becky was with her.

Then on the morning of the fourth day, the wind, which had changed to the southeast, veered to the southwest and by noon, the sea was almost calm. On deck, Julia found that the cow and most of their livestock had been swept overboard, the larboard bulwarks were smashed, and one longboat had been stove in, but otherwise, there was little damage. Though one man had a broken leg, no hands were lost.

As she climbed up to the quarterdeck, she looked at Stephen with a respect that was not new, but one that she had almost forgotten. There were not many masters who could have brought a ship through in such good condition. And only now, sleepless and tired beyond the limits of exhaustion, was he leaving his post.

He nodded at her as she came up to him and said, "Keep an eye on things, Julia. The mates are both as worn out as I am. The men on watch have to be kept at work, though God knows most of them need the sleep as much as I do. I've told Mister Pratt to have me called in two hours."

The pumping continued for most of the day, and two days later, when they sailed through Lyemoon Pass, the *Crystal Star* looked as though she had barely been touched by the storm.

The harbor at Hong Kong was crowded with shipping, more crowded than she had ever seen it before, and the problem of Megan came to Julia's mind. Since she had made the decision that night with Stephen, there had been no chance to speak to her friend.

Megan had been drained by the seasickness and terror of the typhoon. Now she was below, too listless even to be interested in their entry into China. She had come on deck for a few minutes earlier in the morning to catch sight of land, but then she had retired to her bunk.

As they sailed through the anchorage, Julia searched for a familiar vessel. There were quite a few, but one after another she discarded them. Some were too small to be comfortable or too old to be safe. On others, the captains were the problem. It would be pleasant, too, if she could find a ship with the master's wife aboard. Then Megan would have company on the way home.

Two ships she knew were definitely not in the harbor for she would have recognized them anywhere. The *Jewel of the Seas* and *Neptune's Dragon*. She realized she had been looking forward to seeing them both.

David Baxter had sailed three weeks before the *Crystal Star,* and he had planned no stops along the way. Yet the *Jewel* was getting old. She was not the ship she once had been, and she had long since been outdesigned and outdated. There was no reason to be alarmed. The vagaries of wind and sea could postpone her arrival for another two weeks.

As for *Neptune's Dragon*, Cousin William had still been in port in New York when the *Crystal Star* weighed anchor. It shouldn't have been surprising to find that he wasn't here. Yet with the records *Neptune's Dragon* had broken in the past few years, Julia had been half certain he would be waiting for them.

No sooner was the anchor down than the usual village of sampans attached itself to the *Crystal Star*. Above the hubbub of voices calling from below, there was one that was more demanding of attention than all the others. Never before had she heard that voice raised above the slow quiet cadence that set his speech apart from all others, but even with a strange urgency in it that would not be denied, she recognized the voice as David Baxter's.

297

Before searching for him through that motley assembly of watercraft, however, Julia once again scanned the harbor for the *Jewel of the Seas*. There was no sign of her, but she must be here if David was. Perhaps hidden behind some massed vessels. Perhaps in a shipyard undergoing repairs. She shrugged. She would find the ship later, and perhaps David and the *Jewel* would solve the dilemma of Megan. It wouldn't be an ideal solution, yet it was better than none.

When he swung aboard, David seemed strangely altered. His shoulders appeared to be broader than ever and his legs longer. Then Julia saw how poorly the clothes he wore fitted his large, muscled frame. They had been made for a smaller man. And his face was older. So much older than the face of David she had seen little more than four months ago. Or perhaps her memory was playing her false. When had those furrows that etched his forehead and lined his cheeks first appeared? They were too deep for a man of only thirty-four.

She rushed up to him even as he was shaking hands with Stephen.

"What is it, David? What's happened?"

There was a stiffness to his face, and in those grey-green eyes, a weltering pain that she had seen once before. How many years ago? Seven? She could see him once again standing in the door of the office at the shipyard with the sun haloing his hair, almost as speechless as he was now. That time, he had come to tell her of his marriage. What was it this time?

"David?" she asked once again to break his silence.

"The *Jewel* . . ." He stopped as though there was no way to speak the next words.

"What about the *Jewel*? What's wrong?" And she found herself trying to shake his immovable elbow.

"She's gone," he said, and in his voice, there was shame as well as sorrow.

"David! Make sense. Stephen . . ." She looked at her husband imploringly.

"Come, man, snap out of it," Stephen said briskly. "There's brandy below."

Somehow they managed to propel David towards the companionway.

It took two brandies before he would or could speak of it. While he swallowed the burning liquid as though it were water, he kept staring at Julia. Then when the words came, they poured forth in an unending stream that permitted no interference.

"She's gone, Julie. I tried to save her for you." He took a deep breath and looked at her as though he himself still didn't believe it. "Five ships lost that night. I've never seen the harbor so crowded as when that typhoon hit. 'Twas a nightmare. Not a vessel there but that didn't drag anchor. The *Tatsun* lost all control. Came barging down on us, battering at us. There was no getting away from her. She was sinking, determined to take the *Jewel* with her. I could see the deep bay of Cum-Sing-Moon was to leeward of us. It's sand, you know. All sand. Except for one rock. It found us before we were able to bring the *Jewel* up. I'd slipped the cable, hoping for that bay, but I didn't know about that rock. No one ever knew about that rock before. The *Jewel*'s there on Cum-Sing-Moon Island now. Smashed. Lifted so high she'll not refloat till the next typhoon, and then the only way for her to go will be down. I tried to save her for you, Julie."

"I know, David," Julia said quietly, but she couldn't comprehend that the *Jewel of the Seas* was really gone. Not her *Jewel*. Automatically, she said the next thing, the thing that was always first said when a ship was destroyed. "And the men. Were any lives lost?"

"No. Only the ship's," he said with despair.

Julia sat for a moment and looked at the battered face that held so much remorse. She still couldn't believe that the ship was lost, but she felt David's suffering as though it were her own.

"She was getting old, David." She reached out and touched the hand that was clenched into a fist. "Almost ten years old. She was hogged and strained."

David sipped at the third brandy Stephen had poured for him and then looked at the glass, as though surprised to find it in his hand. He spoke to Stephen then, master to master.

"Maybe if she'd been in ballast, but we'd just finished unloading cargo that afternoon. We were due to go to the beach and have her careened for bottom work the morning after the storm struck. We were riding light. Hadn't been for that, maybe she'd have survived."

"I doubt it," Stephen said quietly. For once, he felt nothing but compassion for David Baxter. To lose his ship! It was a nightmare all masters had, and too often it came true.

The reality of the loss finally began to seep through Julia's mind and close behind it came a kind of panic. "Can't we salvage her? Isn't there anything we can do?"

"Nothing that the underwriters can't handle. She was fully insured." David held it out to her, but he knew it was only a crumb. Money could never make up for the loss of a ship. He knew that only too well.

"I want to see her!"

"No, Julia," Stephen said. "Leave it alone."

"I have to. Don't you understand that she was *my* ship? I lived all my life waiting for her to be built, and then I built her."

"You built the *Crystal Star*, too," Stephen reminded her gently. "And you had a large part in designing her. You didn't design the *Jewel*. Your father did."

"I still want to see her!" Julia banged the table with her fist to keep the tears that prickled the lids of her eyes from coming.

Stephen studied her for a moment, saw her tilted chin, saw her eyes enormously blue in her tanned face. Then he looked at David, who looked more miserable than ever after Julia's outburst. He nodded and stood up.

"Very well. We'll go now."

"Now?" Julia wasn't prepared for it yet. Not so soon. To escape the reality, she wanted to run and hide in her cabin behind the locked door, but as she rose, Stephen took her arm.

"Now," he insisted. "The sooner we get this business over with, the better."

Even before they reached the shore, Julia could see the masts . . . the shattered masts . . . skewed sideways away from the water, and then the black hull loomed on the hill. When the longboat grated up on the sand, Julia was prepared for the landing. Before they'd left the *Crystal Star*, she had stripped off her stockings, and on the journey out, she had surreptitiously loosened her shoes. Now she pushed them off, lifted her skirts, and jumped ashore.

The wet sand was grainy and hard under her feet, and as the water swirled around her ankles, she could feel the sand seep and give beneath them. Yet she didn't notice it except for the reassurance of familiarity. The pull and tug of the sea. And she had eyes for nothing except the white-waisted black hull which should have been floating as gracefully and proudly as a swan, but which now lay on her side in the grassy sand with green sea slime drying on her copper bottom.

As she scrambled up the hill with her skirts gathered in her hands, Julia outdistanced the men. There was no one to hear her sobs or to see the tears that were pouring down her face.

"Oh, *Jewel*, my *Jewel*," she gasped as she reached up to touch the transom.

But before she was able to touch it, two bearded men with muskets in their hands came around the ship towards her, and she froze. Scavengers? Already come to tear apart her lovely ship. She wouldn't let them. She wouldn't!

"It's all right, Morris," David shouted from behind her, and then she realized that they were part of the ship's company, standing guard against marauders.

The presence of others helped her regain the control she had lost, but it didn't prevent memories or the anguish that accompanied them.

It had been another August half a world away. Another vessel had been lost and with her the man who should have been captain of the *Jewel of the Seas*. Ten years ago? Where had the ten years gone? It was only yesterday. No, it was ten years, and the storm had been an Atlantic hurricane rather than a Pacific typhoon. Yet storms in their violence took the same toll.

Ten years ago. I was eighteen. So vulnerable. Now I'm twenty-eight. I shouldn't be so vulnerable anymore. But I am. Oh, Jason, my love, my love. Your ship is gone.

The men had walked away from her to inspect the damage. Now as she looked towards them, she noticed that Stephen stood near the bow, a little apart from the others, with his cap in his hand. In the clear, rain-washed air, he seemed terribly alone. Almost . . . vulnerable. And it struck her with great force that he was what mattered. Not a dead man, not a shattered ship, but the living man who was her husband. The past would have to take care of the past. She almost ran across the grass-tufted sand to be with him.

"Stephen," she said as she reached him and held out her hand.

He smiled sympathetically at her and dug into his pocket for a handkerchief, which he handed her.

"Dry your face, love," he said.

"Isn't there something that can be done?" she asked as she mopped away the few remaining tears. "If we were to patch her up and somehow float her off . . ."

"The other side's worse, Julie," David said as he came to join them. With the twist of his mouth and the shimmer of his eye, he asked her forgiveness. "If you want to go aboard and look . . ."

"No, I don't," she said quickly. Then she turned imploringly to her husband. "Stephen, there must be some way?"

Stephen shook his head. "There's no way to get her off, Julie. If there were, she's not worth it. You yourself said that she was old. And she is. She's a tired old lady. You couldn't have kept her profitably on the China run much longer. She's chosen her spot. Let her be."

Julia looked at her husband, at David, at the sailors who had gathered around them. All of them carried their hats in their hands. They reminded her of mourners at a funeral. She felt the same. It remained only for the final words to be spoken.

"I suppose you're right," she said sadly and then she lifted her chin with pride. "She went when she was fully insured, all hands saved, no cargo aboard. She took care of her own. The *Jewel of the Seas*. She broke records in her day, didn't she, David?"

"A few," he said somberly.

Julia nodded and took one long last look at her youth and the ship that had come out of it. They were both gone now, and she felt as old as the figurehead looked. The paint was flaking, her hand chipped. The wood was weathered. White salt streaked down from the wreath of seaweed and roses over the once glossy black hair. Julia turned and, never looking back, walked slowly down to the boat that waited on the shore.

"Let her be," she whispered.

The voyage home was a mixture of many things. Realizing what they had so nearly lost, Julia and Stephen came closer once more. Although it wasn't possible to completely recapture the first spendthrift joy of the early days of marriage, they shared again the happiness of a few hours spent watching the constellations flee across the skies. They smiled at each other as they felt the exuberance of the *Crystal Star* when the wind was steady astern and light enough to carry all her sails. They became one in their rapture on nights when the crests and troughs of waves matched the rhythm of their love.

Julia gave little thought to Megan on that voyage. Cousin William had sailed into Hong Kong a few days after their own arrival and had immediately enchanted Megan. After a long conversation with Julia, he had agreed to take Megan home with him. Although he'd always refused to take paying passengers, he even accepted a young couple returning to the States so that Megan would have company. Julia knew that somehow she would have to cope with Megan's troubles when she got home, but life at sea tended to wash away all problems of the future. As long as the *Crystal Star* rolled across the oceans of the earth, there was no other world.

David had been given command of a homeward-bound ship whose captain was so ill he couldn't continue as master. His skill and abilities were too well known throughout the merchant fleet for Captain David Baxter to remain unemployed for long. No one who had felt the crushing hand of a typhoon blamed him for the loss of his ship. If David arrived home before the *Crystal Star,* he would be the first to break the news of the loss of the *Jewel* to her father. Otherwise she herself would have to do it, and it was a task she did not relish. But that again was something that could be relegated to the future.

However, Clara's health was a problem that could not be ignored. The doctors in Hong Kong had been as mystified as all the doctors before them. They could find neither the cause of nor the cure for Clara's fevers, and she grew no better. Julia, still believing that sun and sea air were the best remedies for any illness, had Becky bring the child on deck as often as the weather permitted. Yet it was Stephen who seemed to benefit her most of all. Knowing that this might well be his last voyage with his daughter, he held her in his arms and told her fairy tales of the flying fish, the whales, the porpoise, and the mermaids who lived below the surface of the sea.

As Julia watched her husband and her child together, she tried not to think of the end of the voyage. Stephen had definitely decided that Clara must be sent home to live and remained equally firm in his determination to keep Julia with him. To be parted from Clara, who was hardly more than a baby, was something that Julia could not accept. Yet to leave Stephen, who was now so happy in the resurgence of their love, would be equally painful. She postponed the decision that she would have to make. After all, as Stephen had said, things had a way of solving themselves.

As they sailed northeastward up the South Atlantic past Saint Helena and Cape St. Roque, Julia was successful in evading the future. Once they crossed the equator, however, time began to shorten. Although they were still thousands of miles from Cape Cod, Julia always thought of the North Atlantic as home.

Despite her reluctance to end the voyage, there were times when the familiar anticipation bubbled up and she found her eyes straying westward. Memories of the Cape with its dunes and wooded hills, its rocks and gulls, its marshes and sunlit creeks beckoned to her. Soon she would walk through the shipyard and call each man by name. She would climb Scargo Hill, smell the sweetness of the pines, and hear the bluejay's call. The December sea became rougher and bleaker as they sailed into winter, and Julia thought with longing of the firelit parlor with her family all around her.

Even before they could see the land, they could smell it, and a blue kingfisher came out to meet them and sit upon the yards as though he were a self-appointed pilot. Then on a morning of cold December rain mixed with light snow when, hoping to be the first to sight it, every hand was on deck, the long-awaited call came from the crow's nest. "Land ho-o-o."

There was a loud, sustained cheer from the main deck, and the men who were off-duty jostled each other as they fought for a place in the ratlines. Though moisture coated the lens of the glass, it didn't take long for Julia to sight the dark cloud on the horizon that was really the land.

On a quickly indrawn breath, she whispered the word, "America!," and the pride and joy that never failed to sweep through her when they returned home held her in thrall. Her land! Not Tahiti or China, not Cape Horn or Java Head. *This* was the land that was truly hers.

Snow lay on the long sheltering arm of Sandy Hook as they passed into lower New York Bay, and the land was bare with winter. When they reached the narrows between Staten Island and Brooklyn, the sun broke through the thinning layer of clouds and illuminated the white forts on the scattered islands and sparkled on the broad rivers that flowed into the Upper Bay. There were large farms on rolling hills, and clustered houses in the villages trailed smoke above the leaf-stripped trees. After China, the land seemed to burgeon with abundance and everything was incredibly clean and well ordered.

304

In the wake of the pilot boat, a few schooners, side-wheel steamboats, and sloops came out to meet them. Merchants, shouting through megaphones, asked for the latest news from the East. Boarding house touts called out the virtues of their establishments to the sailors. Representatives of shipping houses asked for word of their vessels. Journalists bombarded them with a hundred questions.

Once they had anchored off the Battery at the tip of Manhattan to wait for a slip to open up, even more boats poured out of the East River to surround them, and they were boarded from both sides. Julia suddenly realized how disheveled she must look in the sea-stained cloak that covered her fur tippet, shawl, and rough wool dress, and she fled below.

She hurried to tidy her hair and put on the clean damask dress she had planned to wear when they landed, but it was difficult to move around the cabin, which was now cluttered with trunks that were packed and ready to go ashore. She was anxious to hear the latest news and to find out when the packet would be sailing for South Yarmouth, the packet that would carry her home to the Cape.

Yet as she was about to open the door, she hesitated and looked back at the main cabin, which had been her home for so long. The red velvet on the settee was worn and shabby and would have to be replaced before they began another voyage, but the curly walnut paneling still glowed with the same warmth and the brass gleamed in the sunlight that was pouring through the stern windows and the decklight. It seemed small now, but it was full of memories. Here there was happiness and sorrow, laughter and tears, elation and pain. And Stephen.

There was a pounding on the door, and William Thacher's voice booming through the panels startled her out of her reverie.

"Julie, you in there?" He sounded anxious and so terribly impatient, it alarmed her.

"Cousin William," she said as she swung the door open. "Is it Megan? Has anything happened to Megan?"

"No, no. The girl's fine now, she's ashore," he said as he swept her into his arms and planted a kiss on her cheek. "I admit the *Dragon* does tend to roll a bit, but I got your friend here safe and sound just like I promised." Then he held her just a little way off and looked down at her with concern. "It's your father, Julie."

"Papa! Oh, no!" She clutched at him for support as the room

305

reeled around her as wildly as if they were in a gale. "What is it? What's happened?"

"It's all right, Julie. It's all right. He had a stroke. I don't know all the details, but he needs you home soon as you can get there."

"Oh, no!" She looked at him incredulously as the room began to settle down. "He couldn't have had a stroke. He's too healthy. I doubt he's even had a cold more than a couple of times in his life."

"That may be, but he's ailing now." He looked at her gravely while he held her steady with his burly arms. "I been over to the packet. Went there as soon as the *Crystal Star* was sighted. They'll wait for you two hours, but no longer. They've got to catch the tide. You ready to go?"

"No. Yes. Oh, I don't know." She threw herself back into his arms.

He held her for a few seconds, and she was dimly aware that Mister Pratt was shouting orders. There was the rattle of the anchor chain, and then the ship was moving again.

"Steady on, lass," William Thacher said and pulled her away from him once more. "If you've got to fall apart, wait till you're on that packet."

"I will," she said, blinking at him, but there were no tears behind her eyelids, only a terrible emptiness that filled her. "I've got to get Clara. I've got to . . . I don't know."

"All you've got to do is get yourself off this ship. I've already told that girl of yours, that Becky, to have the child dressed in good warm clothes for the journey."

"And Megan? Where's Megan?" Julia glanced wildly around the cabin as though she might find her friend there. "I can't take her home with me if Papa's sick."

"Don't fret yourself," he said as he studied Julia with real concern. He'd never expected her to go to pieces like this. "I've already sent her on to the Cape. Gave her the key to the house in Brewster and a little money to tide her over till I can get there."

"I didn't mean to saddle you with her," Julia said as she tried to concentrate on something outside the fog of pain that filled her. "She's not your responsibility."

"She is now," he said gruffly as he took his arms away from her to see if she were capable of standing by herself. "Maybe I like responsibilities."

"How long have you been in?" she asked woodenly.

"A week," he said gravely. "Been waitin' here for you. Didn't want you to hear about it from anyone but me."

"Thank you, Cousin William." She tried to smile, but it didn't work. Then she walked to the stern windows and, leaning her forehead against the cold glass, was hardly aware of the water traffic of the East River. There were ferries, coasting vessels, packets, and small boats of every description. The number of small steamers had increased in just a few months, but she didn't notice it. The scene moved before her as she fought against the numbed lethargy of her brain. "You don't know *any* details? How bad is he?"

"I don't know, Julie," William said from just behind her. "But he *is* alive. The word I got from your mother said he's frettin' over the shipyard and the doctor's having the devil's own time holding him down. She thinks if you get home, it'll calm him."

"How long . . . when did it happen?"

"Just a couple of weeks ago. Wasn't long before I got in."

She realized that the ship had ceased to move, and the outside world intruded on the silence of the cabin. She could hear the rumble of carts and horses' hoofs clopping over cobblestones. The sounds of land were strange to her ears.

"We're here." She turned away from the window and picked up her peacock blue caped coat. Then she took one long look around the saloon. Lightly she ran the tips of her fingers in a caress along the golden walnut paneling of the bulkhead. Her father. The shipyard. Clara. How long would it be before she sailed aboard the *Crystal Star* again?

"I wish we'd docked in Boston," she said. "It seems so much nearer home."

"Well, there's not many can afford the luxury of Boston anymore. That one percent tax they imposed on auction sales was bad enough, but with the Erie Canal distributing goods across the country, New York is the place to make the most profit on tea and silk."

"I know. Guess we'd best be on our way."

Just as they were about to leave the saloon, Stephen burst through the door. "What's keeping you, Julie? The steward's gone to fetch a couple of porters to take your trunks to the packet."

"I'm coming."

Stephen looked at her, and when he saw how tightly drawn the skin seemed over her bones, how pale her face was, he forgot his impatience. "Julie, I'm sorry about your father."

"Yes. Oh, Stephen." She was suddenly in his arms and the tears of worry that had not come before were loosed. "I don't want to leave you."

"You don't have to, Julie, but your father. . . ." He held her close for a moment and stroked her hair.

"I know."

"You've always gone home ahead of me. It's no different this time. I'll be down in a few days. As soon as the goods are auctioned off."

"Things are just happening too fast."

He tilted her chin so that she was looking into his eyes and he smiled at her. "My lady, this isn't like you."

She nodded and smiled back, but her smile was a little crooked. "I'm ready now."

As they came out of the companionway, Stephen took Clara from Becky and held her up so that she could see the city with its many large buildings, its spires, and the cupolas of its churches. Tied up in Old Slip, the bowsprit of the *Crystal Star* rose high above South Street and threatened to pierce the windows of Delafield's Store.

After one quick glance at the empty quarterdeck, Julia shook hands with the mates and waved to the few men who were still on the ship. Then the five of them were on shore amid the running messengers, the smock-clad porters trundling their loaded barrows, the horse-drawn wagons and carriages. Julia found the cobblestones difficult to navigate after the smooth decks of the ship, and when she looked ahead at the hundreds of bowsprits that arched over the street, she felt slightly dizzy. The street seemed to have taken on the motion of the ship, and while the motion of the ship had never bothered her, the street's imitation of it did.

Clara must have felt it, too, for she fretted in Stephen's arms. He tried to distract her by pointing out the constant movement of vessels being loaded and unloaded by burly longshoremen, barrels and boxes and bales being carted about by porters.

Usually Julia was fascinated by the auctioneers as they stood on the piers chanting forth the glories of goods from all over the world, their voices mingling with other voices that shouted in a hundred languages and dialects. Now, however, there was no enchantment in the scene. All her thoughts were centered on the large white house on the Cape and on the man who lay stricken within it.

A stroke, a stroke, she kept saying to herself until it became a word without meaning. How had it affected his body? His mind? She thought of others she had known who had suffered from strokes, and then she tried to forget them. The paralysis, the deformities a stroke could leave in its wake made her blood run cold. And then she had an even more frightening thought. When one stroke occurred, others could quickly follow.

Throughout the long journey home, she was almost unaware of Becky and Clara. Though William Thacher was ever at her side, she rarely spoke to him. All of her energies were concentrated as she willed the wind to blow harder and speed the packet up Long Island Sound to South Yarmouth. Once ashore, she focused on the large-hoofed horses, willing them to pull the stagecoach faster and faster from South Yarmouth to East Dennis.

Chapter Sixteen

1848

Patches of snow lay like white shadows behind the chinked stone walls, and the leafless chestnut trees were black from days of moisture when the stagecoach pulled up in front of the house. Julia threw open the door even before the footman had the steps in place, and she nearly fell over them in her haste. Without waiting for the others to gather up the gear and follow her, she flew up the walk. As she set foot on the front porch, the door opened and her mother stood there.

"Julie!" Lydia's arms were around her. "We thought you'd never get here."

"I came as fast as I could, Mama. How is he?"

"Not well." Lydia shook her head mournfully. "You've got to prepare yourself. It's his arm. His right arm. He can't use it. Half the time, he just lies there and stares at it."

"I have to go to him, Mama. Where is he?"

"In bed. Keeps saying if he can't go down to the yard, he isn't going to get up at all. It's best he doesn't. Doctor Willett says he's got to rest for a long time, maybe months."

Julia looked at her mother and wondered if she had lived on the brink of tears ever since the stroke. There was a puffiness around her green eyes that almost hid them, and her clothes hung in loose folds. She wanted to put her arms around her mother's frail body and love her, but there was no time for that now.

"Can't Papa get up and sit in a chair . . . or something? I won't have him just lying there staring at his arm."

"Julie," Lydia pleaded. "Go easy on him. He's right sick. And don't go talking to him about the yard or ships or the sea or anything of that ilk. You'll just get him all riled up."

"Mama, what else *is* there to talk about? You'll just have to trust to my judgment. I'm not going to treat him as though he's already dead and buried."

"Dead and buried!" Lydia looked at Julia in horror, then picked up her skirt, buried her face in it, and fled into the parlor.

Julia was shocked by the effect her words had had on her mother, but it was too late to recall them. Cousin William would have to deal with her mother, and perhaps the sight of Clara would cheer her up. Meanwhile, she had better things to do.

Without taking the time to remove her bonnet and coat, Julia ran up the tall narrow stairs, all the while dreading what she would find at the top of them. The door to her parents' room was shut to keep in the warmth of the fire. She hesitated for a moment and then she knocked. There was no answer, so she thought he might be sleeping. Slowly and quietly she opened the door.

But he wasn't sleeping. He was just lying there, staring at the door with deep blue eyes that were filled with a pain that went much deeper than any physical hurt.

"Papa!" She rushed to the bed and, bending over, kissed him on his smooth-shaven cheek.

"Julie." His voice was very gentle as though he were afraid that, if he raised it, he would disturb some delicate inner mechanism. "You're home."

"Yes, Papa." She sat down on the bed next to him and, holding his hand in both of hers, she looked hungrily at his face. Instead of adding lines, the stroke seemed to have erased a few, and there was a sweetness in his expression she had never seen before.

"The voyage." The strong fingers of his left hand clutched at hers. "Was it a good one?"

"Yes, Papa. Very good." And then she remembered the *Jewel.* She couldn't tell him. Not now. And she would have to see to it that no one else let it slip.

311

"Something's happened. I can tell by your face."

"I never could hide anything from you, could I?" She smiled at him. "It's nothing important. We can talk about it later."

"Tell me now."

The tiredness of his voice and the economy with which he spoke worried her. It was as though each word was a carefully considered expenditure. He seemed so fragile. She couldn't leave him here to fret over an unknown. She had to tell him something.

"Well, I have a friend who's in trouble," she began and blessed Megan for giving her something other than the lost ship to talk about. "She has nowhere to go."

"Is she a good friend?"

"A very good friend, Papa. You remember, I told you about the missionaries in Tahiti. Well, Megan's all alone now. Both her son and her husband died in awful circumstances."

"No other family?"

"None that she can go to."

"Then bring her here," he said without further question. He frowned slightly as he examined the face that was so dear to him. Her dark blue eyes were clear and filled with love. Her skin glowed with the special radiance it always had when she returned from a voyage. It made it more difficult to ask her what he must. The same demand had once been made of him, and he knew what it meant to give up the sea. "Will you stay at home . . . for a while, Julie?"

"Yes, Papa. Till I get you back on your feet."

"That's good." He closed his eyes for a second and sighed as though relieved of a burden. "The shipyard needs you, Julie."

She had known it was coming. She knew that it was true. And yet, just for a moment, she fought against it.

"What about Daniel Sears?" she asked.

"Daniel's a good man," he said quietly but firmly. "So's Philip. But it takes more than the two of them. It takes a Howard to run that yard."

"All right. I'll go over in the morning." The immobility of that body that had never before been still made her feel terribly helpless as she fought back the tears. She managed to speak lightly as she patted his hand and rose from the bed. "I'm tiring you, Papa. I'd best let you rest."

"No!" As he pushed himself up on his pillows, Julia could see how difficult it was for him, but the fire was back in his voice. "Don't you go treating me like a damned invalid, too."

"I won't." She couldn't help smiling. "But you're going to have to rest if you're to get better."

"If I'm to get better! That's all I've been hearing from the pack of women in this house, but I never expected to hear it from you. Thought when you came home, 'twould be different."

"It is different, Papa," she reassured him. Suddenly she realized how stifling the room felt, and yet the fire was only flickering in the hearth. In her concern for her father, she'd forgotten she was still wearing her heavy coat. Slowly she began to unbutton it as she watched the man on the bed. What was it that made him seem so ill? The color in his face was good. There was more grey in the black of his hair, but that was to be expected after seven months. But there was a feebleness, a slackness of muscles, he had never had before. He was thinner, too, she thought.

"Good. You're staying," he said with satisfaction as she removed her coat and draped it over a chair. "Take off that damned bonnet, too, while you're about it. I want to get a good look at you."

"Well, Papa?" She smiled at him after she had laid her bonnet on the dressing table. "Will I do?"

"Damned right, you'll do." He smiled, but then as he watched her, his bristling eyebrows met in a frown. "That dithering old fool of a doctor talks like he wants to put me out to pasture."

"Well, he won't," Julia said as she sat down on the bed again next to him. "I won't let him, and neither will you. I'll make you a wager you'll be back on your feet in time for the March launchings."

He grinned at her and a little of the old devilment came back into his eyes. "I won't wager against you. Without you home, I probably wouldn't be able to make it, but you have a knack for getting your way."

"I should. I learned it from you, and I've yet to see you bested."

"Only when you're on the other side of the fence." Then he suddenly saddened. "Or when my body betrays me. You know about my arm, Julie?"

Julia glanced at his right side, where his arm lay immobile on the quilt. "Yes. Mama told me. What does Doctor Willett say about it?"

313

"He won't tell me a damned thing. Just says only time will tell. See what you can get out of that old rascal. If he knows more than he's tellin' me, I'll change doctors."

"That's going to be pretty hard to do considering he's the only doctor for miles around."

"Aye, and he thinks he owns everyone for miles, too." He looked at her in silence for a few moments. Then he said, "So you're really home, my little jewel, home to stay. You heard about the gold in California?"

"A little. We spoke to some vessels heading there on our way home. They were jammed with passengers. I've never seen anything like it. They're all going out to get rich."

"Some will and some won't, but they'll all need transportation. The price for ships is soaring. We're the ones who can get rich. The minute I heard the news, I bought up some old vessels that thought they'd seen their last days. Hold on to them for a couple more months, and then you'll be able to sell them for ten times the cost."

"We can talk about it later, Papa." Julia thought he looked tired, very tired, and she was frightened by the possibility that he might slip away from her.

"Has the *Jewel* arrived yet?" he asked, ignoring her plea.

"Not yet," she managed to say calmly.

"Well, as soon as he gets her cargo unloaded, tell Baxter to set sail for California. Tell him to take tools. Lots of tools. Lumber, pots, pans, food. Whatever he can lay hands on. Jam them into every corner of the ship. He'll make so much money, he can just load up with ballast and go on to China from there."

"I'll tell him, Papa." The conversation was growing more excruciating by the moment. She wanted to blurt out the truth, to tell him that the *Jewel* was lying wrecked on a sandy hill on Cum-Sing-Moon Island, but she couldn't.

"Tell Stephen to do the same thing. He controls the *Crystal Star* now, don't he?"

"Yes. Captain Asa still holds an interest, but Stephen owns forty-eight of the sixty-four shares." Julia thought her mother was right. Too much talk of ships and profit was exciting him. It could only lead to exhaustion. "You can talk to Stephen yourself. He'll be home directly he's disposed of the cargo."

"Shouldn't come home. Send word to him to turn that ship right around and head her for California."

"That's enough visiting for now," Martha Chambers proclaimed as she threw the door open and sailed into the room. The years had done little to change her unlined plump face, her abundant white hair, or her calm, clear eyes, but she had put on a little more weight. "Time for your medicine, Captain."

"Martha, stop telling me what to do. I'll take it in my own good time. Besides I've got the best medicine in the world right here," he growled and patted Julia's hand.

Julia smiled at him. "You know there's no point disputing Aunt Martha. If she says you'll take your medicine, you'll take it, even if she has to force your mouth open and pour it down." She rose from the bed and gave the older woman a quick hug. "I'll see you downstairs after you've dealt with your patient."

"Your room's all ready for you so you can wash up, Julia," Martha said placidly, not in the least disturbed by Benjamin's gruffness. "I put Clara and Becky in Sarah's old room. They'll be close to you there."

"Thank you, Aunt Martha. I'll see you later, Papa," she said as she gathered up her coat and bonnet. Then she blew him an airy kiss from the doorway before she went into the hall. But once the door was closed behind her, she exhaled a great sigh and let her shoulders slump.

Despite her mother's warning, she hadn't really been prepared for the actual fact of her father's illness. The terrible worry she'd tried with so much difficulty to conceal from him now assaulted her, and she walked to the end of the hall and looked out the window that was opposite her door. Because of the L shape of the house, she was able to see her father's window from here, but already Martha had drawn the curtains. As she watched, the winter sun, setting early behind a bank of clouds, shot rays of watered rose over the snow and turned the woods into patches of black silhouettes.

Once the sun had set, she found herself shivering in the biting cold of the unheated hall, and she crossed it to enter her bedroom. There she found warmth and the air of stiff familiarity, as though the room had forgotten her, that always greeted her when she first returned home. Even her portrait and Stephen's seemed to look askance at her. She glanced at the washstand and saw that hot water had been sent up, but she felt too drained by emotion to rinse off the dust of the road immediately. Instead, she threw her coat and bonnet onto the bed and sank down in the small armchair beside the fire, where she had spent so many other hours of sadness.

The first morning was hard. After a sleep that was hardly a sleep so filled was it with nightmares about her father followed by intervals of wakefulness when she lay and stared into the embers of her fire and eventually into the blackness of the unlit room, she awoke with a headache and a feeling of enervation.

As she watched the grey light of early morning filter through the panes of the floor-length windows that led onto the upper porch, she thought of the day with its responsibilities, and it seemed to stretch interminably before her. It would be so much more pleasant to burrow into the warmth of her soft bed and forget the world and its problems. But she couldn't!

Resolutely she sat up and pushed her tumbled hair behind her shoulders just as the door opened and Martha Chambers backed into the room.

"Mornin'," Martha said as she turned to reveal a tray covered with a white cloth. "Thought you might like to take your breakfast in bed. You looked a mite qualmish last night."

The sight of the big cheerful woman brightened the grey morning. Nothing ever really seemed to get Martha Chambers down. As she had during her illness, Julia felt that here was a strength she could draw on.

"You're spoiling me, Aunt Martha. If you coddle me too much, I might just make a habit of it. Then where would we all be?"

Martha put the tray on Julia's lap and glanced at her sharply with concern.

"We'd all be here where we are right now." She went briskly to the fireplace and poured new coals on the grate. "Feelin' sorry for yourself this morning, are you?"

Julia smiled ruefully as she watched Martha get down on her hands and knees to light the fire. It was a job for one of the maids, but no one would dare suggest to Martha that she was getting too old to take care of anything she set her mind to.

"I reckon I *was* feeling a little sorry for myself," Julia admitted as she poured a cup of coffee and inhaled the aromatic steam. "It was a shock to see Papa in that condition and think he might be that way for the rest of his life."

316

Martha concentrated on the fire, but once it was blazing, she dusted off her hands and, pulling a comfortable armchair up next to Julia's bed, plumped herself down.

" 'Tis a drear morning and there's no mistake about that," Martha said. "Colors all your thinking. Now your pa's goin' to be all right. He's as ornery as you are. There's not much'll keep him down."

Julia shook her head as she spread some blueberry preserves on a slice of toast. "It'll be a long time, and I wonder if he'll ever really be the same again."

"None of us stays the same," Martha said briskly. "You're not the same girl you was when I first met you, and that's so much the better. I'm gettin' older, slowin' down. Nothing wrong with that. I can still do my job. Your pa's goin' to be slowin' down, too. Would have even without a stroke. Don't mean he won't be able to do *his* job."

Julia took a long slow swallow of her coffee and then, setting down her cup, looked directly at Martha. "Stephen's going to be upset when I tell him I can't go back to sea with him."

"You've had the best of it, Julie," Martha snorted, "both of you, and don't think you haven't. There's not many sailors and their wives who've been able to stay together long as you have. Count your blessings for the years you've had. I reckon you'll find a way of goin' to sea again one of these days. At any rate, it's best you stay ashore for a while. That child of yours looks meeching to me."

Julia frowned as she thought of Clara. She was so slender and pale until the fever brightened her eyes and colored her cheeks with flame. "Aye. She's never been well."

"Might be she just needs a home."

"But she's had a home! The *Crystal Star* is the perfect place for a child. She has both her parents with her all the time, and you know how healthy the sea is. They send sick people on voyages to recover."

"May be perfect in your eyes, but may not be in hers. We're not all born to go gaddin' about the world, Julie, and that's a fact. She needs friends her own age."

Pushing her tray aside, Julia raised her knees and hugged them to her chest. "I've taken her to play with other children whenever we've been in port, but Clara's shy," she said defensively. "She doesn't take to other children."

"Most likely 'cause she's never known any long enough to make

317

friends. And she needs more than you and her pa and Becky and a shipful of men."

"Well, I hope you're right, Aunt Martha. Maybe you can do her some good. No one else seems able to."

"I intend to," Martha said briskly as she rose from her chair. "You finished your breakfast?"

"Yes. Thanks for bringing it. I feel better already."

"Now you get up out of that bed and start takin' hold of things," Martha said as she picked up the tray. "And don't go thinkin' you're alone. You got me here, Amelia's just down the road, and Daniel and Philip are over at the yard. You've got plenty of help, but you're the one that's got to give the orders."

Suddenly Julia grinned at the older woman. "You really going to let me give orders at this late date?"

"Well, maybe not orders." Martha smiled back at Julia, glad to see that her spirits had risen. "But you make the decisions, and the rest of us will give the orders."

"Like the master of a ship."

"That's what it amounts to. Your pa's been master of this ship for a long time. Now it's your turn to try your hand. Just be thankful he's still here to give advice. I've known a lot of folks killed by a stroke. Where would you be then?"

"You're right, Aunt Martha. I always knew the responsibility was coming. I just didn't expect it this soon."

"Sooner or later, it always comes. Now get dressed and get to work. There's a long day waitin' for you."

Her conversation with Aunt Martha strengthened Julia and helped her through the early hours of the morning. She was able to be cheerful when she paid her father a short visit, to be encouraging with her mother, and to reassure Clara when the child clung to her skirts in the strangeness of the house.

Yet when she stood waiting in her rough shipyard clothes for Ezra to bring out her horse, the loneliness descended upon her again. The clouds were higher and only a light sprinkling of snow fell in the windless air, but Julia pulled her grey cloak more tightly around herself. So often in the past, she and her father had stood together on this porch and planned the day that lay ahead.

Now there would be only one horse, and she had no idea of the condition of the shipyard. Her father had wanted to discuss it, but she had realized very quickly that it excited him too much. At any rate, he knew nothing of the past couple of weeks, for the doctor had forbidden him to see even Daniel after one exhausting visit.

The ride seemed long in her loneliness, and she had to go slowly because winter had already begun its destruction of the road. How many people had walked or ridden this road with her! Her father, Stephen, Jason, Cousin William. She would have welcomed her cousin's hearty presence now, but he'd left the house before her in order to ride over to Brewster to check on Megan.

When she reached the curve at the top of the hill above the shipyard, however, her spirits lifted. The sound of anvils and caulking hammers, axes and men's voices rose to greet her. And there, below on the large railway beside Sesuit Creek, a great ship was taking form. She couldn't see the details distinctly from here, but it was the largest she had ever seen on the ways of the Howard Shipyard. She clucked up her horse and went eagerly down the hill. Why had the thought of running the yard ever intimidated her? This was her kingdom.

After she had dismounted, Julia was tempted to go immediately to the ship to check her lines, to smell the freshness of her new-cut lumber, to run her fingers over the unpainted hull. Instead she shook her head and sighed. The place for her to begin was where she had begun as a young girl. In the office.

When she pushed open the door, Daniel Sears was standing by the tall desk, immersed in the figures he was putting on a piece of paper. He didn't look up immediately, and Julia, wanting to surprise him, stood quietly by the door. It gave her a chance to study him.

He had acquired a natural dignity during the years of his responsibility, yet there was still the awkwardness of youth about him. His black hair showed no signs of grey, and it was hard for Julia to realize that he must be in his early forties by now.

When he did tear his attention away from the paper and saw her, his swarthy face was lit by a smile more welcoming than any she had received since she'd returned home.

"Miss Julia!" He limped quickly to her with his hand held out.

Julia bypassed his hand and gave him a light kiss on the cheek. "Well, Daniel," she said gently. "It's been a long time."

"That it has. Far too long, Miss Julia. You seen your pa?"

"Yes. I've seen him, Daniel."

"Well?" Daniel's worried look included not only a concern for her father's health but for the ships, the men and their jobs, the future of the shipyard itself.

"I don't know, Daniel." She swept off her cloak and threw it on a chair, then went to the stove to warm her hands. "I really don't know. However it comes out, it'll be a long time before he's able to come down to the yard."

"There's no need to worry, Miss Julia," he said quickly as he sensed her discouragement. "I've kept things going. Philip and me. The vessels are comin' along. The accounts are in order, but I don't know about the Captain's finances. You know he's always taken money out of the yard, just left enough for us to run on. Then when we need it, he puts some back."

"I'll have to go through all the papers, Daniel. That's my first job." She sat down near the stove in the chair that had always been her father's favorite and looked around the office. "Where's Towers, Daniel? He's still the clerk, isn't he?"

"Not any more, he ain't," Daniel said with a look of disgust. "Run off to the gold fields like half the fools in the township, even knowing how bad we needed him. Least he could have done was wait till you got home. He lit out of here two days after your pa took sick. Reckon he thought we'd be too occupied to worry about his indenture."

"Well, if he's gone, he's gone. We'll just have to find someone else." Julia frowned as she thought of the length of time and patience needed to train an apprentice. Then she realized that Daniel was still standing and watching her anxiously. "Is there any coffee in that pot, Daniel?"

"Reckon there is, Miss Julia. I've tried to keep most things just like Captain Howard wants them." He went to the stove and picked up the battered pot that had for so long been a fixture in the office. "Can I pour you a cup?"

"I could use one. Pour yourself one too, Daniel. Then sit down and tell me what's been going on."

After Daniel had poured the coffee into the heavy china mugs, he handed one to Julia. Then he slued a chair around so that it was facing her. After he was seated, he leaned forward eagerly with his elbows on his knees and with his cup held between his hands.

"People are clamoring for ships, fast ships for California, Miss

Julia. I don't know what to tell them. I know what orders we've got in hand, but Captain Howard was plannin' on building a ship on his own account. I don't know whether he wants to go ahead with it or whether we should accept somethin' else."

"I don't know, either, and I don't think it's wise to bother him with it now."

"Well, something's goin' to have to be decided soon . . . one way or t'other.

"Something. By someone." Julia made a wry face as she sipped the bitter coffee. It tasted as though it had been made yesterday. "You mean me, don't you, Daniel? I'm the one who has to decide."

"Seems to be the way it falls out."

"How soon do you have to know?"

"Should be decided by the first of January."

"Two weeks," she said thoughtfully. "Well, I have news for you, Daniel. It's not me who's going to decide. It's we. You and me."

He looked at her in dismay and shook his head. "I don't know nothin' about the finances."

"Then it's about time you learned."

" 'Tain't my money, and it's too much responsibility." His face was suddenly closed to her.

"Oh, Daniel," she said as she smiled at him encouragingly, "I think you can handle responsibility. You've been doing it for how many years now? A little more isn't going to hurt you. Besides . . . I need your help."

"I'd do anything in the world to help you, you know that, Miss Julia, but it's a personal matter." Daniel looked doggedly down into his cup of coffee. "If you need help, best you should get it from someone you can trust. A member of the family."

Julia laughed. "If I can't trust you, then I'm in a pretty hopeless muddle. Who else is there?"

"Captain Logan. It's his place."

"What good's my husband going to do me when he's halfway round the world? That's where he'll be going."

"Captain Thacher then?"

"You're not going to keep him ashore, either. No, Daniel. I'm sorry. There's no one but you."

"What's Captain Howard goin' to think about it?" Daniel was still scowling, but Julia could see that he was about to give way.

"He's going to think it's a fine idea when I get around to telling him . . . which won't be for a long time to come." She put down her cup decisively and strode to the desk. "Now let's get to work. Tell me what all these papers are about."

"Those aren't the ones you want to see." Daniel limped to a brass-bound chest and brought forth another sheaf of papers. "I've been savin' these for you."

"What are they?"

"Things the Captain was workin' on when he was struck down. I tended to what I could, but these . . ." He shook his head.

She riffled through the papers but found it hard to concentrate on them while Daniel was standing watching her so hopefully. "So you saved these for me. How could you be so sure I'd get here in time?"

" 'Twasn't much doubt about that. We knew you'd come. The men . . ." He drew a deep breath as though with the remembered weight of their anxiety. "Every day they've been askin' when you'd get here. They've been waitin' for you."

"Waiting for me . . ." She glanced out the small-paned window that looked out over the yard. A pale winter sun had appeared, but it had been so long since the windows had been washed, the day still seemed grey. The men were going about their duties as they always had, but she noticed how often one or another turned his eyes towards the office. Of course they had been worried. Their livelihood and that of their families depended upon the Howard Shipyard. "And I haven't even gone round the yard to say hello to them. Guess that's more important than the papers. What do you think, Daniel?"

"It's right important. They've been a mite nervy ever since the Captain was taken. A lot of them been talkin' about goin' to the gold fields." He shook his head. "First 'twas the railroads; now it's the gold fields. They don't know when they're well off."

"How long since they've had a raise?"

"Been a while."

"Well, the first of the year is coming up. We'll have to see that everyone gets one. If business is going to be as good as you and Papa think, they may as well share in the profit."

"Business ain't been good this year . . . not till the California news come in. Think maybe that's one reason why your pa was goin' to build a ship on his own account."

322

"We'll know more after we go through these." Julia shoved the worrisome papers aside and went to pick up her cloak. "Might as well go out and see if we can't settle things down. I want to see that new ship anyway. Who's she being built for?"

"Captain Seth Siddons over Yarmouth way. Your pa designed her," Daniel said with pride as he opened the door for her. "Had to extend the ways to take her. She's got a length between perpendiculars of one hundred eighty-one and a half foot, a beam of thirty-six foot, and her depth of hold is twenty-one foot."

"What's her tonnage?"

"Captain Howard reckoned she'd be one thousand fifty tons."

Julia whistled under her breath. "That *is* sizeable. There's a lot of work there."

"Yes, ma'am. A *lot* of work."

Their first stop was by the blacksmith's shop, which even on the coldest day was warm and cheerful. Blackie was a tall, intense man who worked in shirtsleeves during the winter and stripped to the waist during the long summer days. Like his father before him, he was well set up, and Julia remembered thinking, when she'd been a child, that the older man looked like the Vulcan of mythology. Now the younger Blackie looked up at her with a welcoming smile, but immediately his eyes returned to the glowing red metal he was pounding into the shape of a strap. His two apprentices glanced at her, but their master had them under too firm a discipline for one to neglect his duty of pumping the giant bellows or for the other to turn his attention away from the blacksmith, who might at any moment demand another tool.

It was enough that she had made her appearance there, and she and Daniel went on to the steaming plant. Here the planks for hulls were bent and curved to the specifications set by the foremen and master carpenters.

At the caulkers' shop, she was met by the gnarled old man who had presided over the seething kettle of tar, the heaps of oakum, the lead, and the containers of ingredients that had gone into the compounding of paint ever since her grandfather's day. The atmosphere in this shop was more relaxed as men and apprentices dropped by to pick up the supplies they needed and spent a moment to gossip.

After they had passed the sawpit, where the broad-hatted men

323

who handled the lower ends of the long-handled saws grinned up at her with sawdust on their faces, Julia realized that her spirits were rising.

The smiles of the men, the warmth of their greetings, their assurances that they were right glad to have her back, made her feel that this was her real home. More real than any ship could ever be, for here she was needed and her long years of training could be put to use. And for the first time, she realized that these men needed her just as surely as any member of her family did. Without her, there would be no shipyard, not for long, and the men would be without employment.

As they approached the large ship, Julia could see her father's deft and daring hand in the lines. There was a round tuck to her square stern, a lower transom, an arch piece, and an upper transom, all of which curved beautifully athwartships. Despite the scaffolding that covered her side, it was obvious that, although her keel was straight, her bilge was well-rounded. The underwater lines of her stem were much like *Neptune's Dragon,* but above water, the bow was padded out in a gentler curve.

Julia thought back to the days when the *Jewel of the Seas* and later the *Crystal Star* had sat on these same ways. The new clipper would have dwarfed them. And at sea? How would Stephen feel when he had to pit his wits against such a ship in a race? When *Neptune's Dragon* had arrived in Hong Kong on her maiden voyage, Julia had realized that the *Crystal Star* had been outdesigned, but only now did she realize by how far. And how far in the past her own talents lay. The *Crystal Star* had been the first and last ship she'd had a hand in designing.

While she inspected the ship and greeted the carpenters and their apprentices, she admired the beauty of the white oak, the live oak, the locust, and the cedar the craftsmen worked so well. She tried not to let them guess how much the size of the ship with her two decks and her twenty-five poop intimidated her. And it was not the size alone.

"Daniel," she said after they had climbed down the scaffolding ladders, "you said my father was talking about building a ship on his own account. Do you know if he made a model of it?"

"He was workin' on it, Miss Julia," he said with a frown. "I seen it in his hands, but I searched the office the day after he was struck down, and I can't find nary a sign of it."

A sudden suspicion occurred to her. "Has Uncle Josiah been around lately?"

"He's been here. Every day. Fired me every day, too." Daniel grinned at her. "But I've kept the door to the office locked. Me and Philip are the only ones have got keys . . . aside from your pa, of course."

"Have you noticed anything else missing?" She still could not dismiss her father's brother from her mind. Long ago, Benjamin had bought out Josiah's share of the yard to put a stop to his meddling ways, but she was sure that her uncle wouldn't be able to resist an opportunity to make trouble.

"No, ma'am, nothin' I know about. Could be some things that were private to the Captain have disappeared, but then I couldn't say."

"Well, I'll have a look at the house. Strange . . ." She stared pensively at the piles of rough lumber, hackmatack, and oak where a couple of carpenters were searching for just the right combination, the proper angle and length of trunk and root, which would match the thin wooden patterns their apprentices helped them hold. "I tried the doors to Papa's study this morning, and they were both locked. I was in a hurry and didn't think much of it at the time. Do you know anything about that?"

Daniel shrugged and shook his head. "Been enough here for me to worry with."

"I hope Aunt Martha has a set of keys. I just don't understand those doors being locked. They never were before." She glanced over at the other ways. Two smaller vessels were there in various stages of construction. Behind them, the gulls were whirling above the incoming tide in Sesuit Creek. "What are those?" she asked.

"A mackerel schooner for Captain Brent over in Wellfleet and a new packet for Barnstable."

"I guess they won't be any problem, but Daniel, I'm not all that sure I can design a clipper. Once Captain Siddons' ship is launched, there's no point in wasting the largest ways on anything else. Maybe I'd better try to get in touch with John Griffith up in New York."

"The naval architect?"

"Yes. He's designed some lovely vessels."

"Miss Julia," Daniel said firmly as he jammed his hands into his pockets and looked at her intently, "you don't need no naval architect. You can do it yourself."

"I don't know." Julia's indigo eyes were filled with misgiving as they swept over the graceful lines of the new ship.

"You learned a lot from the Captain." Daniel refused to be shaken in his belief in her nor was he about to allow her to be shaken in it, either.

"I know, but that was a long time ago. I haven't been near the yard except to visit for years, and there've been a lot of innovations. Things are more complicated than they used to be."

"I've been here, and you've been out there." He nodded towards the Bay. "Most likely you've seen just about every new vessel to come off the ways, no matter where they was built. You must've learned somethin' from them."

"I wonder." Julia looked at the new ship once more. The more she looked at her, the more impossible the task seemed. "Does she have a name yet?"

"I ain't sure. Captain Siddons said he was thinkin' about *Free Wind*. He don't think much of these steamers."

Julia laughed. "Well, that's as good a name as any, I reckon. I can't say I think much of them, either."

At the schooner, they met Philip Sears, and Julia smiled as she watched the two brothers together. They were both dark and had the same intense brown eyes, but where Philip had once also been slender, he now seemed to roll across the ground. Not as bright or as quick as Daniel, he was nevertheless a good man, steady and trustworthy.

"Well, Philip," Julia said as she shook hands with him. "Looks like your wife must be a good cook."

"She is that, Miss Julia." Philip's eyes, almost hidden by his plump cheeks, twinkled, and he patted his paunch with an air of pride.

"Don't let him fool you, Miss Julia," Daniel said. "He's got a lot of brawn beneath that fat of his. I seen him lift his weight more than once."

"What Dan here needs is a wife, too." Philip winked at Julia. "Someone to put some meat on that frame of his."

"No." Daniel's face flooded with color. "Not yet. If you'll excuse me, Miss Julia, I'd best get on back to the office. We've got a load of timber due in soon from Maine, and I've got t'find the papers on it."

Julia watched in amazement as he almost fled from them with his limping stride. Then she turned back to Philip.

"What was that all about?"

"Don't you know, Miss Julia?" Philip was suddenly serious.

"I've no idea. Guess I've been away too long."

" 'Tain't nothin' new." Now Philip seemed uneasy. "He's been carryin' a torch for the same girl for years."

"Well, she's a lucky girl, whoever she is. Why doesn't he propose? It couldn't be his leg, could it?"

"Doubt it. Dan never thinks about that leg of his. Never did consider himself a cripple even when they brought him home from sea with it smashed."

"Who is she, Philip?" Julia glanced over at the office, where Daniel had disappeared. "I'm going to die of curiosity till I find out. Maybe I could help things along."

"I doubt it, Miss Julia. 'Twouldn't do to mention her name. She's a married lady now." Philip looked down at his feet and shuffled them in the icy sand. "Want to see the schooner?"

"Yes." Julia dismissed Daniel from her mind. There were more pressing things to think about.

However, when she entered the office later, Daniel, after a quick glance and a nod at her, returned to the papers he had spread out before him. Julia noticed that his color still seemed high. She pulled a tall stool up beside him and sat down.

"Show me what you're working on, Daniel."

"Yes, ma'am," he said and began to explain the most recent complications in the ordering of supplies, but he avoided looking directly at her.

Finally Julia grew exasperated.

"Really, Daniel, what's the matter with you?"

"Nothin'. Now on the order we've got on Jensen Brothers . . ."

"Never mind that." Julia snatched the letter out of his hand and slapped it on the desk. "What's eating on you?"

He averted his face and looked out the grimy window. "What did Philip say to you?"

"Philip? He showed me the schooner and the packet. They seem to be going apace, and the workmanship is good. You two have done a grand job of holding things together since Papa's been away."

"I mean about me."

"Oh, so that's it. You mean about you marrying?"

Daniel nodded.

"He just said you weren't the marrying kind." Daniel had been her good friend for so many years, sometimes her champion, and she saw no reason for embarrassing him by repeating Philip's remarks. Yet her curiosity wouldn't let her drop the subject entirely. "I always did wonder about it. I know you had the responsibility of your sister and her family for a few years, but now she's remarried and your nephews are grown. All your obligations are over."

"Not all my obligations, Miss Julia."

"Do you want to tell me about them? Maybe I could help."

"No. There's no help to be had." He pushed himself away from the desk and, with his hands shoved deep into his pockets, strolled to the stove. "My obligations won't keep me from doin' my best here at the yard, so don't let that worry you, Miss Julia."

"I know that, Daniel," she said softly, a little ashamed of herself. "I never thought they would. I didn't mean to pry. There's a lot of work to be done in the next couple of weeks. Best we get on with it."

Ignoring the dinner hour, Julia worked on through the day. It was late afternoon and the men were gathering up their tools when a horse and buggy drove into the yard. If someone had come by buggy, they were bound to want to see her, Julia thought, annoyed at the interruption. She was just beginning to get the feel of things.

Chapter Seventeen

1848

When Amelia bounced through the door, however, all sense of irritation disappeared. Only a few golden curls escaped from her red bonnet. Her face was flushed and her cornflower blue eyes sparkled from the cold.

"Julie! You've been home a whole day, and you haven't given me the chance to lay eyes on you," she said as she gave Julia a flurried hug and kiss. "Aunt Martha says you haven't had dinner, and she sent me to carry you home."

"Amelia," Julia said as she stood back and admired the sister she loved so dearly. "You know I'd have come to see you if so many things weren't happening all at once. I think I'll be staying home a while this time."

"Yes." Amelia nodded soberly. "I reckon you will be."

"Well, tell me about yourself," Julia said, trying to forget the sadness of her homecoming. "How are the children and where are they?"

"You'll see them soon enough. I went by the house, and when you weren't there, I left them to play with Clara. You know, she and Hattie always have gotten along well, being so close in age." Despite the sorrow that had fallen over all their lives, Amelia couldn't help her dimpling smile. "Oh, Julie, it's so good to have you home. I know I shouldn't say it, but I hope you'll be here for quite a spell. I miss you when you're away so much."

"I know, Melia," she said, lapsing into the childhood nickname. "I've brought someone home with me I want you to meet. I hope you'll be as good a friend to her as you've always been to me."

"You mean Megan Fairfield?" Amelia asked as she drew her finger across the desk. Then she looked wryly at the dust on the tip of her glove.

"Why, yes." Julia looked at her sister in surprise. "How did you know?"

"As soon as she got here, she sent me a note Cousin William had written. The day after I got it, I took and went right over to Brewster. She . . ." Amelia's cheeks grew even rosier as she hesitated. "She told me her story."

"All of it?" Surely Megan wouldn't tell everything to a stranger. Yet Amelia had a way about her. Everyone seemed to feel that she was a safe repository for their secrets.

"I think so, Julie. It was pretty awful, the poor girl."

"I haven't seen her since I left Hong Kong. How does she seem to you?" Julia carefully wiped the steel tip of her pen and put it in a small drawer in the desk.

"Sad, especially when she first saw my Levi. He reminded her of her little Freddy. But after a while she cheered up. Said she felt she's always known me, you've told her so much about me."

"I guess I have." Julia sighed as she closed the brass top of the inkwell. "I'm going to have to go over to Brewster and see her, maybe tomorrow. I don't know where I'll find the time. Oh, Amelia, there's so much to be done, so much I don't know." She gestured at the papers that were stacked on the desk. "It's like one big puzzle with a lot of pieces missing. If only I could figure out just what Papa had in mind."

Amelia's eyes were round with sympathy as she shook her head. "I wish I could help you, Julie, but you know Mama would never let me have anything to do with the yard. Every time Papa started to talk to me about it, she'd hush him up. The only thing I've been able to do is help Aunt Martha keep Uncle Josiah out of the house."

"He's been at the house, *too*?" Julia paused in her job of stacking papers to look at her sister sharply.

"Yes." Amelia shivered slightly in the room that was rapidly cooling with the coming of night and she burrowed both of her hands into the warmth of her fur muff. "He wanted to come in and straighten things out . . . or so he said. Mama was about to let him into Papa's study, but Aunt Martha sent Ezra to fetch me and I came flying. Got there just in time, too."

"You sure he didn't get a look at anything?"

"I'm positive. When I got there, Aunt Martha had locked one door to the study and was barring the other." Amelia giggled. "That was a sight to behold. She must outweigh him two-to-one. He was so mad, he was just prancing around."

Julia smiled at the picture she could easily visualize. "Well, I'm glad you were able to stop him. He'd destroy us all if he could."

"I know." Amelia stopped laughing and her fair brows drew together in a frown. "Sarah got in there one day, though."

"She did! Did she take anything?"

"No. I followed her into the room. She was going through some papers on the desk, and I asked her what she was doing. She said that, with Papa ailing and you out of the country, it was up to her to take charge."

"What did you do? Sarah can be right formidable when she sets her mind to it." Julia was suddenly aware that the room was growing dark and went to light the lamp that sat on the table near the stove.

"I just called in Mama and Aunt Martha," Amelia said as she followed Julia into the circle of light. "Fortunately Michael was home, too, and you know he's never been what you might call fond of Sarah. Wasn't even when we were courting. I just told her that you'd be home soon and that you were the one to deal with it, that Papa had taught you all his business, and that the world wasn't going to end if we waited a few weeks."

"Sounds as though you've had your hands full," Julia said as she studied her sister, whose soft femininity disguised the very real strength that lay underneath.

"I have." Amelia fished in her reticule. "Here's the keys to the study, Julie. After Sarah left, I locked the doors and demanded all the keys."

"Oh, I'm glad to see them. I didn't know what to think when I found the doors locked." Julia took the keys and looked at them. Then she impishly grinned at her sister. "You mean to say Aunt Martha actually gave up some of her keys."

"She was happy to have them out of the house, that's certain."

"What about the windows?"

"I had Michael fasten the shutters from the inside before I locked the doors, and I've gone in and checked them every time I've been to the house."

"Oh, Amelia, what are we going to do?"

"Go home and get some dinner." Amelia picked Julia's cloak up from where it had been draped over a chair and handed it to her. "Aunt Martha's keeping it warm for you on the north side of the stove. I'll sit with you while you eat, and that'll give Clara a little more time with the children."

"But what about Michael? You said he was home." Julia flung the cloak over her shoulders, but then paused to glance around the office to see what she had left undone.

"Was," Amelia said pensively. "He's gone to California now. Sailed last week."

"I haven't seen him in years. Seems we're never home at the same time. I wish he'd been in the China trade."

"I don't," Amelia said with surprising vehemence. "I got to see a whale of a lot more of him long as he stayed in the Atlantic, but nothing would do but that he must go to California. Cape Horn!" She shuddered.

"Oh, it's not that bad," Julia said as she put an arm around her sister's shoulders. "Not with a captain as good as Michael. I should know. Been around it a few times myself."

"Well, I never heard you with a good word to say for it before, and I've worried about you every time I thought you might be near it, heaven knows."

"And here I am safe and sound."

"I know." Amelia gave her a quick hug. "Oh, Julie, I am glad that I have at least you home for a while."

That evening, Julia sat in her father's study at his carved teak desk and ran her fingers over the smooth white oak of the almost completed lift model. She had discovered it as soon as she'd entered the room. She sighed for, with the windows still shuttered and only one sperm oil lamp for light, it was difficult to do the model full justice.

At first, when she'd found the notes and diagrams that lay beside the model, she'd been horrified. The one figure that stood out above all others was the displacement. Two thousand five hundred and fifty long tons. Daniel had said that the ship that now sat on the railway was one thousand six hundred and fifty. A difference of nine hundred long tons, and this ship would be only two feet longer between perpendiculars.

Now as she studied the model, she could see that she was beamier and much deeper in design than the *Free Wind*. With the flare of the forward sections modified and her upright stem, she would have more cargo capacity. But would she have the speed?

She longed to talk to her father about it. Obviously he must have known what he was doing. Or had he begun to fail before the stroke? No. A stroke was something that happened swiftly.

Ever since the owners had allowed him a free hand, all of her father's ships had been record breakers. The *Jewel*, the *Crystal Star*, *Neptune's Dragon*, each in her turn, and so many, many more. How could she doubt him now?

He had been so tired this evening, she'd been able to stay with him for only a short time. Any discussion of ships or business had been out of the question. She had told him how lovely she thought the *Free Wind* was and he'd smiled, but his interest hadn't seemed to be there. All of his concentration had been turned inwards as he counted the strokes of his heart. How soon would she be able to seek his advice? She shook her head and knew that it would be a long time. She refused to consider the fact that it might be never.

The easiest thing would be to delay, to build a ship for someone else, a smaller vessel of less extreme design. But where was the challenge of that? And her father had obviously wanted this ship built. He had spent many loving hours on the model.

Her head ached with the weight of the day, and she pushed the model towards the back of the desk. There were so many other factors to take into consideration before she would know whether this was the time for the Howard Shipyard to build for itself or for others.

She was so out of touch with the latest news. All anyone wanted to talk about was California. There was a wave of gold fever around, that was certain, but was there really all that much gold in California? And how long would the fever last?

Where was the best profit to be made from it? Her father had mentioned some old vessels he'd bought up, but he hadn't told her where they were or what condition they were in. Probably not very good. How much money had he sunk into them? And how was the rest of their money invested? In working ships? In railroads?

Then she remembered the *Jewel*. She would have to get in touch with the underwriters. The insurance money would help, and the bank drafts David had given her for the goods he'd sold in Hong Kong were upstairs in her still unpacked luggage. There were other shareholders to consider, of course, but eighty percent of the *Jewel* had been hers.

Julia's mind had begun to run in unproductive circles when the door opened and her mother came into the study. She stood and looked down at Julia and then at the model for a moment before she sat down on a side chair that was next to the desk.

"We need money, Julia," she began quietly. "There wasn't much in the strongbox and what was there I've used. Your papa planned to ride over to the bank in Barnstable, but he took ill before he got round to it."

Julia nodded. "I'll take care of it in a few days, Mama."

"A few days!" The fear that Lydia had held at bay while she waited for Julia's return began to cloud her green eyes. "I need it now!"

"Now? Why now? What's so terribly important?"

"Everything's important. The servants. Food. Medicine. The dressmaker. I'd just ordered new clothes."

Julia knew that she would never be able to explain to her mother the machinations of business. She would never understand about banks and lawyers, investments and loans, the need to find the power of attorney Julia knew her father had made out to her several years ago. The only thing Lydia would be able to understand would be actual money in her hand.

"All right. You'll have some in the morning. Stephen gave me what he could before I left New York. It's not much but it'll see us through for a while."

"A while . . . but where's it to come from in the future?" Lydia raised a hand to her mouth and her uncertain eyes were glazed with tears. "Your papa's lying up there helpless. Where's the money to come from?"

"It'll be there same as always," Julia said softly, trying to reassure her mother with a certainty that she herself did not have, not at the moment. "Don't worry about it, Mama."

"How can I help but worry? Here I am, a helpless woman with no sons, only daughters."

334

"I said don't worry!" Julia said more sharply than she had intended. She had seen her mother have hysterical attacks before, and she was just too harassed herself to cope with one of them now. "Everything's fine. Just give me a few days."

"You sure you can handle it, Julia? It's not woman's work. I've always said so. Maybe Josiah . . ."

"Mama! I can handle it! Now just leave me alone so I can get on with it . . . and don't you dare let Uncle Josiah in this house."

"He's your own flesh and blood . . . and he's a man."

"He may be *my* blood, but he's none of yours. You want to lose everything, Mama? You want to kill Papa off? Then you just let Uncle Josiah in this house again."

"Julia!" Her tears forgotten, Lydia straightened up in her chair indignantly. "I tried to bring you up to be respectful of your elders. How dare you speak to me like that . . . especially after what I've been through?"

"I'm sorry, Mama. I'm just tired. Very tired." Julia leaned her forehead on the heels of her hands and tried to stroke away the tenseness of the headache that was growing stronger.

"It is a load on you, isn't it, child?" For a moment, Lydia's voice softened in sympathy, but it was only for a moment. "Well, it's what you always wanted from the day you was born. Played up to your papa to get it." She jumped up from her chair and stood beside Julia with clenched fists. "Oh! If only Nathaniel had lived!"

"He was just a little boy when he died," Julia said wearily. "He might not have suited you if he'd grown to be a man."

"And now you speak ill of the dead!"

"Where's Cousin William?" Julia asked. He was one person who could always be counted on to handle her mother.

"He's deserted us, too. Hasn't been back since he left this morning. Just sent word that he had important business to tend to and that he'd return in a day or two. Important business! I think our business is more important than any foolishness he has in mind."

"If he said he's coming back, he'll be back. Mama, nothing dreadful's going to happen tonight or tomorrow or even next week. Please go to bed. You're overwrought. Do you have any of that tonic Doctor Willett used to give you?"

"Tonic! You and your father are just alike. Every time I turn round, it's, 'Take your tonic and rest.' "

Although it was an effort, Julia pushed back her chair and stood up. For years, she had been a head taller than Lydia, but now the distance seemed even greater, as though her mother had shrunk. She put an arm around Lydia, and suddenly her mother seemed to be the child and she, Julia, the mother.

"Well, if you don't want it, I'll take a little myself tonight," she said soothingly. "We're too tired to talk now. Let's both go to bed."

The tonic had a good effect on Julia, and when she wakened to see the sun rise in a clear sky, she was fresh and rested. She felt almost eager to tackle the problems that had seemed so hopeless last night. At the breakfast table, she was pleasantly surprised to find that her mother was there ahead of her. Lydia had Clara seated next to her and was far more interested in feeding her granddaughter than in her own food.

As she watched them, Julia was struck by how much the two were alike. She'd never noticed any resemblance before. Although Clara had Stephen's grey eyes, the expression in them was far more like that in Lydia's green ones. The child's fair hair was not much darker than her grandmother's white, and they were both pale and fragile. At the moment, they were laughing as Lydia played a mealtime game remembered from the days when her own children were small.

When, upon leaving the house, Julia gave her mother the gold coins she had taken from the leather bag that was locked in her sea chest upstairs, Lydia seemed almost casual about the money. Without bothering to count it, she turned her attention to the child who clung to her side.

Well, Julia thought as she rode through the crisp air to the shipyard, perhaps Clara and her mother were two problems who would take care of each other.

As for her father, he had seemed more cheerful, too, this morning. He'd even initiated a conversation about business, but after he'd told Julia where to find the most important documents and explained to her where he currently had money invested, she had cut her visit short.

Things seemed to be falling into place when Stephen, bringing

336

presents for everyone, arrived home a week later. Work at the yard was going smoothly, and Megan had ridden over to East Dennis one day to see Julia while she was at the office.

Although Julia had suggested that Megan move into the house with her family, she knew the suggestion had not been whole-hearted. Since her mother was sleeping in Amelia's old room, there really was not another to spare in the house unless she took Clara into her own room. With Stephen coming for what would be their last time together before a long separation, Julia hadn't wanted the child's presence during the precious nights that would be left to them.

She had been frankly relieved when Megan said she was happy in Brewster. Looking at the smudges under Megan's dark eyes, Julia had wondered how much truth there was in it. But she had eased her conscience by telling herself that her friend was at least safe for the moment.

When Stephen arrived, she hadn't been expecting him for a few more days. She had just been going over the details of the *Free Wind* and had paused alone in the middle of the yard for a few stolen moments to dream about the new ship's lines when she heard his voice behind her.

"So you're the wild, wicked, infamous Julia."

She whirled around to see him standing behind her. His tall hat was pushed back on his sun-bleached hair, and the slow, lazy grin lighted his face back to the youth she had first met while standing on this very spot.

"And you're Aaron Martin's friend," she replied, caught as he was in the magic of that past day.

"Aye." Then his expression grew more serious but no older as he looked at her with that early longing in his eyes. "I couldn't resist it, Julia. You looked so much as you did when I first saw you. Even the wind has loosened your hair."

She smiled her love at him. "I'm the same. Even after all these years, I'm the same, Stephen."

"Are you?" One tawny eyebrow shot up and he became thirty-six again. "I've been to the house."

"Have you seen my father?"

"Yes. For a moment."

"Then you know."

He was silent for a moment as he glanced at the blacksmith's shop without really seeing it, not even aware of the ringing blows coming from it. When he looked back at her, his eyes were bleak.

"I know you're planning to stay."

"I have to, Stephen."

"Because of your father!" he exploded without warning. "It's always your father, isn't it, Julia? All he has to do is crook his finger and you come running. You've spent the last seven years comparing me to the great Benjamin Howard, and I just don't measure up. He's the magnificent man of ships. He can not only sail them, he can build them. Not a single day has gone by since I first met you that you haven't mentioned his name at least once."

"Stephen! That's not fair!" She was stunned by the sudden viciousness of his attack. She was trembling as she stepped back away from him.

"Oh, yes it is. It's time you heard the truth and took a good long look at yourself. Your father spoiled you from the day you were born, and so you think he can do no wrong. Every day, you take out that pretty little painted picture of him you carry around in your head. Then you look at me and say to yourself, 'No, Stephen Logan isn't the man my father is.' Well, he's a man like any other man, Julia. And you're not the portrait of perfection he shows you in that mirror he holds up to you, either."

"My father's not the only reason I'm staying." She tried to keep her voice from shaking as she spoke.

"Oh, isn't he?"

"No, he isn't, but while we're on the subject of my father, let me remind *you* of a few things." Her eyes darkened into indigo and flashed with anger as she refused to back down any further. With her shoulders squared and her chin lifted high, she shot back at him, "You often said that I'm unlike other women, and that's why you married me. Well, let me tell you, if it wasn't for my father, I wouldn't *be* the woman I am. If he hadn't brought me up the way he did, if he hadn't taught me how to build ships, how to think things out for myself, I'd most likely be content to stay quietly at home while my husband went off to sea. I'd tend the house and raise the children, join the sewing circle and spend my days in endless gossip. Is that what you wanted? You know damned good and well it isn't, and if I'd been that kind of woman, you'd never have looked at me twice."

He whipped off his hat and banged the brim against the flat of his hand. Two workmen, who were carrying a knee for the new ship, glanced nervously over at Stephen and Julia and steered well clear of them. Stephen noticed neither the men nor his surroundings. All he saw was Julia drawn up in her pride, and it fed his fury.

"However he brought you up isn't to the point. The point is that you stood up before an altar and swore that you would forsake all others and keep only unto me as long as we both should live. There was no mention of your father being the exception to that vow."

"Stephen, my father has very little to do with my decision to stay ashore. Look at this shipyard!" The breeze billowed her cloak as she swept her hand around the circumference of the yard. The sight of the men and the vessels, the knowledge that they were being watched, calmed her. She continued in a more reasonable voice, but one that was still firm with resolution.

"Who's going to run this yard? Who's going to see that those vessels slide down the ways come the spring tide? Who's going to see that those men are fed and housed? Who's going to see that my family is taken care of? If 'twas only that my father was ill, I'd go with you. 'Twould tear me in two to leave him in that condition, but I'd do it. But I cannot leave everything and everyone who depends on me."

"You just said it, didn't you?" He, too, lowered his voice, but it was still filled with venom. "Did you hear your own words? It would tear you in *two* to leave him. So that leaves me half. Half a wife. Half a woman."

"Stop it." She stamped her foot on the frozen sand. "Stop it right now. I didn't ask for this responsibility. I never really wanted it. But it's mine, and now I'm learning just what it means. It means *not* always doing the thing you want to do but doing the things that must be done. It means thinking about a lot of other people and not just yourself. You take responsibility the minute you walk onto the quarterdeck of the *Crystal Star*. You think of the ship, the men, the cargo. You go without sleep, often without food to make certain that the ship and all she carries come through safely. You drive yourself into exhaustion, but you don't complain about it. Well, grant me the right to my own responsibility. I can no more leave here now than you can walk off your quarterdeck in the midst of a storm."

"A fine storm!" he said caustically and clapped his hat on his head. Turning abruptly on his heel, he strode in the direction of the new ship.

Julia let him go while she tried to bring her emotions under control. She knew that the argument had just begun, but she couldn't allow it to continue in front of the workmen. Before Stephen and she left the yard, they would have to present a united front.

If only Stephen would be reasonable! she thought as she stood frozen to the same spot where he had left her. Why wouldn't he listen to her? Why would he never consider her point of view?

Finally, when she felt that she was calm enough, she approached him. His back was rigid when she spoke.

"How do you like the ship?" she asked in a neutral tone, which she hoped was pleasant.

His face was stony when he first looked at her, but as he examined her face in the silence that lay between them, his features gradually softened. Then a smile slowly touched his lips. It was full of confidence. He appeared certain that he would win. Julia uneasily wondered what he was going to try next.

"Beautiful," he said quietly. He wasn't speaking about the ship.

There was a pain in her chest as though he had turned a knife there. Or was it she who was turning the knife? All that she knew was that she wanted him, she wanted to go with him, to follow him to the ends of the earth once more. Why could he always do this to her? It wasn't fair! Reminding herself that she must remain calm, she took a deep breath.

"Stephen, please look at the ship."

"If you insist, my lady." The smile was still on his lips as he turned his head slightly and studied the vessel with expert eyes. Julia forgot the ship to study his profile.

"Are you memorizing my features so that, on dark lonely days ahead, you can take out a faded picture to console yourself?" he asked without moving his eyes away from the ship.

"She's a lot like *Neptune's Dragon*, but Papa's made quite a few modifications. I think they're improvements, don't you?"

"It won't work, you know. After a while, you'll forget how I look. You'll lie there at night trying to remember, and all you'll see will be hazy outlines and every once in a while a distinct detail or two."

"She's over a hundred eighty-one feet."

"The *Crystal Star* is over one hundred forty-three. You were always happy enough with her."

"She's a thousand and fifty tons," Julia went on desperately.

"And the *Crystal Star* is only six hundred and fifty. What are you trying to do, Julia? Sell her to me?"

"No. She's being built to order. She already has an owner."

"Then you must be trying to arouse my envy."

"No, no. Of course not."

"Then there's no point in my inspecting her, is there? I'd give almost everything I own to possess her, but not my soul. I only gave my soul for one thing." He stopped staring at the ship and turned back to Julia and there was blue smoke in his eyes.

"Stephen, couldn't you stay, too?" She offered him, as though it were a gift, the only solution she had been able to find. "Please? You could find another master for the *Crystal Star* for just one voyage."

"And what would I do ashore, my lady?"

"You could help me. Oh, Stephen, there's so much to be done. I don't know which way to turn. I need you. I need you to help me make decisions, to help me run the yard, to help me with the other investments."

He just shook his head. "No, Julia."

"Why? Why won't you help me?" She put her gloved hand on the sleeve of his greatcoat.

He covered her hand lightly with his own but he didn't squeeze it. "Because it would be just that. I would be helping you. The decisions wouldn't be mine, the yard wouldn't be mine, the investments wouldn't be mine. The *Crystal Star* may not be a small empire, but she is mine."

Clouds had begun to pile up in the northwest, and as they hid the sun, the wind veered and began to blow the stinging sand.

"I'm cold, Stephen. Very cold. Let's go over to the office."

"Are you cold, my lady? That's strange. So am I." He tucked her hand under his arm.

They walked across sand that yielded underfoot with the melting snow. Stephen looked around the yard as though he had never seen it before and nodded to the workmen they passed. However, none of the men came up to greet him for the two walked in a frozen silence that left questioning looks in their path.

When Stephen had taken Julia's cloak and hung it up together

341

with his own greatcoat on pegs on the wall, they both turned to the stove. There was still silence. For both of them, there were memories in this small room, and now once again a plan had to be made for their future.

"I didn't see Clara at the house," Stephen finally said.

"She's over at Amelia's," Julia answered, relieved that her husband had decided to defer their previous conversation. "I wasn't expecting you or I would have made sure she was home."

"It's just as well. Clara wasn't foremost in my mind. Is she still running a fever?"

"No. I wouldn't have let her go out if she had been."

"Why not?" He shot an intense glance at her from beneath a lifted brow and then walked away from her to inspect the lift model that lay on the desk. "You had her up on deck when she ran a fever."

"That was different," Julia said to his back.

"Why?" he asked without turning.

"The weather was better."

"Yet her health is better here."

"At the moment."

"Is she happy?" He turned to face her with the model in his hands. "Does she enjoy being home?"

"Yes." Julia looked at him, perplexed. There was some reason other than Clara's health behind all these questions. "After the first day, she started settling in. She's making friends with Amelia's Hattie, and when she's home, she follows Mama everywhere. She even takes a nap with her."

"So I was right about Clara?" He was paying no attention to the model he held. All of his concentration was focused on her. "She's better off ashore?"

"Well, for the moment, but she's been just as well many times at sea." Damn! she thought. He's trying to put me on the defensive again. Well, I won't let him do it.

"You won't admit that I'm right?"

"I'll admit that you're right, Stephen, until something proves you otherwise," she said and tried to control the flash of anger that could grow into an explosion.

"Very well." He put the model back on the desk and strolled casually towards her. "If I'm right about Clara, isn't it just possible that I'm right about other things?"

"Of course, you are. You're often right."

"Usually." He stopped just in front of her and his voice was as expressionless as his face.

"Yes, usually." But her eyes didn't give ground.

"Then just keep that in mind when it comes time to sail."

Julia sat down next to the stove and pushed the wind-tumbled hair away from her face. She might have known he hadn't dropped the subject. Once Stephen was set on something, he'd never drop it, just try a new tack. It was an admirable quality in a master, but an infuriating one in a husband.

"Stephen, you're right when it comes to commanding a ship, when it comes to trading, but it doesn't mean that you're right when it comes to things you know little or nothing about."

He sat down on the table in front of her and swung one leg while he watched her. "Yet you believe in my judgment strongly enough to want me to stay here and help you make decisions."

"Yes."

"Then what is it that I know little or nothing about?"

"Papa, the shipyard, the whole situation. You've only been home a few hours, if that long. How can you know what has to be done?"

"You're taking a lot of factors into consideration, aren't you?" he said, never taking his eyes from her.

"Yes. A lot of them."

"Have you taken your husband into consideration?"

There was no anger, no laughter between them, only a protective numbness that was as hard and clean as the icicles that hung from the eaves, and each was encased in his own thoughts.

After a few minutes, it was Julia who spoke. "Since the day we were married, Stephen, you've always had first place in my consideration. For six years, I've thought of no one but you. Now I must think of other things."

"I don't recall anything in the marriage service about six years. I thought it was till death do us part."

"It is. I'm your wife. I'll always be your wife."

Abruptly he stopped swinging his leg and his very stillness was searingly intense. Only his eyes and lips showed any movement. "Then come with me, Julia."

She rose and went to the desk, where she lifted the large model he had earlier held. She turned to face him with it in her hands.

343

"Do you see this, Stephen? Did you really look at it?"

He didn't move nor did he look at the model. He looked only at her. "Another of your father's ships or is that the model for that one out there?"

"Another one," she said with her shoulders held very straight despite the weight of the model. "I have to build this ship, Stephen."

"Why? Why you?"

"Because there's no one else."

"Are you going to build it for me?"

"If you wish."

"You know I can't afford a new ship!" He stood up and began to walk towards her with his arms held out as though he would take the model from her. "With one more voyage . . . with you at my side . . . I could afford it."

The door opened and a gathering wind swept through the room. Daniel Sears pulled off his cap and shut the door behind him. He was immediately aware that he had broken into what appeared to be a very private conversation.

"Pardon, Miss Julia, Captain Logan, I didn't know you were here. Welcome home, sir."

"Thank you, Daniel," Stephen said. "I was just leaving."

He dropped his arms and went to the wall where his coat was hanging.

"It's nothin' that can't wait." Daniel, flustered, turned to the door. "I'll come back later."

"No. You'd better stay and confer with Miss Julia. She may not be here long, and I suggest you take advantage of every moment." Stephen shrugged into his coat and buttoned it with ceremony. Then he picked up his top hat and, with a half-bow, saluted Julia with it.

"Miss Julia," he said as he put it on at a rakish angle. "I'll see you at home. I trust you'll be there before dark."

"Yes. Before dark." She realized she was still holding the model. Though it was growing heavy, she clutched it tightly against her body as she watched her husband leave.

"I'm right sorry, Miss Julia," Daniel said after Stephen had gone. "Seems I've come at the wrong time."

"No, Daniel. You've come at the right time." She turned and carefully put the model on an oak table at the back of the room. "What did you want to see me about?"

344

"Well, Christmas is less than a week away, and the men have been talkin'. You know Captain Howard usually gives them a bonus about this time of year."

"Oh, yes, the bonus. Money." Julia went to the tall desk and hoisted herself up onto the stool. She looked vaguely at the papers that covered the surface of the desk.

"You all right, Miss Julia?"

"Me, Daniel?" Her laugh was short and bitter. "I'm fine. Just fine."

"It could wait another day. . . " Daniel's brown eyes were soft with concern. He wanted to go to her, to comfort her as he had when she was a child, but he didn't dare. The wall of years between them was too high now.

"No." She leaned her cheek on the palm of one hand and looked towards the stove that was burning low. "Figure out what the bonuses should be and let me know how much. I'll get the money somehow."

"Captain Howard was always the one to figure that out before, Miss Julia," Daniel reminded her gently.

"Yes. So he was, but it looks like it's your turn now, Daniel."

Daniel fidgeted beside the door with his cap in his hand and then went to stand beside the stove. He picked up a cup, thought better of it, and put it down again.

"Well," Julia said sharply. "What is it?"

"I'll figure it out for you, but I'd rather the men didn't know 'twas done by me."

"Why? Are you afraid of them?" Julia knew she shouldn't be taking out her unhappiness with Stephen on Daniel, but somehow she couldn't help herself.

"No, ma'am." Daniel, understanding her unhappiness though not the reason for it, forgave her and spoke to her with gentleness. "But I reckon they'll work better if they believe it was you that done it, that you spent some time thinkin' about them."

"Isn't it important to them that *you* think about them?"

"I wasn't born a Howard, Miss Julia."

"It's a pity. You should have been," she said under her breath.

"What, Miss Julia?" Daniel had heard the words but couldn't believe them.

"Nothing, Daniel. Figure out the bonuses. I've got to ride over and see Captain Chase at the Marine Insurance Company before dark." She got up wearily and went to pick her cloak off the wall.

"Is there anything else? I won't be back today."

"Just one thing, Miss Julia."

"Well, what is it?" she asked as she tossed the rough cloak around her shoulders.

"Captain Logan. . . "

"What about Captain Logan?" Her eyes warned him not to go beyond bounds.

"He said you might not be here long."

"Don't pay any attention to him, Daniel. I'll be here." She swept out of the door before he could ask more questions.

Daniel went to the window and watched her as she mounted her horse and trotted out of the yard, but the question was still in his eyes. When he could no longer hear the horse, he took off his thick jacket and hung it on the peg where hers had hung. Then he went to the chest where the payroll records were kept.

On Christmas Day, extra leaves had to be put in the dining room table, but Stephen and Cousin William were the only men present. Sarah and her husband, Aaron Martin, had been invited, but they preferred to spend the holiday with Aaron's parents. Thomas Benjamin, Sarah's child, was their only grandson and they doted on him.

It was the first Christmas Julia and her family had spent at home in years, and with the addition of Megan, Amelia, and Amelia's three children, the house should have been filled with gaiety. Yet the absence of Benjamin at the head of the table would have made a mockery of it if it hadn't been for the children's enjoyment.

Even for the children, however, the joy was damped with constant reminders to keep their voices lowered. Each one had paid a brief visit to Benjamin to wish him a happy Christmas, and even though he had looked forward to seeing them, he was exhausted before it was over.

Julia was concerned about the effect the excitement might have on him. Although on some days he was stronger than on others, his condition remained essentially unchanged. When she had quizzed Doctor Willett on it privately, he had just told her that it was too early to tell, but that her father positively must not be worried about any matters, whether they were business or private.

Stephen was uncommonly slow that night, Julia thought as she lay in bed and watched him remove his clothes with great deliberation. He'd also been brooding and silent for most of the day, even when he had sat in her father's chair at the head of the table to preside over the Christmas dinner. To get away from the children's chatter, he had taken a long walk alone after the meal, and when he had returned, he'd shut himself up in her father's study.

When at last he had his nightshirt on, he came and sat on the edge of the bed, but made no move to get under the covers with her. Instead, he stared at the fire.

"Aren't you cold?" she asked when she could stand it no longer.

"Cold? I suppose I am. Something I must get used to, mustn't I?"

"Not tonight, Stephen."

"Not tonight?" He turned to look at her and then reached out a hand to spread her blue-black hair across the white pillow. His fingers were gentle as he traced the bones of her face. "Do you know what loneliness is, my love?"

"Yes. I know."

"I don't think you do. Loneliness is an empty space, a hole that cannot be filled. Loneliness is the weather side of the quarterdeck and a vacant captain's cabin. It's the sea when I can't look at it through your eyes. It's the wind when I can't hear it with your ears. It's salt when I can't taste it on your lips."

"It won't be long, Stephen."

"Won't it? Seven months, nine months, perhaps longer. And at the end of that time, what then? Another nine months?"

"Just one voyage."

"Just one and then another and another. Or perhaps this will be my last voyage, the one when I don't return and the months turn into years and the years into eternity."

"Stephen, don't!"

"Don't." He shook his head slowly and all the sorrow in the world was in his smile. "Don't what? Don't love you with every beat of my heart? Don't long for you with every muscle of my body?"

He leaned forward and kissed her eyelids.

"Close your eyes, my pretty Julie. Don't look ahead to what will come. See only the surface. Listen only to those who call the loudest, not to the one who loves you the deepest."

She looked up at him through half-closed eyes and ran her hand up his arm. Through the thin lawn of his nightshirt, she could feel the strength of his muscles. "Come to bed, Stephen."

"During the storms, I used to think of you, my treasure, so vulnerable below in my cabin. I fought the winds, the waves for you with every trick I could muster. You were in my keeping."

"You're a good master, my love. Others went down when we survived."

"For you."

"Not just for me. For the ship, the men, the cargo."

"No, my sweet. For you. To see your smile, I drove the hardest bargains. To hear your laughter when we broke a record, I drove the ship and the men almost past endurance. For you."

"Stephen . . ."

"If you'll just come with me, my love, I'll take you places you've never been. We'll stop in Australia. I'll take you to France. You've always wanted to go there. You've never seen Copenhagen in the spring. We don't have to go back to China." He stretched full length on top of the quilt and put an arm on each side of her, imprisoning her. As he stared down into her eyes, his were full of promises and hope. "I'll give you the world, Julie."

"Oh, Stephen, you know I want to come. God knows, I want to come."

"But you can't."

"I can't."

He rolled away from her and, locking his hands behind his head, stared at the shadows that flickered on the ceiling.

"Is that how you sent him away, the other one? Jason?"

"Stephen, that's not fair. You'll come home. I know you will. My being with you has nothing to do with it."

"I might come home . . . someday . . . and then again I might not. I might decide there are other places I'd rather be. Why should I come home to a woman who cares so little for me? One who can do so well without me?"

Julia rolled onto her side and propped her head up with one hand.

"I *love* you. Can't you understand that? How can you ever doubt it? I'll miss you probably more than you will me."

"That would be impossible."

"Oh, Stephen." She rolled closer, trying to nestle her head on his shoulder, but he lay unmoving, still watching the darkening ceiling, and his shoulder was unyielding.

"I'm leaving tomorrow, Julia."

"Tomorrow!" She sat bolt upright. "Why?"

Now he looked at her. "Why not? I'm a sailor and a sailor's job is to sail."

"But so soon! You've only been home a few days."

"By the time I reach New York, the *Crystal Star* will be out of drydock. There's a cargo to be found, a crew. I must be about my business."

"You won't reconsider? Let someone else take her? For just one voyage?"

"No. You'd enjoy California, Julia. Think of the excitement. Gold and thousands of men willing to spend every cent they have for passage to the gold fields."

She lay down and turned on her side so that her back was to him. There was nothing more to be said. Presently Stephen crawled under the covers and put an arm around her.

"You'll come with me, sweet Julia, pretty Julia," he whispered as he held her close with one hand cupping her breast.

"Stephen . . ." His hand was warm despite the cooling room and the gusts of rain that rattled the windowpanes. Warm and strong and melting.

"You'll miss me too much," he murmured as he kissed the nape of her neck, her ear. "Do you know how many nights there are in seven or eight or nine months? You're not used to doing without, Julie."

She twisted in his embrace until she could see him. "Oh, Stephen, I do love you, only you."

"Then you'll come."

She shook her head.

"I'll be in New York for two weeks before I sail. You'll come. I know you will. I'll look for you on every packet."

She started to answer, but his lips found her open mouth and he kissed her hungrily, demandingly, and his hands roamed over her body in the private places that were known so well only to him.

The next morning, the glory of the night might never have existed. Rain had coated the world and then frozen it. The early sun glittered off of every surface. It should have been beautiful, but it made Julia think of the treacherous ice that could cover masts and yardarms, sails and rigging.

Stephen had scarcely spoken to her this morning after her negative reply to his final repetition of that one question. Waiting

349

in the front hall for the stagecoach, she looked at him and thought that he, too, seemed to be made of ice this morning.

When the four horses finally pulled the coach up by the side of the road, Ezra and the footman carried Stephen's sea chest down to it. Julia and Stephen paced slowly behind it. She felt as though she were in a funeral procession. Just before they reached the end of the walk, he turned and gave her what at best was a dutiful kiss.

"Oh, Stephen, do we have to part this way?"

"We don't have to part at all, my lady." There was no emotion in his voice or on his face. It was a look that he might have given any member of his crew.

She pressed her lips together as he doffed his hat to her and then swung onto the stagecoach. As soon as he was aboard, the footman slammed the door, hopped up onto his seat, and they were off. It was only a moment before they had rounded the far curve, and she knew that she would not catch sight of them again.

Looking across the ice-coated marsh, light glittered blues, yellows, reds as brilliant as crystal. Crystal, she thought. Crystal shatters. I wonder if stars do.

Chapter Eighteen

1849

The weeks that followed into the new year and beyond were a torment to Julia. Although she heard nothing from Stephen, she was constantly aware of his presence in New York. At night when she tossed in her lonely bed, she could feel him calling to her just as her body called for him. Each night when the coals in the grate tumbled into a few red embers, she would decide to go to him. Yet when she wakened to daylight, she knew that she could not.

Then one day, she received a short note from him. He was sailing with the morning tide, and it had taken the letter four days to reach her. He was gone.

There was relief, for now she had no alternative. There was also an aching emptiness in knowing that he no longer walked the land as she must.

Usually she was able to concentrate on the business at hand as she sorted and straightened and planned. Too often, however, thoughts of him stole into her mind and she would find herself staring vacantly at the papers she had been studying while she tried to cope with the darkness that lay like a physical weight within her.

One morning in late January, the weather turned warm with the false breath of summer, and Julia carried the lift model of the ship that was yet to come down to the beach with her. She had decided to follow her father's original plan and build it. If nothing else, she was sure she could sell it once it was completed. As she knew from the number of inquiries she had received, the demand for clippers, large clippers, was growing every day.

The only problem was that she still felt unsure of her ability to build such a ship, and the constant interruptions upon her time both at the yard and at home made it difficult for her to puzzle out the complications such a vessel would have.

She spread her cloak in the lee of a dune and laid the model beside her. The secret, she felt, lay in the way of the waves, but this morning there was only a light ripple on top of the water, and the ebb and flow of the high tide made only a dreaming sweet sound as it rattled the pebbles in their perpetual music.

Idly she watched the vessels that sailed in the far distance. There were fewer now than there had been in her childhood, for most of them avoided Boston in favor of New York. As she watched a small old-fashioned barkentine tacking her outward-bound way through the light, variable airs, Julia thought of the days when she and Stephen had set sail from Boston. She wondered if those aboard had the same joyful hopes she and her husband had once shared. Most likely they did although of a different kind, for they were undoubtedly bound for the gold fields.

And Stephen? What of him? If he'd had favorable weather, he would be in mid-Atlantic heading south. She offered a short prayer that all was going well with him.

Aside from that farewell note, she hadn't heard from him, and she wondered at his silence. By now, he should have had an opportunity to send her a letter by a homeward-bound vessel. She herself had sent several, but they would probably not reach him until after he arrived in California. Not if he drove the *Crystal Star* in his usual ruthless manner.

She sighed. He probably still hadn't forgiven her for what he considered her desertion. But there was more. Even though he had been completely unreasonable, two things had become signally apparent. His need for her and his loneliness. Perhaps the two things were really one. Why hadn't he let his need show more over the years? Or had he? And was she at fault for not listening? The possessiveness, the jealousy that had irritated her so. Perhaps they had been his way of speaking, of telling her how essential she was to him.

On their last night together, she had thought he had only been trying to sway her into coming with him when he had spoken of his loneliness. Yet now that they were parted for the first time in their marriage, she could look at him from a distance, and what she saw was a lonely man. It wasn't only that his profession required the separation of himself from others. Even when he was ashore, he had many acquaintances, but no real friends aside from herself and Captain Asa. All others, he held slightly away. Almost as though, if they came too close, they might discover some weakness or flaw. But was that really true or had her sight become distorted as she tried to explain away his cold anger?

She scooped up a handful of dry, grainy sand and let it trickle through her fingers as though she would find the answer there. Digging deeper, she discovered that the sand was still icy beneath the sun-warmed surface.

That same night, he had said this might be the voyage from which he would never return. But those had only been words heaped upon the thousand other words of his persuasion. Hadn't they been?

It couldn't have been a premonition. No. It couldn't have been. She dusted off her hands and picked up the lift model and, putting it on her lap, she stroked it like a cat. The smooth texture of the wood was soothing, almost as soothing as the wavelets that lapped the beach.

Suddenly, as she stared off at the sails on the horizon, she could see this future ship as a living creature. Every detail, from the placement of the ribs to the arrangement of the furnishings in the captain's cabin, came to her. The masts would be tall and raking, well fitted to carry the maximum in sail. Her mainmast would be eighty-four feet from heel to cap, and her main yard would be seventy-eight feet from boom iron to boom iron. With her crossed skysail yards, she would be a magnificent sight. Julia knew how to build that ship!

And she would give it to Stephen.

If she couldn't be with him, he would have the thing he most desired. The fastest, most beautiful ship in all the world.

Perhaps by the time it was built, she would even be able to sail with him again. Her father would recover, at least enough to manage the yard with Daniel in a position of increased responsibility. She knew he would. And Clara would have outgrown the fevers of early childhood. Megan would have borne her child by then and would be settled one way or another.

Yes. It would work out. All she had to do was build the ship. Then everything else would fall into place. She sprang up filled with new energy and purpose.

When she reached the top of the dunes and could see down into the yard, she noticed several horses and a buggy. That meant a lot of visitors. Well, it wasn't unusual. Word had spread about the building of the *Free Wind,* and people often came to take a look at her. Julia found them an irritation, for they interrupted the men and herself when every hour was needed to complete the ship in time for the March high tide. Yet she supposed the visitors were a necessary evil. They were potential customers, and even when they weren't, they spread the fame of the Howard Shipyard.

She hurried across the yard to the office, nodding to the visitors she knew, but not pausing to talk. If they had anything important in mind, they would seek her out. Just now, she wanted to make notes about the unborn ship while the details were still fresh in her mind. When she went through the open door of the office, however, she saw that the future would have to be delayed for the present.

Megan, whose pregnancy was now obvious beneath a bombazine dress that was as black as her eyes, was sitting quietly in a chair in the far corner and Cousin William was standing protectively beside her, but the other four men were in the center of the room.

Daniel Sears, with his smaller stature and wiry body, seemed dwarfed by David Baxter, who towered above him. The smile David gave her was meant to be impersonal, but he couldn't hide the welcoming warmth in his grey-green eyes. The well-tailored suit and vest he wore indicated that he had come for some formal reason. Unlike most sea captains, he normally preferred the casual clothing he wore at sea while he was at home.

Yet well-attired as he was, no one could outshine Hiram Richardson, who was as always dressed in the very latest fashions and whose chestnut hair was trimmed to perfection. By the set of his bulky shoulders and the vibrancy with which he moved, he dominated the room. Seth Siddons, with his lanky frame draped in a somber frockcoat, seemed like a shadow beside the merchant.

"I was just comin' to fetch you, Miss Julia," Daniel said as he separated himself from the group. "Seems there's been some changes."

"Changes?" She handed the model to Daniel and looked at the other men. "What changes?"

She couldn't understand why these three men should be together and yet they seemed to be. Captain Siddons would be here about the *Free Wind,* but what connection could he possibly have with David Baxter and Hiram Richardson? And they with each other?

"It's a little late to make any radical changes in the *Free Wind,*" she said to Seth Siddons, who had his lantern jaw set but looked a little embarrassed.

"It's not changes in the vessel, ma'am," Captain Siddons said. "It's a change in ownership. Captain Richardson here wants to buy her."

"How very pleasant to see you again, Mrs. Logan." Hiram Richardson was circumspect in his bow, but his smile was as warmly flattering as it had ever been. "I've always wanted to own a Howard ship, but this seems to be the only way I could obtain one. Your father has never answered my letters, and when I've seen him, he's always claimed to have a backlog he couldn't handle."

"I see." The news was not particularly pleasant to Julia, and she was thankful Stephen wasn't present to hear about it. He would sooner or later, though, and it was not apt to improve his temper. After the business of the opium, they had seen Captain Richardson from time to time but had never had any further dealings with him. She glanced at the customer who, only a week ago, had been so pleased with the progress of his new vessel. "Well, that's your privilege, Captain Siddons. The ship is being built for you, but you're entitled to do what you will with her. I think you're making a mistake, though."

"Could be. But it's necessary." He clamped his mouth shut, and Julia knew that nothing she could say would make him reconsider.

"Very well." She turned back to the merchant. "I hope you're not considering any major changes, Captain Richardson. We've less than two months, and if we're not able to launch her then, you'll have another six months to wait, and of course we'll have to charge you a fair sum for tying up the ways."

"Oh, no. No major changes. A few trifles perhaps. We can go into them later. I believe you know Captain Baxter." He nodded at David. "I've arranged for him to take command of the *Free Wind.*"

"Yes. We're old friends." It felt strange to offer him her hand, but in the presence of others, nothing less formal would do. "So you're deserting the Howard Line, David."

"Yes." He held her hand in his huge one for a moment. "I didn't have a contract with the Line, just one for the ship, and I doubted you had anything for me. I didn't want to bother you with it after hearing about your father."

"You're right. We don't have anything now that the *Jewel* is gone." When he suddenly released her hand and she saw his large jaw tighten, she realized that he'd misunderstood her. She continued quickly. "It's not the *Jewel*. No one can blame you for that, certainly not me. But the other vessels are all in good hands, though maybe not as capable as yours. All that's left are a few ancient ones I'm going to dispose of. You wouldn't want them, anyway."

"No," he said a little stiffly. "Not if what I hear of them is true."

"It's true." With her eyes, she begged him not to let her unthinking words build an unneccessary barrier between them. When she saw the beginnings of a smile touch his lips, she tried to remember what she had been saying. Yes. The cast-off vessels. And she felt a little ashamed and apologetic about them. "They're not in the best condition, but they're likely good enough to get to California. I'll make no pretense as to their seaworthiness to any prospective buyers."

"Let the buyer beware." Hiram Richardson winked at her, which did not endear him to her in the least.

"The *Free Wind* is a good, seaworthy ship, Captain Richardson," she said coolly.

"I'm sure of that, my dear. I meant no offense." His clear blue eyes were as innocent as a boy's. "In fact, I admire your father a great deal for having had the foresight to buy those old tubs when they were still available for a song. It's something I overlooked."

"That's not like you, Captain Richardson," Julia said sweetly.

"It's something we might discuss when you come down to Boston to supervise the rigging of the *Free Wind*. You will do me the honor of staying at Louisburg Square as my guest, won't you?"

"I'm afraid that's not possible," Julia said sharply. The impropriety of what he was suggesting was absolutely insulting. "As soon as the *Free Wind* is launched, we start laying the keel for our next ship. Philip Sears is one of our top foremen, and he'll supervise the rigging of your ship."

"Is he capable?" The merchant looked as though he doubted it very much.

"He's more than capable," Julia said and her voice was tinged with ice. "He's been a master shipbuilder for years. How many, Daniel?"

"Twelve," Daniel said tersely.

"And this will be your next project?" Hiram Richardson gestured towards Daniel, who was still holding the model Julia had thrust at him.

"That's it," Julia said.

"May I see it?"

When Captain Richardson held out his hands for it, Daniel lifted his dark eyebrows at Julia. She nodded and he handed it to the merchant prince.

The other men, including William Thacher, crowded around him, and Julia folded her arms and leaned back against the desk. She watched them resignedly. The day was going by and so little had been accomplished.

"Daniel," she whispered, "you'd best get on back to work. No point in their wasting your time, too."

"Will you be all right, Miss Julia?" He glanced suspiciously at Hiram Richardson. He hadn't felt right about the man from the beginning, and after listening to the conversation, Daniel was sure his worst suspicions were confirmed.

Julia nodded. "I can handle it."

Megan had been so quiet in the corner, Julia had hardly been aware of her presence, but now that the men's attention was immersed in the model, she realized that she'd completely ignored her friend. She went over to her.

"Megan, are you comfortable?"

"Yes." Megan's smile had none of her old elfin gaiety, but at least misery no longer completely obscured it. "I probably shouldn't have come when you're so busy, but I did want to talk to you privately."

"This shouldn't take too long."

"That's all right, Julie. Take as long as you wish. I'm enjoying the show."

Well, I'm glad *you* are, Julia thought as she returned to the group of men.

Hiram Richardson looked up as she returned. "Beautiful, Mrs. Logan. Truly beautiful. Who will you be building her for?"

"My customer prefers that I don't disclose the name."

"Are you sure you have a customer?" For a moment, the shrewd merchant appeared in place of the affable gentleman. "I'd like to bid on her."

"In addition to the *Free Wind?*" Julia asked skeptically.

"Yes, indeed. My resources are not exactly limited."

"Well, if my customer decides to sell, I'll tell him that you're interested. She'll be more expensive than the *Free Wind,* though."

"I'd expect her to be. My estimate is that the *Free Wind* ready for sea will be approximately seventy thousand dollars. Am I right?"

"Most likely. You're right about most things, aren't you, Captain Richardson?"

"I try to be." He handed the model to David. "We must be getting back to Yarmouth. I'm staying with Captain Siddons, and Mrs. Siddons is expecting us for dinner."

Julia suddenly remembered her manners. Her father had always shown warm hospitality to his customers and suppliers alike, even when he hadn't greatly cared for them.

"I'm sorry that I can't ask you to dine with us, but with my father so ill, it's impossible."

"I understand, my dear." He picked up his black silk top hat. "I'll stop by tomorrow to see how things are going and have a chat with you about the *Free Wind.* It will be a pleasure working with you."

"Indeed, Captain Richardson." She hoped that her smile looked natural.

When they had gone, she turned to David Baxter. "I'm surprised to hear you're working for him, David."

"Why? I've nothing against the man, and he's offered me a generous salary." He grinned at her. "After all, you'll be working for him, too."

"Not for long!" At the sound of hoofbeats outside, she glanced toward the door, but they were quickly gone. Then she looked back at David. It was good to see that some of the lines which had suddenly appeared in his face after the loss of the *Jewel* had been erased by his voyage home. His color was fresh and he seemed comfortably at ease with himself again. "I really think you ought to reconsider, David. They say he drives his masters harder than they drive his ships."

David shrugged and his massive shoulders threatened the seams of his coat. "Once I'm at sea, I can do as I please. He can't follow me there."

"He may ship a supercargo with you," she warned.

"Makes no difference to me," he said with an amused smile. "We've already agreed on terms. If he sends a supercargo along, it'll give me that much more free time ashore."

"You getting lazy, David?"

"Nope. Just getting rich. One of these days, I aim to have you build a ship for me."

"When that day comes, you just let me know." Her smile was a promise. "Till then, I wish you luck with Captain Richardson."

"Julia, I . . ." His eyes clouded as he spoke. Then he glanced at William Thacher and Megan.

"Yes? What is it?"

"Nothing that won't keep. I'll just go back down and take another look at my new command." He laid the model on the table near the stove and picked up his hat. "I hear your husband sailed for California without you."

"Yes, he did."

"So you decided the sea wasn't for you after all?"

"It wasn't my decision to make."

He hesitated and seemed to be on the verge of saying something once again. Instead he turned towards the door. "Captain Richardson has set me the job of watching the *Free Wind* to completion, so I'll be around if you need me for anything."

"Good. I hope that means Captain Richardson plans to stay away."

"Reckon it does. He doesn't strike me as a man to stand around and shuffle his feet." He nodded at Megan and William. "Mrs. Fairfield, Captain Thacher."

Julia was thoughtful as she watched him stride across the yard. What had he been about to say? Well, it made no difference. She was sure she would have no problems with him about the *Free Wind,* and it would be good to have him here for a while. At the very least, he would serve as a buffer between Hiram Richardson and herself.

"Julie, you seem to have enough on your hands at the moment. I'll come back later, whenever it's convenient for you," Megan said as she rose from her chair.

"What?" Julia had just been wishing that there was another vessel in the Howard Line for David. Somehow his sailing someone else's ship seemed to create a distance between them.

With an effort, she turned her attention to Megan. "No, no. Don't go. Stay and have a cup of coffee with me. I could use one about now. I'm sorry I don't have any tea."

"If you have some milk to go with it, I'd like some coffee."

"Cousin William, how about you?"

"No milk. Just make it black and sweet."

Julia was relieved to find the coffee pot was full. Daniel must have filled it just before she'd arrived. And she hadn't offered any to her guests! Well, I can't take care of everything, she thought crossly. But Papa did.

"Well, Megan," she said after she had set the coffee cups in front of them. "You wanted to talk to me privately."

"We both do," William Thacher said. "Appears I've got another stubborn woman on my hands."

"Julie," Megan said earnestly as she stirred the milk into her coffee, "I can't really accept Captain Thacher's hospitality any longer. He's very kind, but I know he's itching to get back to sea."

"Nothin' of the sort!" William snorted. "Been promising myself a holiday for a long time."

"Then why are you always wandering down to the beach with your telescope?"

"Just checkin' on what's goin' in and out of Boston."

"And wishing you were out there." Megan smiled fondly at him. Then she looked at Julia. "He won't leave as long as I'm there," she explained. "He says the babe might come at any time, and I might be alone."

"That's true," Julia said thoughtfully. "It's about time for you to move over to our house. Now that Stephen's gone, there's plenty of room."

"No. I think the best thing for me to do would be to go on back to Maryland." There was a certain defiance in the glance she shot at William. It was obvious that they had discussed this before. "I was low when I was in Tahiti, but things look different now."

"Have you written to your family?" Julia asked. It really might be the best solution.

"Yes."

"What do they say?"

"Well . . ." Megan looked down at her still untasted coffee and stirred it with great care as though her problems would dissolve with the sugar. "They haven't answered yet. I suppose they haven't had time."

"There's been time and plenty of it," William grumbled. "And she's written more than once."

"Did you tell them the whole story, Megan?" Julia asked gently.

"Yes." As she looked at Julia, there was a little sadness mixed with the candor in her black eyes. "I couldn't lie to them and then have them discover the truth after the baby was born."

"Well, if your family won't answer your letters, there's no point in going home to them," Julia said briskly. "Besides you shouldn't do any more traveling while you're in that condition."

"But, Julie, I can't have the baby in your house. Not with your father the way he is." The more they talked about her situation, the more embarrassed Megan became by the trouble she was causing. She moved restlessly in her chair.

"Why don't you go on up to the house and talk to Papa about it? He was sitting up when I left."

"Have you told him . . ." Megan's spoon was suddenly still as she stared at Julia in alarm.

"Yes," Julia said with great frankness. "I haven't told anyone else, but I really had to tell him. You can see that. And you can also see it hasn't affected his attitude towards you. He's always asking when you're coming over again to yarn with him about the islands. It gives him something to think about. Keeps him from worrying about the shipyard."

"But *you* have to worry about the shipyard." Megan pushed back her chair and stood up. "Julie, I'm sorry to interfere with your work. When you talked about it in the past, I never envisioned how large it was or how much responsibility you would have. In a way, you're lucky, though. You can *do* things. I've sat by the hour and wracked my brain trying to find a way to support myself and my child. The only thing I know is missionary work, and that's impossible now."

"Well, don't fret about it," Julia said with an open smile. "Everything will work out. Just concentrate on getting that baby into the world in good shape."

"But you don't know what it's like." Megan took a deep breath and leaned on the back of the chair as she looked from Julia to William. "You've both been kind, but . . ."

"Don't start in on that again," William warned her.

"I *have* to," she said with a kind of desperation. "I have to make you understand what it's like being dependent on people who aren't my own family."

Julia, alarmed by her tone of voice, got up and went to put an arm around her. "Megan! You're like a sister to me. We all love you. And once your baby's born, you'll be a lot of help around the house. We can always use an extra pair of hands."

"That's what I've been tellin' her!" William slapped the table with his open palm. "My house hasn't looked so good since you lived there a few years back, Julie, and that I'll swear by the mainmast. She keeps those girls moving."

Megan shook her head impatiently. "You still don't understand. It's not the same as having your own money . . . or making it some way or other."

Oh, why do people have to make such a pother about things that aren't really important, Julia thought irritably as she moved away from Megan, whose attention was focused on William. Then she felt guilty. After all, she'd never been in Megan's situation and so she couldn't possibly understand how she felt.

Still, it was hard to concentrate on Megan's problems when there were so many other things clamoring for her attention. Inadvertently she glanced at her desk, which as usual was piled high with papers. And no clerk! At this rate, she'd never be able to set down her plans for the new ship. She shook her head and tried to concentrate on Megan again. Megan! Of course!

"I'll tell you how you can make some money," she said, suddenly enthusiastic. "You write a fair hand. How are you in arithmetic?"

"Quite good, actually." Megan looked at Julia hopefully. "I had to be in order to stretch our money as far as I did in Tahiti. George never could be bothered with worldly things."

"Then you can give me a hand with some of our correspondence." Julia went to the desk and began to sort through the papers. "I'll fix up something comfortable for you here."

"But will the men accept a woman in the office?" Megan followed Julia eagerly to the desk, but she didn't dare believe that she would really be given the chance to prove herself.

"It's where I started, and I never noticed anyone ever thought the less of me for it."

"You were your father's daughter."

"Be that as it may, no man around here had better dare say a word against it," Julia said briskly. "Not while *I'm* running this yard."

"It *would* make me feel better if I were earning my keep in some way." Megan turned and looked at William rather wistfully. "What do you think, Captain Thacher?"

"Don't ask me. Julie runs this show."

"Then I'll start right now," Megan said decisively and began untying the black ribbons of her bonnet.

Julia paused in her search through the papers and looked hesitantly across the desk at Megan. "You won't mind the men swearing? They won't do it on purpose in your presence, but sometimes they tend to forget."

"Lord, no," Megan laughed. "I doubt they can come up with some of the things those whalers said."

Julia smiled. "I wouldn't be too sure of that. The men used to try to hold their tongue when I was around, but I had a pretty ripe vocabulary by the time I was fifteen. Not that I've dared use it, of course, but there've been times when I've been tempted."

She pushed aside the papers on the desk. They all required too much of her own time and attention. Instead she went to the nearest chest and pulled out a letter file. Riffling through it, she pulled out a few items. They were rather dull ones she'd been putting off, but they had weighed on the back of her mind as some of the many things she would have to get to the minute she could breathe.

"You can work at the table near the stove," she said as she looked at Megan's girth. "I doubt you'd be comfortable at the moment on a high stool."

"I doubt I'd fit on it," Megan said with the first gaiety she'd shown in a long time. She looked expectantly at the papers as though her salvation were written on them.

After Julia had started Megan on a few simple letters, she picked up her cloak. "I have to go out in the yard and see what's going on. If anyone wants me, Megan, tell them I'll be over near the schooner for a while."

"I'll come with you," William said as he shrugged into his greatcoat.

"You tagging after me? I remember when 'twas the other way around."

"Aye. It's always a pleasure to tag after a pretty woman."

Once they were outside, Julia said, "I hope I'm doing the right thing. I don't want to tire Megan out."

"Seems to me she gets more tired out doin' nothing than she does when she's occupied." William pulled out his pipe and a much worn leather pouch of tobacco. His fingers worked automatically as they strolled towards the creek. "Julie, I don't know as I think too much of the idea of her movin' into your house."

"Well, she has to sooner or later. I never meant to saddle you with her, and if I know anything about you, Megan was right when she said you're itching to get back to sea."

"Maybe I'm settlin' down in my old age."

"Maybe, but I doubt it." She smiled as she looked up at him affectionately. The golden hairs still outnumbered the white ones in his beard, and his far-seeing green eyes sparkled with the lustre of youth. Despite his weight, the sea had kept him trim. "You've got a long way to go before you get old."

William struck a match and cupped his hands around the pipe to shield the flame from the breeze. When he was satisfied that it was drawing well, he glanced sideways down at Julia.

"I'm a couple of years older than your father and look what's happened to him. Makes a man stop and think."

Julia glanced around at the three vessels on the ways, at the men whose joy in the warmth of the day showed in their work. Her father should have been striding through the yard, directing the work, chastising and praising, as she had so often seen him.

"Papa's only fifty-five. It shouldn't have happened to him."

"No, that it shouldn't, but it did," William said gruffly, "and I don't think he's in any shape to listen to a child bein' born in his house."

"I've thought about that," Julia said as, turning her back on the yard, she wandered towards the bank of the creek. "When the time comes, Megan can go over and stay with Amelia. It's not all that far from us and I've already talked to Amelia about it."

"And Amelia's three young ones?"

"They can come stay with us. 'Twon't be for long, and Mama would enjoy having them around."

"Julie, I'm tellin' you, Megan's better off in Brewster. There's a good midwife lives just down the lane, and she'll have peace and quiet to recover her strength after. Then I'll go on back to sea, and Megan can have some privacy. Something she'll never get in that house of yours."

"But Megan can't stay there forever," she said. "What if Samuel marries and wants to bring his wife to live there?"

"Samuel?" Benjamin pulled on his pipe reflectively as he thought about his younger son. "Don't know that Samuel will ever marry. He's a quiet one. Strange. As a youngster, he was always full of life . . . like his mother . . . but he's changed. Think it had somethin' to do with some girl jiltin' him, but I've never been able to get any details out of him. He's my son, but I can't say I ever rightly knew him."

Julia thought of Samuel, so unlike Jason. Slender and short, there was a tautness, a constant alertness about him, and although he had his mother's brown eyes, there was nothing gay or melting about them.

"I've only run into him two or three times over the years," she said. "He seemed . . . distant. I thought it was because I'd been Jason's wife and I'd married someone else."

"Nope. That's just Samuel's way. You heard from Stephen yet?"

"No. He wasn't too happy when he left. I don't know *why* I can't make him understand that I can't possibly sail with him," she said impatiently.

"Most likely he don't want to understand."

Two fishing boats sailed into the creek and tied up at the wharf opposite the shipyard. The gulls that had followed them, screaming with excitement, circled overhead and made powerful swoops at the boats.

Once their racket had subsided a little, Julia said pensively, "You know, the last night he was home, Stephen said he might never return from this voyage."

"Stuff and nonsense! He'd drive a ship to hell and back to return to you, and you know it . . . and so does he."

"He might have been thinking of . . . of other things."

"Don't you worry about that, neither. That husband of yours runs in luck. Got you to marry him, didn't he?"

"I don't know how lucky *that* makes him." Talking about Stephen made her restless and she started in the direction of the schooner.

"Plenty. There's a few things about him I've noticed over the years. A typhoon nearly wrecks his ship. He ends up in Tahiti and comes out with silver in his pocket. Gets attacked by a pirate war junk and comes out practically unscathed with greater profit than if he'd stayed cozy in the harbor. The market closes up in Tahiti, but by stopping there, he escapes bein' wrecked by the typhoon in Hong Kong."

"So you really think he's lucky?" Julia asked hopefully. She wanted to believe him. When the sea wanted a man, she took him, no matter how great his ability or his knowledge of her ways.

William glanced sideways at Julia as they came to a stop near some of the men who were driving caulking into the seams of the schooner. The impact as hammers met caulking irons gave off a measured, rhythmic music, but William wasn't aware of the sound as he studied the young woman at his side. He didn't know what nonsense was filling her head now, but he'd known her for too many years. 'Twas sure to be something about the sea and its ways. Since there was no reasoning with her on that score, he could only reassure her.

"Aye, he's lucky. Got a lot of sense, too. How many sails has he lost over the years? How many spars? How much damage has he sustained?"

"Not much, I guess. Not compared to some."

"Now, don't you go worryin' about him, Julie." William knocked the ashes from his pipe against the rough wood of the schooner's scaffolding. "You got enough else to fret you."

"I suppose." She glanced absently at the windlass a couple of men carried past them. Then she straightened her shoulders and looked directly into William Thacher's green eyes. "I've made up my mind, Cousin William, and I've decided Megan has to come to East Dennis. That way I can keep an eye on her. Then I want you to go back to sea."

"You decided what the moon and stars are goin' to do, too?"

"What?"

"Well, looks to me like you're takin' over the job of runnin' the universe."

"What's the matter? Did I sound too bossy?"

"A mite."

"I'm sorry, Cousin William, but there are so many problems, little ones as well as big ones, I guess I've found the only way to get through them is to make quick decisions for once and for all and then forget them."

"Too bad Stephen isn't here to help."

"Oh, he's like you. Can't stay away from the sea."

William's eyes twinkled. "Sounds like someone else I could name who's not too far away at the moment."

Julia thought with longing of the vision of the new ship she'd had such a short time ago. For a moment, she could see her again, could feel the motion of the waves beneath her keel, and she sighed.

"Reckon you're right," she said.

Chapter Nineteen

1849

The next morning, Julia rose well before dawn in order to be at the shipyard with the first light. Although the days were growing longer now, every daylight hour was precious, especially in good weather. The men came to the yard with their lanterns lit and returned in the same way. As she stood in the center of the yard and watched them approach down Sesuit Neck Road on one side and across Toct Bridge from the village on the other, they reminded her of winter fireflies gathering for the festival of sunrise.

Rubbing her hands in front of a fire made of scraps, which had been lighted to warm the men after their long cold walk, she became aware that a man was standing behind her and had been for some time. She turned to find that David Baxter was staring down at her with his hands stuck into the deep pockets of his peacoat. The visor of his cap was pulled down over his low forehead so that it hid his eyes. Yet there was a suggestion of bemusement in his smile that was probably not a smile at all, but just the way his lips were made.

"Well, David, you're here early," she said.

"Aren't you cold standing out here?" He tried to see her face by what light the fire afforded, but it was hidden in the shadows cast by the hood of her cloak.

"No. I like to see them coming. With the men, the yard wakens and lives."

"And as long as they think you'll be here watching for them, they know they'd best arrive on time."

"It doesn't hurt. If I was you, I wouldn't try to climb the scaffolding up to the *Free Wind* till it's lighter. It's a little rickety."

"After climbing rigging in the dark most of the years of my life, I doubt I'm in much danger on a scaffolding."

"I suppose not, but I won't be responsible if you break a leg." She turned to greet the men who were gathering around the fire, and then she strolled to the office, where the watchman had kept the stove glowing through the night. David followed her.

The office seemed stuffy after the crisp air of early morning, and she took off her cloak and tossed it over a chair. While she lit the sperm oil lamp, David unbuttoned his coat, but then he stood by the door as though uncertain whether he would stay or go. Julia, anxious to get to work, made no gesture of hospitality.

"You have something you want to discuss with me?" she asked as she set the lamp on the table.

"Yes." He drew one hand out of his pocket and held it out to her. "I wanted to return this to you. You forgot to take it with you a few years back, and I salvaged it from the *Jewel.*"

She held out her hand and he dropped onto her palm the delicately carved flying fish which he had offered to her years ago.

"I told you I couldn't take it then, David. I still can't. You should have given it to your wife as I suggested." Although she didn't understand why it should be so, there was something too personal about this small figure. Perhaps it was only because he himself had carved it.

"I wanted you to have it. I still do. Cynthia wouldn't appreciate it."

"Why not? Have you ever offered it to her?"

"No. Not this, but others. She calls them my whittlings."

"Do you still carve?"

"Yes. There's not much else to do at sea. I've quite a collection at my parents' house. You'll have to see them when Cynthia arrives."

She took a sharp breath and her fingers involuntarily clutched the fish. Feeling the wood bite into her flesh, she opened her hand and made sure that she hadn't harmed it. "When Cynthia arrives," she repeated slowly as she examined the carving. "She's finally coming then?"

"Aye. She should be here in two, three weeks."

"After all these years of refusing to leave England? Why now?"

"I told her she'd either come or I'd no longer support her." Whether it was the light cast upwards by the lamp or whether it was his true expression, David's triangular eyes looked hard and the lines about his mouth were deeper. It was the first time she had seen his gentleness stripped away. "I sent her passage and enough money to last the voyage and told her that was the last she'd have from me till she arrived in America."

To avoid seeing the strange harshness in his face, Julia held the small flying fish close to the lamp and noticed how the wings were carved so finely they seemed almost translucent. What kind of woman could his wife be that she would scorn such a pretty thing?

"You haven't mentioned her for a long time. How often have you been able to get to England since you were wed?"

"Twice in almost eight years, and even then I only had a few days to spare. I hardly felt I knew her. I did find out that I don't care for her friends, though."

"What's wrong with them?"

"They're . . . I don't rightly know how to describe them. Maybe giddy is the right word."

"I never knew you to be against laughter."

" 'Tisn't a matter of laughter. There are other things." He took off his cap and slapped it against the palm of his hand. Then he laid it on the tall desk. "I swear, there's nothing in this world they take seriously. I knew they were making fun of me behind my back. The thing that hurt most is that she seemed to be leading them on."

"Then I think you'd be content to leave her in England." If only he would. But it seemed it was too late for that now.

"I need a wife, Julia," he said and his eyes never left her face while he spoke. "I want children of my own. I need to think of someone waiting for me when I'm away, someone who'll think of me and write to me."

"She writes to you now, doesn't she?"

"Rarely, and then only when she wants more money."

"You think you'll change her just by bringing her here?" The sharpness of her own voice surprised Julia.

"If I can get her away from those friends of hers, I think she might change."

"Might change for the worse, too." Even as she spoke, Julia wondered why she was arguing against Cynthia's coming. It couldn't make any difference. Still she persisted. "She'll be right lonely in a strange land without them."

"She'll make other friends here. Better friends. You'll be one, won't you, Julia?" His eyes were softer now, almost pleading.

"I won't have the time, David. I'm sorry," she said abruptly and tried to ignore his look of pained surprise. No, she thought. I'd never be able to become a friend of Cynthia's.

She handed the fish back to him.

He shook his head and plunged his hands deep into his pockets. "It's yours, Julia. I carved it for you and no one else."

"All right." She put it on the table next to the lamp. "I'll think of you when I look at it. It's getting light, David. I must get to work."

"Aye. I suppose I must, too." He began to button his jacket. "Can't have my new employer arriving to find me idling on the first day on the job. Though I doubt he'll be here before the middle of the day."

"I hope not. I have enough to do without coping with Hiram Richardson."

David paused and looked at her searchingly. "What is it you don't like about him, Julia?"

"Is it so obvious?"

"It's very obvious. I'm sure even he picked that up yesterday."

"Then I suppose I'll have to make more of an effort to hide my feelings till he leaves, won't I?" She turned the wick of the lamp down and then blew out the flame.

" 'Twouldn't hurt, but what is it you have against him?"

"Let's just say it's something out of the past and let it go at that."

"Is it something I should know?" He picked up his cap, but still he watched her. "After all, I'll be working for him."

"No. It's nothing that need ever concern you. I would advise you to keep Cynthia away from him, though."

"Julia, if he's ever hurt you. . . ." He took a step towards her as though he would protect her.

"He never had the chance. Nor will he." She went to the desk and picked up one of the letters Megan had written for her yesterday. After glancing from him to the door, she began to read it. When she heard the door open and shut, she didn't look up.

The wind had veered to the north and the deceptive balminess of the day before had gone when Hiram Richardson arrived at the yard. He swung up the high scaffolding ladders as blithely as a man half his age to find Julia on the deck of the *Free Wind*.

She had seen him coming across the yard with his greatcoat whipping in the breeze before he had seen her, and now she pretended concentration on the handsome workmanship of a brass-laid capstan made of locust and mahogany.

"Good afternoon, Mrs. Logan," he said as he approached her and raised his tall top hat to reveal his abundant chestnut hair. "I trust I'm not intruding."

"She's your ship, Captain Richardson. You have the right to come aboard any time you please." Then Julia realized she'd sounded abrupt and decided she had better try to be pleasant to him. If he felt aggrieved, he could very well decide to find a thousand petty things wrong with the ship, which would necessitate her sending a crew of workmen to Boston to satisfy him. She smiled as she said, "I'll have one of the men show you through her."

"Why, I'd hoped you'd do that yourself, my dear." His smile was affable, but there was a coolness in his light blue eyes, and she could sense the strength that lay behind his courteous words. What he was saying was tantamount to an order.

How would her father have handled it? He would have graciously shown the man the ship while concealing his true feelings. She shrugged.

"I'd be delighted to, but some of the men who've worked on her are better qualified than I am to explain the details," she explained.

"Oh?" He studied her intently. "I understood from Captain Siddons and your foreman that you were running the yard. I found it a little difficult to believe that a woman could be giving the orders, but they convinced me that it was so. Or have they misled me?"

This was more than an indirect order. It was a challenge . . .

and an insult. Julia lifted her chin and looked at him squarely.

"No, Captain Richardson. They did not mislead you. I am running this shipyard." She knew that she would have to be his guide, but the thought of climbing down into the holds with him was not at all appealing, and it was definitely not something she wanted to do alone. "However, I've been home for only a few weeks and so haven't been present for most of her construction. If you don't mind waiting, I'll send for Daniel Sears so that he can accompany us."

"Oh, there's no need for that," he said, relaxing to the point where he allowed a twinkle to show in his eyes. "I went over the ship yesterday with Captain Siddons and Captain Baxter. There are just a few things I wanted to discuss with you."

"I'd still prefer Mr. Sears's presence," she said and gave him what she hoped was her most innocent smile. Let him make of it what he would.

"Of course. Perhaps it's well to have a man along. He undoubtedly *would* understand the details of shipbuilding better."

Better than what? Julia thought. A woman? Oh, Captain Richardson, that is not a way to become a friend of mine. She wondered how she had ever thought him so charming. Well, that had been almost seven years ago, and she'd been a lot younger then.

"Have you seen Captain Baxter today?" Hiram Richardson had seen the involuntary lift of her chin, the flash of her dark blue eyes, and the set of her shoulders after his last words and thought it safer to find a new subject.

"He's been here since daybreak," Julia answered shortly. Surely he didn't expect her to keep track of his captain's comings and goings. David wasn't in *her* employ.

"I hope he's aboard. I'd like to have a few words with him."

"I'm sure he is, but he could be anywhere." Julia was determined she was not going to interrupt another apprentice's work in order to send him searching through the ship.

"Well, perhaps we'll run across him." Hiram Richardson began to stroll aloft and Julia went with him. She kept reminding herself that he was her guest.

"Do you plan to run this shipyard with women?" he asked as he idly ran his hand along the polished rail.

"What a strange question." Julia looked at him in astonishment.

"A natural one I should think." He offered her his arm as they reached the bottom step of the elaborate ladder that led to the poop deck. "You've only been home a few weeks and already you have a lady clerk."

"What are you talking about?" Julia had touched his arm lightly as they ascended the steps, but now she dropped her hand and turned to confront him.

"I stopped by the office to see you when I first arrived, and . . . Mrs. Fairfield, is it? . . . told me where I might find you."

"Oh!" Julia had been so immersed in other problems she had completely forgotten that Megan was coming. "Mrs. Fairfield isn't a clerk. She's a friend of mine and is trying to help me out until I can find a new clerk. Mine ran off to the gold fields."

Hiram Richardson shook his head as he continued to walk aft. "So did a couple of my lads. Broke their indentures. But I never considered filling their places with *women.*"

"Why ever not?" Julia was beginning to burn. If he wanted to be outrageous, then so would she. "Mrs. Fairfield has twice the brains of most men I know. I wish it *was* possible for her to remain with me, and I'd hire as many more like her as I could find."

"Well . . ." Hiram Richardson's smile revealed his perfect teeth. "I wouldn't think a shipyard is any place for a lady, which Mrs. Fairfield so obviously is, especially for one in her, ah, delicate condition. I can't understand a gentleman who'd allow his wife to leave her home in order to drudge in a shipyard."

"Mrs. Fairfield is a widow and makes her home with me." Julia was becoming more irritated with this man all the time. It was obvious that whatever he said about Megan he must be applying to herself as well.

"Oh, is she?" He grasped the spokes of the large wheel and gave it a twist. It turned easily in his hands and he nodded. Then he looked at her with an expression that had suddenly become very much interested. "A recent widow, I presume."

"That's a little indelicate, Captain Richardson." Julia's eyes were hard as she stared at him. "Of course, she's recently widowed."

"And still grieving?"

"Yes. Still grieving. I asked her to help me in the shipyard to take her mind off of her sorrow."

"She'll soon be over that when her child comes. Fairfield," he mused as he looked down the length of the ship that was now his.

373

He was pleased at what he saw. A true clipper. The newest and the best. "Is she any relation to the Fairfields of Mystic?"

"No. She's from Maryland." Julia wondered why all his interest in Megan. Surely her secret was a closely kept one. "I don't recall where her husband was from originally. I believe he was born in England."

"And her husband was a sailor?" he asked casually as he wandered to the chart house to peer through its windows.

"No. A missionary." Julia wished Daniel would come. She was tired of discussing Megan instead of business.

"A missionary." He turned away from the chart house and began to pace the length of the poop as though he were measuring it with his legs. "Seems unlikely. She doesn't appear to be the kind of woman I'd always associated with missionaries. So delicate. It must have been a hard life for her. You'll have to bring her down to Boston once she's recovered from her . . . grief. I'd be delighted to entertain you both."

Why, you old reprobate, Julia thought. Don't you ever stop trying? She wondered how many women had seen his lady's bedroom since he'd shown it to her.

"Mrs. Fairfield is a very religious woman, Captain Richardson, as I'm sure you can appreciate. I doubt she'd enjoy worldly entertainments. A quiet life is more to her taste."

"With that sparkle in her black eyes?" He had reached the taffrail and now turned and looked directly at her. "How well do you really know your friend, Mrs. Logan?"

"Quite well," Julia said sharply, "and I'll thank you not to cast aspersions on my friends in my presence."

"Oh, I meant no harm," he said hastily. "It just seems a pity to bury a lovely woman like Mrs. Fairfield up here on the Cape. She would make a lovely adornment to Boston society."

Julia pressed her lips together and stared down the length of the ship. Daniel, having just climbed over the rail, came limping towards them rapidly.

"We can get on with the inspection now that Mr. Sears is here, Captain Richardson," Julia said coolly. "I'm sure you're anxious to do your business and get back to Boston as soon as possible. After all, we don't want to bury you up here, too."

* * *

374

It was a relief to Julia when Hiram Richardson, after having made very few changes, left the Cape a few days later. With Megan installed in the house and her father showing slow signs of improvement, life settled down to a series of short days and long nights. Clara was moved into Julia's bedroom, and sometimes her presence made the nights less lonely for Julia. At other times, it only served to emphasize the fact that the child was there and the father was not.

Julia would kneel beside the trundle bed and listen to her daughter's breathing, which was barely more than a whisper. She would run her fingers over the delicate cheek and wonder how she could have borne a child so unlike herself. Except for an occasional fleeting expression, she was not like Stephen, either.

It was difficult for her to understand Clara. Instead of enjoying a romp with her cousins outside in the snow, she preferred to remain in the house close to her grandmother's or Aunt Martha's skirts. Although she prattled to the two older women, she had little to say when Julia returned home from the shipyard in the evening. At first, Julia had thought it was because Clara was tired after a long day, but when she found the same behavior occurring on Sundays, she was puzzled. It was true that she often shut herself up in her father's study on those days in order to do the thinking and planning she was unable to accomplish during the week, but she always tried to find time to spend with her daughter. Yet it was only when Clara was asleep that Julia could feel that she was really her child.

Her child and Stephen's.

Then she would stretch out in her own bed, which seemed too wide for one person. Closing her eyes, she would try to project her mind across the many miles that separated her from her husband and send it winging to the *Crystal Star*. Was Stephen lying as lonely in his bed as she was? Did he imagine her there beside him and remember other nights and other years? Or was he sleeping soundly with no thought of her, no wish for her, no need for her as she had for him? Often when she woke at night, she found her pillow soaked with far more tears than she had shed before she slept.

As the work went forward on the *Free Wind*, Julia saw more of David Baxter than she ever had before, and yet he seemed more

375

distant. When she climbed aboard the ship, he would wave and then disappear below. If she had business in the holds or between decks and found him there, he would greet her with his ever-present gentle smile and find some errand that took him on deck. She was mystified and a little hurt for she had always considered him one of her few true friends, a man she could rely upon when all others failed.

One day she saw him alone in the chart house and decided to confront him. There was little chance for privacy amongst the workmen who swarmed over the ship, singing and talking as they went about their work, but they were not likely to invade the small house this afternoon, especially if they saw her talking to David through the many windows that lined its walls. If he wanted to evade her, there were two exits, one opening onto the deck and the other leading below, but she hoped he'd stay. The day of launching was fast approaching, and when the ship went to Boston, he would be aboard. They'd had only that one real conversation since he had been hired as master of the *Free Wind*, and then, she realized, she had been rather abrupt. She hadn't meant to alienate him.

"How do you think you're going to like her?" Julia asked as she opened the door from the poop deck.

David pushed his cap back on his dark blond curls and smiled. "She's a lovely ship," he said quietly.

While he watched her and waited for her to speak, David gave her no reason to feel awkward, and yet he did. Perhaps it had something to do with the sadness in his eyes, a sadness that had been there almost constantly since he'd arrived home. She noticed a few drops of paint on one of the cut-glass windows and studiously scraped at it with her fingernail. It was easier to speak if she didn't look at him.

"What is it, David? Why are you avoiding me?"

"I didn't mean to avoid you, Julie," he said gently.

"But you have."

"Maybe I have." He leaned back against the cabinet that was specially built to hold the charts and watched her. A curl had escaped from her chignon and was caressing the nape of her neck. He longed to go to her and tuck it in. "It wasn't intentional. I guess I've had a lot on my mind lately. I spend more time thinking than I do talking."

376

"Is it because you're worried about the *Free Wind?*" she asked as she continued to scratch at the glass.

"No. It's not that."

"Can't you tell me about it?"

He shook his head even though she wasn't looking at him. "There's not much to say."

"Then maybe when Cynthia arrives, you'll be able to talk to her. You shouldn't cut yourself off from other people."

"That's one of the things I've been thinking about. She's not coming."

"She's not?" Julia whirled around and looked up at him, the drops of paint forgotten. "I thought . . ."

"I got a letter instead. Do you want to see it?" Moving away from the cabinet towards her, he reached inside his peacoat and pulled out an envelope. It had obviously received much handling.

"No. A letter between a wife and her husband is a private thing." She really didn't want to see Cynthia's handwriting.

"Yes." His face fell as he replaced the envelope. "I reckon it is."

"If you want to tell me about it, David, that's different."

"It just says she's not coming."

"Does she say why?"

"Yes. She says she has no intention of setting foot in a wild country populated by barbarians like me and my countrymen."

Julia looked out the window at the hills and the snug houses that nestled amongst firs and winter bare trees. Smoke rose from their chimneys, and from across Sesuit Creek, she could hear the East Dennis church clock faintly striking the hour.

"It's hardly what I'd call a wild country. As for barbarians, I've met a lot of the English in Hong Kong. Are they supposed to be more civilized than we are?"

With his hands plunged deep into the pockets of his coat, David just shrugged. "It isn't Liverpool."

"Maybe not, but we do have cities. She could live in Boston or New York and see a lot more of you than she does now."

"I reckon that's what it all boils down to. She doesn't want to see me," he said in a voice that would not admit to emotion.

"Not even when you refuse to support her unless she comes?"

David leaned against the polished chart table and stared down through the dimly lit doorway that led to the officers' quarters.

"She may not have seen much of me, but evidently she knows

me well enough to recognize it as an empty threat. I sent her some money after I received her letter. She is my wife and I can't let her go in want."

Julia shook her head and the woolen scarf that covered the top of her head slipped down and allowed a few more curls to escape. "Maybe if you'd held to it, she would eventually have come."

"Maybe. It makes little difference to me now whether she comes or not."

"David," she said slowly as she knit her delicate black brows in concentration. "Why don't you apply for a job on the Liverpool packet clippers? I'm sure the Black Ball or the Dramatic Line would be happy to find a captain of your caliber was available. That way you could be with her quite often."

He shook his head and smiled at her with indulgent amusement as though she were a child. "I'd never be content shuttling across the Atlantic and back, not after I've been able to stretch my legs around the world. Besides, on the packet lines, you have to spend as much time pleasing the passengers as you do sailing the ship. It's not for me."

"But if it would help your marriage?"

"No. There's not the money in them that there is in the China clippers. Julie, I'm so close to having my own ship built, every dollar makes a difference."

"So a ship means more to you than a wife does," she said softly.

"I know ships and I love them." He ran his hand over the gleaming mahogany of the chart house wall. "They respond to me in a way my wife never has. I hardly know the woman, and now I don't think I care to know her."

"Maybe you've never really given her a chance."

"I've given her every chance in the world."

"David, I've never thought of you as being hard. You were always kind to me, to everyone." She put her hand on his arm and looked up at him earnestly.

"It's not difficult to be kind to you, Julie." He lightly patted her hand and then wrapped his fingers around hers. She was shocked to find them tingling and she quickly pulled her hand away, aware of how visible they were to the workmen.

"And yet your wife . . ."

David stuck his hands back into his pockets and paced to the windows from which he could see over the dunes to the Bay that lay beyond them. Julia knew he was looking in the direction of Provincetown. Three thousand miles over the horizon lay Liverpool.

"Eight years and never a word of kindness from her. At one time, I did think of going into the packet service so that I could see more of her. When I mentioned it in a letter, all she asked was how well it paid. I told her it wouldn't be as much, and she was completely against the change." He swung around and looked directly at her. "Do you still want to call me hard, Julie?"

"Give her just one more chance, David," Julia said as she thought of Stephen and how he had left her. "Go over to England and talk things out with her."

"No. She's had her last chance," he said almost savagely. Then he rubbed his forehead before he continued more calmly. "I have a couple of friends, one on the Red Star Line and the other on the Dramatic Line. I'd asked them to call on her when they were in Liverpool, to make sure she was all right. They both came back with the same story, not that they relished telling it. There's a man living there."

"But he could have been a caller, just as they were, or maybe he's a relative of hers." Julia wondered why she was defending Cynthia unless it was to see David's eyes alight with laughter again. She realized once more how dear he was to her.

"Cynthia doesn't have any close relatives left. No, Julia. I'm afraid it's true. Captain Ford checked into the man. Seems he's named Prudholm, a draper's assistant, but evidently he's been unemployed for some time. Makes me wonder what my money's buying."

Talking about it didn't seem to help David for he stared out the window with unseeing eyes. There must be some way to shake him out of his gloom.

"What are you going to do about it, David?"

"Nothing. What can I do?"

"Well, if I was you, I'd go over there and straighten her out," Julia said vehemently. "Bring her back by force if necessary. After all, it's your right as her husband."

"That isn't my way, Julia. I hope you know me better than that. Besides, I don't think I really want to have anything to do with her anymore."

"Then get rid of her."

"You mean divorce?" He was suddenly alert with a spark of

379

hope in his eyes. It was obvious he'd never considered it before.

"Yes."

"What good would that do?" The spark was extinguished as swiftly as it had been lit. "No decent woman would marry me after a divorce."

"You never know. Why don't you try it and see. You'd be no worse off than you are now."

"No. It's not my way, Julia."

"I am sorry, David. I wish things hadn't worked out this way."

"Are you, Julie? Strangely enough, I feel rather relieved."

"Then you shouldn't spend all your time thinking about it," she said impatiently. "All you're doing is brooding. It doesn't suit you, David."

"Brooding?" He finally smiled at her, even though it was a little crooked. "Do you think that's what I'm doing? No. I'm just thinking about life. What is the point of it all?"

"Does it have to have a point? Isn't it enough to be alive and to know there's a God who watches over us?"

"I have to have more," he said and the yearning gave his face the look of a dreamer.

"You have the *Free Wind*. The sea's lying there waiting for you. Eventually, you'll have your own ship. You just said a little while ago that a ship means more to you than a woman does."

"That's not completely true. What I said was a ship means more to me than Cynthia does. I wasn't speaking of women in general."

"Well, David, life's a lonely business."

"For you, too, Julia?"

"For everyone."

When the day for the launching of the *Free Wind* arrived, crowds gathered from all over the Cape as well as on specially chartered vessels from Boston, and newspaper reporters descended upon them armed with notebooks, but Julia was not present. It was the first time in her life that she'd been ashore and yet not been able to witness a launching.

She had wakened in the early morning filled with anticipation of the gala day ahead and equally filled with dread of an accident. As the ships grew larger and larger, Sesuit Creek seemed to shrink. Its banks and wharves appeared to be edging closer to each other.

Just as she was washing her face, Megan opened her door and

leaned against it as though by holding onto the knob she would support herself. Her black eyes were enormous in her pale face as she glanced at Clara, who was still sleeping in her little bed.

"Julie," she said in a voice that was not much louder than a whisper. "I have to go over to Amelia's. Now."

"Are you sure?" Julia asked, but she quickly rinsed the soap from her face. According to Megan's calculations, the child wasn't due for another two weeks. Plenty of time to get her comfortably moved.

"I'm positive, and Freddy came fast. This child will probably be in just as much a hurry."

"Well, we can't go out in our robes and slippers. Go back to your room and lie down. I'll send Aunt Martha to help you dress and Ezra off to fetch Doctor Willett."

"The doctor? I thought the midwife . . ."

"Now just do as I say." Julia put her arms around Megan and propelled her out of the room. She didn't want to tell Megan that the doctor himself, after having noticed Megan when he had come to check on Benjamin, had suggested that it might be best for him to be present at the delivery.

All the plans they had laid so carefully for transferring Megan to Amelia's house at the proper time were destroyed by Martha Chambers's first words upon seeing Megan.

"She stays here," the white-haired woman said calmly as she came out of Megan's room. "There's no moving her now. You go in and sit with her while I see to getting Doc Willett to come here instead of Amelia's."

"Clara . . ." Julia started to say.

"Becky can carry her over to Amelia's. I'll tend to what needs tending," Martha said firmly and marched down the stairs.

"Julie," Megan said as Julia entered her lavender and white bedroom. "I'm scared."

"There's nothing to be scared of, Megan. Lots of babies come a little early." Julia pulled up a straight chair and sat down beside the bed.

"I know, but why are you sending for the doctor instead of a midwife?" Megan held out her slender hand, and when Julia took it within her own, she found it cool.

"Because last I heard the midwife was over in Dennis with Mrs. Murray. Doctor Willett's handier. Probably better, too."

"Julie, you won't leave me, will you?"

Julia thought of the launching. She should be on her way to the shipyard this very moment, and here she wasn't even properly dressed yet for such an occasion. Then she saw the terrified pleading in Megan's eyes.

"No, Megan. I won't leave you." She patted the hand she held, but she couldn't resist glancing at the light that filtered between the almost closed curtains. A golden glow was dispelling the early morning greyness.

There might still be time after the baby was born to get to the yard before the launching. Megan had said her babies came fast. And if she couldn't make it, Daniel would just have to handle it. A launching in the Howard Shipyard without a Howard presiding. It had never happened before, Julia thought uneasily. She hoped it wouldn't bring bad luck. Amelia had planned to take the children to see it. Maybe she still would. Then there would at least be a Howard present. Likely Sarah and Josiah would show up, too, but she didn't know what kind of luck they would bring.

Megan gasped and then she said with an effort, "I hope I won't disturb your father. I'll try to be quiet."

"Don't fret about him," Julia said, although she herself was a little concerned. "Noise isn't going to hurt Papa. It never did, and I can remember times when he's raised a ruckus himself."

"But he's so ill."

"He's getting better. You just think about yourself now. Never mind about other people."

Megan's hold suddenly tightened on Julia's hand and her body stiffened with pain, but she made no sound other than a sharply drawn breath.

When Martha returned, the pains were coming faster and faster, and Julia was relieved to see Doctor Willett follow her into the room. She patted Megan's hand and put it on the quilt.

"Julie, you promised not to leave me."

"I'll just be gone a minute. I have to send word to the yard."

"Oh!" There was guilt mixed with the fear on Megan's face. "This is launching day. Go on, Julie. Never mind what I said. You have to go."

"No. I've seen a hundred launchings. I'll be back as soon as I've sent word to Daniel." Julia slipped quickly from the room as the doctor began his examination.

Although Megan had expected a fast delivery, the hours stretched on. Doctor Willett left Megan to pay a morning visit to Benjamin, and Martha took Julia's place by the bedside. Julia rose and stretched. The fire was so hot, the room was stifling, and she went to open the curtains. All morning she had been hearing the wind rising in the trees, and now she looked out at the giant spruces at the back of the house. A north wind. The worst possible for launching the large clipper ship. She hoped it would die down before the tide reached its highest mark.

"Close the curtains, Julia," Martha Chambers said. "This child is cold."

"I'm sorry." Julia quickly pulled the curtains to again. Even in the lamplit room, she could see that Megan was shivering. She had forgotten how easily Megan was chilled. The years she had spent living so near the equator had thinned her blood, and whenever possible she stayed near a fire.

Then Megan screamed as her body arched and she clung to the sheets that were twined around the posts at the head of her bed.

"That's right," Doctor Willett said as he entered the room. His eyes twinkled behind his spectacles and he rubbed his hands in anticipation of the new life to come. He often thought he should have been born a woman so that he could have been a midwife. Though there were rewards in restoring people back to health, there was nothing like a good healthy birthing. "You go right ahead and use those lungs of yours, young lady. That's what they're for."

"Captain Howard . . ." Megan moaned.

"I just been to see Captain Howard, and he said, 'Tell that girl to yell.' Says you're botherin' him a lot more by bein' so quiet and that you're to yell nice and loud so he'll know what's goin' on."

Megan didn't acknowledge his words but lay exhausted and pale with her eyes closed. It has been going on too long, Julia thought, although she knew it was possible for the labor to last many more hours. But how could Megan, with her small bones and delicate body, stand much more? She remembered seeing her friend poised, ready to dive into that mountain stream pool in Tahiti. The leaves had dappled her ivory body with shadows and her hair had streamed like a silver river down her back. Now it lay matted and dark with perspiration.

Julia tried to remember how it had been with her when Clara

was born. There had been pain, yes, but she couldn't possibly have suffered what Megan was suffering. She glanced at her watch. Only ten minutes had passed since she had last looked at it, and yet it seemed an hour. She glanced her question at Doctor Willett and he shook his head.

When Julia drew out her watch again a few hours later, she realized that it was time for the launching. She wiped Megan's forehead and said the soothing things that meant nothing. Then she handed the cloth to Martha and, with a feeling of guilt, tiptoed out of the room. She hoped Megan wouldn't know she had gone, but she was irresistibly drawn to the upstairs porch that fronted her own room. Although she couldn't see the shipyard from there, she would be able to see the wind blowing through the tall marsh grass. It would give her some idea of what conditions would be like at the yard.

Once she was on the porch, the wind pierced its cold through her wool dress, but the sun shone bright in a painfully clear, high blue sky. She held her breath. Now. They must launch now or it would be too late. The tide would come this high only twice a year, and when it came, it gave them little time to float a ship and tow her over the bar. Then from across the marsh, there came the faint noise of a crowd. Were they cheering or was it the proclamation of disaster? She strained to hear, to distinguish, but the sound was so far distant. They must be cheering. They must be. There. It was gone.

In its place, there came a scream so high, so tortured, it couldn't have come from a human throat. Julia flung open the door and ran down the hall to Megan's room. As she reached the doorway there was another cry, but this one was even higher pitched and angry.

"A boy," Doctor Willett said, but Julia hardly heard him as she rushed to the bed to look down at Megan's face. It was peaceful now, but Julia couldn't be sure whether any breath passed between those lightly parted lips.

"Julie," Megan sighed.

"Yes, Megan, I'm here. I'm here." Relieved she sat beside the bed and took her friend's hand.

Megan's eyes fluttered open, but it seemed difficult for her to focus.

"What . . . what does he look like?"

384

"Well, he don't look like you." Martha already had the child bundled in a soft blanket and laid him down beside Megan. "Must look like his father."

"He has red hair, Megan," Julia said quickly. But how in the world could the child have red hair?

Megan smiled and pulled the baby closer to her. "It runs in my family," she murmured. "My mother and two of my sisters."

Martha took the child from Megan and handed him unceremoniously to Julia to hold while she and the maid Janet attended to Megan. Julia walked to the door with him to see him in a better light, and she examined the incredibly tiny face. She wasn't sure. He was so red and wrinkled, but she thought his skin was a little darker than might ordinarily be expected. Yet with red hair, she hoped any inheritance he might have received from his Polynesian father would be overlooked. If only his hair would stay red after the first fine down disappeared.

Before the women had finished, Megan had fallen asleep, and Julia looked questioningly at Doctor Willett. He nodded and followed her out the door.

"Is she going to be all right?" Julia whispered when they were safely in the hall.

"Don't you worry about that one," he said. "She may be small, but she's made of steel. Just give her a little time to rest up, and she'll be running rings round the lot of you."

"Are you sure?" Julia asked suspiciously. Doctor Willett had a way of saying that all his patients were going to get well, but there were quite a few graves in the cemetery that would give lie to his faith.

"Can't guarantee anything," he said quietly, and Julia knew that, out of his tiredness, he would speak the truth. "You know there're still risks. Always are after a birth, but there's nothin' wrong with her now that time won't cure."

Julia nodded. "Why don't you go down and get something to eat. Maryanne's keeping some food hot for you."

"I will." The doctor took off his spectacles and wiped them on a clean handkerchief. Without their protection, Julia could see how truly weary he was, and she wondered how old he could be. He had been a fixture in their lives for so long.

A good man, she thought as she watched him go down the

stairs. Then she crossed the hall to her father's room.

"Look what I brought you, Papa," she said as she opened the door. "It's a long time since a boy was born in this house."

Lydia and Benjamin were sitting in comfortable chairs that looked out over the marsh, but neither one was relaxed. They both had been waiting for so long. When Julia entered the room, they looked up at her expectantly. Her father started to rise, but then thought better of it.

"Well, it's about time," he said. "As I recollect the last one was me and that was fifty-five years ago."

Lydia rose and took the baby from Julia and walked with him to the window. She began to croon a small unworded song to him.

"Bring him over here, Lyd," Benjamin said. "I want to get a look at the young rascal, too."

"I hope it didn't bother you too much," Julia said as she searched her father's face for signs of strain. He looked well, however. Better than he had since she'd been home. "There was really no time to move Megan."

"Bother me!" Benjamin snorted. "Life don't bother me. This house has been silent as a tomb too long, everyone tiptoeing around, talkin' in whispers. That young fellow's goin' to stir things up."

"Not too much, I hope," Lydia said as she held the baby down for him to see.

"Red hair!" From beneath his bushy brows, he shot a look up at Julia. "Now that's interesting."

"It runs in Megan's family," Julia explained.

"Hmmm." Benjamin tentatively touched the newly soft tiny cheek with the tip of one finger. "Wonder if that means she'll be goin' back to Maryland."

"Why should she go back to Maryland just because the child has red hair?" Lydia asked, instantly alert. "I thought she didn't have any kin left there."

"She has some that are a little . . . distant," Julia said. "I doubt she'll go back."

"She's all right, isn't she?" Lydia asked as she went back to her chair and sat down with the child still in her arms. She evidently had no intention of giving him up.

"Doctor Willett says she came through it fine."

"That's good." Lydia smiled down at the baby. "It'd be a terrible thing for the boy to be left an orphan. Bad enough being born without a father."

"Oh, I don't think he'll lack for love," Julia said while she watched her mother.

As Julia was returning to Megan's room with the baby, there was a loud knocking at the front door. The house was so turned upside down, she wasn't sure where everyone was or if anyone was free to answer it. Of the maids, Becky was with Amelia helping her care for the children, Janet was with Aunt Martha in Megan's room, and Maryanne was most likely seeing to it that the doctor got a good meal. It might be someone with news from the shipyard. Forgetting that she still held the baby, she started down the steps, but Maryanne came dashing out of the dining room.

"Don't come near the door, Miss Julia," she warned when she caught sight of Julia, "not with that baby. I'll see who 'tis and send them on their way."

"No, don't. It might be something important. I'll wait here."

When the door opened to admit Hiram Richardson, Julia was unpleasantly surprised. She had presumed that he, as owner of the *Free Wind*, would be aboard the ship on its journey to Boston, and the ship should be over the bar and well on her way by now. In her anxiety, Julia held the baby a little closer.

"What happened?"

Hiram Richardson whipped off his hat and handed it to Maryanne. "Good afternoon, Mrs. Logan. That's just what I came to find out. What *has* happened?"

"The *Free Wind*. Why are you still here? Did something go wrong at the launching?"

"Oh, no." He smiled up at her and smoothed back his chestnut hair with one hand. "The launching went smooth as glass. No need to concern yourself. I didn't mean to intrude, but your foreman explained why you weren't present. I came out of concern for Mrs. Fairfield. How is she?"

Julia went down three more steps so that she could speak more softly. "She's asleep. The doctor says she should be all right."

"The *doctor?*"

"Yes. He felt there might be complications and wanted to be here."

"Such a delicate young lady. She should have someone to take care of her." He came up the steps until he could see the child. "Boy or girl?"

"A boy."

Hiram Richardson studied the small face though he made no attempt to touch the child. What surprised Julia was the longing she saw in his own face, and she remembered his telling her years ago of the son he had lost even at the moment of birth when he'd lost his wife as well. She'd never realized before that he had any tenderness except a rather artificial one that he used to gain his own ends.

"Well, when that lad grows up, she'll have someone to care for her," he said finally, "but there are many long years ahead."

"Yes," Julia agreed. "Now you'll have to excuse me, Captain Richardson. He's barely an hour old, and I have to return him to his mother."

"Of course. I'll be sailing with the next tide aboard something a little more comfortable than a jury-rigged ship, but please give Mrs. Fairfield my warmest congratulations." He made no move to leave, but kept his eyes on the baby until Julia turned and went back up the steps.

Chapter Twenty

1849

The young men were leaving the yard. Julia had been able to keep them at work on the *Free Wind* only by promising them all a substantial bonus after the launching, and lured by the promise of extra money with which to start their expedition, they had remained. Now there was no staying them. The call of the gold fields, the promise of a fortune to be had just by picking nuggets out of a stream, was a magnet that could not be ignored.

The morning after the launching, Julia herself had paid them off and wished them luck. Now in the quiet of their departure, she sat alone in the office and wondered where she could find replacements for them. There were still vessels to be built. With the men who remained, she could build only one ship, and that might take a year rather than the six months she had allotted for it. The two smaller ways would have to sit empty.

No. She couldn't allow it to happen. With the current demand for vessels, she couldn't allow the Howard Shipyard to sit partially idle. She would have to raise the wages once more and try to entice experienced craftsmen to move to East Dennis. It would mean that she would have to charge higher prices for the vessels, but there should be no difficulty in finding buyers at any price now.

Just how long the demand would continue was another question.

And would she be able to finance the new ship for Stephen out of her own funds? If he arrived home in time, he could sell his shares in the *Crystal Star,* but what if she didn't even hear from him in time? Then she would simply have to sell the ship to someone else. Six months from now, there would still be a good market.

When the door opened, it disrupted her train of thought and she looked up from the sheets of paper she had covered with figures.

She had said good-bye only this morning to red-headed Paul Kelley, who was Daniel and Philip Sears's nephew, when he had appeared amongst the men who would be leaving. Now wearing his newly purchased high boots and with a slouch hat in his hands, he stood before her. Did that mean he had changed his mind and planned to stay? She hoped so, for he was a good carpenter. She could remember him as a child, hanging around the yard, begging for scraps of wood so that he could build things, especially boats.

When Daniel followed him into the room, she was sure Paul meant to stay. She smiled as she looked at the two men questioningly, but Daniel leaned against the door jamb with his arms folded across his chest and watched his nephew.

"Miss Julia," Paul said uneasily, "I understand you have some vessels for sale."

That certainly didn't sound like staying. Julia stopped smiling. "I have a few. Why?"

"Well, ma'am, I'm a member of the East Dennis Mining and Trading Company. There's thirty-two of us, and we'd like to buy one of your vessels."

Julia glanced at Daniel, but his eyes were still on his nephew, and she could not read his expression.

"They're not in what you'd call good condition, Paul," she said gently. "You plan to sail her round the Horn?"

"Yes, ma'am. An older ship's what we're lookin' for. Most likely we couldn't afford one in real good condition. Besides I doubt there's any to be had. We figure there's enough of us from the yard here to keep her patched together till we get to San Francisco."

"You part of this company, too, Daniel?" Julia asked the foreman suspiciously.

Daniel just glanced at her and shook his head. Then he went back to watching the young man. Julia knew that, after Paul's father had been lost at sea, Daniel had taken the boy under his wing. She guessed he must be here in the role of that dead father.

"And who's going to sail this vessel once you've got her?" Julia asked more sharply than she had intended.

"Oh, we've got plenty with sea experience and a couple who've been mates."

"You'll need a captain," she warned him.

"We know that, ma'am," Paul said earnestly, his vivid blue eyes sparkling with enthusiasm. "We'll elect him. We all have equal shares, and we're goin' to run everything on democratic lines. A vote from every man on everything, from running of the vessel to the prospecting, mining, cooking, and carpentry."

"Well, I've never heard of anything save a fishing boat could run along those lines successfully. I just hope you get there without too much bloodshed. And whoever you elect will have to know how to take sights. Otherwise, you'll never find the Horn, much less California."

"There's several who do. Will you sell us one of your vessels, Miss Julia?"

"You'll have to pay the same as any other buyer, Paul. I can't afford to do you any favors. The bonuses set me back quite a bit. Your uncles can tell you that."

"We're not asking any favors, ma'am." Paul was insulted. "We was just hopin' you'd sell us one of your best vessels, seeing as how you know us. Uncle Daniel said you might."

Julia glanced at Daniel again, but he maintained his role of silent observer. Did he actually think she might cheat the boy? But no. He wasn't watching her. All his attention was centered on his nephew.

"I only have five left," she said reluctantly, "and I really don't know their condition firsthand. I haven't seen them. All I have are reports on them. And I'd better warn you, the best ones went first."

"Yes, ma'am." Paul fidgeted with his hat and was obviously impatient. Julia wondered if he was even listening to what she was saying.

"Well, you can have your pick of what's left," she said finally. "I'll give you a list with the prices so you'll know where to find them, and I'll give you two weeks to decide before I accept any other offers. Go take a look at them, but look at everything else you see for sale, too. You might find something better."

"Yes, ma'am."

"And you be sure to let Miss Julia know the minute you decide against one," Daniel warned him with the stern look he gave the newest hands. "She's bein' right generous, and there's no reason for her to lose a sale on your account."

"Yes, sir."

The two men stood, Paul with eager anticipation and Daniel with stolid resignation, while Julia found her master list and copied the five vessels out for him. There were actually seven, but she would not under any circumstances sell two of them to Paul and his friends, nor would she sell them to anyone going to California. She was determined on that. They sounded too rotten to make it around the Horn, if they even got that far. She wondered what her father could have been thinking of when he purchased them.

"Make sure you take plenty of supplies, Paul," she said as she handed him the list.

"Oh, we'll take plenty to last us the voyage," he said.

"I'm not talking about the voyage alone. You'll need more when you get to California. With the thousands of men pouring out to the gold fields, there's going to be a shortage of food, shovels, cloth. Some you can use and some you can sell. You'll need the money to buy it back again."

"We'll get the money up in Sacramento," Paul said with excitement. "It's just lyin' there in the streams, waitin' for us."

"Do you really believe that, Paul?"

"Yes, ma'am. Why you must have read it in the papers yourself. How Lieutenant Loeser was just ridin' his horse along and spotted a nugget they say is worth over five thousand dollars."

"That may be, but I doubt you'll find many like that. You take as much in the way of goods as your vessel will hold. Might be worth a lot more than five thousand dollars. Now you tell the rest of your company what I said and see to it they do it."

When Paul looked dubious, Daniel spoke up. "Do like Miss Julia tells you, boy. She's been all over the world and knows how trading's done."

Paul looked from his uncle to Julia and back again. He stuck one hand in his pocket and swayed back on his heels as he considered how he could explain.

"I don't know as we could afford it, ma'am. Not after we pay for a vessel and the supplies to get us there. And we'll need a little money set aside for a rainy day once we get there."

"Don't take money. Take beans, flour, shoes, nails, whatever you can find that's cheap. They're going to need everything out there in that wilderness. For a while, it won't matter what you take. You'll make a profit on it and a good one."

"Yes, ma'am." Paul shifted from one foot to another and glanced down at the list in his hand. His face brightened as he looked at it. "Guess I'd best get goin' if we're to see all these in two weeks."

"Of course." Julia stood up and offered him her hand. "I really do wish you luck, Paul, and hope you come home a millionaire, but if you don't, you'll always have a job here."

"Yes, ma'am. Thank you, ma'am." He took her hand and gave it a quick nervous shake. Then he ducked his head at her and went quickly out the door.

Through the window, she could see the group of similarly clad men who rushed over to him as soon as he appeared. They were good men, all of them. She only prayed they would make it to California and back safely.

"Well, Daniel?" she said. "I hope I'm doing the right thing."

"You can't stop them, Miss Julia, no more than you can stop herring swimmin' upstream come spring. They're goin' to buy something."

"I know, but if anything happens to them in an unseaworthy vessel I sell them, I'd have it on my conscience the rest of my life."

" 'Twasn't as if you hadn't warned them." Daniel limped across the room and pulled some papers out of one of the chests.

"Seems every man under forty, and some that's over, is heading west. Soon there'll be nothing but old men, women, and children left on the Cape. Aren't you tempted to go, too, Daniel?"

"I've thought about it," he said. "Can't deny that."

She had only meant it as a jest. Was Daniel seriously considering joining in the madness? It was a thought that had never entered her head before. He couldn't! What would she do without him?

Turning toward her, he saw the alarm in her eyes, and said soberly, "I'm not leavin', Miss Julia. I've thought it would be nice to come home with money, better myself. But then I wondered what that money would buy. 'Twouldn't make me a different man, and 'tis certain it won't bring the things I want."

"What *do* you want, Daniel?"

"Nothin' worth talkin' about." A shadow crossed his face and then was gone. "Besides with my luck, I'd most likely lose everything I have."

Relieved, Julia looked out the window again. Paul's group was leaving the yard. Even from the distance, she could see the excitement in their long strides and waving arms.

"I envy them in a way," she said. "To be young again and off to a great adventure."

"You're still young, Miss Julia," Daniel said softly as he moved to stand beside her and look out the window."

"Not so young as I once was." She slowly swept her hands up the sides of her face, pushing back the tendrils that would never stay under control. "I'll be twenty-nine come summer, and the year after that, thirty. Life seems to be slipping through my fingers and disappearing like sand."

Daniel laughed at her. "When you get to be my age, you'll think that's young."

After Daniel had left, Julia sat thinking about the freshness and fervor of youth, the rainbow that arched the sky and promised you that a pot of gold waited for you somewhere just out there. She hadn't really expected her rainbow to end in a pot of gold as Paul did. What had they been looking for, she and Stephen? Well, perhaps for Stephen, it *had* been a pot of gold, and he had done well enough. But for herself, what had she been seeking?

When she was as young as Paul, she had told herself it was the sea. Yet now she realized that the sea had always been with her. It was there, just beyond the dunes. Aboard ship, she had gloried in it, it was true, but it had not really been what she lacked. The travel, the foreign lands? No, for while they had fascinated her, they were not really what she had been seeking.

Happiness, perhaps? She had found it many times, and yet happiness was not a thing that would stay. It, too, like life, just slipped away when you weren't looking. She knew she wasn't happy now. The bright expectancy she had seen shining on Paul's face had depressed her. Once she and Stephen had worn that radiant glow.

Right now what she wanted was Stephen. She had to admit it. The days were so busy, and when the nights came, she was too tired to do anything but sleep. It was a way to keep from thinking about him. Even a letter would help. But though there had been many reports from those who had sighted the *Crystal Star,* she'd had no word from him, and each day that took him away from her doubled the time it would take a letter to return.

She looked down at the desk and realized that she had torn a sheet covered with calculations into tiny shreds. Her fingertips were black with india ink. Well, she would have to begin all over again.

When the open carriage swayed into the shipyard on a morning in early June, Julia was halfway up a tall ladder with the chalk in her hand. For the last two days, she had been surveying the frames of the latest ship, the ship she was building for Stephen. Hours had been spent imagining what the vessel would look like when oak planks covered these frames, and whenever she had seen an unsightly bulge, an unpleasing curve, she had mounted the ladder and marked with chalk the inch or even eighth of an inch that must be filled out or shaved off.

One husky man held the ladder for her and moved it according to her whim while the carpenters followed her trail as they smoothed and corrected the shape of the ship to come. It was tedious work and yet she enjoyed it more than she did many of her chores in the shipyard. In this attempt at perfection, there was a challenge that pleased her.

"Miss Julia," an apprentice with sawdust in his hair called up to her. "Mrs. Martin's here to see you."

"I'm too busy to come just now," Julia called back impatiently. "Tell her if she wants to wait, she's welcome to use the office."

What could Sarah want here? Julia wondered as she drew a line on the giant frame. She had seen little of her sister in the six months she'd been home. Although Sarah, with her young son, Thomas Benjamin, often visited their mother and father, ordinarily she was there during the hours Julia spent at the yard. Their only contact had been casual greetings at church and an occasional Sunday dinner at home, where she arrived in great ceremony with her child and her husband, Aaron Martin, in tow.

The lack of contact was something Julia did not regret. So often her sister brought turmoil with her when she came. Even her father complained about Thomas Benjamin. Sarah could not bear to discipline her only child and would allow no one to speak against him. As a result, running wildly through the house, he excited the other children into a fever of giggles and shouting which often ended in a fight.

Julia reluctantly put the chalk into the pocket of her gingham dress. There was no use trying to concentrate on the ship while her thoughts were on her sister. Might as well face Sarah and be done with it. Then she could get back to more important matters.

After climbing down the ladder and dusting the chalk from her hands, she started for the office, but across the road, she saw the flash of a yellow parasol near the blacksmith's shop. That surprised her for Sarah disliked dirt, and the soot of the shop should have discouraged her. However, Julia reminded herself, the master blacksmith was quite handsome and very well set up. Sarah always had had an eye for a good-looking man.

"Hello, Sarah," Julia said as she came up beside her sister and Thomas Benjamin. "I thought I'd find you in the office."

"Not on such a beautiful day," Sarah said, smiling sweetly as her black lashes fluttered over her dove grey eyes. "Besides I thought it was time Thomas Benjamin took an interest in the shipyard. After all, it will belong to him someday."

"Not entirely," Julia said. "Papa has four other grandchildren at the moment and perhaps more to come."

"Well, I think Thomas Benjamin would be the obvious one to manage the yard. He's the eldest and by far the brightest of them all." With one daintily gloved hand, Sarah smoothed her already smooth light brown hair beneath the brim of her flowered hat. Her look was one of satisfied certainty.

Julia had no intention of ever allowing Thomas Benjamin to have a say in the yard, but she decided not to argue. It was pointless. Whatever happened would happen many years in the future.

"Don't you think he's a little young to be involved in it yet?" she said simply. "He is just six years old, isn't he?"

"None too young to begin learning, and he's very clever. He spends a lot of time at the saltworks with Aaron and Grandfather Martin. You should hear his comments when he comes home. He knows ever so much more about it than most of our workmen."

"Well, if you just want to show him the yard, please do so, but I must get back to work." Julia began to move away from the blacksmith's shop. "It was nice seeing you, Sarah."

"Oh, but Julia, I want to talk to you." Holding her son's hand, Sarah followed Julia, but not before she had tossed an over-the-shoulder smile at the good-looking blacksmith. "I've been hearing rumors that I find a little disturbing."

"Most rumors are disturbing because there's very little truth in them. If you came for advice, I'd suggest you ignore them."

"But I think there is some truth to these rumors."

"Then we'll talk in the office. There's more privacy there."

"Can't we talk over there?" Sarah nodded towards the new ship. "I've been hearing so much about it, I'd like to get a good look."

Julia shrugged. "If you wish. There's not much to see yet, though."

"Perhaps it will give Thomas Benjamin a feel for it. As Papa's namesake, I'm sure he's inherited his talents."

Julia looked down at her nephew, who was straining at his mother's hand as he tried to hurry her forward. His auburn hair would be like his father's when he was grown, but his eyes were the same soft grey as Sarah's. Where the boundless energy came from, she didn't know. He was never still unless he slept, and he often cried himself to sleep in exhaustion. The poor child. When he didn't irritate her, she felt sorry for him. There seemed to be little thought behind his constant nervous activity.

"Well, I don't know about a name having anything to do with inheritance, but seems likely since you named him first after Aaron's father, his real talents must lie in the direction of the saltworks."

Julia led the way across the road and had to slow her pace for her sister, who was picking her way gingerly over the packed sand.

"So that's the famous ship you're building for yourself," Sarah said as they approached it.

Julia glanced sharply at her sister. Whenever Sarah used that tone of voice, nothing but trouble was bound to follow.

"I don't know how famous she is," Julia said dryly.

"Oh, everyone knows about it. How you're building a ship some say will be too big to launch. What really interests me is the way you're using Papa's money to make your own fortune when he's too ill to know what you're doing."

"Papa knows what I'm doing," Julia said curtly. She didn't feel like playing games with Sarah today. Or any other day for that matter.

"Does he? Isn't that strange. I tried to bring the subject up only yesterday, and he said he wasn't feeling well enough to discuss business. In fact, he said he knew nothing of what was going on in the yard. Said you were handling everything and that he trusted you implicitly."

"What's strange about it? He knows basically what's going on, but Doctor Willett doesn't want him to be bothered with details yet."

"He really knows?"

"Of course, he knows."

"Well, it does seem odd he never offered to build a ship for Aaron and me."

"Why should he? What would you do with a ship?"

"The same thing you do with yours. Hire a captain and make some money."

"I'm not building this ship for a hired captain. I'm building it for my husband. I'm sure if you'd asked Papa to build a ship for you, he'd have been glad to. He does it for customers all the time."

"But then we'd have had to pay for it like customers."

"Sarah, if you think I'm not going to pay for this ship, then you're very much mistaken."

Sarah's eyes narrowed below her delicate black eyebrows. "Where'd you get the money?"

"Like you, Sarah, I'm married to a successful man, and I'm certain Aaron could purchase a ship just as easily as Stephen can." Julia was not about to tell Sarah about the *Jewel of the Seas*. So far she had been successful in keeping the news of the ship's destruction from her father, and Sarah was sure to find delight in running to him with the information.

"What do you know about Aaron's finances?" Sarah asked sharply.

"Just about as much as you know about Stephen's, which is nothing."

Sarah looked after her son, who was approaching the large stack of timbers that was halfway across the yard. She preferred not to

398

look at her sister. If Julia saw her face, she might guess on what short reins Aaron's father kept him. Barely enough to get by, she thought, and though she ranted at Aaron and was always sweet to his father, the old gentleman kept the running . . . and the profits . . . of the saltworks firmly in his own hands.

"You'd best watch your son," Julia said as her eyes followed the direction of Sarah's. Men hurrying through the yard with boiling pots of tar or giant knees would have little time or thought for a small skittering child.

"Thomas Benjamin isn't interfering with the yard."

"I'm just concerned that he might get hurt."

"You mean you just don't want him here . . . nor me neither. Papa used to bring you down to the yard when you were that age, and no harm ever came to you. Of course, *I* was never allowed to come. Even when I was older, if you'll recollect."

"What I recollect is that I wasn't allowed to run free like that. Papa kept a sharp eye on me till I was a good bit older. What was it you wanted to talk to me about, Sarah?"

"I just wanted to see the ship." Sarah sauntered closer to the scaffolding and looked up at the hollow ribs that still had the rich scent of fresh-cut oak.

"Well, you could have seen her without calling me away from my work."

"Oh, Julia." Sarah's eyes opened wide in mock distress. "You're so important. I tend to forget that sometimes. I really do need for you to remind me occasionally."

"It's important that the work be done."

"Yes. You must rush and finish that ship for your precious husband. By the bye, have you heard from Stephen recently?"

"Yes. Just the other day. He's well." It was a lie. She had yet to hear from him, and from the smug cat smile Sarah gave her, she suspected that her sister knew it was a lie. How did she find out these things? But then Sarah always did.

"How nice," Sarah said airily. "Well, we mustn't keep you from your *important* duties any longer."

"Thomas Benjamin, get down from there!" Julia shouted.

The boy had begun to climb up the pile of logs, and she knew how precariously balanced the great limbs and hackmatack roots were. She ran toward the woodpile with Sarah following close behind her. Before they reached it, however, the wood started to move and the boy with it. Three of the men nearby dropped their tools and, with giant strides, were there before Julia and Sarah. With great gentleness and strength, they managed to move the logs that pinned Thomas Benjamin down and lifted him kicking and screaming from the pile.

Sarah practically snatched the child from the men's arms and rocked him in hers as though he were still a baby.

"Is he all right?" Julia asked.

Sarah glared at her and then set the child on the ground and began to inspect him for damage. There was a cut on the boy's cheek and he rubbed his right leg, but he never stopped howling.

"There, there, love," Sarah crooned as she wiped his cheek with her lace-fringed handkerchief. "It's all over now. We'll go and see if Granny doesn't have a nice big piece of chocolate cake for you."

"I think you ought to check his leg, Sarah."

"His leg's all right, but it's no thanks to you that he wasn't killed. If you hadn't yelled at him like that, nothing would have happened. You startled the poor darling."

"I warned you the yard was dangerous, Sarah. From now on if you can't supervise him properly, I'd suggest you keep him away from here."

"Oh, you won't get rid of us that easily, Julia. We'll be back. I won't have my son cheated of his inheritance."

Sarah took the parasol she had dropped from the man who offered it to her and twirled it as she raised it. Taking her son by the hand, she made her way mincingly through the yard to the carriage.

It was later that day when Aaron Martin rode into the yard. The sun had set, and in the long summer twilight, Julia was locking the door to the office. Aside from the watchman who was making the first of his rounds, the shipyard was deserted.

Julia looked up and watched Aaron come towards her. He still sat his horse with his old elegance and his clothes fitted him as neatly as ever, although they had to be ordered in a larger size than when he had tried courting Julia. Above his cravat, she could see the beginnings of a double chin.

There was a general slackness, a softness to his entire appearance which made her compare him unfavorably with Stephen. Though they were close to the same age, Stephen, with his hard body and his quick, lithe movements, seemed years younger than this man who seemed to have settled into middle age. Yet his plumpness gave Aaron's face the unformed features of adolescence.

"Hello, Julia," Aaron said as he reined in his horse beside her and raised his silk top hat to expose his auburn hair. "How are you?"

"I'm fine but rather puzzled," she said as she slipped the key into her pocket. "Why am I honored by visits from both you and Sarah on the same day?"

"Well . . . it's a matter of business," he said, and the horse, as though sensing his rider's uneasiness, skittered a few steps away from Julia.

"I'm sorry, but I'm just leaving. If you want to discuss it on the way home, you're welcome to ride with me." She walked briskly to the mounting block where one of the apprentices had left her horse saddled and ready for her.

Once they had started up the road, Julia looked at him questioningly. "If you have business to discuss, I'd advise you to get on with it. As soon as I get home, I'm going to have a nice long bath, and then I'm going to have supper."

"I came because Sarah asked me to," he said almost in apology.

Julia sighed. She usually enjoyed this peaceful ride when the birds were settling down in the fading light. It was one of the few moments of the day when she had time to be herself, unbeholden to anyone. She wished that Aaron was anywhere but beside her.

"Sarah's already seen me. Why did she send you?"

"It's about that ship you're building."

"What about the ship I'm building?"

"Well . . . Sarah tells me you're building it on your own account."

"And what if I am?"

"Sarah thinks we ought to be allowed to see your accounts . . . just to keep everything square."

"Aaron Martin!" She turned sideways in her saddle to fix him with her flashing eyes. "What damn business is it of yours?"

"Now, don't get upset, Julia. Sarah says that, as long as you're not doing anything dishonest, you should be happy to show us your ledgers."

"Dishonest!" Julia glared at him until he seemed to shrink in his saddle. "You are not going to see the ledgers unless Papa gives you permission to do so. The yard, the ship, none of it is any of your business, and I'll thank you and your wife to take your long noses out of it."

"Be reasonable, Julia." His soft brown eyes pleaded with her. "All Sarah wants is to ensure that her interests aren't being overlooked."

"Sarah's interests? What interests? Last I heard Papa owned the yard. When did Sarah acquire an interest in it?"

"She hasn't yet, but she will someday . . . after your father's death."

"You ghouls!" Julia looked at him in horror. "What are you doing? Praying for his early demise? He's improving every day, and I fully intend to make sure he lives to be a hundred. So you just get any ideas of a quick inheritance right out of your minds."

"Julia, you know he could go at any time. Sarah says that once a person's had a stroke . . ."

"*Sarah says, Sarah says.* Don't you have any ideas of your own, Aaron?" Then she laughed derisively. "How could I forget? It's just that I've been away so long. Of course, you never had an idea in your life. As I recall, you used to quote Stephen like a parrot. Now it's Sarah."

He drew himself up with dignity. "I must remind you that Sarah is my wife, and as such, it is my duty to look after her inheritance."

"Get it through your head, Aaron, Sarah doesn't have an inheritance. No one can have an inheritance until someone dies, and I've just told you that no one is going to die. Papa has put his affairs in my hands until he is able to cope with them. If he's satisfied to trust in my judgment, then you and Sarah will just have to follow suit. Sarah has no rights and you are not going to see the ledgers until Papa agrees to it."

She swung down from her horse and handed the reins to Ezra, who came hobbling out of the carriage house.

"Good night, Aaron," she called over her shoulder as she swirled toward the house.

Julia was in the bathtub, soaking away the grime and sweat of a busy day in the shipyard, when she heard her father's roar. Jumping out of the tub, she pulled her light silk robe around her and ran to his room. Her father was still roaring.

"You whimpering lap dog, you spleeny coward, son of a sea

402

squid, get out of my house and stay out!"

When she saw how red her father's face was as he stood and shouted at Aaron, Julia went swiftly to his side and put her arms around him.

"Hush, Papa. Don't fret yourself. 'Tisn't worth it."

"Do you know what this son of a bitch just asked me?"

"I know, Papa. He wants to see your accounts. I've already told him he couldn't. Here. Sit down." She pushed him into his chair and glanced over her shoulder. "Get out of here, Aaron."

"You told me I needed his permission to see the ledgers."

"Well, you're obviously not going to get it, so go away."

"Damned right, he isn't going to get it," Benjamin simmered. "And if you ever show them to him, I'll disinherit you."

"It's all right, Papa."

"I . . . I didn't mean to upset you, Captain Howard. It was just a simple matter of business."

"Yes. My business, and after today, it will *never* be any business of yours or of that mealy-mouthed wife of yours."

"Now, Papa, you don't mean that. Aaron, will you please just go." She saw that her mother, Martha, and Megan had gathered in the hall. "Aunt Martha, send for Doctor Willett."

"I don't need any damn doctor," Benjamin said.

"Well, it won't hurt to have him look at you."

"Get your eyes off my daughter, you son of a sea cook," Benjamin growled at Aaron, who still had not moved.

When Julia looked up at him, he seemed to be frozen to the spot and he was staring at her. Suddenly she realized that the light silk robe clinging to her wet body left her all but completely revealed.

"Get out," she said in a low threatening voice. "Get out of here before I send for some of my men to throw you out."

"*Your* men?" Aaron, stung, rose to her challenge with a sneer.

"Yes, *her* men." Benjamin's eyebrows bristled at his son-in-law.

Martha Chambers decided to take things into her own hands and moved swiftly into the room. Before he knew what had happened, she had taken both of Aaron's arms from behind in a tight grip, turned him around, and propelled him out of the room past the women in the hall. She was pushing him toward the stairs before he realized the woman's strength and grabbed the bannister to support himself against a fall.

*   *   *

403

By the time Doctor Willett arrived, Benjamin was sitting peacefully eating his supper.

"What's this I hear about you having tantrums, Ben?" The doctor peered over his spectacles at his patient.

"Tantrums, ha!" Benjamin waved his fork at him. "Just defending the ship against pirates. Tried to sneak aboard when my back was turned. Want some supper?"

"No. I just left a fine one sittin' on my table to come over here and tend a crazy fool who don't have the brains to look after himself. As I recollect, I told you not to get excited."

"Did me good." Benjamin grinned at him. "Haven't felt so young in months. I'm not goin' to have any more namby-pamby from you."

"You want to live to see your grandchildren grow up?"

"I want to *live*. I don't want to sit around here cooped up in this room the rest of my life."

"I told you you could go downstairs once a day."

"Still not exactly what I call living. I go down and sit in the parlor or out on the porch and watch the rest of the world out there goin' about their business. But me? You've got my own daughter locking me out of my study."

"It's for your own good, Ben," the doctor said soberly as he felt his patient's wrist. "Julia, you out there in the hall?"

She slipped in, a little embarrassed that her father should know that she had been eavesdropping.

"You got all the keys to that room?" the doctor asked her.

"All of them," she said firmly and looked at her father.

"Well, you just keep them . . . and don't leave them lyin' around where your father can lay hands on them."

"I mean what I say," Benjamin stated. "I'm not goin' to be treated like an invalid one day longer. There are ways of breaking down a door."

"And you're not goin' to attempt any of them. Not for another week."

"Another week?" Benjamin fixed the doctor with his penetrating blue eyes while he considered it. "And after that, what?"

"After that, we'll see." The doctor snapped his case shut. "Doubt you did yourself any damage today, but it might show up later. If next week this time, you're still improving, then I'll give you one hour a day."

"One hour a day for what? For living? God's sake, that's just enough to tantalize a man without satisfying him."

"For one hour a day, you can go into your study and do whatever you've a mind to. If that works out, then you can go in for two hours a day."

"And what about the shipyard? What if I want to spend my hour a day over there?"

"You stay away from that shipyard. First thing you know you'll be climbing ladders or chipping away with an adze, and I won't be responsible."

"Who asked you to be responsible?"

"You did and your wife and your daughters."

"Are you sure he's all right, Doctor Willett?" Julia asked. "His face was red as a flannel petticoat a while ago."

"*If* he gets his rest tonight and takes his digitalis like he's supposed to . . . and most particularly, if he stops havin' tantrums . . . I can't see there's much to fret about."

"What am I supposed to do? Lie here and let everyone walk all over me?" Benjamin growled.

"That's about what I had in mind, Ben," the doctor said mildly. "Never seen anyone who succeeded in using you as a doormat yet, though."

"Never will, neither," Benjamin muttered after the retreating backs of the doctor and Julia.

One day in mid-September, when the heat of summer had fled with the passing of an offshore hurricane, Julia looked around the shipyard and was well content. With her offers of high wages, she had been able to draw many experienced, mature men from smaller yards, and she found that they proved better and more efficient workers than the men they had replaced. There was still a fair proportion of younger men in her employ, those who either had no funds to take them to California or who had family responsibilities that tied them to the Cape. Boys were brought to her for apprenticeship and she accepted the best of them. By the time they were old enough to find their way west, she hoped the California craze would have subsided.

It was good to have Papa back, she thought as she made her way to the office. As yet he could only spend an hour or two a day at the shipyard, but his presence and advice were strengthening, not only to Julia, but to the men as well. He preferred to sit in the sun just outside the office where he could watch the comings and goings and the work of the men. Julia had assigned one apprentice as his messenger, and he kept the boy so busy, she was considering taking on another to wait attendance on him.

There was always a chair beside his, which was usually occupied by a visitor. Today, she could see, it was Captain Asa Crofton, who still owned quite a few shares in the *Crystal Star*. She wondered if he had merely come to yarn with her father or whether he'd had word of Stephen. Her husband hadn't seen fit to communicate with her since that ice-cold day last December when he'd taken his leave, but he had written a couple of notes to Captain Asa. She quickened her step. It helped to know that Stephen was alive and well, even if he was still angry with her.

"Here 'tis," Captain Asa said, holding out an envelope to her as she approached the two men. "Your young man's bad as all the rest. A real scalawag."

Julia glanced at him sharply, but decided not to comment until she had read the letter.

SAN FRANCISCO
MAY 25, 1849

DEAR CAPTAIN ASA,

Upon arrival, the entire crew including the two mates jumped ship and headed for Sacramento. The gold fever has reached incredible proportions. Not one vessel arriving here has been able to muster enough men to set sail again.

All of the merchandise has been auctioned off at prices that far exceeded our expectations, and I was most anxious to return home for a new cargo. However, it seems the *Crystal Star* must lie idle until I can round up a crew, which does not seem a likely occurrence for some time to come.

After due consideration, I have come to the conclusion that the only profitable way to spend my time is to follow the crew to the gold fields. I have taken the *Crystal Star* to Benicia, where I believe she will be safer than in San Francisco. I have paid the watchmen to keep an eye on her.

406

If you can find another vessel upon which to ship cargo, I would advise you to do so. Pork and beef are selling for between forty to sixty dollars a barrel as is flour. Tea, coffee, and sugar go for four dollars to the pound, and a pair of cowhide boots sells for forty-five dollars. I expect these prices will hold for another few months. As you can imagine, picks, shovels, and tin bowls are also much in demand as are spirits of any kind and quality.

Please be assured that I will sail at the first opportunity. I remain,

Yours very truly,
STEPHEN O. LOGAN

Julia stared at the abrupt ending. No word for her. Not even a word about their child. And he was off to seek a fortune in gold, too. So this was his way of paying her back. She'd be willing to wager that, if she'd been along, he would have found a crew quick enough. He wouldn't have taken her up to the hills nor would he have left her alone on the ship in Benicia, wherever that was, that was certain.

Really! He was as bad as Paul and all his friends.

She was so angry her hands were shaking when she wordlessly handed the letter back to Captain Asa.

"He remains mine very truly," Captain Asa snorted. "He remains in California, that's what he remains."

"Well, if he can't get a crew together, I don't suppose he can do much else except remain," Benjamin said mildly.

"Stuff and nonsense. There's vessels returning every day."

"You read about any in the papers?" Benjamin asked. "Must have missed my notice."

"Then how'd this letter get here?" Captain Asa demanded.

"Most likely down the West Coast on one of those new Pacific Mail Steamship Company vessels, across Panama, and then onto an Atlantic Steamship Company vessel bound for New York."

"Hmpf!" Captain Asa spat out a stream of tobacco juice. "You notice the date on that letter? I suspicion it was written the minute he had his anchor down. You hear from him yet, Julia?"

"No, Captain Asa." She shook her head, still shocked by the news the letter contained. "No, I've heard nothing."

In a daze, she wandered through the shipyard, without a glance at the ship she was building for him, and over the dunes to the beach.

The tide was out, and on the flats the clammers were hard at work with their rakes, but there was no one here on the higher sand to disturb her thoughts.

Launching would be on the next full moon, and although she'd frequently written to Stephen about the new ship, he'd not given the slightest indication that he was interested. Now that he'd caught the gold fever, he wouldn't be coming home in time to take command. Would he ever come home? she wondered in anguish. He had threatened not to return that last night, but she hadn't really taken him seriously. Yet it seemed possible he meant it.

She was defeated. She couldn't hold back the ship for him. Not any longer. Another man would own her. Another man would sail as her master.

But Stephen, why must you be this way? she thought as she sank down on the warm sand and stared sightlessly out at the sails that clung to the far horizon.

You need me as much as I need you, and you know you do. Why must you be so stubborn and proud? How much would it cost you to write even the shortest note to me? I know you haven't forgotten me anymore than I have you.

The same blood courses through our veins. At night, I wake to the touch of your lips only to find that you're not there. Are you dreaming of me then out there in your lonely tent on the dark hills of California? Or are you awake and thinking about me, longing for me just as I long for you?

You're lonely and you know you are. I can no more imagine you joining in the fellowship of a company than you could join your crew in a glass of grog. How can you be content with none but strangers around you, with no one who loves you, cares for you? With no one who needs you as I do?

Chapter Twenty-One

1850

The long and lonely months dragged by as the trees turned to the gold and flames of autumn only to lose their leaves under the northerly winds of winter. The snows came and melted. Spring unfurled in all its youthful glory, which brought more pain to Julia than all the other seasons combined. Vessels were launched to make way for new ones that rose on the ways until they, too, were launched.

It was late June and the midday sun was at its peak when the signals, hoisted on the highest hills of the Cape, finally sent the word from Provincetown to Boston that the *Crystal Star* had been sighted homeward bound. For days, Julia had been watching the hills for the message to be telegraphed, and now that the moment had come, it seemed unreal. Eighteen months had gone by since Stephen had left the Cape, and for the first year, she hadn't heard from him directly.

Only a few months ago, in January, a letter had finally come, and then it had been short and terse. Written in November, Stephen had said that he was sailing from San Francisco for Canton. After that the notes had begun to arrive, charting his way around the world from Canton, from Anjier, from the Cape of

Good Hope. The latest had been sent from Liverpool, where he had gone to sell his cargo of tea, and that one had been no more affectionate than the rest.

As she rode her horse over the path between the tall green marsh grass that was filled with the blackbird's song, Julia wondered what her feelings truly were. When the signal had first been hoisted, she had been elated. While an apprentice had saddled her horse for her, she had stood impatiently by, and then she had practically snatched the reins from his hand in her excitement to be gone to the top of Scargo Hill. It was one of the tallest points on the entire Cape, and from there she would be able to sight the *Crystal Star* long before the ship was visible from the shore or the dunes.

However, after cantering wildly along the sand roads for half a mile, she had suddenly been toppled from her joyous heights. Reining in, she slowed her horse to a walk while she tried to understand her strange mixture of emotions.

Stephen had been away so long and his short letters had been those of a stranger addressed to a stranger. She had filled hers with news of Clara, of the shipyard, of the gossip of the shipping world that she had gleaned from newspapers and from the men who returned home briefly from the sea. Yet she had to admit it had been difficult for her to express any warmth or love to the man who had written to her with none.

After she tethered her horse to a tree, she slowly climbed the narrow crooked path that was sheltered from the sun by the overhanging branches of the massed trees. She remembered how, in the past, she had fairly flown up the path with the telescope clutched in her hand. Never before had she felt any reluctance. Never before had she been so deeply hurt.

And she needed time, she thought as she reached the small clearing that overlooked the curve of the Bay from Provincetown almost all the way to Sandwich. After the months of endless days when it seemed the time would never pass, now she felt that he would be here too soon. She wasn't ready for him.

There were sails scattered across the water, but she couldn't distinguish those that belonged to the *Crystal Star*. It would be a while. She brushed pine needles off of a fallen log and sat down to wait.

She wanted him. She knew she wanted him. Through those

nights when her body had kept her from sleep, she had remembered in detail the clean scent of his body, the feel of his hand cupping her breast, the taste of his .lips upon hers, the rich laughter when he first came to her, the languorous look of content in his grey eyes when they lay at peace together afterwards. With every sense, with every muscle, with every pore, she had remembered him and ached for him. It brought a pain that had driven her to walking through moonlit halls and empty rooms. There had been nights when it had driven her over lonely roads to pace beside the sea until dawn came to give her release.

But did he still want her? How could the man who had written her those terse notes feel anything for her? There were other women in the world, and for a famous sea captain as attractive as Stephen, many of them would be available. Were they able to give him a satisfaction she could not? Were they more adept at pleasing a man? Had he found them more beautiful, more seductive than she could ever be? And was there perhaps one woman?

Then anger made her spring up from the log to train her glass on the waters north of Provincetown. He was her husband! He had no right to treat her this way! He had left her in coldness with no attempt to understand why she must stay. During the months of strain and worry over her father, over the yard, over Megan, she had received no support from him. First he had sent her only silence, then those abrupt notes that were no better than silence. Never once had he shown concern for her problems. Never once had he asked about Clara. Instead he had tried to fill her with guilt for not tossing everything over her shoulder and sailing gaily away with him.

She moved restlessly around the clearing, snapping twigs from bushes, pausing to train her glass upon the water.

He was the most selfish man who had ever lived! The most unbearable!

Then why did she want him back again? Because she did. Her eyes filled with tears when she thought of the gay fantasies he would spin to make her laugh, of the love and generosity he could show in so many subtle ways, of his tenderness when she had been carrying Clara.

She wiped her eyes against her sleeve and raised the telescope once more. And there was the *Crystal Star!* Home, she thought. The ship that had been more truly her home than any other she had lived in. Every plank in the deck, every creaking of the hull, was dearer to her than the walls of the bedroom that had been hers since childhood or the sigh of the spruces that had sung her to sleep. The *Crystal Star* was so tiny when seen from this distance, she felt she could hold it in the palm of her hand.

And though the distance was too great to see a man, she could imagine Stephen standing silent on the quarterdeck, observing, always observing, the workings of his ship. Did he turn his face towards the Cape? Did he, with his telescope, pick out Scargo Hill and know that she was there?

He did! She was sure of it. She felt the bond that had always been between them, holding them together, turning them into a single being with two bodies. It was almost visible as it stretched across the miles that separated them.

Oh, Stephen!

And then she felt nothing. The bond was gone. Dissolved back into the depths of her imagination from which it had sprung, she thought wryly.

As she watched the ship running taut before the wind, she waited for the return of that magic moment. She would go to Boston to meet him! The packet was scheduled to leave tomorrow. He would have to stay in Boston until he had disposed of his cargo, and they would have those days together.

Then her shoulders sagged and she lowered the glass.

She couldn't go. She had been going to fly to the man she had known and lived with for seven years, but the man who stood on that quarterdeck was a stranger. He had to have changed or he would have sent her some token of love, of understanding, during the past year and more. She couldn't go to the city and expose herself to his repudiation. He had not asked her to come. If he wanted her, it would have to be he who made the first move.

But what if he doesn't?

If he simply takes on another cargo and sails from Boston without coming, without making any attempt to see me, how will I live? And if he's still carrying that anger around with him, he's quite capable of doing it. That's certain.

The *Crystal Star* had long since disappeared from sight by the time Julia finally made her way down the hill that was now shadowed by the setting sun. When she arrived home, her father was sitting on the front porch waiting for her.

"You missed dinner and supper both," he said as she sat wearily down in the chair next to his.

"I know, Papa. I'll get something to eat in a few minutes."

He looked at her curiously. After he had heard news of the sighting, he'd expected her to come tearing home filled with elation at the prospect of seeing her husband after so long a separation, but she sat slumped in her chair like an old woman.

"You want to talk about it?" he asked.

"There's not much to talk about," she said leadenly as she took off her bonnet and tossed it on the floor beside her. She swept her hair back from her face with both hands and then leaned her head against the back of the chair. The boards of the porch creaked as she began to rock slowly. "It's the *Crystal Star,* that's certain, and she's bound for Boston."

"You don't seem too happy about it."

"I don't know whether I am or not." She stared straight ahead at the gold-washed hills that rose on the far side of the darkening marsh.

Benjamin rubbed his chin as he rocked back and forth for a few silent moments. It was hard to find the right words. Most everything he thought of seemed to phrase out wrong.

"Thought he was the right man for you," he finally said. "Maybe I was wrong."

"You were right. He was." There was an abruptness in her voice that didn't invite any further discussion along that line.

"You goin' down to Boston tomorrow?" Benjamin asked as he tried to tackle whatever was worrying her from a new angle.

"No. I don't think so."

"The yard won't suffer if you do now that I'm able to get around."

"That's not the reason."

Benjamin leaned forward in his chair in order to get a better look at her face. Even in the soft evening light, she looked strained and tired. Damn it! She wouldn't even be thirty till next month. He wasn't going to have it.

"Julie, I've tried hard not to pry, though I must admit, at times it's taken considerable restraint on my part."

"I appreciate that, Papa."

"Well, now I'm going to do some prying," he said firmly and his bushy black brows drew together in the concern that was beginning to pain him. "What's going on between you and that young husband of yours?"

"Nothing, Papa," she said, still staring across the road at the marsh. In the gathering dusk, the fireflies were just becoming visible. "That's just it. Nothing."

"Then best you make something happen!" He almost shouted at her in his effort to shake her from her lethargy. He did startle her into sitting up straight and looking at him.

"What?"

"Go on down to Boston and see him," Benjamin said more quietly now that he had her full attention. "It's been a long time. He'll be expecting you."

"I'm not so sure he wants me," she said. Bewilderment and hurt lightened the blue of her eyes.

"He wants you."

She shook her head. "No. If he wants me, he'll have to come for me."

"Pride, Julie!" He struck his knee with his fist. "That's nothing but pride."

"Maybe it is." She raised her chin defiantly at him. "And if it is, it's your fault. You're the one who taught it to me. Besides I won't go crawling to him, not after the way he's treated me."

"How's he treated you?" Benjamin preferred her temper to the numbness she had been displaying.

"He's ignored me."

"Never beat you up, has he?"

"Stephen!" Her eyes flew wide with surprise. "No. Of course not."

"Threatened you?" he persisted.

"Not that way. His anger's cold. He just . . . removes himself. Do you know what I mean?"

Benjamin nodded. "Better than being hot-headed."

"Is it?" she said pensively. "I wonder."

"If he comes, you goin' back to sea with him?" He tried to sound casual and pretended to concentrate on slapping a mosquito that had landed on his leg.

"I don't know."

He drew a deep breath as he prepared to say what he didn't want to say, and he wondered how much truth there was in it. Still, this was his Julie, and what he wanted for her was happiness, no

414

matter what the cost to him might be. He remembered all too well how much he had missed her in the years she had been away. It would be hard to give her up again.

"If you're fretting about the yard, don't. I'll be around a few more years."

"As long as you take care of yourself, you will be, but I don't trust you." She frowned mockingly at him, but her anxiety about him was so real she forgot about Stephen for a few seconds. "The minute I'm out of sight, you'll be down there from sunrise to sunset, driving yourself the way you always do."

"No, no. Don't you worry about that." He smiled as he reached across and squeezed her arm. "I can make you that one promise. Age and a stroke have taught even me a few lessons. You know damned well you want to go back to sea, so go. If you don't, you might spend the rest of your life wishing you had."

"I may not have any choice in the matter," she said quietly.

"Well, I'll tell you, Julie. Lately I've had a lot of time for thinking." The creaking of his rocker played a counterpoint to the pipings of the marsh frogs and underlined his words. "I've been wondering if I did right bringing you up the way I did. I never meant to, but I tied you to the yard just as surely as I was tied to it. I handed on to you a responsibility I never wanted myself."

"It's something I wanted, Papa," she said earnestly and her voice reassured him. "After watching you take dreams and turn them into reality, I wanted to do it, too. Think of the vessels we've built. Some of them have been record-breakers, some of them not, but they've all been good, sound craft. And you've designed ships the world said couldn't be built. Look at the letter we got from David Baxter just yesterday. After that eighty-one-day run from New York to China, the British Admiralty went and asked permission to send their surveyors down to take off the lines of the *Free Wind* while she's in dry dock at Blackwell. That's something."

"It don't mean much. Not if there's something else you'd rather be doing."

Even though it was now too dark to see his expression clearly and the lamplight streaming through the tall windows only served to silhouette his features, she could hear the yearning in his voice.

"You still wishing you were at sea, Papa?"

"No," he sighed. "Not any more. If I'd been at sea when I'd had that stroke, I'd likely not have lived to tell the tale, and I've found what a dear thing life is. But when I'm gone, Julie, sell the yard. Don't let it tie you to the land."

"I'll *never* sell it," she said indignantly. "After all the work you and Grandfather put into it, I'd never even consider it. It's the Howard Shipyard and it's going to *stay* the Howard Shipyard. You've got grandsons coming along, you know."

"Aye, and neither Sarah's Thomas Benjamin nor Amelia's Levi has got what it takes. Wish you had a son, Julie. Maybe you will yet."

"Maybe, but I wouldn't count on it." The thought of a son brought Stephen all too strongly to mind. She slapped at the mosquitoes that were gathering around her ankles. Then she stood up. "If I'm going to eat, I'd best go in and see what Aunt Martha saved for me."

"Go on down to Boston, Julie," he said as she passed in front of him and the lamplight from the parlor illuminated her features.

"No, Papa. I stay here."

A week went by and there was no word from Stephen. The only news she got was from the papers and from Captain Asa. As the days passed, Julia became more and more convinced that Stephen was going to sail without coming to see her. Finally she could stand it no longer, and on the eighth day, when she heard that the packet was arriving from Boston, she left the shipyard abruptly and went home to pack a bag. It was better to face Stephen on no matter what terms than to live in this limbo of uncertainty.

She had her brush and comb in her hand ready to put them into the bag when she heard footsteps on the porch, then on the front stairs. She stood frozen, staring at the bedroom door, for there were no other footsteps like those in the world. She had heard them on the quarterdeck, in the cabin, and on the roads of the world.

When he reached the door, he didn't enter, but stood framed in the afternoon sunlight that came pouring through the hall window behind him. He leaned against the jamb and stretched an arm against the other side of the doorway. He looked long at her, flicked a glance at the open bag on the bed, and then looked back at her again. One eyebrow shot up and his smile was only on his lips, not in his eyes.

"Running away, my lady?"

"No." Julia found it hard to speak around the lump that had suddenly formed in her throat. "I was going down to Boston to see you."

"Why didn't you come before?"

"You didn't ask me."

"You're my wife!" He stiffened and dropped his arm, but he made no move towards her. "Do I have to *ask* you, for God's sake? I expected you. Every day I expected you. When you didn't arrive on the packet, I waited for the stage coaches. You knew I was there. You were watching from Scargo Hill when we sailed by the Cape."

"You couldn't have seen me."

"I didn't need to see you. You were there."

"Yes, I was. I was there. Do you know how long *I've* waited, Stephen? Do you know how long it was before you even bothered to send me a letter?"

"It was a long time," he said evenly. "It'll be a long time again. I'm sailing for California in two weeks. Are you coming with me?"

"If you want me."

"*If* I want you!" In two strides, he was across the room and his arms were so tight around her, she could hardly breathe. She dropped the brush and comb as her arms went around his neck.

"Oh, Stephen," she whispered as his lips fluttered over her face and hers tried to follow his. She wasn't aware that she was crying.

He pulled her with him to the door, which without releasing her, he slammed shut and locked. Then they were sitting on the bed and he was drying her tears with his handkerchief.

"So you missed me, my lady."

"Oh, yes." She reached up to touch his face, but his image was blurred by the tears that were still welling up in her eyes.

He gently swung her around so that she was lying in his arms with her head in the hollow of his shoulder. She had forgotten how safe she could feel when he held her so.

"Julie, Julie," he said huskily as he kissed the hollow below her throat. "There's no other woman like you in the world."

She didn't have to ask him, she *wouldn't* ask him, but she knew that he had been unfaithful to her. Strangely enough, it didn't matter. What mattered was that no one else had satisfied him. He had come back to her with his love intact.

His light brown hair was soft and thick as she buried her fingers in it, and she could smell the clean salty scent of his skin. She thought that, even in the dark, she could never mistake his rich personal fragrance for that of another man. With the tip of her tongue, she lightly tasted his neck just below his ear.

Almost immediately, his lips were upon hers, and they clung together, their hands still, while they sampled and explored every corner, every curve of each other's lips. There were tingles and small shocks that lengthened as they grew into each other once more. Their hands, their lips, their bodies, their very breath moved together and became one long before the final completion.

As she began to surface slowly from the tidal depths, the first thing she was aware of were Stephen's eyes, blue in their greyness as they clung to hers, and then she knew his hand was gently stroking her cheek. She smiled at him, and with the radiance of his face, he became again the young man she had married so long ago.

"Are you happy?" he asked as though he couldn't see it on her face.

"Oh, yes, yes," she whispered. "Did I make you happy?"

"Julie, my Julie." He kissed her lightly on her nose and then on the corner of her eye. "You're as much woman as any man could want."

She pulled him closer in her arms, and they lay in the quiet yet glorious union of their souls as well as of their bodies. Somewhere in the house, there were voices. Clara calling to her grandmother, Aunt Martha good-naturedly chivying the maids in the kitchen, where pots clanged and cutlery rattled, yet it was all far away, the sounds of a distant world.

Later when Julia wakened, Stephen was still asleep, and as she listened to the light sound of his breath, she leaned on one elbow and watched the way his golden brown eyelashes lay against the darkness of his tanned skin. His lips curled into the innocent smile of boyhood and she wondered if he were dreaming. Then he opened his eyes, instantly awake, and his smile grew wider though older.

Oh, I love him, I love him, she thought with a kind of desperate wonder.

"I built you a ship," she whispered, giving him the only gift she had.

"You wrote me. Where is she?"

"We had to sell her when we didn't hear from you. Don't you remember?"

"Yes. Well, there are other ships. What about the one that's on the ways now?"

"She's already been sold. I'm sorry."

"The *Crystal Star* will do for another voyage." He stretched his arms high above his head as he spoke, and Julia watched the powerful muscles moving in them. "Have your father build the next ship for us. I have enough now to afford her. Or have you sold that one, too?"

"No. With each ship we've built, I've held off as long as I could, hoping you'd write and say you wanted her. You know that. I offered them to you, but you never answered."

"I know." He brought his arms swiftly down and pulled her on top of him so that she was lying on his chest. "I had to see you first. I had to be sure of you before I could be sure of anything else."

"You couldn't have wanted to see me very much," she said as she propped herself up with an elbow on each side of him and looked down at his face.

"I did, Julie, I really did. You don't know how very much I wanted to see you."

"And California?"

"What I wrote was true." He swirled her hair around until it was a curtain around both their faces, enclosing them in a private world. "Almost no ships got away, and there were no men to be hired. In order to set sail, I had to pay from one hundred twenty-five to two hundred dollars a month for some of the worst and greenest men I've ever sailed with. There was no one aboard who could navigate except me. Don't you believe me?"

"I believe you." She was willing to believe anything if it would make Stephen happy. "Yet you're going to California again?"

"With cargo rates going for forty dollars a ton? I'd be a fool not to."

"I heard they were getting sixty dollars now." She pulled her hair back so that she could see him more clearly and kissed him on the chin.

"No. That's for the newest clippers. We can't get that for the *Crystal Star.*"

She thought about the *Free Wind.* David Baxter was getting sixty dollars a ton. So were *Neptune's Dragon* and all the ships that had been built in the Howard Shipyard in the last five years.

"If only . . ." she started to say, but he stopped her with a long and sweet kiss that brought her down to his side.

"There are no if only's," he said as he released her lips. "There is only what is. On our next ship, we'll be getting top dollar because we're going to have the fastest and the largest money can buy."

"What was California like?"

"Exciting, dirty, and hot."

"Did you like it?"

"Ummm," he said as he buried his face in her hair. "I like this better."

"Tell me."

"There's not really that much to tell. Even before all the sails were furled, most of the men jumped ship. Didn't wait around long enough to be paid off. I ended up finishing the furling myself with a little help from the mates and the steward. Then they took off, too."

"What's San Francisco like?"

"It's a strange place." He lay back with his hands behind his neck and stared at the ceiling as though he could see through it to the scene he described. "Shacks, frame buildings, tents. When I was there years ago, my uncle had a couple of vessels droghing hides in California. In those days, the mission was called San Francisco, but the settlement was called Yerba Buena. There wasn't much there except for the presidio, the mission, and a half-dozen buildings. Now there are hundreds of structures of one sort or another, and the streets are nothing but mire. Everything is filthy. That's what I remember most. The dirt. You think you'll never get clean."

"And the gold fields?"

"They're not much better. The sun beats down on your back, and your legs freeze while you pan for gold in those icy streams. Not enough food and you're exhausted before the day's half over. When the sun goes down, you think you'll never be able to straighten up again."

"Did you find any gold?" She pushed back the hair that had fallen over his forehead so that she could gaze at his cleanly chiseled features.

"Oh, yes. It's there." He caught her hand and kissed it. "I did well at first, but then more and more men came pouring up into the hills and it was harder to find a good spot. And the sites were getting smaller as the fields became more populated. I made thirty thousand dollars and spent five thousand for supplies and getting the *Crystal Star* back in condition to sail. That's all I wanted to do after a while. Get away from the crawling hills, the filth of the town, and put to sea."

"Thirty thousand dollars for just a few months work!" She sat back on her heels and looked down at him with astonishment.

"Twenty-five." He grinned at her.

" 'Tis a wonder you came back at all."

"It wasn't worth it. I watched fortunes made in the fields and lost in the saloons. It could have happened to me."

"But you're not a gambling man . . . except for an occasional wager on a race."

"It's different out there. Panning for gold is a gamble. It becomes a way of life. There were some who stayed away from the saloons, but there wasn't much place else to go except to the fields. I'd go into town and have a drink or two and watch them. Some of us were able to stay away from the tables, but when you see that much money changing hands, it's a powerful temptation. Sooner or later, I would have played, and sooner or later, I would have lost. That's when I decided that, no matter how much it cost, I had to get out of there."

"But you're going back." She ran her fingers through the darker hair on his chest.

"Not to prospect for gold. To trade. And as soon as the trading's done, I'll leave."

"If you had trouble with the crew before . . ."

"I won't this time. I have a plan."

"What?"

"Let's wait and see if it works." He winked at her and touched her lips lightly with one finger. "I'll have to have good mates, though. Men I can count on not to desert the ship."

"Stephen, with all that money, don't you think you ought to buy a new clipper now? There's a lot of difference between forty and sixty dollars a ton."

"There is. And even more of a difference when it comes to getting a cargo for England. Ever since Britain repealed the

Navigation Laws last year, those Englishmen in China have been fighting for cargo space on the fastest clippers for their really choice teas." His eyes lit up with laughter. "The joke of it is that the English tubs are sitting at anchor in the harbors out there while our American ships are taking all their trade."

"Oh, Stephen, we *have* to have a new ship. With all that money you made in California, surely you can afford one."

"It won't be that easy to find one. *You* should know that."

"That's true," she sighed. "If only we hadn't sold the one that's building now. She'll be launched come fall."

"Any chance of buying her back?"

"I doubt it, but we could try."

"It's not the end of the world, Julie." He pulled her down to him again and buried his face in her neck.

"No, but to think I designed that ship and she can't be yours."

"It's my own fault." Holding her face between his hands, he gazed directly into her eyes. "Look, sweetheart, if we sail in a couple of weeks, we'll be back within the year. By then, your father will have a ship built, rigged, and ready for us. Meanwhile, we won't have lost any time. If we waited for this ship to be ready, it would be winter before we could sail. It'll work out. You'll see."

"Stephen?"

"Hmmmm?"

"I've designed another ship. The model's already finished. Do you want to see it?"

"Now?"

"Yes." She threw back the covers and had one leg over the side of the bed before he pulled her back.

"Not now. Most emphatically not now. What I want to see is you."

"But the ship . . ."

"Hang the ship." He pulled her closer and whispered in her ear while nibbling on its lobe. "Don't you agree?"

"Yes," she said and trembled as the excitement only he could transmit flowed warmly through her body. "Hang the ship."

The staircase was so narrow, Stephen had to follow Julia down the steps, and yet it was hard for them to be even so short a distance apart. His hand strayed to her shoulder, and she put hers up to clasp it. When they reached the bottom, neither could resist the temptation of one final kiss before they went into the parlor to join the family. It was unfortunate that Clara was standing in the doorway of the dining room and saw them.

"Let my mother alone!" she shouted, and with her blonde braids flying, she came whirling down the hall and began pummeling Stephen with her small fists.

"Clara! What a way to behave with your papa," Julia said as she scooped up the little girl. "Here he's come all the way from California and China just to see you."

Clara's eyes opened wide, and as she stared at her father, her thumb went into her mouth. When Julia tried to take it away, Clara resisted and firmly kept her thumb where it was, but her eyes never left her father.

However, when Stephen reached out and took her from Julia, the thumb came out of her mouth and she struggled wildly to get down.

"Clara, Clara, don't you know your papa?" Stephen asked and tried to kiss her soft cheek.

"No!" Clara howled and kept on howling until the tears were pouring down her reddened face. Finally disgusted, Stephen put her down with a thump on the floor and squatted beside her while he kept her imprisoned with his hands.

"Stop that!" he said sharply.

In surprise, Clara did stop and stared at him balefully.

"Stephen, she's only five years old," Julia said softly. "You've been away a good part of her life. Give her time to get used to you again."

"Do you remember the ship, Clara?" Stephen asked and this time his voice was warm and gentle.

She nodded slowly and once again her thumb sought her mouth.

"Don't you remember how I used to tell you stories about the whales and flying fish?"

Clara just stared at him.

"Well, do you see that chest?" He nodded at his sea chest, which was on the floor near the front door.

She glanced at it and then quickly back at him again.

"I have a present in there for you. I'll find it for you when I unpack tomorrow morning. You would like a present, wouldn't you?"

423

Clara looked uncertain, but eventually she nodded. Then she noticed that her grandparents and Aunt Megan were standing in the doorway of the parlor, and she suddenly broke away from her father's grasp and ran to Lydia. Once she was safely swathed in her grandmother's full skirts, she ventured to peer out at Stephen.

Stephen stood up and dusted his hands. "Didn't you ever talk about me while I was gone?" he asked Julia and it was an accusation.

"Of course, I talked about you. We all did. For a long time after you left, she kept asking where you were."

"Papa's at sea," Clara said from the muffling folds of figured green silk.

"You see?" Julia flashed back at Stephen.

"But it hasn't been that long." He was perplexed as he looked at the saucerlike grey eyes that peered out at him. "How could she forget me?"

"She says goodnight to your portrait every single night," Lydia said as she petted Clara, "but there's a right smart difference between a daub of paint and a living man. Young ones need their fathers around them, not gallivanting off to sea."

"Lydia," Benjamin cautioned her. "Stephen makes his living from the sea. Now don't go holding that against him."

"He could make a good enough living right here on land. The place he belongs is in the shipyard. The young are supposed to relieve their elders of their burdens when the time comes, and what good's that yard if it don't provide a living for our children and their husbands?"

"I'm sorry, ma'am, but I'm afraid I wasn't cut out to be a shipwright."

"I've never seen such a family for running off to sea. Next thing you know, Julia will be going back with you."

"I am, Mama. Stephen sails in two weeks and he's taking Clara and me with him."

"Good, good." Benjamin beamed at Stephen and clapped him on the shoulder. "Glad to have you home, son, and you're welcome to stay as long as you please. Just wish it was going to be longer. I want to hear all about California."

"You're *not* taking Clara back to sea!" Lydia pulled Clara even closer to her.

"Of course we are, Mama," Julia said impatiently. "Look what's happened already. It's time she got to know her father again."

"You don't want to go back to sea, do you, Clarie?" Lydia looked down at the child who was still half-hidden in the protection of her skirts.

"No!"

"Mama!" Julia flashed a warning look at Lydia. "Clara, remember what fun we had on the ship? You had your own lovely bunk and Becky was with you."

Clara suddenly let go of her grandmother's skirts and ran past her parents down the hall to the dining room. They could hear her calling, "Aunt Martha, Aunt Martha."

"Mama, I wish you wouldn't encourage Clara in her stubbornness," Julia said. "You've spoiled her to death, and I don't know how we're going to handle her once we get aboard ship."

"Spoiled her, hmpf!" Lydia glared back at Julia. "The poor mite. Her father goes off to sea and leaves her, and her mother spends all her time at a shipyard. Might as well be an orphan the way you two treat her."

"Nonsense, Lydia." Benjamin took his wife's arm and led her back into the parlor. "Is this any way to greet your son-in-law when he's finally returned home?"

Megan, who had been hesitating just inside the door, glanced after them and then turned to Stephen. "I think this is going to be a family discussion. You'll have to excuse me, but I do want to wish you a welcome home."

"Don't go, Megan," Julia said. "You're part of the family now, and we're not going to have any discussions, anyway. Stephen is Clara's father, and if he decides he wants her to go to sea, then she's going to sea."

"I'm not so sure I want to take her," Stephen said slowly.

"What?" Julia felt the blood drain from her face. Had he suddenly changed his mind and decided he'd rather sail alone? "But Stephen, you said you wanted me to come with you."

"I said I wanted *you* to come. I didn't say anything about Clara." He looked at the dining room doorway, which was empty, and there was a wondering hurt in his eyes. "If the child doesn't want to come with us, she doesn't have to."

Then he turned to Julia with a look so naked in love and appeal that Megan disappeared into the parlor.

"Julia," he said, "I've spent a lot of time alone these past few months, and I've discovered what's of real importance to me in this life. This afternoon only reinforced the conclusions I'd already reached. The two things that come first are you and the ship. You because you *are* you. The ship because that is my life as a man and a provider. It's what I can *do* and do well, better than most. Much as I've thought about it, I've found that I can place neither of you above the other. I have to have you both. After that, the rest of the world can go hang. Clara's my daughter and I love her, but if she doesn't want to come to sea, then we'll leave her home."

"But Stephen . . ." She laid her hand on his sleeve. "You know so well what it's like to be a small child without parents."

"It's not the same thing." He glanced at the dining room door and then at the one that led to the parlor. "I was a small child without love of any kind. Clara has an abundance of it. She's also needed and wanted by your mother and, I suppose, others. Don't give up your life . . . our lives . . . for the sake of a child who's happy where she is."

"I . . . I won't," Julia faltered and wondered what she was promising. She knew that she was promising something. "But give Clara time. It's just that children have such short memories."

"Of course, I'll give her time. But we don't have much of that." Then he smiled and took her hand, which he tucked under his arm. "We'll be at sea again soon, Julia."

When they entered the parlor, Benjamin winked at Stephen and gestured at a tray that had been set up on a side table. "I'm only allowed one tot a day, and I think this is as good a time as any to have it. You got a good steady hand there for pouring?"

"Steady as they come, sir." Stephen grinned back at Benjamin and released Julia's hand.

As Julia sat down on the sofa and watched him pour the drinks, she glowed with pride and happiness. He was so trim in his black frock coat, and he carried himself with the proud assurance of a man who has all life under control. She couldn't help but notice that the hand that held the decanters was steady. Evidently he had that problem well under control, too. Everything would be all right now. It would be all right as long as they lived.

Once he had handed his brandy to Benjamin and sherry to the three women, Stephen sat down next to Julia and stretched his legs out before him.

"Ah, it's good to be home," he said with a long sigh.

"Well, I'm glad to hear that from you," Lydia said. "I never was quite sure you considered it home before."

"Why not? It's more a home than I've ever had." He raised his glass in salute to Lydia and gave her his most disarming smile. "Here I have a mother and father, a wife and a sister all gathered around the family hearth. Speaking of sisters, where's Sarah?"

"She hasn't been by for a couple of days," Lydia told him, "but I'm sure she and Aaron will stop in when they know you're home."

"I'm sure they will. I can't wait to see dear sister Sarah."

"I never knew you were so fond of Sarah before," Lydia said with a perplexed look.

"Stephen, stop it," Julia said. "He isn't fond of Sarah, Mama. He can no more abide her than she can abide him."

"But that's precisely where her charm lies. I have never known anyone who hated me so thoroughly in all my life. There's absolutely no one I'd rather do battle with. Yes, it's good to be home."

Yet Stephen was home for only a week, and then he was gone on the packet to Boston. During his brief stay, he set out to win Clara over, and he succeeded. First came the doll he had brought her from England, and then came the short walks when he would take her with him and tell her stories. They were mostly of his childhood, and on the few occasions when Julia accompanied them, she found herself learning more about the boy he had been than she had ever known before. So often when she had asked him, he had refused to talk about those days. With his own child, however, he was somehow able to forget the pain of loneliness and remember the joys that were illuminated by the distance of things past.

Before he left, Clara was thoroughly enchanted with him and ignored her grandmother and Aunt Martha whenever he was near. Julia marveled at her husband when he sat with Clara in the kitchen while she had her supper. He made gravy lakes in mashed potato mountains and persuaded her to eat all the green pea boulders so that they would not roll down the mountains and crush the people below. Clara ate with a heightened appetite, and gales of her laughter filled the sunny kitchen. Stephen had never shown so much patience with the child, not even during the days of her illness at sea.

For the first two days after Stephen had gone, Julia's time, when it was not consumed by the thousand details of packing, was spent at the shipyard. She had carried so many things in her mind, and now it was necessary to explain to her father, Daniel, and Philip how she had planned things and what the schedules were. Megan, who still enjoyed her role as clerk, sat by and recorded the most important items, and Benjamin would wink at Megan and say, "Strange how Julie thinks I've never had the managing of a shipyard before."

Over the months of Megan's stay with them, a close relationship had grown between Benjamin and Megan. He treated her as though she were another daughter, and she responded with affection. He often seemed fonder of her son, Robert, than he was of his own grandchildren. To him, the boy, with his red hair, sparkling black eyes, and lightly tan skin, was a creature to be protected, and for Robert, Benjamin was the only father he had ever known.

Julia was content to leave the Fairfields in her father's care. So long as he lived, she would never have to worry about Megan and her child.

It was her own child she had to worry about, for three days after Stephen had left the Cape, Clara came down with a high fever. It was the first she had had since they had come ashore to live.

Chapter Twenty-Two

1850

Julia learned about Clara's illness when she went home with her father for dinner in the middle of the day and found Doctor Willett's horse and buggy at the hitching post. Everyone had been well when they had left the house that morning, and at first she felt only curiosity and mild surprise. After all, if it was anything serious, they would have sent word to the yard. Most likely her mother was having another one of her megrims.

But when Maryanne greeted them at the door with the news that it was Clara who was sick, she flew up the stairs with a heart that seemed to skip every other beat. The awful thing was the anger she felt at the same time. Anger at her own sick child. Shocked at herself, she tried to push the anger away, but it wouldn't go. The fear that inspired it was too great. What if this meant that she wouldn't be able to sail with Stephen?

In her bedroom, she found her mother and Aunt Martha with the doctor. Clara had moved in with Lydia while Stephen had been home, but as soon as he had gone, she had returned to her little trundle bed in Julia's room. Now she lay on her mother's wide bed and her face was wet with tears and perspiration.

"What is it?" Julia asked as she bent over her daughter. "How could it have come on so fast?"

"I don't know." Lydia's green eyes were framed by wrinkles of worry. "She started crying and saying she didn't want to go to sea, and before I knew it, her forehead was blistering hot."

"Were you scaring her with stories of the sea, Mama?" Julia, ready to turn her ire in any direction but Clara's, looked sternly at her mother.

"No. Of course not. I wouldn't do such a thing," Lydia protested, but she seemed more defensive than resentful in her denial.

Julia glanced at Aunt Martha, and the older woman's usually smiling face was stony as she looked at Lydia.

Sitting down on the bed beside Clara, Julia stroked her hot head and said, "What is it, love? What's the matter?"

"Don't want to go," the child sobbed. "Don't want to go."

"Don't you want to see Papa?"

Clara hiccuped and looked hopefully at Julia. "Tell Papa to come home."

"He can't, sweetheart," Julia said as she blotted Clara's tears with her handkerchief. "Papa has to go to sea to make money for your food and clothes and all your playthings. There aren't many little girls who can go with their papa when he's working, but you can. Aren't you lucky?"

"No." Clara's face crumpled and she began to cry again. "I want Papa here."

"Well, let me talk to Doctor Willett for a minute. Then I'll come back and you can tell me all about it." Julia brushed the soft fair hair back from Clara's high forehead once more, then rose and went out of the room followed by the doctor.

"Well?" she asked as they walked down to the other end of the long hall where they wouldn't be overheard.

He clasped his hands together behind his spare back and shook his head. "Nothin' much I can tell you. You know that child's been having these spells all her life."

"I know, but I thought she'd outgrown them." Julia wiped her damp hands against her skirt. "She's been fine the past year or so."

"Aye," he said as he looked at her over the top of his steel-rimmed spectacles. "Just reinforces the opinion I've always held. 'Tis more a matter of temperament than real sickness."

"But the fevers she runs!" Julia looked at him in astonishment. "You can't lay them to temperament."

"The human body's a strange animal," he said and brought out a large handkerchief to wipe his face and bald head, which glistened in the midday heat. "If you'd seen what I've seen, you'd know how people can will themselves into illness. Usually means they're unhappy and figure by gettin' sick, they'll get their way."

"No!" Julia's denial was vigorous. "Clara's way too young to think like that. Why, it's been going on practically since the day she was born."

"Look, Julie, you listen to what that child's saying. She don't want to go to sea."

Julia couldn't believe it. She wouldn't believe it. "That's only because Mama tells her awful tales about it. It's got nothing to do with her being sick."

"Don't it?" He gave his face one final pat and then stuffed his crumpled handkerchief into his pocket. "It's like you said. Clara's been ailing ever since she was born. Now, you may like the sea, but I've always thought you were a mite peculiar that way. Keep that child ashore and give her a chance."

"But Doctor Willett, you don't understand." Julia leaned against the bannister that guarded the stairs and looked down the hall at her room. She felt as though her carefully constructed world was falling apart. The parting with Stephen when he'd left for Boston. It had been so joyous in their shared anticipation of the voyage that lay ahead. Now . . . "I have to go. I've promised Stephen. If only you knew . . ."

"I do know," he said gruffly. He'd always been fond of Julia, and after observing her for the past year or so, he understood the dilemma she faced. He tried to stay out of his patients' private lives, but he rarely succeeded. Being a childless widower, he tended to look upon them all as part of his family. "God gave me eyes to see what goes on around me, and it didn't take me long to figure it out. Go join your husband and go to sea with him. Nothing's stopping you. But leave the child ashore."

"But I'm her mother! I can't just go off and leave her." Even the thought of it was inconceivable.

"There's plenty of women in this house to take care of her."

"No! No one else could care for her, love her the way I do. How could I desert her?"

" 'Tisn't rightly what I'd call desertion. You'll be back. And it's a sight better than bustin' up your marriage on the one hand or ruinin' the child's health on the other."

"But if she needs me . . ." Julia nervously took a few steps in the

431

direction of her room and then came back to face the doctor. "If she needs me, I'll be thousands of miles away. I won't even know when she's sick . . . or happy . . . or anything."

"Well, that's up to you." Doctor Willett pulled a large watch out of its pocket and studied it carefully. "I've left some medicine with your mother and Martha and told them how to use it since they were here when I arrived."

"Meaning I wasn't," Julia snapped at him. She hadn't meant to, but she felt as though he was tearing her apart.

"Meaning anything you want it to mean, Julie," he said calmly as he put his watch back into his pocket. "I've got to get on my way. There's other people waiting. I'll be back before evening."

"Yes. Thank you, Doctor Willett," Julia said in a voice that was subdued with embarrassment. "Good-bye."

She watched him as he went down the stairs and then turned to find Martha Chambers standing behind her with her arms folded over her ample breast.

"You've been listening?" Julia asked her, hoping for comfort.

"The question is, have you?" Martha made no move of sympathy towards Julia but remained just as she was.

Julia caught her breath. There was something almost fierce about the older woman. "What do you mean?"

"I mean listenin' to the doctor. May be true your mother's been filling the child's head with a lot of nonsense, but I doubt Clara's rigged right for the sea. When you brought her home, she wasn't much more than a shadow. Didn't hear a laugh out of her for nigh on two months. Now look at her. Twice the weight she was. Learned how to play, too. You just go on with Captain Logan and leave her here with an easy mind. I'll see she comes to no harm."

"Oh, Aunt Martha." Julia shook her head. "I wish it was so simple."

Martha allowed herself a small smile. "As I recollect, you always did like to make complications where there wasn't none."

"But what if Mama keeps filling her head with nonsense, telling her stories about terrible disasters?" Julia said with real distress as she imagined her daughter abandoned and frightened. "She'll spend half her time fretting for fear Stephen and I'll be shipwrecked."

"I'll see to it that she don't fret."

"I'm beginning to think you're all trying to push me off to sea so you can have Clara for yourselves," Julia snapped.

432

"You know better than that, Julie," Martha said placidly.

"Yes, I do. At least as far as you're concerned. I'm sorry, Aunt Martha."

"No harm in speaking your piece. You'd best get back to the child."

When Julia returned to her room and saw the high color on Clara's cheeks and the distress written in every line of her face, she made one decision.

"Clara, sweetheart," she said as she dampened a cloth in the bowl of water and wiped her daughter's hot forehead with it. "You don't have to go to sea if you don't want to."

"Truly?" Clara asked, and her grey eyes were pleading.

"Truly."

"And Papa will come home?"

"No, darling. Papa can't come home." Then to see what effect it would have on the child, she added, "I might have to go take care of Papa. He'll be so lonely without either one of us to look after him."

"Yes." Clara yawned as the medicine began to take effect. Before she closed her eyes, she looked at Julia and then at her grandmother with a peaceful smile.

When the next morning she found Clara completely recovered, Julia began to believe that Doctor Willett knew what he was talking about when he labeled her illness a matter of temperament. Yet how could he possibly be right about her leaving her daughter, even in the hands of those who loved her?

As she set out at mid-morning to join her father at the shipyard, she longed for Stephen's presence. Why had Clara waited till he was gone before she took sick? If only she could discuss it with him, perhaps he wouldn't be so adamant in his insistence that she sail with him, perhaps now he would understand. Yet even while she wished for him, she knew what his answer would be.

When she reached Sesuit Neck Road, she reined in her horse. At the end of that long tree-tunneled road, the shipyard waited for her, but she didn't feel that she could concentrate upon its problems until she had solved her own. She turned her horse in the other direction and followed the highway until she reached the winding road of soft sand that led to the larger beach. She needed the sea.

At the top of the dunes, she halted more from habit than any

433

desire to watch the white, sun-reflected sails in the distance. Yet even as she glanced absently at them, she felt their call, and the longing to follow them surged up in her as strongly as it had when she'd been a child. It made no difference that now she'd experienced the wildest fury winds and waves could produce. The glorious sensation of living through them and coming out of them onto the long, rolling swells of the sunlit Pacific was something the land could never duplicate. And the days of doldrums and headwinds only made the tradewinds the sweeter. She could almost smell the flower-filled fragrance of the islands, the spice-laden winds of the East. And California? What was it truly like? No one could truly render with words the sensation, the completeness of a land.

Almost in a dream, she tethered her horse to a stunted tree and made her way down the shifting sand to the summer beach. The tide, rushing in, grasped at the shore with a gentle crash that echoed down the beach and then pulled the pebbles and sea wrack back to it with a tinkling music that sounded like laughter. Gulls, terns, and sandpipers paraded its edge hoping for a stranded sea creature. A group of children playing nearby danced in the wake of the ebb to run shrieking from the incoming waves that clasped their bare feet.

How she would like to give all this to Clara when she was older, but how could she ever transmit the magic of sight to one who was blind?

She walked a distance from the children, then sat down on a piece of driftwood and took off her own shoes and stockings. When she reached the water, she scooped up her skirts and played her own game with the waves. When her hand got wet, she licked it and tasted the salt of the sea.

As the tang of rough crystals touched her tongue, she could hear the echo of other voices.

"Go join your husband and go to sea with him. Nothing's stopping you. But leave the child ashore." Doctor Willett's voice was kind but gruff as he tried to conceal his compassion.

"You go on with Captain Logan and leave her here with an easy mind. I'll see she comes to no harm." And Martha Chambers meant what she said in that warm, no-nonsense voice of hers.

"The two things that come first are you and the ship. I've found that I can place neither of you above the other. I have to have you

434

both." Stephen's voice, like his face, was naked with the appeal of his love.

I can't give Clara a love of the sea, Julia suddenly realized. No more than Clara can take mine away. They're right. I have to give her the chance to grow up where she'll be healthy and safe. Clara isn't me, and if I tried for a thousand years, I could never turn her into me. She's separate, herself. We're two completely different people. It would be nothing but pure selfishness on my part if I took her away from the place where she's happy.

On the other hand, I can't let Clara mold my life, either. I can't let her turn me into someone I'm not. I can't let her take away my happiness. She has Mama and Papa, Aunt Martha and Amelia and Megan, all here ready to surround her with love. Stephen has only me.

And I need him.

The edge of a wave touched her bare feet, and as it receded, it left a hem of foam like the ermine border of a queen's robe. Julia scooped up a bit of the soft white fluff and held it up to the sun. Miniature rainbows sparkled in the tiny bubbles.

As the foam dissolved into the air, so did the doubts that had burdened Julia's mind. There was only one path for her to take. The one path she was born to take. It wasn't only Stephen who called her to come.

Although Julia knew that she had made the right decision and went about her tasks with a lightened spirit, it was still not easy to think of leaving her daughter. From then on, wherever she went, she tried to keep Clara by her side. Listening to her chatter, joining in her laughter, Julia felt that she was closer to the little girl than she had ever been before. She wondered if it were because she now was able to enjoy Clara as Clara and not as the child she had expected her to be.

At night before she went to sleep, Julia would kneel beside Clara's trundle bed, and as she prayed for God to take care of her daughter, she watched the play of moonlight on that small, sleeping face. If she wavered for a moment, she would remember the thin child who had tossed with heat and sickness aboard the *Crystal Star*. No. Clara belonged to the land and it was here that she must stay.

* * *

435

The days were gone almost before they had begun, and then after a swirl of activity, Julia found herself on the wharf surrounded by her family while boxes, crates, and barrels were swung aboard the packet. There had been a fog earlier in the day, but the hot summer sun, in dissolving it, had left only a light mistiness in the air as a remembrance.

The straw bonnets and gaily colored parasols that crowded the wharf lent an aura of festivity to the day. Orders were shouted, friends called to one another, and small boys watched enviously while a couple of their not much older counterparts deftly carried out the mate's orders.

For Julia, the familiar bittersweetness of departure was more intense than it had ever been. When they had driven up to the wharf, the sight of the schooner that would carry her on the first leg of her global journey had made her catch her breath with an excitement that was always new. Already a part of her had begun the voyage.

Yet as she tried to talk to those she would be leaving behind, their pensiveness, which showed only in an occasional glance or a difficulty with words that were intended to be cheerful, magnified the sense of sadness Julia felt over the long separation that was about to begin.

"Papa, is there anything I've forgotten to tell you? About the yard? About the business I handled for you while you were ill?"

"No. Nothing." He leaned upon the silver-headed cane he had begun to use and smiled down at her. As always he could read her thoughts, and now he tried to reassure her. "We'll begin work on your ship in just a few months, and when you sail into Boston next year, you'll find her waiting for you. Don't you worry about us while you're gone, Julie. There'll be nothing you can do till you're home again."

"I'll try not to, Papa."

"And don't go fretting about Clara. You've made the right decision."

"Have I?" She looked up at him hopefully. In his dark blue eyes, she read a firm certainty. "I think so, too. At least, I hope so."

They both glanced over at the child, who was standing beside Lydia. Her grey eyes were wide, and Julia couldn't decide whether it was in wonder at the bustle around her or whether the child had finally realized that her mother was really going to go away and leave her.

"Clara," she called, and when her daughter ran to her, she bent down and held her close. She was so small. How tall would she be when the *Crystal Star* sailed back into Boston Harbor? Would her cheeks still be rosy with health? Someone else would teach Clara her first lessons. Someone else would kiss her finger when she pricked it over her sampler. Julia had a sudden impulse to swoop the child up and carry her on board the packet. There would be enough time in Boston to buy some material for clothes. "Are you sure you don't want to come with me, sweetheart? You still may."

With her arms around Julia's neck, Clara clung tighter to her mother, but she shook her head so vigorously, her bonnet slid back to reveal her high forehead.

"Well, you don't have to if you don't want to." Julia smiled into the eyes that were so solemn beneath their fair brows. She held Clara a little away as she inspected the delicate face and touched the child lightly beneath her rounded chin. "You'll be a good girl while I'm away, won't you?"

"Yes, Mama," Clara said and an answering smile lightened her face. She was obviously relieved that there was not going to be a last minute change in plans. It reassured Julia to see that smile. Clara would be all right.

"And you'll remember me, Clara? You'll say a prayer for me every night?"

"Yes, Mama."

"They're ready for you to board," Benjamin announced gruffly.

Julia glanced up at him and saw that there were tears in his eyes. She gave Clara one final kiss.

"I love you, Clara. Don't you ever forget that."

Clara reached her arms up to Julia's neck once more and returned her kiss with a moist one. "Love you, too, Mama," she said gravely.

Julia couldn't bear it. If she held her daughter for a moment longer, she would cry, she would stay, she would take Clara with her. The break must be made. Now.

She straightened up and clutched her father's arm. "Good-bye, Papa. Take very good care of yourself."

"I will. Don't cry, Julie."

"I'm not. At least no more than you are."

"Am I? Yes. I suppose I am."

She stared at his face one more long moment, each of them saying without words all the things they knew lay in the other's heart.

Then she was surrounded by a flurry of arms. Her mother, Megan, Amelia. There were laces, muslin, silk, and the scent of lavender engulfing her. Even Lydia managed a weak smile while Amelia displayed her deepest dimples and Megan's voice was silver with light laughter. There were injunctions to write, to take care, to come home safely. With the excitement of the future rising in her again, Julia broke away from them and hurried to the gangway.

Daniel Sears, standing beside it, was waiting for her. When she gave him her hand, he held it for a moment.

"Take care of Papa for me, Daniel."

"I will." His brown eyes were soft with concern. "Take care of yourself, Miss Julia."

"Write to me, Daniel." She was surprised to hear herself say the words. It was something she had never asked of him nor had she ever thought of it before. "Let me know how things are going."

Daniel nodded. "I planned on it."

The other passengers had all crowded by her onto the schooner, and she was aware that the captain was looking at her with impatience. She dropped Daniel's hand and lifted the skirts of her blue muslin dress as she went up the gangway. Once on board, she found an empty spot at the rail and then stood looking at her family. She felt she should call out to them, but there was nothing left to say. Instead she just looked at them and tried to memorize the way they stood in that small group. She wished she had a picture of her mother in her green silk dress bending over Clara as she encouraged the child to wave. There was her father flanked by Amelia on one side, tall and slender in her primrose dress, and by Megan, tiny and delicate in her rose-grey silk, on the other.

A short distance away were the servants with Amelia's children and Megan's Robert. She looked for Daniel, but he was gone from beside the gangway. Then she spotted him rowing across the creek to the shipyard. She lifted a hand to wave to him, and he shipped one oar to return her farewell. The bank beyond him was lined with men who raised their caps and hats to her when she extended her wave to include them all. They should have been at work, not idling about to see her off, but she forgave them.

All these, who meant so much to her, she had seen so many times before, but she hadn't really looked at them. Now she tried to turn them into portraits that she would carry in her heart.

Then the tide turned, the lines were cast off, and the sails were raised. The rushing ebb of water carried the schooner quickly out of Sesuit Creek, and the wharf, the shipyard, and her loved ones were gone. The familiar beaches were deserted as the packet swept by them, but on the high dunes there were the eternal watchers of the sea and of the vessels that plied their trades upon her surface.

Most of the passengers soon went below to stow their belongings and to seek a bit of comfort in the walnut-panelled saloon, but Julia remained on deck. As they left the calmer waters of the Bay and the Cape dwindled behind them, Julia felt the land and all the troubles it could hold relinquish their grip upon her. The sea, with sunshine sparkling on her lightly riffled surface, laughed in happiness at a summer's day, and Julia, feeling the rise and fall of the deck beneath her feet, wanted to laugh with her.

She felt lighter than she had for months. For years? The sea breeze swept her clear of all doubts, of all sadness, and left her cleanly stripped. She was herself, Julia, without adornment. There were no other eyes or minds to mold her into the person they wished to see.

But there would be one mind, one pair of eyes, she thought joyfully. Stephen would be waiting for her in Boston with all the love he had shown on his short visit home. They would be starting again as they had in the early days of their marriage, but this time, they would have a deeper understanding of each other's needs. This time, nothing could be allowed to come between them.

And for the first time since Clara had been born, they would be truly free and alone together with only the sea and the ship as their world. Free to watch the ocean's double rainbows together, free to trace the hours of night by the wheeling of the moon and stars, free to seek their fortune on the trackless highways of the globe.

She could see his grey eyes smoke blue with loving laughter. She could feel the hardness of his body pressed against her own and the tenderness with which his arms would hold her. Once more, she would be able to watch him without interruption as he, her captain, standing on the windward side of the quarterdeck, drove his ship from ocean to ocean.

He would show her the golden hills of California, the smoking city of Liverpool. Once more she would hear the music of the boat

439

people's voices, their flutes, and their drums drifting across the water at Hong Kong. She hadn't realized before how homesick she was for the excitement and intrigue of that island nor how she had missed the adventure of sailing through the Straits of Sunda. Together they would share that world where, as the sea displayed her many temperaments for their entertainment, no two days were ever exactly the same.

Soon, soon, the dancing waves seemed to say as they lapped against the bow. You'll be with Stephen, and it will all begin again. Soon.